THE TREASURE OF
SANTA
CATALINA
ISLAND

EAN

ISBN 978-1-7331824-0-9 $16.99 U.S./$22.99 Can.

9 781733 182409

51699>

THE TREASURE OF

SANTA
CATALINA
ISLAND

BY

MIKA BÓWYN

 **A MACKENZIE MILLES** ADVENTURE

Library of Congress Control Number: 2019906998

ISBN 978-1-7331824-0-9

10 9 8 7 6 5 4 3 2 1

First United States paperback edition, 2019

Cover art and content
Copyright © 2019 by Mika Bówyn

ARISTEIA® BOOKS
NEW YORK

for my Dad

Contents

v

The path ahead not only leads to where you've never been. It also keeps you close to all you never want to leave behind.

— Fire-Walker

1993

14 years before the release of the first iPhone.
12 years before streaming video would be available.
4 years before people started watching movies on DVDs.
3 years before the first Google web search.

In 1993, it had been 85 years since the Chicago Cubs
last won a World Series.
Their next World Series win wouldn't happen
for another 23 years.

In 1993, it had been 48 years since the Chicago Cubs
had last won the National League Pennant.

In 1993, it had been 48 years since the infamous
'Curse of the Billy Goat' had been placed on the Chicago Cubs
by Billy Goat Tavern owner William Sianis.

In 1993, it had been 42 years since the Chicago Cubs last held
Spring Training at the Wrigley Field facility on Catalina Island.

In 1993, a 12-year-old girl named MacKenzie Milles
did something bravely heroic, and made an extraordinary
secret discovery about the Island of Santa Catalina.

Chapter 1
TRAJECTORY

If a player on the opposing team hits a home run into the stands at Wrigley Field, the crowd throws the ball back. It's tradition. This does not apply to foul balls. MacKenzie's dream was to catch and keep a ball at Wrigley. This meant it would have to be either a home run ball hit by the Cubs, or a foul ball hit by either team.

MacKenzie and her mother did the math on this about a year before MacKenzie's mother died. It was not complicated. There were many more foul balls hit than home run balls, and roughly half the home run balls had to be tossed back onto the field anyway. Conclusion: sitting in foul territory provided the best opportunity to catch and keep a ball. MacKenzie and her father had later refined this by determining that at Wrigley, more foul balls were hit to the right-field side than to the left. Consequently, they always sat in foul territory in right field.

MacKenzie had never caught a ball at Wrigley in all her twelve years, which included six years of fairly regular attendance. She and her father now had season tickets, and they never missed a home game. But that was about to change.

Today was perfect for baseball. It was a hot Chicago afternoon, and the July sun baked the tens of thousands of weekend fans packed into Wrigley. In the right-field upper deck, MacKenzie and her father sat slathered in sun block, surrounded by smells of hot dogs, cheap beer, peanuts, cigarettes, and bag cotton candy. The static muttering of transistor radios and portable televisions droned, and the roar and murmur of the crowd rose and fell like beach surf.

MacKenzie made pencil notations on her scorecard with her left hand, and kept her right hand jammed securely into her second-baseman's glove, ready for her first foul ball. Today, as usual, no fly balls had come her way.

To make matters worse, the Cubs were losing. Unfortunately, this also was not uncommon. The Cubs often lost. But as MacKenzie's mother used to say, anyone can like a team that wins all the time. To like *your* team even when they lose takes genuine devotion; sticking with something unsuccessful until it succeeds builds character, she had said.

MacKenzie and her father were building character again today. It was the bottom of the eighth inning. The Cubs were down to their last out and in need of anything resembling a hit.

"Rally caps, Dad," instructed MacKenzie, and rotated her baseball cap around on her head so the bill and the Cubs logo faced backward, and the back of the cap faced front.

"Whatever works," her father replied hopefully. The logo on his cap said 'Illinois Wildlife Conservancy' and had an icon of a buffalo on it. He obediently rotated it around so that it too faced backward.

From MacKenzie's radio, the words of announcer Harry Caray, perennial voice of the Cubs, crackled as he delivered the play-by-play commentary. The living soundtrack to Cubs' home games, the nationally-beloved sportscaster's distinctive and uniquely appealing gravelly voice was rich with the whimsically-flavored exclamations of his colorful personality, and endearingly peppered with sporadic unintentional mispronunciations and slurred renditions of players' names.

"*Bautista comes set. He winds up. Now the pitch. And how about that! Biggio gets a piece of it, and it's a long drive to right field! But no, he was just ahead of it, and this one's going to hook foul toward the right-field seats...*"

MacKenzie was already on her feet. Letting her scorecard,

program, and pencil drop, she flipped down her sunglasses and thumped the pocket of her glove with her left fist, ready for the catch.

Everyone in the right-field bleachers was on their feet, hands in the air, hoping for a shot at the incoming foul. Keeping her eye on the ball, MacKenzie stood on her seat to get a view over the heads of the fans rising in front of her. She couldn't believe what she was seeing. For the first time ever, a foul ball was heading straight toward her.

The clamor of the crowd grew as the ball hurtled closer. The hands in front of MacKenzie stretched higher. She reached with her feet for higher ground, stepping up now onto the back of her seat, keeping her eye on the ball, and steadying herself in this precarious position with her left hand on her father's shoulder.

"I've got you," MacKenzie's father assured her over the din.

The world got louder and louder, and time slowed and slowed until suddenly everything was silent and frozen for an instant. One second MacKenzie thought she had the ball in her glove, and the next she knew she didn't. Just as fortune had sent the ball straight for her, destiny had placed the hand of another fan directly in the ball's path at the last possible moment.

There was an eruption of cheering and vaunting celebration, and the teenager who had snagged the catch gripped the ball and pumped his fist triumphantly in the air.

It was this scene that MacKenzie and her father were now watching on their living room television that evening. A Chicago cable channel replayed all Cubs games on a time-delay, so fans who had attended the game could later see the same game on television.

"*Nice catch, fella*," lauded the voice of Harry Caray from the television. "Another lucky fan nets a souvenir, and the count on Biggio goes to oh-and-two." On the television screen, MacKenzie and her father were momentarily visible in the crowd before the scene cut back to play action at home plate.

On the couch, MacKenzie nudged her father, who needed no prompting to spot them. "Look, Dad," she pointed. "It's us. There I am not catching that ball."

"You and those foul balls keep converging," observed MacKenzie's father.

"What's 'converging'?"

"Heading for each other. Getting closer together. 'The pitch and the swinging bat were converging just before the hit.' Et cetera. One of these days you're going to actually catch one, you know."

This prognosis did little to console MacKenzie. "Well," she said. "I suppose we should at least be excited that it's our first time ever on TV."

"It's all about trajectory," continued her father, launching himself on a philosophical tangent. "If the ball has the right trajectory, it doesn't matter if someone tall is in front of you. There were tall people in front of that young man, but the ball went into his hand. That's because the ball had the right trajectory for him to catch it. Someday, MacKenzie, you too will be in exactly the right place at just the right time."

"What's 'trajectory'?"

"The direction something is going in; the precise path that something travels along. 'The rocket's trajectory had it heading for the moon.' Et cetera."

"Is that literal or figurative?"

"In this instance, it is literally the exact path the ball is traveling. Figuratively, your trajectory is that you are on a path whereby you are getting closer and closer to the day you catch your first foul ball."

MacKenzie sighed, unconvinced. "Since we know how this game turns out, we know the trajectory of the Cubs for today: they're on a path to losing ten-to-one."

"Yes," agreed her father, "I'm afraid so. Sadly, it won't be the first time the miracle of pre-recorded television has enabled us to re-experience a loss."

"I suppose you'd rather watch the news now?" MacKenzie suggested.

"It's your call. But I do feel as though the news might be less depressing."

"I'll start dinner." MacKenzie pressed the channel selector on the remote and switched the program to a news broadcast.

"Thanks, Mac. I'll be in to help in a minute."

"Uh-huh..." MacKenzie replied dubiously. Climbing over the back of the couch, she headed into the kitchen and prepared to cook pasta. The voice of the newscaster followed her from the living room.

"*...and these recent concerns,*" the television blared, "*have led to stepped-up government efforts to address this disturbing surge in the theft and black-marketing of bomb-grade plutonium. At the Lawrence Livermore laboratory in California, site of the most recent incident, officials were unavailable for comment on—*"

"Dad," MacKenzie called in from the kitchen. "What is that guy talking about?"

"Sorry, I can't hear you," her father replied loudly. "I've got the news on."

MacKenzie left a box of linguini on the counter and returned to the living room. "I said..." she began purposefully, "what's all that bomb stuff about?"

Her father lifted the remote long enough to mute the television. "It's your basic twentieth-century cloak-and-dagger fare: the good guys are trying to make it harder for the bad guys to be bad."

"Is our country one of the good guys?" asked MacKenzie.

"Not according to the bad guys."

"What's plutonium?"

"Something twelve-year-olds should avoid."

"Does it have any other particular qualities?"

"It's a substance."

"Substance?"

"Stuff," said her father. "It's stuff."

"Oh, I see."

"Radioactive stuff."

"And?"

"And it's used in nuclear power plants."

"That government guy on the news last night didn't say it the way you do," said MacKenzie. "He pronounced it 'nuke-yoo-ler'."

"He's an idiot."

"What's 'bomb-grade' plutonium?"

"Plutonium that can be used to make a nuclear bomb."

"Is that bad?"

"Extraordinarily."

"And this stuff is being stolen by the bad guys?" asked MacKenzie.

"Bad guys are stealing it to sell to other bad guys," replied her father.

"This is supposed to make it easy for innocent young children to sleep at night?"

"The aforementioned children are not supposed to be watching news stories about bomb-grade plutonium."

MacKenzie nodded. "I know," she said. "They're supposed to be making dinner."

"Actually," her father said, getting up from the couch, "they're supposed to be getting help from their father while they make dinner."

MacKenzie was skeptical. "I'll believe that when I see it."

"In that case," he began, turning her around and steering her back into the kitchen, "you're in for a surprise, because—"

He was interrupted by the ringing of the phone.

"I'll just go ahead and make dinner then," MacKenzie said wryly. "While you're on the phone."

"Very amusing. I'll be off in a minute," he insisted, taking the receiver off its hook on the wall in the kitchen. "Hello. Milles Residence. John Milles speaking."

MacKenzie ran water into the pot slowly enough that she wouldn't disturb her father's conversation, and so she could listen in.

"Yes," he was answering. "Yes, I have... Yes, that is odd, I agree... How long has it been happening? Oh, I see... No, you're right. It should be looked into immediately..."

MacKenzie put the pot of water on the stove, turned on the gas, and put the lid on the pot.

"No, of course..." her father was saying. "There seems to be little choice." He glanced over at MacKenzie. "Well, no, to be honest, it's not convenient. However, under the circumstances..."

MacKenzie was fascinated. Because of his work in wildlife conservation, her father often had phone conversations that were enigmatic to MacKenzie until he explained them to her. But this one seemed different. His voice was an unusual mixture of concern and excitement that she couldn't remember hearing before. Hardly able to wait for him to hang up so she could find out what was happening, she lifted herself lightly onto the counter top, sitting on the tiled surface and settling back against the teak wood cabinets to listen further.

"That soon, eh?" John was saying with a certain degree of resignation and reservation. "Yes, I expect that does make the most sense..." As he talked, he began to pace slowly around the kitchen chairs and table in as broad a circuit as the length of the telephone cord would allow. "Alright, that will have to do... Yes, please do call me back once you've made all the arrangements... No, no, just two.

For me and for my daughter MacKenzie. She's twelve. Very well... I'll talk with you soon... Yes, thank you very much... Good-bye."

John hung up the phone and looked tentatively at MacKenzie.

MacKenzie pushed an errant wisp of strawberry blonde hair from her eyes. "Give me the bad news first," she instructed with grim resolve.

John sighed and sat down uncomfortably in one of the kitchen chairs. "You're not going to like it..."

"I can tell."

"We leave tomorrow."

MacKenzie was appalled. "What?" she nearly yelled.

"First thing in the morning, I'm afraid."

"For where?"

"California."

"Ugh! No way."

"I'm sorry, Mac. Way."

"For how long?"

"I don't know, exactly. A while. Indefinitely. Weeks, at least."

"Dad! Our season tickets!!"

"I know..."

"My friends!"

"I know..."

"DAD!!!"

"Look, don't you want to hear the good news?"

"There isn't any!"

"Um, actually, there is."

"This stinks!"

"We're going to Catalina Island."

There was a pause. MacKenzie's outrage subsided slightly as she processed this information. "That's the Cubs' old Spring Training camp..." she said at last.

John nodded. "That's right."

"Is there any other good news?"

"Yes. Catalina Island is a beautiful place."

"Great... Anything else?"

"Yes."

"What?"

"Your pasta water is boiling over."

"Cute. Really..." MacKenzie took the lid off the pasta water to abate the boil.

"I'm sorry, MacKenzie. Really."

MacKenzie irritably gripped a sheaf of linguini in both hands and broke it with a fierce crackling snap into two fistfuls of splintered pasta which she dumped unceremoniously into the water. "You want to tell me why we're going?"

Her father smiled and nodded. "I thought you'd never ask..."

Chapter 2
STRANGER

Their flight from Chicago's O'Hare Airport left the next morning. They landed in Los Angeles three and a half hours later, though on the clock it was only an hour later because they had crossed two time zones. After a forty-minute taxi ride to the coast, they were on the docks at the port city of Long Beach, where they waited for the arrival of the next Catalina Express boat to take them to Catalina Island.

The friendly piers of the Catalina ferry were small, clean, and welcoming, and just beyond the reach of the forbidding industrial megalopolis of Long Beach that encroached from all sides. Even the bright morning sky seemed to darken to an autumnal gloom where it touched the iron and steel and soot of the harbor city.

Long Beach was a locus of maritime commerce, and one of the busiest container complexes in the world. It bustled, but not with life. Inexorable and mechanized, it seethed like a giant dirty robotic-insect nest. Towering bug-like gantry cranes the size of skyscrapers crawled on rails, looming over an endless grimy sprawl of tens of thousands of freight containers. The redolence of the sea soured amidst the bleak atmosphere of the vast grim industrial landscape, and was deadened by fetid noxious fumes and the stench of diesel exhaust and petroleum.

In valiant contrast to the coarseness of the surrounding city was the august colossal ocean liner *Queen Mary*. This elegant relic of an earlier age was permanently berthed as a tourist attraction less than a mile from the Catalina ferry terminal. Once the pride of Royal British steamships, she retained her imposing dignity despite decommission, immobilization, and conversion to a hotel. But even her majestic proportions were dwarfed by the enormity of the industrialization rising around her.

MacKenzie looked from the modern grime and sprawl of commerce that had overrun the coastline, to the old-world stateliness of the *Queen Mary*. Rising proudly from the uppermost deck, the three huge red elliptical funnels with black tops unmistakably distinguished her as a steamship of long ago, and created along the vast span of her topside a silhouette as distinctive as a classic city skyline.

She had been berthed facing west. Her bow pointed seaward, toward the Pacific, as if she were longing to escape the industrial squalor of the Long Beach docks and the dereliction of her grandeur.

No, not longing, MacKenzie thought. *Waiting. She believes she'll be back at sea someday. And she knows a secret. After sixty years, she knows so much. But she knows a secret that has something to do with me...*

Vaguely seeking some sort of clue, MacKenzie looked hopefully toward the odious Long Beach container complex. A labyrinthine chaos of steel-railed transport tracks, polished and filthy, gleamed back at her and revealed nothing. Her gaze was drawn back to the *Queen Mary*, over the bulwarks and gunnels, down the length of the promenade deck railings, beyond the prow, and finally out to the ocean. *Somewhere out there*, reflected MacKenzie, *is Catalina. That's the exact path I'm on: a straight line between here and Catalina...*

Standing at her side, MacKenzie's father was also looking out over the water. "'Twenty-six miles across the sea,'" John sang softly to himself, "'Santa Catalina is a-waitin' for me...'"

"What are you singing, Dad?"

"Something from before your time."

"I like stuff from before my time," MacKenzie reminded him. "You know that."

"'Twenty-Six Miles' is the name of that song. It was a big hit about thirty-five years ago. It went to Number Two on the charts in 1958, and was written and recorded by a group called The Four Preps."

MacKenzie thought about this for a moment. "Is it really twenty-six miles from here to Catalina?"

Her father smiled and shook his head. "No. It makes for a charming song title, but the actual distance is closer to twenty-two miles. And it really is Santa Catalina, but everyone just calls it Catalina."

"And when we get there, we're really going to be taking care of sick buffalo?"

"Not *we*, my dear. *I* am going to be attending to the buffalo. You are going to be otherwise occupied having fun."

"Fun doing what?" she asked with annoyance.

"The island is beautiful, and there's lots to do there. Hiking, bicycling, sea kayaking, snorkeling..."

"I thought you'd never been there before."

"I haven't."

"Then how do you know so much about it?"

"Because of all the buffalo there, the CIC have called upon me for my 'expertise' many times, and I've learned a lot about the island from them."

"I forget what the CIC is..."

"Catalina Island Conservancy."

"Right. Like the IWC is the Illinois Wildlife Conservancy," MacKenzie remembered.

Her father nodded. "Very like," he said. "Except the CIC are also the primary owners of the island."

"But they've never asked you to go there before."

"They've never had a problem this serious before."

"Last night, you said the entire buffalo population of the island has signs of an illness."

"Yes," said John. "It's very mysterious, and it's alarming."

"So, I don't want to go bicycling or snorkeling," said MacKenzie. "I want to help you solve the mystery of the sick buffalo."

"Listen, Sherlock Milles. I promise to keep you apprised of all developments as they unfold, and you can keep my thinking steered in the right direction. And," he went on, "I know you'll be wanting to check out the old Cubs' stomping grounds. Maybe you can turn up a mystery there. Maybe you'll meet a nice, cute boy..." There was a hint of teasing in this last comment.

"Back off, Dad," MacKenzie admonished.

"'Water all around it everywhere,'" John returned to the song. "'Tropical trees and the salty air. But for me the thing that's a-waitin' there: romance...'"

"Dad!" she advanced with a more menacing tone.

John put his hands up in a mock gesture of defensive innocence. "Just kidding!" he protested.

"I don't want to go sea kayaking or meet some 'nice cute boy'," MacKenzie muttered with frustration. "I want to do something that matters..."

"Maybe you can find the missing treasure..." suggested someone from behind who apparently had been listening to them.

MacKenzie and her father turned to see who had insinuated himself into their conversation. A man about John's age wearing dark clothing and a dark leather jacket had appeared as if from nowhere. He stood there looking more out at the sea than at them. With bright, piercing sea-blue eyes, he was taking in the ocean with a quiet thirst as if it were a view he didn't get to see often. He was very handsome, MacKenzie thought, although there was something about him she didn't like. Nevertheless, out of courtesy and curiosity she responded with civility to his intrusion.

"What treasure?" she asked.

"Supposedly there's a cache of treasure hidden somewhere on the island." His voice was deep and had an air of easy authority to it. "I don't know the story..."

"What's 'cache'?" MacKenzie asked her father. "Is it like 'cash'?"

"It is if you have a lot of it," John replied. "Hoard. Stash. A great big amount of something hidden away. 'Deep in the cave, the dragon jealously guarded his cache of gold.' Et cetera."

MacKenzie turned back to the stranger. "How do you know about the treasure?" she asked.

"It's island lore," the man answered. "There are more details, I just don't know them. Some of the local islanders could tell you..." He seemed to have lost interest in the topic as quickly as he had brought it up.

"I'm John Milles," said MacKenzie's father, extending his hand in greeting. "And this is my daughter MacKenzie."

The stranger paused for a moment, as if he hadn't quite expected this development and wasn't sure what to do. Then, with a slight shrug, he seemed to have made a decision, and shook hands with MacKenzie's father.

"Trelain," he stated simply.

"Pleased to meet you, Trelain," John said politely.

"Likewise," he replied, and then said to MacKenzie, "So, you want to do something important?"

There was an uncomfortable pause before MacKenzie answered, "That was a private comment between me and my dad."

Trelain regarded her for a moment. "My apologies," he said at length. "Looks like your ship's coming in," he said, looking toward the Catalina Express boat that was now approaching the dock.

"Are you heading out to the island?" John asked.

The trace of a smile seemed to appear for a moment on Trelain's face, as though there was something about this question which he found secretly amusing. "I won't be taking the boat with you," he replied. "I'm just stealing a few minutes to enjoy the view. I don't... I don't get out as much as I'd like. Sorry for intruding on your conversation," he said, and turned to leave.

"It's no problem," John reassured him. "No need to rush off. It looks like they're going to be a little while off-loading the boat before we can board."

MacKenzie was looking at the *Queen Mary* again.

"That's kind of you," Trelain said to John. Noticing MacKenzie's distraction, he followed her focus. "She's a big, beautiful old ship, isn't she," he mused.

"She's beautiful," agreed MacKenzie. "She seems almost as big as the *Titanic*."

"Bigger," Trelain corrected her.

"No way..." MacKenzie said with mild disbelief.

"But it's true. She's one hundred thirty-six feet longer than *Titanic*. She's higher, and she has four more decks. And of course, the *Queen Mary* had one thousand and one successful trans-Atlantic crossings. *Titanic* had... well, fewer than that."

"You mean, like, zero?" contributed MacKenzie.

"Yes," Trelain confirmed.

"*Titanic* had *four* stacks on top, however," added John.

"Ah," remarked Trelain, and the deep sea-blue of his eyes sparkled. "That is one of my favorite details of *Titanic*. She did have four stacks, but the fourth was a buffalo."

"What are you talking about?" asked MacKenzie. "How can a smokestack be a buffalo?"

"He means it was a fake," explained John.

"That's right," Trelain went on. "The designers of *Titanic* wanted her to look more impressive, so they gave her a fourth stack.

But she only had twenty-nine boilers, so she only needed three stacks. The fourth stack didn't do anything. It was just to buffalo people into perceiving the ship as big and powerful."

"That's pretty tricky," MacKenzie observed with disapproval and admiration.

Trelain looked out to the ocean. "Things often are not what they appear," he said vaguely.

"I suspect *Titanic* would have appeared pretty formidable even without the fourth stack," John said.

"I think the *Queen Mary* looks pretty impressive with only three," said MacKenzie.

Trelain looked over toward the looming industry of the Long Beach complex. "They could never build a ship like the Queen Mary today," he said thoughtfully. "In 1950, The Empire State Building in New York City was built in only fourteen months. That was forty-three years ago. But in the same city of New York, they've been working on a subway tunnel, the shortest one in the system, to go underground a distance of one quarter mile. They've been working on it for twenty years. It still isn't finished. The first four hundred miles of track in the New York City subway system only took eighteen years to build, from 1904 to 1922.

"Now, look at that train terminal over there," Trelain continued, pointing to a large area of construction and railroad sidings in the distance. "That's the mouth of the Alameda Corridor. It's going to be a twenty-mile-long railway for trains to connect with the port in L.A. The first ten miles will be a trench, most of it below ground level. It's going to take them nine years to complete."

"That seems like a long time," MacKenzie said uncertainly, not sure how the conversation had come around to underground railways.

"And yet," Trelain continued, "most of the tunnel work has already been done by nature. This is an active fault area. Over two million years ago, magma in this region carved out huge, lengthy underground tunnels called 'lava tubes.' All they have to do now is tidy up a lava tube, and suddenly it looks like they've done a lot of construction work."

"Well, if you're set on digging a long underground train tunnel," John commented, "it sounds to me like a sensible way to take advantage of a geological opportunity."

"Oh, it is," Trelain agreed. "It's just intriguing how much goes on under people's noses, and they have no idea or any interest in what's really going on..." He looked back out over the ocean toward Catalina. "Now, take Catalina Island, for instance..."

MacKenzie and John followed Trelain's gaze and looked out over the water. Gulls circled lazily. The sun shone brightly, and sunlight glistened in trembling sparkles on innumerable low waves.

They turned to see what Trelain was about to say next, but he was gone.

"That was weird," decided MacKenzie.

"What a curious individual," her father agreed.

"He certainly liked to talk about unusual stuff," MacKenzie added.

By this time, the Catalina Express boat was ready to receive new passengers and had begun boarding.

"Okay," John said with enthusiasm. "Looks like it's our turn at last."

MacKenzie and her father gathered their bags and headed down the gangway.

Chapter 3
DOLPHINS

The Catalina Express was the passenger ferry between the Port of Long Beach and Catalina Island. There were few boats in the fleet, all collective referred to as the 'Catalina Express'. At less than a hundred feet in length and able to hold about one hundred fifty passengers, none of the boats was large. The name of the boat MacKenzie and her father were on was the *Avalon Express*. Of its sunny sundry passenger-mix of tourists, sightseers, travelers, picnickers, hikers, explorers, beach-goers, and returning Catalina residents, some were already settled in the inside cabin seating, and most were topside, standing at the deck railings to take in the sun, sights, and salty zephyr of the departure from Long Beach.

MacKenzie and her father leaned on the railing at the bow as the boat first backed out of the slip and away from the dock, then came about to motor slowly past the breakwater and head down the channel out of the harbor.

They had been underway in open sea at moderate speed for only a few moments when a flotilla of numerous quick-moving dorsal fins unexpectedly broke the surface of the water and swiftly surrounded the boat. A group of over two dozen capering bottlenose dolphins was playfully escorting the vessel. Propelled by the effortless strength and agility of their powerful flukes, the spirited animals easily kept pace with the forward speed of the boat, racing alongside mere feet from the hull, gliding torpedo-like through the water, breaching the surface, spouting spray from their blowholes, leaping in long airborne arcs forward through the air, cavorting in the breakers, and speeding with daring and carefree boldness across the bow of the boat just ahead of the cutwater.

It became apparent that this was a familiar ritual for both the captain of the *Avalon Express* and the dolphins. Perhaps to accommodate the paying crowd, perhaps yielding to a personal indulgence, perhaps wanting to indulge the frolicsome whimsey of the gamboling convoy, the captain continued to let the ship run at slower than cruising speed. The delighted onlooking passengers were amazed and entertained with the graceful animals' extraordinary antics. It was perhaps the dolphins themselves who enjoyed the performance most of all, the motion of their bodies expressing their joy, and the long narrow mouth lines of their rostrum snouts seemingly curved in irrepressible grins.

MacKenzie picked out one dolphin to watch over the side. She could see it clearly in the water just below the surface, and followed it with her eyes as the surface of the ocean rushed past, amazed at how a creature could move so skillfully and so fast through the water with so little effort. She wondered if she had ever had as much fun enjoying doing something as these enchanting animals seemed to be having.

After nearly ten minutes of fun and awe, it was apparently time to get underway in earnest. There was lag of several moments between when the timbre of the engines changed and the boat actually began to increase in speed. But with their extraordinary sonar sensitivity, and no doubt from their familiarity with the ritual of this game, the dolphins responded instantaneously to the change in engine sound. They gave a last gleeful parting leap and then scattered into the depths of the sea without a trace, well before the speed of the boat had changed.

So exhilarated was MacKenzie by this experience of magical creatures she had never seen before, that she didn't want to talk or interact with her father or anyone. She later explained it to her father as the feeling you get at the end of a movie which has touched you, and you want a few moments to think about it and process it and feel it privately, before the intrusion of talking about it, or talking about anything, with anyone else.

She leaned her chin on her fingers as her hands and arms rested on the rail. Looking out over the water, she let her thoughts and feelings about the dolphins swim through her mind. She let herself savor the taste and smell of the briny spray and the sound of the sea wind rushing past her ears, and she let herself become lost in the soothing rise and fall of the bow as it thumped and slapped and surged through the undulating waves in a rhythmic up and down dance between boat and ocean.

The tiny water in the distance didn't seem to move at all, and the water directly over the side seemed to be racing past. The nearby water all around was big with swelling waves that moved hugely up and down and had small caps of white foam at their tops, frothing and folding and disappearing over and over with the wind and the motion of the water.

The force of the oncoming buffeting wind grew as the boat continued to pick up speed. MacKenzie's silken strawberry blonde hair suddenly became like an animal that had waited all day for its beloved owner to come home and could now release all its pent-up energy and express its joy at reunion and freedom without restraint. It whipped uncontrollably about her face. No amount of hooking it behind her ear or changing the direction she was facing would tame it. At last she gave up trying to compel it to behave, and acclimated herself to—for now—experiencing the world through a crazy diaphanous gauze of impetuous hair frolicking with abandon about her face, which had now become her hair's playground.

It occurred to her that at this moment her hair was like the dolphins, playing for the sheer joy of playing, untamed by anyone or anything, and simply rejoicing and dancing. She had never been a fan of her own hair before. In general, she found it plain and unglamorous and unremarkable. But figuratively seeing in her hair the similarity to the newly beloved dolphins, and as she now literally could see the world around her only through the giddy veil of her hair whose acrobatic antics had taken over her face, she suddenly had a newborn fondness for her hair, and she laughed without realizing it from the sheer joy of enjoying how many new ways of seeing she had experienced in such a brief span of time.

"Need a hair elastic for that?" her father's voice asked near her ear. In order to be heard over the rushing wind, he was having to speak loudly. But the wind was winning, and it blew away his words almost before MacKenzie could hear them.

MacKenzie shook her head. Her hair played along.

"No thanks," she said.

"Hair scrunchie?" he offered.

"Dad, do you even have a hair scrunchie?"

"No," he admitted.

"Hair elastic?"

John shook his head. "No, I'm afraid I actually don't have one of those either."

MacKenzie smiled, unsurprised. "Well, it was thoughtful of you to offer, anyway," she said loudly into the wind and sea spray.

MacKenzie's father strategically had an Illinois Wildlife Conservancy knitted hat pulled over his Illinois Wildlife Conservancy baseball cap to keep it from blowing off.

MacKenzie's Cub's cap was strategically folded and stuffed in a back pocket of her jeans so that it wouldn't be blown overboard.

"It is less windy on literally any other part of the boat than the bow," John said loudly into the unrelenting wind. "There's much less wind at the stern, but it's a bit crowded and engine-noisy there. But if we move from here a bit more to the starboard side, we can at least hear each other speak," he suggested.

"Okay," she agreed, nodding.

The farther they headed out to sea, the more sunny and

cloudless the day became. Off the stern, gulls nonchalantly chased after the boat, gliding effortlessly above the wake. They adjusted the position of their bodies but never needed to flap their wings, riding the wind with expert proficiency, casually eager for any tasty fish morsels churned up by the ship's screws.

"You were right about the wind," said MacKenzie, as she and her father stood together looking out to sea at the rail by the forward starboard entrance to the boat's lower inside cabin. "It's still nice in this spot, but now we can hear each other."

"You seem less miserable about the trip than you did last night," John suggested hopefully.

"The dolphins are amazing, Dad," said MacKenzie. "They're beautiful and amazing."

Her father smiled and nodded. "Your mother always said, no one can make the best of a difficult situation better than our little MacKenzie. You're very positive, Mac. You're always looking for ways to help things turn out better."

John teared up slightly. It may have been from the sea spray and headwind of the boat's rapid forward motion over the Pacific Ocean water. MacKenzie suspected it was because her father had mentioned her mother. Her father always got misty and lovingly sentimental whenever he talked about her mother. MacKenzie did too. They both missed her very much. They were moving forward with their lives without her, because they had no choice. They weren't wallowing in the past. They were just treasuring all the time they had once had together as a family. MacKenzie's mother was gone, but she was part of their thoughts and their lives every day, and she always would be.

Her father now half-lifted his sunglasses from where they had been resting idly above the brim of his cap, and he moved them down and settled them into place over his eyes.

"No fly balls out here," he explained. "But lots of sun and wind.

Sam Foster produced the first pair of celluloid sunglasses in 1929. Edwin H. Land, inventor of the Polaroid camera, sold the first pair of polarized sunglasses in 1936."

MacKenzie nodded patiently at this information, pulling her own flip-down sunglasses from her black-denim jacket pocket and settling them into place on her own face.

"Dolphins sleep with one eye open," said John.

"How is that possible?" MacKenzie asked.

Her father shrugged. "They're dolphins," he said, as if that explained it.

"How do they do it?"

"One side of their brain sleeps at a time," said her father. "And the eye that goes with that half of their brain closes. The other half of their brain is partially awake, and the eye that goes with that side of their brain stays open. While they're half sleeping, they regularly switch back and forth between which eye is open and which side of their brain is partly awake."

"Why do they do that?" asked MacKenzie.

"Like humans, who are mammals," John explained, "dolphins, who are also mammals, need about eight hours of sleep per day. But they also need to stay alive. Staying alive for a dolphin includes important activities like watching out for sharks who want to eat them, continuing to move so they don't get cold, and continuing to regularly surface so they can breathe in air from above the water."

"That's kind of amazing," said MacKenzie. "Dolphins are so cool. I love them."

John nodded. "They are extraordinary. And they're not the only animals with a one-eyed sleep strategy. Mallard ducks, who are not mammals, sleep as a group, in a row. The ducks on either end of the row sleep like dolphins, with half their brain partly awake, and one eye open for danger. All the ducks in the middle of the row get to sleep with both eyes closed."

"I hope they take turns being on the ends," said MacKenzie. "Otherwise it wouldn't be fair."

Her father smiled. "Few things in life are fair," he said. "And even fewer things in nature are fair. But in this case, the Mallard ducks do take turns with where they are in the row."

MacKenzie nodded and looked out thoughtfully over the water.

A few moments later, she turned to her father, her sunglasses aimed intently at his sunglasses. "We need to talk," she said.

Her father nodded agreeably. "Let's talk," he said. "What do you want to talk about?"

Chapter 4

BUFFALO

"**B**uffalo," said MacKenzie.

"Fake funnels on an ocean liner?" asked John.

MacKenzie shook her head, well aware her father knew exactly what she was talking about.

"No. And not buffalo mozzarella cheese, either."

"Technically, it's *mozzarella di bufala*," he said, gesticulating theatrically with his hands in the warm ocean wind and bright sunlight, and pronouncing it with an Italian flourish.

MacKenzie shook her head again. "I'm not interested in cheese right now."

"I thought it was your favorite food group."

"It is. Duh. I'm just not interested in talking about cheese right now. By the way, why do they call it buffalo mozzarella?"

"It's made from buffalo milk."

"Seriously?"

"Seriously. It's made from the milk of Italian water buffalo. Some of the best comes from the Campania region of Italy. Just this year, they got a trademark. Buffalo mozzarella is made in many countries, but only cheese made in Campania is allowed to call itself Mozzarella di Bufala Campana™. Superscript 'tm'. Trademark. It's kind of like how only sparkling wine made in the Champagne region of France can be labelled as 'Champagne'. By law, all other sparkling wine has to call itself 'sparkling wine'."

"Hmm..." said MacKenzie. "At that Conservancy party you took me to in June, they were serving from bottles that said 'California Champagne'..."

Behind his sunglasses, John smiled. "Very astute, Sherlock Milles. Per usual. Yes, some California sparkling wines still get to call themselves 'champagne'. That's because of a legal loophole, left over from the eighteen hundreds."

"Eighteen hundreds. That's the 19th century."

"Correct."

"What's a 'loophole'?"

"Literally, it's a slot or narrow opening for things to go through. Medieval castles had arrow loops in the castle walls, small slits to less-dangerously shoot arrows out of. Figuratively, a loophole is a place in the rules where someone forgot to make the details specific, and people have used that place as a way to avoid following the rules."

MacKenzie nodded. "Like, if the teacher says you can't talk unless you raise your hand, so you just raise your hand and keep on talking. Because she forgot to say that you have to raise your hand and also wait to be called on."

"Hmm…" replied John thoughtfully. Sounds like you're speaking from experience…"

"Details matter," said MacKenzie evasively.

"Indeed," agreed her father.

"Buffalo," repeated MacKenzie. "The four-legged kind. The kind that live on Catalina Island. You didn't give me any details. All you told me last night is that the buffalo on Catalina are sick."

"And as I told you last night, that's all I know. I'll know more once we get to the island and I talk to the Catalina Island Conservancy people."

"I get that. But from what they told you on the phone, what do think might be going on?"

"Clues, Sherlock Milles. We need more clues. I don't yet have enough information."

MacKenzie grudgingly nodded with reluctant understanding. "Dad, how are there buffalo on Catalina?" she asked.

John nodded. "They're not indigenous to the island. They were brought there during the filming of a movie in 1924."

"What's 'indigenous'?"

"Native. Something or someone that's always been there, or comes from there naturally. 'Buffalo, also known as American buffalo, also known as bison, are indigenous to North America, but they are not indigenous to Catalina Island.' Et cetera."

"And they were brought there for a movie?"

Her father nodded again. "Fourteen of them. Brought by boat. It was for some of the scenes in a silent movie called *The Vanishing American*. It was referred to as a 'western', but it wasn't your typical 'cowboy' movie. It was about the mistreatment of the North American indigenous peoples, the Native American Indians, while America was becoming America."

"That sounds serious," MacKenzie said earnestly. "Have you seen the movie?"

"I have. Once. A long time ago. It is not a happy movie. But the issues it tries to address are important. But it is, after all, a Hollywood movie, so it doesn't show things to be as bad as they actually were. Most of the movie was filmed in the American mid-west. In Monument Valley, Utah."

"Why didn't they just film the buffalo scenes in the mid-west? Wouldn't that have been easier?"

"It certainly seems like that would have been easier. But *The Vanishing American* movie was based on a book by a writer who was famous at the time. His name was Zane Grey. He was also a dentist. He also lived on Catalina, and so somebody made the decision to film the buffalo scenes from the movie there on Catalina Island."

"That's kind of weird."

"What's also weird is that all the buffalo scenes shot on Catalina were cut from the film. They ended up never being in the movie."

"That's really weird. But, why are there still buffalo on the island?"

John adjusted his sunglasses. "Well, it turns out the movie crew couldn't round up the fourteen buffalo they had brought, so they just left them there."

"That's crazy."

Her father nodded. "But it's a craziness Catalina has ended up benefiting from. The herd has grown and thrived steadily over time, and they've become hugely popular with tourists. Tourism is an important part of Catalina's economy. And the local island people love having the buffalo there. They've become part of what makes Catalina Catalina."

"And the buffalo aren't a danger to the environment, even though they're not…indigenous?"

Her father smiled. "Bonus points to you for using your new word accurately."

From behind her sunglasses, MacKenzie smiled back. "Thanks."

"And the answer is no, the buffalo do not pose an ecological threat to the island's wildlands or its ecosystem. They may even be helping it. Though, herd size matters. At some point, someone's going to need to do a study to figure out what is the best number of buffalo for the island, and make sure the herd numbers don't go too far above or below that number."

"I'm proud of you, Dad," said MacKenzie. "You totally know your buffalo facts."

Her father smiled. "Thanks, Mac," he said. "Buffalo are one of my specialties. I'm not as famous as Zane Grey was, but in the environmental community, I'm known as 'the bison guy'. Which of course is why we've ended up here on a boat to Catalina…"

MacKenzie nodded, and looked down for a moment at the authentic Chicago Cubs watch wrapped colorfully around her right wrist at the end of her jacket sleeve. "Will we be able to see any Cubs games on TV while we're in Catalina?" she asked.

"We won't be able to see any of the WGN-TV telecasts," her father replied. "Only the games that are nationally televised. I'll see if I can get a hold of a short-wave radio. We might be able to pull in the WGN 720 AM radio signal. Maybe we can listen to tonight's game."

"It's Monday, Dad. Today's Monday. We don't play the Rockies until Thursday. It's an away game."

"Oh, Mile High Stadium. That's nice thin air. Maybe we'll finally get some runs."

"That would be a breath of fresh air, alright," agreed MacKenzie.

"High altitude air isn't necessarily fresh," said her father. "It's just thin."

"I was being figurative," MacKenzie explained. "Not literal. How does thin air help home run balls?"

"More trajectory details," said John. "Higher altitude air has less air pressure. Balls hit at Mile High will travel on average thirty-two feet farther than they would at Wrigley Field."

"That's kind of cool."

"It's great for the Rockies, it's their home field."

"Well, the air doesn't know the difference between a Rockies hit and a Cubs hit, so maybe we'll have a good day on Thursday."

"Someday, someone is going to make the Rockies start using a humidor to prepare all the baseballs for the games."

"What's a humidor?"

"A special container that controls humidity."

"What's humidity?"

"How much water there is in the air."

"What difference does that make?"

"In the summer, the difference is that we all get extremely uncomfortable when the humidity goes up."

"But what difference does it make in baseball?"

"More like, what difference does it make in 'a' baseball. If a baseball is more humid, it slows down. If the baseballs at Mile High were all stored in a humidor to make them more humid, that could cancel-out the advantage of less air pressure."

"But, in the summer, when it's humid at Wrigley, it doesn't seem like there are less home runs."

"Not less," said her father. "Fewer. Fewer home runs."

"Whatever."

"Details matter."

"Cute. But finish the explanation."

"This will sound confusing…"

"Try me."

"A humid baseball travels less far, but humid air makes a baseball travel farther."

"You were right," said MacKenzie. "That's confusing."

Her father nodded sympathetically. "What time is Thursday's game?" he asked.

MacKenzie pulled out her schedule, holding it tightly to ensure it wouldn't blow away over the side.

"Hmm…"

"Problem?"

"I was wrong. It's not an away game. It's a home game. We play the Rockies at Wrigley on Thursday."

"Being wrong builds character," said her father. "Look how much character I have."

"I love you, Dad."

"I love you too, honey."

"Thursday's game starts at 7:06 p.m.," MacKenzie reported, still studying the schedule.

"Catalina's in the same time zone as the rest of California," said her father. "So that's two hours behind Chicago time."

"So Thursday's game will start at 5:06 p.m. on Catalina?"

"Correct. I should be able to get my hands on a short-wave radio by then."

MacKenzie nodded, and then folded her Cubs schedule and stuffed it back into a jeans pocket.

"How long before we get to Catalina?" she asked.

John slid back one sleeve of his windbreaker to look at his chronograph watch. "The boat ride's about an hour," he said. "So we should be there in less than thirty minutes."

MacKenzie nodded. "Okay," she said, looking pointedly at her father's sunglasses through her own sunglasses. "So, what happens when we get to the island?"

Chapter 5
AVALON

About half an hour later, as the *Avalon Express* slowed its engines and crept gently into Avalon Bay, all passengers were at the boat rails, savoring the sights and sounds, and taking in all the sublime summertime beauty of Catalina Island's small and welcoming city of Avalon. The water of Avalon Bay was vividly clear, gradually shifting in hue from deep turquoise to light aqua the closer it was to the shore. Below the surface, large flat brilliantly-colored orange fish were everywhere. On the surface of the water of the small crescent-shape harbor, dozens of anchored sailboats bobbed placidly in the deeper water, and in the shallower water dozens of kayakers actively paddled about in brightly colorful sea kayaks. Along the white sands of the shore, people lounged soaking in the sun and sights, and waded and swam and played. The full expanse of the small narrow beach was plentifully populated with frolicking happy beach-goers.

The *Avalon Express* docked, and the warm air of the shoreline breeze filled with the cheerful animated noise of excited visitors already enchanted by the loveliness of Avalon, happy to be exiting the ferry to begin whatever Catalina adventures were ahead for them.

Carrying their bags, MacKenzie and her father made their way with the other passengers off the ferry, walking down the boat gangway to the dock, then up the ramp to the pier. Someone seemed to be expecting their arrival. A friendly-looking man wearing a brightly colored shirt with a Catalina Island Conservancy logo on it was waiting to greet them just past the top of the ramp.

"Davenport's the name," said the friendly man. "Ed Davenport. You can call me Ed. I'm from the Conservancy."

Davenport was tall, but not as tall as MacKenzie's father. He had a friendly smile and rosy skin that looked like it was always sunburned. He looked down at the logo on his shirt for a moment and tapped it. "Catalina Island Conservancy," he went on. "I'm the Director of Conservation and Wildlife Management. The four-legged critters are my specialty. The Catalina Island foxes, and the bison. John Milles, I presume? I recognized you from your photo in the *Nature* journal magazine. You and I spoke on the phone yesterday."

John nodded, lifting his sunglasses off his face and up onto his cap. "Yes, we did. Pleased to meet you, Ed," he said, shaking hands with Davenport. "This is my daughter MacKenzie."

MacKenzie followed her father's lead and flipped up her sunglasses. "Pleased to meet you, Mr. Davenport," she said politely as Davenport shook her hand.

"Either of you ever been to Catalina before?" asked Davenport.

MacKenzie shook her head.

"No, we haven't," said John. "We're happy to be here now, though. We're sorry for the circumstances that have brought us here. But we're glad to be here."

"Well, we're awfully glad you're here, too," said Davenport. "Welcome to Catalina Island, The Magic Isle. The Isle with a Smile," he added, smiling broadly to demonstrate.

MacKenzie smiled back politely.

"What happens first, Ed?" said John.

Davenport nodded. "Well, let's step over here to the side a minute. Just want to help get you two oriented a bit before I take you to where you'll be staying."

Davenport politely took MacKenzie's big Cubs duffel bag from her, and he led MacKenzie and her father several steps away from the flow of off-loading ferry passengers.

Davenport looked at MacKenzie's Cubs hat, her Cubs backpack, her Cubs duffel bag, and John's Cubs windbreaker jacket. "Cubs fans," he said, nodding. "I figured you might be, coming from Chicago and all. Full disclosure, it's actually pretty well known that The Bison Guy is a Cubs fan," he added, giving MacKenzie a friendly wink and smiling at her father.

"It's all true," said John amiably. "We're proud loyal die-hard Cubs fans."

Davenport nodded. "I think you're going to like the living accommodations we've arranged for you."

"That sounds enticing, Ed," said John. "Thank you. We're looking forward to seeing whatever you've arranged for us."

Davenport nodded again. "So, briefly," he began, "this is Avalon, the only city on the island. It's not very big. Only about one square mile. But it's very beautiful and has a lot of fascinating history. Right now, we're looking out at Avalon Bay. You can see the beach is shaped like a crescent, which is why the main street that runs along it is called Crescent Ave. We're here at the south end of the harbor. That beautiful round big building there at the north end is one of the most famous buildings in Catalina. That's the Casino. Not for gambling. Casino means 'gathering place' in Italian. Fancy old-world Hollywood movie theater and ballroom. All Art Deco. Masterpiece. Finished in 1929. Another of the island's treasures given to us by William Wrigley, Jr. You should take a tour inside. Tickets are free, but you have to get them in advance."

"I think just MacKenzie will be doing the sightseeing, I'm afraid," said John.

Davenport nodded. "Yep, I guess that's right. We're going to be needing your expertise elsewhere, all right."

For no reason she could identify, MacKenzie suddenly felt as though they were being watched. She looked away from the direction of the Casino building and scanned across the Avalon Harbor beach toward the shore-end of the pier. And then her pulse raced.

Someone was watching them. Some mysterious man. Or at least, he was watching all the passengers from the ferry leaving the pier, and for a moment seemed to be looking right at her. The mysterious man was tall. He had short-cropped dark hair, and was wearing a suit that seemed like it was trying to be summery but was too dark for summertime. He was looking around, acting as though he was trying not to be noticed, which to MacKenzie's eye made him stand out. Had he really been looking directly at her and her father and Mr. Davenport? She could not be sure because he was wearing sunglasses. He was a large man with broad shoulders who appeared very physically fit. He turned his head, and MacKenzie could see that he had a long scar on the right side of his face that ran from next to his ear down to his jaw.

In alarm, MacKenzie looked back up at her father. Davenport was still explaining to him some of the local highlights, and saying something about the palm trees. Her father glanced down at her, recognizing that something was going on in her mind, but he continued listening politely to Davenport.

MacKenzie looked back toward the mysterious man, but now he was gone. She looked quickly around to see what direction he might have gone off in, but she could not see him anywhere.

Davenport was now picking up MacKenzie's duffel bag, and John was picking up his, and they turned to start walking.

"All set, Mac?" her father asked her, which MacKenzie knew meant that her father had realized something was up, and he wanted to know if she was alright.

MacKenzie nodded. "All set, Dad," she said, to let her father know that what she needed to talk with him about could wait.

The three of them walked together, proceeding forward the rest of the way along the pier toward the shore.

"All this," Davenport was explaining, gesturing around them with his free hand. "The landing for the ferries, and what we're walking on right now, this is the Cabrillo Mole. And up ahead is the Cabrillo Mole Ferry Terminal. Juan Rodríguez Cabrillo was a Spanish explorer, and in 1542, he was the first European to set foot on the island. So, he's got some things here named after him."

"I thought a mole was a little furry creature that digs tunnels underground," said MacKenzie.

Her father nodded. "You're right, that is a mole. But 'mole' is a homograph, which means there is at least one other word with the exact same spelling that is actually a completely different word, with a different definition. In this case 'mole' means pretty much the same thing as 'pier'. Like what we're walking on right now. It's like a pier, but it can also be called a mole."

MacKenzie shook her head. "So, then what's the difference?"

"The difference," replied her father, "is that water can flow under a pier, and a mole is solid, usually solid ground and rock, and no water flows under it."

MacKenzie nodded. "Okay," she said. "That makes sense. Now I get it."

Davenport was grinning. "Well now," he said. "Between the two of you, that is an impressive amount of brain power."

"It works out pretty well," said John, "because MacKenzie likes to observe and think and learn and understand, and I like to talk."

Davenport laughed. "Well, sounds like you two have it all worked out just fine," he said, smiling.

"Mr. Davenport," said MacKenzie. "Since Cabrillo found the island, is he the one who named it Catalina?"

Davenport smiled again. "Well, now that is a very good question, MacKenzie. And the answer is no. There's another layer to that story. You see, Catalina is one of the Channel Islands. And Cabrillo was the first European to explore the Channel Islands, and he had a fleet of ships. The ship that he himself sailed on was the flagship, and she was named *San Salvador*. So, Cabrillo named this island after his flagship, and he named it San Salvador. That was in 1542. But then in 1602, another Spanish explorer named Sebastián Vizcaíno came along. He was really more of a soldier and more interested in making money than Cabrillo. Vizcaíno had been given the job of mapping the California coast, and finding safe harbors for Spanish ships carrying lots of gold. So Vizcaíno traveled around, stopping at a lot of the same places Cabrillo had been to. Vizcaíno didn't often stay in any of them very long. When he came to this island, he stayed just long enough to change the name. He renamed it Santa Catalina in honor of Saint Catherine."

MacKenzie nodded. "So Catalina is just short for Santa Catalina."

"Yep, that's just right," said Davenport.

"You have a lot of really interesting information about Catalina," said MacKenzie.

Davenport smiled. "Well, thank you kindly, MacKenzie. I'll just tell you, anyone who works or lives on Catalina is here for just one reason. We love this island. And when you love something, you love knowing as much about it as you can."

John nodded in agreement at this.

"Now, MacKenzie," Davenport went on. "Up here on the left as we go under the overhead, there are places to get tickets for lots of the activities available to do in Avalon. At that place right there, Avalon Blue Line Baggage, you can rent a locker for the day for cheap. Great for stashing your street clothes if you're going to be doing some swimming or sea kayaking, or suchlike."

MacKenzie nodded. "Thanks, Mr. Davenport."

They passed through the overhead-covered area of the open-air terminal and stepped off the end of the mole onto a blacktop transportation area.

"Golf cart's right this way," Davenport announced cheerfully. "By the way," he added, pointing. "That big white mansion way up there at the top of that hill? That's Mount Ada. It's the house that Wrigley built. Now it's a fancy hotel. Back in the day, Wrigley lived there with his wife, Ada. He named it after her. That's why it's called Mount Ada.

"The ball field the Cubs used to practice on during Spring Training was over on Banning Drive, not too far from where we are. Now it's the Catalina Country Club. Nothing left of the old ball field except a plaque they put up saying what used to be there. But it used to be the Cubs' practice ball field. Wrigley had a clear view of the field through binoculars from his house. He used to watch all the practices from up on Mount Ada. Any player he didn't think did a good job during practice, he made them go up all those steps to his house after practice to explain themselves. True story. It was a famous punishment. The greatest players, back in the day, all prided themselves on never having to go up the steps after a practice."

"Wrigley was an owner who was extraordinarily involved in the Cubs and their success," said John.

Davenport nodded. "Yep," he agreed. "Legendary. And his family after him. The story goes, Wrigley had three loves in his life. His family first, Catalina second, and the Cubs third. And he brought all those loves together here."

"And to think he made his great fortune by selling chewing gum," said John appreciatively.

MacKenzie nodded. "The only kind I chew," she said, pulling a stick of Wrigley's Spearmint chewing gum from her jacket pocket to demonstrate. She unwrapped it and popped it into her mouth, before stuffing the Wrigley wrapper back into her pocket.

"That shows good taste," said Davenport, and laughed at his joke.

MacKenzie smiled at him politely.

"Okay, folks," Davenport announced. "Here we are. Hop right in."

They had arrived at a small blue golf cart parked against one of the curbs, and Davenport was putting MacKenzie's duffel bag onto a stowage shelf at the rear of the little vehicle. John put his own duffel on the shelf next to MacKenzie's.

"You'll notice pretty quick," Davenport was saying, "there aren't many cars on Catalina, and even fewer trucks. Golf carts aren't only used by visitors. They're used by pretty much everyone who lives on the island. Three main ways to get around: electric golf cart, bicycle, and human feet. Keeps things nice. Peaceful and quiet, clean air, and no traffic jams."

John slid his sunglasses back into place, and MacKenzie followed his lead and flipped hers back down. The three of them slid easily into the small cart, Davenport behind the wheel, John on the passenger side of the front bench seat, MacKenzie settling herself in the middle of back bench seat. Davenport turned the key and put the vehicle into motion. The electric motor operated in near silence, with little more than a soft whir whose volume changed with the speed of the cart. It was quieter than the sound of the small rubber tires on the pavement as the vehicle turned and moved forward out of the transportation area and onto the road.

Chapter 6
COTTAGE

After less than a minute's drive toward the Crescent Avenue beachfront, Davenport pulled over to a curb near the beach for a moment, and the cart came to a silent stop.

"Now, I can't drive us through the most interesting part of Crescent Ave," he explained, turning and pointing, "because that portion is a walking mall. But there are lots of fun stores and shops there. Most, of course, are a bit touristy. But they've all got plenty of authentic Catalina flavor to them. And of course, there are plenty more stores and shops on the side avenues. But MacKenzie, you'll want to stop in at Big Olaf's ice cream and Lloyd's of Avalon Confectionery. That is, if you have a taste for ice cream, chocolate, pastry, and candy. Which I know I certainly do."

MacKenzie smiled and nodded. "That sounds good to me, Mr. Davenport. Thank you."

Tourists and visitors and locals bustled with calm happy animation in colorful summer beach clothing and accessories as they strolled and shopped and socialized along the busy length of the shop-filled side of Crescent Avenue. The opposite side of the avenue was the start of the Avalon Bay shore. From the close-by sands of the cozy and populated beach came the summertime-leisure redolence of cigarettes, sunscreen, music from radios, people casually talking and laughing, energetic teenagers gregariously interacting, and gleeful children playing.

"Catalina is quite a lovely place," said John thoughtfully. "It seems frozen in time. Not in a depressing way. Just in an escape-from-everything-and-everywhere way."

MacKenzie nodded. "I like it here," she agreed. "It's like you said, Mr. Davenport. It seems kind of like magic. Interesting, fun, safe, beautiful, and magic."

Davenport smiled broadly. "Glad you two like it so much already," he said.

He put the cart back into motion, and they continued on their way.

Davenport took them on a short round-about sight-seeing route that included a turn onto a short stretch of Clarissa Avenue. "That's where I work," said Davenport, pointing as they drove by. "That's the Catalina Island Conservancy main building. John, you and I won't be going there tomorrow. We'll be heading to a Conservancy wildlife station further up in the hills."

The last stop on the driving tour was the site of the long-gone Cubs practice field which had been replaced with the Catalina Island Country Club.

"The country club clubhouse," Davenport explained as they drove past, "is actually the same structure that Wrigley built for the Cubs. But the ball field where the Cubs used to practice, just below what's now the Catalina Island golf course, that's long gone. Like I said, nothing left of the old days except a plaque saying the Cubs' practice field used to be there."

After a few more turns, they were suddenly into a more rural part of town. The road began to incline, and they were going steadily uphill.

"This is Avalon Canyon Road," Davenport explained. "I've got maps to give to both of you. There aren't that many roads on the island. It's pretty easy to not get lost."

"Where are the buffalo?" asked MacKenzie.

Davenport nodded. "They don't roam anywhere near Avalon. They stay in the interior, up in the wildlands, within the largest middle portion of the island. Which is most of the island, and away from where a lot of people are living. You won't find bison here at the east end of the island, and you won't find any at the west end past Two Harbors."

"What's Two Harbors?"

"I'll show you on your map when we get to where you're staying. But Two Harbors is a small low-lying area that almost looks like it's separating the west end from the rest of the island. Back in the day, it was called 'the Isthmus'. Fewer than three hundred people live in the village there, but a lot of tourists go there. It's very nice there, and there's lots to do if you like enjoying interesting animals in their natural environment, nature on land, nature on the water, and marine nature under the water. A lot of hikers and boaters go there. A lot of divers like to go scuba diving there."

"What's an 'isthmus'?"

"Isthmus describes a particular land area," John explained. "An isthmus is a thin strip of land, with water on two opposite sides, and connected land on the other two sides."

"Yep," said Davenport. "That describes Two Harbors all right."

The cart slowed and Davenport pointed to the left. "And here we have the Joe Machado ball field," he said. "It's not in the best shape. We're working on ways to raise money to help it. But it's conveniently right here at the end of the road where you two are staying, in case you want to have a game of catch, or suchlike."

The cart turned off to the right, leaving the weathered and faded asphalt of Avalon Canyon Road and entering a rough dirt road. After a short drive uphill on the rocky dusty path, they came to stop in front of a lone cottage with paint so faded there was no way to know what the color once had been.

Not too big, not too small, MacKenzie thought to herself. *But boy, it sure does look old.*

They all climbed out of the golf cart. Everyone took off their sunglasses and stood for a moment looking together at the cottage.

"It's a bit of a fixer-upper," Davenport said, more as a report than an apology. "But don't worry," he added with a smiling laugh. "We don't expect you to do any restoration or repair. We could have put you up in fancier accommodations, but we'd like to keep your presence here out of the mainstream. Don't want to alarm the tourists with concerns about the local wildlife. And the Conservancy owns this residence, so it's no cost to us, and we can just forward what we would have spent for a nice hotel into your pay, John. And of course, it's just up the road from the ball field, which I thought you two Cubs fans might enjoy."

"This will be fine, Ed," said John. "Thank you."

"You bet," said Davenport. "And if you change your minds, we can of course move you to a nice hotel. Though, I'm hoping you'll be able to solve our mystery for us before too much time goes by."

John nodded. "Of course."

"Yep," Davenport went on. "It's not the oldest house on the island. Not by a long stretch. But of all the houses on the island, this little cottage has probably changed the least in the last forty or so years. It's only been lived in by one family since the Cubbies stopped using it for player housing back in '47. Nice couple. Lots of people would like to live on Catalina, but there aren't a lot of homes here. So as you might imagine, buying a home on the island has a waiting-list 26 miles long..." He paused for a laugh at his own joke. "You see what I did there? 26 miles? Like the song?"

MacKenzie nodded politely. "That was a good one, Mr. Davenport."

John smiled with kind politeness at the witty remark.

Davenport cleared his throat. "Ahem... Well," he went on. "Anyway, the lovely old couple who lived here all those years passed away about two months ago. Within a few hours of each other, actually. They were still very much in love. Lovely people. They bequeathed their home to the Conservancy. They loved Catalina almost as much as they loved each other."

"That's so very sweet," said John earnestly.

MacKenzie nodded. "I'm getting the feeling," she said, "that nearly everything about Catalina has some kind of a story behind it."

Davenport nodded. "You've got that right," he said. "Usually more than one story. Usually layers and layers of story. This cottage, for instance," he continued, "used to be housing for Cubs players during Spring Training. Over the years, some very famous players have stayed here. All the other original Cubs player housing is gone, or has been renovated. But not this little gem. This house is pretty much the same house it was in 1951."

"Is that the last year the Cubs were here?" asked MacKenzie.

Davenport nodded. "Yep. William Wrigley, Jr. bought much of Catalina Island in 1919, then bought most of the ownership of the Cubs in 1921. After that, the Cubs trained on Catalina every spring from 1921 to 1941, and from 1946 to 1951."

"1941 was the start of World War II," said John.

"Yep, that's right," said Davenport. "Catalina was controlled by the U.S. Military during the war years. The Cubs resumed having Spring Training here after the war, in 1946."

"Why did they stop coming after 1951?" asked MacKenzie.

Davenport nodded. "Well, partly because there was famously bad weather on the island in the spring of '52. But it was mostly because Wrigley's son, Philip K. Wrigley, had to make a lot of important new decisions about the team, and one of them ended up being that the Cubs would no longer train here. You see, when William Wrigley, Jr. died in 1932, his son Philip, or PK as everyone called him, took over control of the team. Took control of the chewing gum business, too. PK wasn't as much of a character as his father had been. Kind of quiet and low key. But PK loved the Cubs nearly as much as his father had. In fact, in 1961, PK turned the chewing gum business over to his own son, William Wrigley III, but PK chose to keep being in charge of the Cubs."

Davenport unhooked a walkie-talkie from his belt and depressed a button on the side of it with his thumb as he spoke into it.

"Dave, it's Ed," said Davenport, and then released his thumb.

"I've got you, Ed," a friendly voice squawked back from the device.

"Dave, I'm over here at the Englewood residence with John Milles and his daughter MacKenzie," Davenport went on, with his thumb pressing the button. "I've got Bertie here," he began. "That's the name of this old girl," he explained aside to John and MacKenzie, affectionately patting the front hood of the golf cart. "And," he went on into the walkie-talkie, "I'm going to leave Bertie with them after I show them around inside. How about you come on over and pick me up here in about ten minutes?"

"Will do," squawked Dave's voice from the walkie-talkie. "Welcome to Catalina, Milles family."

Davenport nodded. "Thanks, Dave," he said. "Out."

The walkie-talkie squawked again and was silent.

"See that long extension cord over there, coming out from the side of the house?" Davenport went on, pointing. "That's for golf-cart charging. Trust me, it takes hours just to put a few minutes of juice into these batteries, so you'll probably want to just leave Bertie plugged in whenever you're not taking her out for a spin."

"Understood," said John, smiling.

"If it works for you," Davenport went on, "I'll come back in a couple of hours, and take you two out to dinner. Not around Crescent Ave. That area's a bit noisy and public and touristy. But I know a nice quiet eatery a few blocks away from Crescent with terrific food, nice atmosphere, and not too many tourists. It's used more by locals than by visitors. You two okay with Italian food?"

MacKenzie nodded eagerly.

"You said the magic words," said John, smiling again. "That will do for us quite nicely. Thank you."

"That's terrific," said Davenport happily. "John, we're going to need a lot of your time tomorrow. If you're both comfortable with this idea, I can get MacKenzie some passes for kayaking, or a glass-bottom boat tour, or whatever she wants to entertain herself during the day tomorrow. Catalina is exceptionally safe."

John looked at his daughter. "Mac?" he asked.

MacKenzie nodded. "That'll be fine," she said without hesitation. "I can take care of myself. I don't mind being on my own. I like exploring."

Davenport smiled appreciatively. "Well, that's terrific. You two are real troopers. Thank you both."

John lifted his large Cubs duffel bag. "Any supplies inside?" he asked. "Or do we go shopping and start from scratch."

Hooking his folded sunglasses into the front of his shirt, Davenport nodded and politely picked up MacKenzie's duffel bag as MacKenzie was slipping her backpack over one shoulder. "We've stocked it for you with same basic staples," he said. "But I'm sure you'll want to head to that Vons store we passed on Metropole and pick up your preferences as you like."

"Staples?" asked MacKenzie.

"In this particular context," said John, "it means the basic things or the most simply important things, especially regarding food. 'They went to the store to buy bread, cheese, coffee, and other staples.' Et cetera."

MacKenzie nodded her understanding, and the three of them walked toward the front door of the cottage.

"Mr. Davenport," said MacKenzie, "Do you know anything about geology?"

"Budding geologist, too, eh?" he said with a friendly smile and a wink at MacKenzie's father.

"The range of MacKenzie's interests," said John, "is unlimited and uncontainable. I never know enough to keep up with her questions."

"I see," said Davenport, as the three of them stopped and put their bags down on the small slab of old concrete at the foot of the cottage front door. "Well, you're in luck, MacKenzie. Geology is one of my specialties."

"Buffalo is one of my Dad's specialties," MacKenzie said proudly.

Davenport nodded. "It certainly is. Your dad's The Bison Guy. That's why we asked him to come here."

"Mr. Davenport," MacKenzie went on, "were there ever any volcanoes in Los Angeles?"

Davenport had to do a double take. "Well," he said slowly. "That's quite an impressive question. Your father was right about the formidability of your questions."

"What's formidability?"

"The noun form of formidable," said John. "How challenging something is. 'The knot looked easy to untangle, but once they tried to untie it, they realized its formidability.' Et cetera."

"Well," said Davenport, "the answer is no. There have never been any volcanos in Los Angeles. If you want a volcano, you'd have to go the Mohave Desert. That's in San Bernardino. That's the closest one."

"So, if there was never a volcano in Los Angles, how can there lava tubes there?"

Davenport did another double take, and glanced at John.

"I warned you," John said to Davenport with a smile.

"Lava tubes, eh?" said Davenport with a raised eyebrow. "Well, since you asked, lava tubes can form without an actual volcano. Especially in a place like Los Angeles with all its faults…" He paused for a laugh at his own joke. "You see what I did there? 'With all it's faults'?"

MacKenzie nodded politely. "That was a good one, Mr. Davenport."

Davenport cleared his throat. "Ahem, well," he went on. "You can have lava tubes forming from magma. The magma doesn't have to come from a volcano, per se."

"I know per se," said MacKenzie quickly. "It means 'in itself, of itself, by itself'. Like, 'chocolate is not bad for your teeth per se, it just matters how much sugar is in it'. Et cetera."

Davenport laughed a big hearty friendly laugh. "Oh, you are your father's daughter, alright," he said smiling. "And so yes, that would explain your Los Angeles lava tube. Or tubes. Magma, but no volcano. But probably from magma about three or four million years ago."

"Thank you, Mr. Davenport. That explanation makes sense."

Davenport lifted his hat for a minute and scratched his head before putting his hat back in place. "Funny thing," he said. "There's a lot of Catalina lore. That is, a lot of stories from the history of the island, many of which may or may not be true. Like the story about the treasure. Well, there's some old Catalina lore about a lava tube. Not much detail to that story. Even less detail than the treasure story."

"There's that treasure story again," said John thoughtfully.

"Come again?" asked Davenport.

John smiled. "Catalina treasure and lava tubes arrived together when they first entered our lives earlier today. I'll explain tonight at dinner."

Davenport nodded, pulling a set of keys from a pants pocket. "Well, I like stories," he said with enthusiasm. "And I'm looking forward to hearing that one."

He unlocked the front door and opened it, and they all picked up their bags and headed inside.

Chapter 7

DINNER

Just as Davenport had finished showing MacKenzie and her father around the cottage, Dave from the Conservancy arrived out front in a Conservancy golf cart. Everyone was introduced, and with a friendly reminder that he would return to get them for dinner in two hours, Davenport drove off with Dave in the golf cart.

MacKenzie and her father went back inside to get settled in and start to unpack. The cottage was very old, but it was clean. The walls, floors, and ceiling looked as though they hadn't been touched in fifty years, but the furniture was all new. There were clean new towels everywhere, the beds had been made and had brand new mattresses, and there were clean new sheets and pillows and blankets. As small as the cottage was, there nevertheless were three bedrooms. Davenport had explained that was because the cottage had once housed six Cubs players at a time, two per room.

John let MacKenzie chose which room she wanted first, and then he chose for himself one of the remaining two. They did not spend time doing more than a cursory job of starting to unpack, because they wanted to do some shopping, and still have time for a game of catch before Davenport returned to get them for dinner.

They climbed aboard Bertie, and John drove them back down Avalon Canyon Drive and over to Metropole Ave where the Vons was located. Both John and MacKenzie were pleasantly amazed at how easy it was to find a place to park, and at how many different kinds if items the store had in stock, even though it was not that large.

After an enjoyable and successful shopping expedition, they drove Bertie back to the cottage, and after plugging her in to charge, they brought their groceries inside and got to know the kitchen better by putting away all they had bought.

Unpacking again only long enough to unearth their baseball gloves and a ball, they left the cottage and walked down the dusty and rocky dirt road, and crossed Avalon Canyon Road to get to the ball field.

The day's sunlight was fading, but there was still sufficient light to easily see each other and the ball. As they had been doing for years, they used playing catch as a backdrop for talking about whatever was on their minds, with the rhythmic alternating muffled pops of the back-and-forth hardball landing in one baseball glove then the other as the soundtrack to their talks.

MacKenzie told her father about the mysterious man she had seen at the Cabrillo Mole. Her father always took what she said seriously, and he did not dismiss her account of what she had seen and what impression it had made on her. But he also cautioned her that it was entirely possible it had simply been somebody looking for someone, and may even have found who they were looking for and then left with them. MacKenzie was not satisfied with this perspective, but she grudgingly accepted that that, or something equally unsuspicious, was an entirely possible explanation. She always felt better about everything after talking with her father, and she felt better about the mysterious man situation after discussing it with her father. And besides, playing catch with her father always made everything better anyway. But she couldn't shake the nagging feeling that the mysterious man still seemed to her to be suspicious.

True to his word, Davenport returned about two hours after he had left, and drove the three of them in a Conservancy golf cart to the special Italian restaurant he wanted to share with them. And as he had promised, there were few tourists dining there, and the eatery was populated almost entirely by local residents.

"So," Davenport was saying as they waited for their first course to arrive. "I don't want to talk shop at dinner tonight. But John, there's been a new development that I just wanted to briefly pass along to you tonight. We'll go over it in more detail tomorrow. But you know on the phone last night I told you we were sure it was the whole herd that had been affected. Well, we got some new field-testing results back late this afternoon, and it's not the whole herd. It's actually specific clusters. That means we may be looking for something specifically environmental."

John nodded. "Yes, we'll discuss this more tomorrow. And of course I need to look carefully at all the field-testing results you and your team have come up with so far. But yes, that already sounds less like a disease or sickness they might be giving to each other. It sounds to me more like there might be hot-spots of something in the environment that's affecting them adversely."

"What's adversely?" asked MacKenzie.

"It's an -ly adverb," said John. "It means in a way that is bad or harmful or prevents something good from happening."

MacKenzie nodded her understanding.

"But like I said," Davenport went on, "we're not going to talk shop at dinner tonight. So, that's all we'll say about that for now. But speaking of tomorrow, I realized I forgot to give each of you your maps of the island. They've got the whole island on one side, and a street map of Avalon on the other. I'm afraid not having them earlier must have made finding your way to Vons needlessly complicated."

John shook his head. "MacKenzie has an uncanny sense of direction. She goes somewhere once—she knows it forever, no matter how complicated. A place she's never been—it's like she's been there before. It's rather remarkable."

Davenport nodded. "Well, that's certainly a handy and impressive talent," he said smiling.

"Thank you, Mr. Davenport," said MacKenzie.

Davenport was wearing a casual blazer with the Conservancy logo on the lapel, and he reached into an inside pocket and took out two maps. "Well," he said, "again, my apologies for not giving you these earlier. I've written some phone numbers on each of them," he went on, pointing. "This is my number at the Conservancy, and this is my home number. And this is the phone number of the cottage. And of course the Conservancy pays the phone bill, so you should feel free to make any calls you'd like, and don't worry about any long distance charges."

"That's very kind of you, Ed," said John, taking the two maps and handing one to MacKenzie. "We really appreciate it."

Davenport smiled. "We appreciate you up-ending your summer to come here and help us," he said earnestly. "By the way," he went on. "I know I showed you the two bicycles that are there for you in the garage, but I forgot to tell the combination for the locks. They're both the same: 1, 2, 3. Really just a formality to lock the bikes if you're leaving them for a few hours someplace like Crescent Ave. There's not really any crime in Avalon. But it helps to keep visiting folks from thinking there are free bikes lying around for them to use."

MacKenzie nodded. "I'll make sure I lock the bike I'm using tomorrow whenever I'm not riding it."

"That's terrific, MacKenzie. Thanks. Oh, that reminds me..."

Davenport reached into another inside pocket of his blazer and pulled out a small stack of what looked like large tickets. "These are the passes I promised you," he said, handing the stack to MacKenzie. "Kayaking, snorkeling, glass-bottom boat riding, the trolley tour, and suchlike. They're only good for tomorrow, but I'll get you some more for Wednesday."

"This is so generous," said MacKenzie enthusiastically. "Thank you so much, Mr. Davenport."

"You're very welcome, MacKenzie," said Davenport, smiling

broadly. "John," he said, "we're going to get a fairly early start tomorrow morning, if that's alright with you. Okay if I come by to pick you up at around 7:30?"

MacKenzie's father nodded. "That will be just fine. We're both earlier risers, and I don't expect the two-hour time difference to give us much of a jet-lag problem."

"Oh," said Davenport. "Sleeping. That reminds me. Please don't leave Bertie's keys in the ignition when she's not in use. Like I said, there's not really any crime in Avalon or anywhere on the island, but it's just a good habit that we all follow. If you wouldn't mind."

"Makes good sense to me," said John, reaching into a pants pocket and then holding up Bertie's keys and the keys to the cottage. "We're pretty used to not leaving things unlocked."

"Oh," said Davenport again, reaching into another pocket of his blazer. "I almost forgot." He pulled out a set of keys and handed them to MacKenzie. "You'll want to have your own set of keys to the cottage. You'll likely be doing plenty of coming and going while your dad's not there."

MacKenzie politely took the keys from Davenport. "Thank you very much, Mr. Davenport," she said.

Davenport nodded. "I've a bit of a hard time keeping track of everything I'm supposed to be remembering sometimes," he said. "Which reminds me…"

Davenport reached yet again into his blazer while MacKenzie and her father put their sets of keys into pockets of their own.

Davenport took out a folded letter-sized piece of paper and opened it.

"So, MacKenzie," he began. "Your lava tube question intrigued me. I have a friend, an old friend—that is, a friend who is very old—who lives overtown. That is to say, on the mainland, near San Pedro. Folks on Catalina don't say 'from the mainland', we say 'from overtown'. So, I put in a call to my friend from overtown, who knows quite a bit more about geological things than I do, and I asked him about lava tubes in Southern California. Well, he told me a few things, and then was kind enough to write a few details down and fax them to me. So, I know a bit more than I did when you asked me before."

Davenport looked at the paper for a moment, then continued. "Briefly," he went on, "for some time reference, the Channel Islands were formed about 14 million years ago, by volcanic activity. Catalina is one of the Channel Islands, but it wasn't formed until about 2 million years ago. And not by volcanic activity, but by tectonic plate activity."

"I know what tectonic plates are," MacKenzie said quickly. "We learned about them in science."

"Well, that's just fine," said Davenport, "because they can be hard to explain. So, the edges of a tectonic plate, wherever they're touching the edges of another tectonic plate, well, they often don't play nice with each other. And at those places you end up with things like volcanos and earthquakes. And at a lot of those place, even if you don't have volcanos, you might still have magma."

MacKenzie nodded with enthusiastic recognition. "We studied volcanos and magma when we were studying tectonic plates," she said.

Davenport nodded. "That makes good sense. They all go together. Well, at a lot of those places where the edges of different tectonic plates aren't getting along with each other, you end up with faults. And faults cause earthquakes. Mother Nature's just always shifting things around, and sometimes with spectacular results, and sometimes with disastrous results."

He paused to check the paper again. "Okay," he went on. "So, running right through Long Beach is a particularly nasty fault called the Newport-Inglewood Fault."

"Like where we're staying," said MacKenzie. "We're staying in the house where the Inglewoods used to live."

John shook his head. "No, the couple who lived in the house where we're staying spelled their name starting with an 'E'. The fault that Ed is referring is Inglewood starting with an 'I'."

"Well, it sounds exactly the same," said MacKenzie.

Her father nodded. "Not exactly the same, but yes, they sound very similar. And also, they're two completely different names that are spelled differently by one letter."

MacKenzie nodded. "Sorry for interrupting, Mr. Davenport."

Davenport smiled. "No need, MacKenzie. Making observations and asking questions is what smart people do."

"Thank you, Mr. Davenport," said MacKenzie.

"So," Davenport continued, "the Newport-Inglewood Fault is over 30 million years old. And in 1933, the Inglewood-Norfolk Fault moved in a big way, and caused a terrible earthquake in Long Beach. And why do I mention that? I'll just tell you why. Because it apparently was connected to something that happened seven years later, in 1940."

He checked the paper again, and then went on. "In 1940," he continued, "they started building the Long Beach Naval Shipyard. At least, that's what it's called now. It was called something different in the beginning, and they've changed the name a couple times since then. But when they first started to dig at the site where they were going to build, they discovered something under the ground, and they called in some geology specialists. Well, they thought they'd stumbled across a giant underground cave. But it turned out they'd dug into part of a giant lava tube. It had been formed by flowing magma. They estimated it had been formed over 2 million years ago, around the same time Catalina Island was being formed. And they estimated that the tube used to be much farther underground, but the 1933 Long Beach Earthquake had raised one end of the lava tube up closer to the surface of the ground.

Davenport put his finger on a place on the paper to get his bearings, then went on. "So, after that," he continued, "they called in the Army Corps of Engineers, and then apparently nobody ever heard of that lava tube again. They may have sealed it up, they may have adjusted the location of the shipyard. But that was the last anyone's ever heard about it. According to my old friend."

He looked at the paper once more before going on. "And," he continued, "the only other lava tube story for that area has to the do with the new Alameda Corridor. My old friend said a completely different lava tube was discovered very near the surface of the ground, right along the path of where they're building the new 20-mile-long below-ground train route. It's not underground per se, but it's below the level of the ground. And that means an awful lot of digging. But after discovering the lava tube, suddenly there's now going to be a whole lot of digging they won't have to do. Now, according to my old friend, no one's supposed to know about that lava tube detail. For several reasons, supposedly so the general public doesn't get scared about huge underground holes beneath their feet. But my old friend says the real reasons probably have more to do with money."

MacKenzie and her father looked at each other.

Davenport looked puzzled for a moment. "Was it something I said...?" he asked.

John nodded. "Yes, it was something you said."

"We already knew about the Alameda Corridor lava tube," said MacKenzie.

Davenport looked even more puzzled. "Well, how ever did you know about that?"

"We met a very odd fellow near the dock in Long Beach while we were waiting for the Catalina ferry," said John.

MacKenzie nodded. "He was pretty weird. But he's the one

who mentioned the Catalina treasure story, and the lava tubes, and the Alameda Corridor."

"How very peculiar," said Davenport.

"First he spied on me and my Dad's private conversation," said MacKenzie. "Then he said a bunch of weird things, and then he was gone, like he'd never even been there."

John nodded. "To be honest, it was really a bit odd. He was a strange fellow."

"But thank you for getting all that information, Mr. Davenport," said MacKenzie. "It's really interesting. I think it all means something. I think it might all be connected."

Her father looked at her. "You're taking a long lead at first base, there, Sherlock Milles."

MacKenzie nodded. "Don't worry," she said. "I'm keeping my eye on the ball."

Davenport smiled and re-folded the page he had been holding. "Well, there's one thing for sure," he said, tucking the paper back into an inside pocket of his blazer and glancing toward the approach of their waiter. "Here comes our food."

Chapter 8
FRIEND

The next morning, MacKenzie and her father woke up early and had an early breakfast together. Despite what her father had said to Davenport about not expecting to be affected by jet-lag, MacKenzie nevertheless was in slow motion and feeling foggy as her body tried to adjust to the two-hours-earlier-than-usual wake-up. Davenport arrived to pick up John at 7:30, and offered to put MacKenzie's bicycle on the rack at the back of the cart and give her a lift to Crescent Ave. MacKenzie thanked him and said that since she was having a slow pace getting warmed up for the day, she would just bike down there herself in an hour or so.

"Ed," John was saying. "I'll be back to the cottage by about four this afternoon?"

Davenport nodded. "We won't be working past 3:30 today."

John nodded. "Okay, Mac," he said. "I'll see you back here at the cottage around four, and then we'll take Bertie over to the Vons and pick up some things for dinner."

"Bertie," MacKenzie repeated with a smiling laugh. "Okay, Dad. That sounds good. Good luck today. See you later, Mr. Davenport."

"Thank you, MacKenzie," said Davenport. "Enjoy your day in Avalon."

"I will. Thanks again for the passes."

"You're quite welcome."

John was handing MacKenzie a small wad of cash. "Remember to keep putting on sunblock," he said. "And before you go in the water, make sure the closure seals on your scuba pouch are tightly zipped, or it won't be fully waterproof. And remember to put anything that matters into the pouch."

"You mean, like my watch?"

John nodded. "Your watch, your map, your money, anything that doesn't know how to swim."

"Got it, Dad. Love you."

"Love you, honey," said her father.

She kissed her father good-bye, and Davenport and her father slid into the Conservancy golf cart and drove off.

About an hour later, MacKenzie had bicycled down to Crescent Ave, locked her bike to a bike rack, and had strolled around sightseeing some of the sights and shops and the beach for a while before heading over to the Cabrillo Mole to rent a sea kayak at the Wet Spot Rentals booth. She first used one of the passes given to her by Davenport to rent a locker. She had worn her bathing suit in anticipation of water activities, and she stashed the rest of her clothes and her shoes in the locker. After closing and locking the locker, she secured the locker key safely inside her waterproof scuba pouch which was clipped to a waist-belt she was wearing that went with the pouch.

MacKenzie didn't mind being barefoot. She had what her father always called 'summer feet', meaning that she spent so much time barefoot, the soles of her feet had become tough and strong and well-used-to walking on all kinds of surfaces at all different temperatures.

She put some extra sunblock on her nose and the tops of her ears, then zipped it into her scuba pouch with her locker key, her cottage keys, and her money. Using another one of the passes, she rented a sea kayak and signed up to go on a kayak sightseeing tour of the coastline and local waters. After zipping the rest of the passes into her pouch, she was outfitted with a colorful life-vest, a colorful sea kayak, and a colorful paddle, and soon she was out in the water of the harbor, bobbing and practicing paddle-strokes with the rest of the people waiting for the tour to get underway.

And then she saw the mysterious man again. He was standing at the top of the beach on Crescent Ave. And just like before, he seemed to be looking around at all the people, as if he might be trying to spot someone. MacKenzie's heart raced, and she looked around to see if anyone bedsides her was noticing him. Even though to MacKenzie his appearance and behavior seemed to stand out, no one else appeared to be noticing him. And then, just like before, when she looked back he was gone.

MacKenzie heard some soft splashing in the water near her, and she turned to see a friendly-looking boy who was not a member of the tour group paddling up next to her.

"Hey there," he said, sliding his sunglasses off and up into his hair. "If you don't mind my saying, you're not holding that paddle the right way."

The boy seemed slightly older than MacKenzie. He had sea-and-sun-bleached wavy hair, piercing blue eyes, and a genuine smile which he was now flashing at her.

"Hey there, surfer dude," said MacKenzie, smiling back. "Okay, so, what am I doing wrong?"

The boy held up his own paddle. "You need to have your hands facing this way, and positioned like this," he explained, demonstrating.

MacKenzie nodded, and re-positioned her hands on the paddle the way he was showing her.

"That's it," the boy said approvingly. "You've got it just right now."

"Thanks for the help," said MacKenzie.

"I'm Erik," said the boy. "I live on Catalina. My mom works

conducting the trolley tours, and my dad is a graduate-school professor. You have kind of an accent. Are you from Boston?"

MacKenzie shook her head. "Chicago," she said.

"I've never heard that accent before." said Erik. "It's a nice accent."

"Thanks. My name's MacKenzie."

"Hi, MacKenzie," said Erik, letting go of his paddle with one hand and reaching over toward MacKenzie's kayak to shake hands with her.

"Nice to meet you," said MacKenzie, letting go of one end of her own paddle to flip up her sunglasses and shake his hand. "I'm here on vacation with my dad. He's a buffalo specialist. He's here doing research on the Catalina buffalo."

"That's pretty cool," said Erik approvingly. "Cubs fan?" he asked, glancing at her Cubs baseball cap.

MacKenzie nodded. "It's true," she said. "Me and my dad are proud loyal die-hard Cubs fans."

"How about your mom?" asked Erik.

"She's not alive anymore," said MacKenzie.

"Erik's face turned serious. "I'm sorry," he said quietly.

"Thanks," said MacKenzie. "She was a proud loyal die-hard Cubs fan, just like me and my dad."

Erik didn't say anything for a moment. His and MacKenzie's sea kayaks bobbed in the low slow waves of the harbor, slightly apart from the rest of kayakers there for the tour. In a large kayak not far away, the kayak tour guide seemed at last ready to get the tour started.

"You must be pretty excited about all the Catalina Island connections to the history of the Cubs," said Erik.

MacKenzie nodded. "I am," she said. "I really like learning about it all. When you love something, you love knowing as much about it as you can."

Erik nodded emphatically. "I know just what you mean," he said. "Say, listen," he went on. "That kayak tour's pretty good, but it's kind of slow, and there's a lot of cool information about the island they don't give you. If you want, I could show you around and give you a better tour. If you want."

There was something charming and innocent and unthreatening about Erik, and he had a kind of energy and enthusiasm that MacKenzie liked. And MacKenzie was adventurous, and liked to do things her own way, apart from the rest of the herd. She had always been that way. Her father always said, she wasn't ever trying to be different. She just was different. And she was impulsive. And so, on an impulse, she decided to take Erik up on his offer.

"Okay," she said decisively. "But I have to be back by the end of tour, to return everything I rented."

Erik shook his head. "No, you don't. Just go talk to the tour guide. I know him. He's a nice guy. His name's Kyle. Just tell him you've changed your mind about the tour, so he can take you off his list. Then you can just keep using all the gear for as long as you want. They'll charge you more when you get back, though. They rent by the hour."

MacKenzie nodded. "That's okay," she said. "Alright, back in a second."

She paddled her way up to the tour guide and told him that one of her friends had showed up, and that she was going to be kayaking with him instead of going on the tour. The tour guide crossed her off his list, and reminded her that she would still be charged by the hour for the gear. She assured the guide that she understood, thanked him, and then paddled her way back to Erik.

"You're doing a really good job of paddling properly," said Erik.

MacKenzie smiled. "Thanks," she said. "I was watching some other kayakers go by, and I think I figured out how to do it."

"You're a quick learner."

"Thanks," said MacKenzie, flipping her sunglasses back down into place. "Okay. So, what happens first?"

Erik smiled and nodded. "Okay, then," he said happily, putting his own sunglasses back on. "Just follow me out of the harbor, and then we'll go side-by-side and I'll show you some cool stuff and tell you lots of really interesting information about everything."

MacKenzie smiled back and nodded. "Got it," she said. "Let's go."

And off they went.

As they made their way out of Avalon Bay, Erik told her all about the history of the distinctive Green Pleasure Pier near the Casino, and he told her much more information about the history of the Casino, and about all the famous old Hollywood stars who used to spend so much time on the island.

Erik led the two of them as far west as Frog Rock, then back past Avalon Harbor, now heading east. Erik talked the whole time, and he was helpful and entertaining and informative. He had grown up on Catalina, and loved the island, and seemed to know everything about it, particularly the island wildlife, and especially the history of the island. And he knew how to spot things. At Frog Rock, he had pointed out a bald eagle that was perched proudly atop a great rocky ledge at the shoreline. Even with the distinctive brilliant whiteness of its head, MacKenzie would never have noticed the eagle if Erik hadn't shown her it was there. He pointed out swimming turtles, and he told MacKenzie all about the large flat vividly orange fish that swam in calm swarms near the coastline, the famous Golden Garibaldi fish of Catalina.

"Up ahead is the Seal Rocks," Erik explained as they approached what looked like a small cluster of tiny tall little islands just off the rocky shoreline. "You can see how they got their name."

MacKenzie could see how. Over a dozen seals were lounging on the rocks like emperors whose reign was eternal, sleeping or flopping their bodies casually into more comfortable positions, basking in the sun and sea spray, and giving out a periodic bark to make some sort of seal announcement to the world.

"It's amazing," MacKenzie said in happy awe. "Seeing real animals in real life is so very different than seeing them in pictures or on tv."

Erik nodded as they continued to paddle slowly toward the rocks and the seals. "Even though I've lived here my whole life," he said, "I don't ever get bored by seeing all the different wildlife of the island. It's always still really exciting. It's fun getting to show you everything, Mac," he said. "It's exciting to show things to someone who's seeing them for the first time, if it's somebody who really gets it and really appreciates it."

They had been kayaking together for almost two hours by now. MacKenzie couldn't remember at what point Erik had started calling her by the shortened form of her name. She tried to figure out how she felt about that, and decided that she kind of liked it.

"Do you have any brothers or sisters?" Erik asked.

MacKenzie shook her head. "Just me and my dad."

Erik nodded. "Same with me. No brothers or sisters. Do you have any hobbies?" he asked.

MacKenzie nodded. "I collect baseball cards," she said.

Erik smiled. "That sounds so cool. Do you have any that are really valuable?"

MacKenzie shook her head. "Not really. My dad takes me to baseball card conventions. A lot of the cards that I really want are too expensive. What condition they're in makes a lot of difference. The ones in good condition are really expensive. My most valuable card is a 1954 Topps Jackie Robinson Brooklyn Dodgers card. The condition's not that great. But I really wanted one of those, and I couldn't afford any of the ones in better condition."

"So, you don't only collect Cubs cards?"

"Well, I have more Cubs cards than anything else. Especially a lot of new ones. I buy new ones all the time. They really don't cost very much new. But I have cards from lots of teams. Do you have a hobby?"

Erik was uncharacteristically silent for a moment. Then he said, "You're gonna laugh."

MacKenzie smiled. "I might," she said. "But probably not. It's not polite."

Erik nodded, and took a breath. "I like trains," he said.

"Not surf boards?" MacKenzie asked in genuine surprise.

Erik laughed. "No," he said smiling. "I've done some surfing, but I don't even own my own board."

MacKenzie looked at him. "So, you mean, trains, like, trains on train tracks?"

Erik nodded. "I've always loved trains. Ever since I was a kid. I really like locomotives, and I especially like the engineer and motor-man controls. I love all the dials and levers and knobs and switches that the engineer has to totally understand in order to make the train operate properly."

"That's a really cool hobby," said MacKenzie earnestly. "How did you ever get interested in that?"

"My dad travels a lot giving lectures," said Erik. "And once when I was little, he took me and my mom with him to a lecture overtown in Sacramento. And while we were there, they took me to the California Railroad Museum. It changed my life. Seeing those amazing old trains was the most exciting thing that had ever happened to me. And, my parents are both old-movie buffs, and they showed me a silent movie made in 1927 called *The General*, about a train during the Civil War. *The General* was the name of the train in the movie. The star of the movie was a famous actor named Buster Keaton. He's amazing, Mac. So funny, and such a genius with doing incredible stunts. He did all his own stunts. Really incredible. And then I was totally hooked. I was a trains fan for life. And also, even today I still think *The General* is one of the greatest movies ever made."

MacKenzie smiled. "That's a good story, Erik," she said. "I like it a lot."

"Thanks for not laughing," said Erik.

MacKenzie smiled. "Erik," she said, "what's that thing around your wrist that looks like a giant tooth?"

Erik lifted his right arm up to display it better. "It is a tooth," he said. "Shark tooth. I found it on the ocean floor the first time my parents ever took me scuba diving, in Monterey. I liked it so much, my dad drilled a hole through it and made it into a bracelet for me."

"It looks sharp," said MacKenzie. "How do you wear it without slicing your arm open in a bloody mess?"

Erik laughed. "It is sharp. But it only cuts if it's at just the right angle. And I like it too much not to wear it. I haven't cut myself on it yet."

"It looks dangerous," said MacKenzie. "But it's pretty cool. I like it."

"Thanks," said Erik, glancing at his diving watch. "You getting hungry yet?"

MacKenzie nodded. "Starving," she said.

"Okay," said Erik. "You want to head back to the harbor and get some lunch?"

MacKenzie nodded. "That sounds good."

"Speaking of scuba diving," Erik said, getting ready to turn his kayak around. "As part of your tour, I want to show something before we leave the Seal Rocks. You see that small red thing with the diagonal white stripe floating in the water over there?"

"Yes," said MacKenzie. "I noticed that. It's floating near that little boat that has nobody in it. What is it?"

"It's a scuba diving marker buoy," said Erik. "They're always red. Technically, it's a 'surface marker buoy', or SMB, but a lot of divers just call them 'blobs'. I don't know why. Maybe some of the old ones looked like red blobs. But it means someone's diving in that spot. And that's probably their boat."

A small empty dinghy with an unusually large and strangely-shaped outboard motor had apparently been anchored and was gently rising and falling with the small gradual swells of the ocean water.

"There's lots of kelp here," explained Erik. "On the surface it looks like a slimy mess. But below the water, the stipes—those are the stems—the stipes are straight like tree trunks. They're still wiggly, because it's seaweed. But every stipe is attached somewhere at the bottom of wherever the sea floor is, and every stipe goes from the bottom all the way up to the surface. So, this slimy mess on the surface is just like floating tree-tops. If you're snorkeling or scuba diving, and you're swimming through kelp underwater, it's like flying through a forest. If the sunlight is streaking through on an angle, it's like a magical forest. Really cool."

"It sounds amazing," said MacKenzie.

Erik nodded. "I'll bet whoever's diving here, they're probably enjoying that incredible experience right now."

MacKenzie poked at some of the kelp amassed at the surface in the water next to her. "Seems like they deserve the reward, if they swam down through this top part. It's pretty gross."

Erik laughed. "You definitely feel differently about the gross part after you've seen the beautiful part." He checked his watch again. "Okay, sorry I slowed us down. Let's head back and get some food."

MacKenzie smiled. "I'm very ready for that," she said enthusiastically.

They had just paddled their kayaks in a half-rotation to be nosed toward the direction they had come from, when bubbles from below suddenly began frothing the surface of the water near the dinghy. In a moment, the bubbles had become more bubbles, and then up from within the bubbles came the snorkel, facemask, breathing regulator, and head of a scuba diver emerging upward, breaking through the surface of the water.

Chapter 9

DIVER

The diver appeared to be a woman. She had surfaced next to the dinghy, and after taking the breathing regulator out of her mouth, she unfastened the front clasps of the straps attached to her air tank. While still remaining in the water, she then reached behind her head to the top of the scuba air tank on her back. Grasping it by the top, she easily slipped the tank and its harness up and off over her head as easily as if she were taking off a T-shirt. Hoisting the scuba tank with its various attached hoses trailing two regulators and two dial gauges, she swung it all smoothly through the air, up and over the side of the dinghy so that it landed gently and carefully-placed just inside the small boat.

Reaching down to her waist, she unfastened her weight belt and lifted it dripping out of the water, hoisting it upward over the side of the dinghy, then lowering it into the boat next to the air tank.

Disappearing back under the water, she apparently swam beneath the dinghy, and appeared a moment later on the opposite side. With the heaviness of the weight belt and the air-tank apparatus now positioned on one side of the dinghy to offset some of her weight, the diver grasped the top edge of the opposite side of the boat and pulled it down toward her. With a powerful dolphin-kick of her swim-flippers, she propelled and elevated herself up out of the water. In a single continuous fluid motion, like a smoothly-executed gymnastics move she swung one leg up and over the side into the boat as the rest of her body followed with a three-quarter-rotation turn, and suddenly she was completely aboard in a comfortable sitting position atop one of the thwarts. It was an artful and impressive display of strength and agility and experience.

"That was a nifty water exit," Erik said to the diver with admiration. "You have to be strong and coordinated and have good timing. Not easy."

"But you sure made it look easy," said MacKenzie.

The diver had apparently already been aware that MacKenzie and Erik were there in their kayaks when she had surfaced. She now glanced at them politely and took off her dive mask and snorkel, shaking some of the sea water out of her long blond hair.

"Hi there," she said them. "Katie Coleridge," she added, by way of introducing herself.

"Hi," said Erik. "Erik Roebling."

"Hi," said MacKenzie. "MacKenzie Milles."

Katie nodded politely. "Pleased to meet you," she said, starting to busily organize and arrange her diving gear in the boat.

"Where's your buddy?" asked Erik.

Katie shook her head. "No buddy today. Just me."

"You shouldn't be diving without a buddy," said Erik. "It's not safe."

"I know," Katie replied, nodding her head in agreement. "And you're right. I don't do it very often. But sometimes I have to. So," she went on, "are you two just kayaking around looking for divers to say hello to?"

Erik shook his head apologetically. "We didn't mean to intrude," he said. "People's business is their own business. We were just sightseeing the Seal Rocks, and talking about your blob, I mean, about your SMB. We were actually about to head back to Avalon for lunch when you surfaced. We thought it would be rude to just leave without saying hello."

Katie looked up from what she was doing and smiled at them. "Well, you two are very polite," she said.

To MacKenzie, Katie looked young, but she guessed that Katie really wasn't too much younger than her father.

"You're very pretty," said MacKenzie.

"Thanks, MacKenzie," said Katie, smiling again. "So are you. Sorry, Erik," she added. "It's a girls thing."

Erik smiled. "I understand," he said. "I don't get it, but I understand."

"Well, you both really are unusually polite," said Katie.

"Thank you," said MacKenzie.

Erik was eyeing the unusual-looking outboard motor with interest. "If you don't mind my asking," he said to Katie, "what kind of motor is that?"

"Electric," said Katie. "It's new. Much better for the environment. No pollution, much less noise."

"Does it hold a charge?" asked Erik

Katie shook her head as she unclipped a scuba pouch and an underwater-writing clipboard from her narrow diving belt. "Not for that long, unfortunately," she said. "But it's powerful, and it holds enough charge for short trips. It's technically a hybrid. It does have a gasoline-powered dynamo to charge the battery if I get into trouble."

"That's smart," said Erik.

"Why do you wear weights under water?" asked MacKenzie.

"If I'm going for a longer dive," said Katie, "even in warm water I wear a wetsuit. The wetsuit wants to float. My tank wants to sink, but not as much as my wetsuit wants to float. So the weights make up the difference. They all balance each other out. That leaves me at zero, which is where I want to be. I've set the weights for this wetsuit and this tank, but actually with a little bit extra. So I blow air into this vest while I'm underwater, or let some air out, if I want to be a little above or below zero. It's easier to add or remove air from the vest underwater than it would be to try to remove some of the weights underwater."

"Are you doing research?" asked MacKenzie. "My dad's doing research on the Catalina buffalo. That's why we're here."

"Where's your mom?" asked Katie.

"She's not alive anymore," said MacKenzie.

"Oh," Katie said, stopping what she was doing to look at MacKenzie. "I'm very sorry."

"Thanks," said MacKenzie.

Erik and MacKenzie dipped their paddles into the water for a moment to keep their kayaks from drifting away from the dinghy.

"Yes," said Katie. "I am doing research. My specialty is marine life, but especially coral. I'm doing research on the coral around the Seal Rocks. I'm doing some work for the USC Marine Science Center," she said, patting the side hull of the dinghy where a green circular logo read 'USC Wrigley Institute for Environmental Studies'.

MacKenzie looked at the stern of the boat, nearly entirely visible with the outboard motor temporarily tilted and raised out of the water. The name *Ada* had been painted or applied as a decal in stylized red cursive lettering with a thin white outline around the letters.

"Your boat's named *Ada*," said MacKenzie. "Is it named after William Wrigley, Jr's wife?"

Katie nodded. "It certainly is," she said.

"Katie, where are you from?" asked MacKenzie.

"I live in San Diego," said Katie. "My work is based there. Where are you from, MacKenzie?"

"Chicago," said MacKenzie.

"How about you, Erik?" asked Katie.

"Catalina," said Erik. "I live here with my mom and dad. I've lived here my whole life."

Katie smiled. "You're lucky. This is one of the most beautiful magical places on earth. So, you two said you had been about to head back for lunch. You must be pretty hungry by now."

"Would you like to join us for lunch?" asked MacKenzie.

"Mac," said Erik. "I'm sure Katie has plans of her own. We've already interrupted her day and her research enough, I think."

Katie looked at Erik and thought for a moment. "Roebling…" she began. "Are you related to the Brenda Roebling who does the trolley tours?"

Erik nodded. "That's my mom," he said proudly. "She does tours on the trolley, the open-air tram, and the Inland Expedition bus."

A look of smiling recognition came over Katie's face. "Oh, that's great," she said. "I took one of your mom's tram tours. She's really good. She makes everything really interesting, and she really knows what she's talking about. And she knows a lot about the island."

MacKenzie nodded. "That sounds just like Erik," she said.

Katie paused and looked at them. "How long have you two known each other?" she asked.

Erik looked at his diving watch. "About two hours," he said.

Katie laughed. "You are both very polite and very charming and very interesting. Sure. I'd love to have lunch with you. My treat, okay?"

"Wow, that's great," said MacKenzie enthusiastically. "You don't have to treat us, though. It will be nice just to have you with us for lunch."

Erik nodded. "There's no need to treat us, Katie. We'd be happy just having you join us for lunch."

Katie smiled. "You two really are polite. Well, we'll see about treating. For now, why don't you two start back. I'll meet you on Crescent, and then Erik can decide where we should go for lunch."

"That sounds great," said Erik.

"Thank you, Katie," said MacKenzie, smiling.

"Okay," said Katie. "Off you go."

And then, not far from where the three of them were bobbing in the water, over two dozen dolphins from nowhere suddenly broke the surface of the water and began leaping playfully through the air.

Katie and Erik and MacKenzie all stopped what they were doing and turned to watch the sudden spectacular performance.

The show didn't last long. The dolphins had been gleefully frolicking for less than a minute when they suddenly all turned in the same direction and began swimming off at top speed, leaping and diving and arcing over the surface and racing forward, away from the island, in the direction of the mainland. They were traveling so fast, they disappeared from view almost as suddenly as they had appeared.

"Well that certainly came out of nowhere," said Katie thoughtfully.

"It's just like what the dolphins did with the ferry when we first left Long Beach," said MacKenzie. "Only, now there's no boat."

Erik nodded slowly. "Yes, it's like they're playing their chasing show-off game with an invisible boat that we can't see."

"Erik, have you seen them do that before?" asked Katie.

Erik nodded. "I have. But only here at the Seal Rocks. I've never seen them play that invisible-boat chase game anywhere except here."

Katie nodded. "I've seen them do it here, too. It's unusual. They usually only do that with actual boats, and usually just larger boats, like the ferry."

"Could they be chasing a submarine?" asked MacKenzie.

"I suppose…" said Erik doubtfully. "I don't think there are any submarines around here…"

Katie nodded. "From below the surface, I once saw them do it while I was diving. There was nothing under the water that I could see. It's like you described it, Erik. It's like they're playing their chasing show-off game with an invisible boat."

"Well," said Erik, "they certainly seemed happy, anyway."

Katie nodded. "No creature knows how to enjoy life more than a dolphin," she said. "Alright, you two. Start paddling. I'll be motoring past you in a few minutes, and I'll meet you on Crescent whenever you get there."

Chapter 10
LUNCH

A few minutes later, Katie waved to them as she motored past in the dinghy named *Ada* and continued on her way, as MacKenzie and Erik paddled their way back to Avalon Harbor, a return trip made slightly slower because they spent the whole time chatting with each other.

When at last they arrived, Erik went to pull his kayak up onto the shore and lock it to a kayak rack, and MacKenzie went to the Wet Spot Rentals booth to return her rented kayaking gear, and happily discovered that the pass Davenport had given her covered all the extra time she had been out.

She retrieved her street clothes from the locker, paused to put some more sunblock on her nose and the tops of her ears just in case, and found Erik waiting for her at the end of the Cabrillo Mole.

The two of them made their way toward Crescent Ave to look for Katie, and Erik was happily surprised to find that Katie was over at the departure area for the trolley tour, talking with his mother.

Erik introduced his mother and MacKenzie to each other, and asked his mother if she wanted to join them for lunch, but she was about to head out with another tour group.

Since MacKenzie was such a fan of Italian food, and since, as Erik himself made clear, he was always in the right mood for pizza, and since Katie was perfectly happy to eat Italian food, the three of them decided to have lunch at the same little restaurant where MacKenzie had had dinner the night before with her father and Davenport.

Erik kissed his mother good-bye, and he and MacKenzie and Katie headed to lunch.

As they finished eating, with Katie sipping her coffee and MacKenzie and Erik sipping their sodas, the inevitable topic of dessert came up.

Katie checked her diving watch. "No dessert for me, I'm afraid," she said. "I have to get back to the Marine Center. But Erik, maybe MacKenzie would enjoy a visit to Big Olaf's ice cream."

Erik nodded enthusiastic agreement. "For sure," he said. "And maybe also Lloyd's of Avalon Confectionery."

MacKenzie smiled. "I've heard of both those places. That sounds like a delicious plan."

Their check arrived, and MacKenzie and Erik both reached for their pockets, but Katie was quicker than they were and had already handed her credit card to their waiter.

"My treat," Katie insisted firmly with a smile. "No protesting. You two can treat me next time."

"So, you'll have lunch with us again?" MacKenzie said hopefully.

Katie nodded. "That would be fun," she said. "And this lunch with you two today has been fun," she added. "Thank you for inviting me."

"Are you married?" MacKenzie asked her.

Katie lifted her left hand and waved her fingers showing no ring.

"Do you have a boyfriend?" asked MacKenzie.

"Mac!" Erik exclaimed. "That's people's private business!"

"It's just a polite getting-to-know-you question," MacKenzie protested innocently.

Katie smiled. "Do you have a boyfriend, MacKenzie?"

MacKenzie rolled her eyes. "I'm twelve," she said firmly, as if that answered the question.

"I had my first boyfriend when I was in kindergarten," said Katie.

MacKenzie smiled. "That's adorable!"

"It wasn't so adorable when he broke my heart and started liking a different girl when we got to first grade," said Katie.

MacKenzie nodded. "You deserve better," she said decisively.

Katie smiled. "Thank you, MacKenzie. That's very kind of you."

"Katie," asked MacKenzie. "Would you like to please come over to our cottage for dinner tonight?" She turned to Erik next to her. "Maybe you would like to please come to dinner tonight too?"

Erik shook his head. "My dad's going overtown first thing in the morning, and he's going to be gone for a few days doing lectures. I want to spend some time with him and my mom together tonight before he leaves."

MacKenzie nodded. "That's what I would want to do, too," she agreed.

Katie was looking at the two of them, smiling. "Okay, MacKenzie," she said. "That's a lovely invitation. I accept. Thank you very much."

MacKenzie beamed. "Really? Oh, that's awesome!" she said excitedly. "Thank you, Katie!"

Katie smiled. MacKenzie pulled out her map to show Katie where the cottage was, and described precise driving directions for how to get there. Katie was familiar with the location of the Machado ball field, so she expected no difficulty with finding the cottage.

MacKenzie and Katie exchanged phone numbers, in case anything unexpected came up, and MacKenzie suggested that Katie could show up any time after 6:30, which was around the time she and her father usually had dinner.

They all left the restaurant together. Katie thanked them again and said good-bye, and headed off to her golf cart.

MacKenzie and Erik made their way first to Big Olaf's ice cream, where they had towering colorful ice cream desserts, and then made their way to the Lloyd's of Avalon Confectionery to have their sugary after-dessert dessert.

Erik then went with MacKenzie to help her reserve a ticket for herself for a tour of the Casino. The two of them then exchanged phone numbers, and agreed to get together again first thing in the morning. They walked to where Erik had locked his mountain bike to a bike rack, said their good-byes, and Erik pedaled off toward his home.

On her own again, MacKenzie took the tour of the Casino building, where she learned about what Art Deco was, and all about the history of the magnificent ballroom and the famous celebrities who used to spend so much time on the island, and all about the vast and beautiful movie theater, which still showed movies, and which was where Erik had told her he was going with his parents later that evening to see a current modern-day movie.

Afterward, when she was unlocking her bike from the bike rack, MacKenzie realized she had been anxiously looking around for the mysterious man, and she was both relieved and disappointed that he was nowhere to be seen.

Given how early in the afternoon it still was, she was happily amazed at how much had happened to her during her first day in Avalon, and she was feeling light and free and relaxed as she pedaled her way back toward the cottage.

On her way, she passed Davenport driving in a Conservancy golf cart and heading in the opposite direction, likely having just come from dropping John off back at the cottage.

Davenport smiled and waved a big friendly hand at MacKenzie, and slowed to a stop just long enough to have a quick friendly exchange with her as she politely pulled her bike over to say hello.

"Did you have a fun day?" he asked.

MacKenzie nodded and smiled. "It was great. Thanks so much for the passes."

"Glad to hear," said Davenport, smiling broadly. "I've left more passes for you for tomorrow with your dad. He's waiting for you at the cottage."

"That's awfully generous of you, Mr. Davenport," she said with great appreciation. "Thanks so very much."

"Any time," replied Davenport cheerily. He waved and drove off, and MacKenzie waved good-bye and pedaled the rest of the way to the cottage.

Chapter 11
RADIO

As she had guessed, her father had left everything locked so that she could have the satisfaction of needing to use her keys. After unlocking the garage long enough to stash her bike inside, and after unlocking the front door of the cottage long enough to come inside, she made her way through the entryway and into the living room just as her father was coming into the living room from the kitchen.

"Hi, Dad!" she said happily, throwing herself into his arms and hugging him hello.

"Hi, honey," he said. "You are home very promptly. Right on time. It's not like you. Everything okay?"

MacKenzie laughed. "Everything's fine," she said taking off her scuba pouch and her sunglasses, and tossing them onto the one of the living room armchairs next to a large brown paper bag. "I'm on Catalina time. 'Twenty-six miles across the sea,'" she sang cheerily, bouncing up onto the back of the couch to sit closer to her father's eye level. "'Santa Catalina is a-waitin' for me...'"

"Hmm..." her father observed. "Either you had a really good day, or you're up to something sneaky, or possibly both..."

"Nonsense," she said brightly. "I'm just being me. How was your day? Did you learn anything important about what's happening to the buffalo?"

"I'll tell you all about it while we're playing catch. How was your day on your own in Avalon?"

"I made a new friend today, Dad."

Her father smiled. "Of course you did."

"I like meeting new people," she said with enthusiasm.

Her father nodded. "I know you do. And you're very good at it. People like you."

"Thanks, Dad."

"Who's your new friend?"

"His name is Erik. He's fourteen. He lives on Catalina. He's lived here his whole life. He's really fun. And I met his mom, too. She does trolley and bus tours around the island."

"Well, that really does sound like you had a fun day."

MacKenzie nodded. "We went sea kayaking together. I'll tell you all about it while we're playing catch. Dad, is it okay if Erik comes over for dinner tomorrow?"

"Of course. He could have come over tonight."

"His dad's about to go out of town," MacKenzie explained, "so he's spending tonight with his mom and his dad."

"He sounds like a very nice boy," said her father. "Yes, of course he can come over for dinner tomorrow night."

"Thanks, Dad!"

MacKenzie paused for a moment, then cautiously proceeded. "So," she went on slowly, "it would have been okay if Erik came over for dinner tonight? Even if I had just invited him out-of-the-blue without you and me talking about it first?"

Her father nodded. "Of course, honey. You don't always need to check with me first. It would have been totally fine."

"Okay," MacKenzie said carefully. "That's really good to hear, because I did invite someone else to dinner tonight."

Her father raised an eyebrow with suspicion. "Yes, and...?"

"She's really nice, Dad. You'll like her. Her name is Katie, and she's a scuba diver, and she lives in San Diego, and she's doing research on coral for the USC Wrigley Marine Center. And she's really pretty, and very smart, and lots of fun to be around. And she was really nice to me and Erik, even though she's never met us before and we just barged in on the research work she was trying to do scuba diving at the Seal Rocks. And she kind of knows Erik's mom. And then Katie took me and Erik to lunch after we invited her, and we had yummy food at the same Italian place where you and me and Mr. Davenport had dinner last night. And she's super friendly."

Her father folded his arms in dissatisfaction. "Mac," he said sternly. "Are you trying to fix me up with someone again?"

"Why would you say that?" she asked innocently.

"Because," her father said, "you're always trying to find a nice person for me to spend time with. Because you think I miss having someone. Because you don't want me to be lonely."

"Would that be so bad if it was true?"

"Mac. I have you. That's all I need."

"I love you, Dad."

"I love you too, honey."

MacKenzie leapt from the back of the couch and gave her father a hug, and then looked up at him intently. "Okay," she said. "So, then I'm not trying to fix you up with someone. We're just having a new friend."

"MacKenzie Milles," he said looking down at her. "You do realize I'm not an idiot, correct?"

She nodded. "Correct. You are the smartest person I know, and you are the best Dad in the whole world."

Her father shook his head. "You may think you're being devious, young lady, but you're not. You're being obvious."

"What's 'devious'?"

"Being skillfully sneaky to get what you want. 'The girl tried to be so tricky that no one would realize what she was really up to.' Et cetera."

"There's no 'devious' in that example sentence."

John nodded. "That's my point. You think you're being

devious, but you're so obvious that 'devious' didn't even make it into the example sentence."

"Oh, yes," she agreed, nodding emphatically. "That's totally me. I'm obvious. If I was up to something, you'd know it. So, nothing to see here."

John gave her an exasperated loving smile. He lifted her baseball cap, mussed her hair affectionately, then put her cap back in place on her head.

MacKenzie always liked when he did that, and she grinned happily.

Her father sighed heavily. "You are a piece of work," he said. "We'll discuss this later."

"You're the best, Dad," said MacKenzie.

Her father looked at her. "Would this be a good time for me to tease you about your new friend Erik?" he suggested.

MacKenzie gave her father a frown of dissatisfaction. "Dad!" she said indignantly. "Come on already! We're just friends."

Her father nodded. "I'll just take that as a no."

"Thank you!" MacKenzie replied with exasperation.

"So," her father went on, "then would this be a good time for me to tell you that I got us a present?"

"Really?" MacKenzie's eye lit up with eager interest. "I like presents. What is it?"

"Well," her father explained, "it's *kind* of a present. We can't keep it. But I think you'll like it."

"The short-wave radio!" MacKenzie guessed jubilantly.

Her father nodded. "We can use it for as long as we're here," he said, walking over to one of the armchairs. "Ed borrowed it from a friend, so we have to take very good care of it."

He reached into the large brown paper bag and lifted the big black short-wave radio out, holding it by a thick black strap attached to large chrome guard-bars mounted at opposites ends of the housing.

"Dad!" she exclaimed excitedly, dashing over to look at it. "It's as big as a suitcase! It's so cool!"

"A small suitcase, maybe," suggested her father.

"That is so cool-looking!" MacKenzie gushed, visually drinking in every detail of the new object. "It looks like a giant transistor radio, only from a science fiction movie. There are so many dials and knobs and things. Erik will love this. He loves control panels. I mean, he mostly likes control panels for trains, but he still likes controls. He will love this! Do you know how to work it? Does it work? Will it pick up WGN 720? What's that big t-shaped bar sticking out of the top?"

Her father laughed and lowered the radio by its strap to a gentle rest on the top of the coffee table. "Okay," he began. "So, yes, I know how to work it. You may have chosen to forget, but I was born in 1949. I grew up listening to short-wave radios. And yes, it works. Ed's friend uses it all the time, and Ed and I tested it at the Conservancy to be sure, it works fine. This rotating bar sticking out of the top is the antenna. The base of the antenna says 'Direction Finder', but really it's the antenna. You swivel it around to get the best reception you can for the channel you want. And I have no idea if it will pick up WGN. It should, but I thought you and I would try that out together."

MacKenzie was enthralled. "It's so cool-looking!" she repeated, unable to take her eyes off it. "Can we try it now?"

Her father shook his head and looked at his watch. "Listen," he said. "We want to have time to play catch. And we have to take Bertie over to the Vons for some shopping, because apparently we're having a guest for dinner."

"Bertie!" repeated MacKenzie, laughing. She gave her father another hug. "Thanks, Dad. You're the best. Really."

Her father smiled. "Okay. Vons first, then we'll see how much time we have for catch when we get back."

"Since we're having company," said MacKenzie, "can we have a fire in the fireplace? Mr. Davenport said it was safe to use. And there's all that firewood stacked up in the backyard."

"Are you willing to be in charge of bringing firewood into the living room without making a mess?"

"Do I still get to help make dinner?"

"Yes."

"Okay then. Deal."

"Deal. Now go get yourself into the golf cart."

"Bertie!" MacKenzie sang out joyfully, and headed toward the front door.

Chapter 12

GUEST

By 6:30, MacKenzie and her father had done all their shopping at Vons, plugged Bertie back in to charge, unpacked all the groceries, headed down to the ball field for their game of catch, shared with each other all the highlight details of their day, returned to the cottage to get showered and cleaned up, and had all the makings of dinner well underway.

The cottage doorbell rang. It was the first time MacKenzie had heard it ring. Like the rest of the cottage, its simple two-tone sound had a charming old muted soft-spoken quality that seemed to fondly and quietly echo decades of past visitors.

"I'll get it!" MacKenzie called out authoritatively.

She ran to door and threw it open to reveal Katie standing on the other side.

"Katie!" MacKenzie cried out happily, and threw herself gently into Katie's body with an affectionate hug.

"Hi, MacKenzie," Katie said cheerily.

MacKenzie stepped back politely. "Come on in. You smell good."

Katie laughed and stepped through the doorway into the front entryway. "Thanks, MacKenzie," she said.

Katie was wearing jeans and a black sweater. MacKenzie decided she looked even prettier than she had at lunch, or even when she had first come out of the water at the Seal Rocks and was shaking the water out of her hair while sitting in Ada. MacKenzie tried to figure out if Katie was just naturally pretty, or if she was wearing make-up but had put it on so well that it couldn't be noticed, but it was a mystery she couldn't solve.

MacKenzie took Katie by the hand and led her into the living room at the same time that John was coming into the living room from the kitchen.

"Dad, this Katie. Katie, this is my Dad."

John and Katie both smiled at each other politely and shook hands.

"Hi, Katie," said MacKenzie's father. "John Milles. Pleased to meet you."

"Katie Coleridge," said Katie. "Pleased to meet you, John."

"MacKenzie is a big fan of yours," said John. "It's very nice of you to come over for dinner."

Katie smiled. "MacKenzie and Erik are such lovely people," said Katie. "They completely charmed me, and I couldn't resist."

John nodded. "I haven't met Erik yet, but it's very like MacKenzie to be a magnet for kindred spirits. From what I hear, the three of you had a nice lunch together."

Katie nodded. "It was a lot of fun."

"What are 'kindred spirits'?" asked MacKenzie.

"A kindred spirit," said John, "is a person who likes what you like, feels the way you feel, sees the world the way you see it. 'The moment she met him, she could tell how much they were alike, and she knew she had found a kindred spirt.' Et cetera."

MacKenzie nodded. "Thanks, Dad."

Katie was holding the thin round handles of a narrow paper bag in one hand, and she handed it to John. "I brought some wine for dinner," she said. "I hope red is okay."

John smiled and took the bag she was offering. "That's very nice of you," he said. "Thank you."

"I know," MacKenzie said, looking pointedly at her father. "I can't have any. Don't worry, I won't ask."

"Did you have soda with lunch today?" her father asked.

"Maybe..." MacKenzie replied evasively.

"So, then, just water for you tonight at dinner?"

"Dad. There was way more sugar in the desserts we had than in the soda."

Her father looked at her. "That information is definitely not helping you at the moment."

"Dad," MacKenzie said importantly. "This is a very special occasion. Katie is a very special friend. I think it's probably okay if I have soda with dinner."

Her father rolled his eyes. "Fine," he said with half-hearted resignation. He turned to Katie. "She runs the house," he said. "I just try to stay out of the way."

Katie smiled at them both.

"Just so you know," MacKenzie said to her, "I have the best Dad in world." And she gave her father a loving hug.

Katie's eyes glistened slightly for a moment as she smiled thoughtfully at MacKenzie and her father.

"MacKenzie, I brought you a little present," said Katie, reaching into a pocket of her jeans.

MacKenzie's eyes lit up. "You didn't have to do that, Katie," she said earnestly. "Just you being here for dinner is the best present."

"Thank you, MacKenzie," said Katie. "But really, it is a very little present. It's not especially valuable, but I think you might like it."

Katie opened her hand and held it out toward MacKenzie. It held something small and dark and round and flat.

"Thank you so much, Katie," said MacKenzie, gently taking the object from Katie's hand. "What is it?"

"It's a penny," said Katie. "I found it on the ocean floor during one of my dives at the Seal Rocks. It's dated 1951. That's the last year the Cubs had Spring Training here on the island."

"Oh my god..." said MacKenzie breathlessly, turning the coin over in her hands and studying it with great care. "This is so incredibly cool… What an amazing present. Thank you!"

Katie smiled. "I hope you like it."

"I love it! Dad, look what Katie gave me!"

MacKenzie held the sea-and-time-weathered coin out to her father. John took it from MacKenzie's hand for a moment and examined it, before carefully handing it back to her. "That's a wonderful gift," he said. "There's all kinds of history and significance going on in that little coin."

"I love it…!" MacKenzie said, holding the coin with great care and looking up intently at Katie. "Thank you, Katie."

Katie smiled. "You're very welcome, MacKenzie," she said, and turned toward John. "She's exceptionally gracious and polite," Katie said to him with impressed appreciation.

John nodded. "I don't know where she gets that from. But it is one of her many admirable qualities. She makes me proud of her every day."

"When I'm not being annoying," MacKenzie clarified.

John smiled. "Mac, you being annoying is a luxury I would not ever want to live without."

MacKenzie beamed and looked at Katie. "See what I mean? No one has a better Dad than me."

"Okay," said John. "You two hang out here and chat, and I'll go finish up dinner."

"Dad," MacKenzie protested. "Remember? You promised I could help make dinner."

John looked at her. "Honey," he said. "You've been helping to make dinner. You've practically made it all already, all by yourself. I just stood around and talked while you did all the work."

MacKenzie nodded. "So it only makes sense that I should see the project through to its final proper completion," she said matter-of-factly.

Her father rolled his eyes and smiled affectionately at his daughter, and Katie grinned at them both.

"Who's going to haul in the firewood?" John asked MacKenzie.

"Oh," said Katie in happy surprise. "Are we having a fire?"

MacKenzie nodded. "I love fires," she announced enthusiastically. "We don't have a fireplace in Chicago."

"What a lovely idea," said Katie. "I like fires too."

"Okay," said MacKenzie. "I've got this all figured out. You two sit here and chat, and I'll go haul in the firewood. Then, Dad, you can make the fire, and I'll finish making dinner. Dad, did you tell Katie about the short-wave radio yet?"

"MacKenzie," said her father. "We've all three of us been standing here together the whole time."

"Well, I think you should tell her about it. It's really interesting."

Katie grinned again and John smiled patiently.

"MacKenzie," her father said, lifting up the bag Katie had handed him. "I'm going into the kitchen to open the wine and pour two glasses for Katie and me. And a glass of soda for you. Why don't you show Katie around the cottage, and then you can be in charge of hauling firewood and finishing dinner, and I'll get the fire started."

MacKenzie nodded. "Deal," she said. "Okay, come on, Katie. I'll show you my room. Oh, wait. First I'll show you the dining room where we'll be eating."

Katie and John smiled at each other, and John turned to head back into the kitchen as MacKenzie took Katie's hand and led her into the dining room.

"What a charming cottage this is," Katie remarked.

MacKenzie nodded. "Like everything else on Catalina," she said, "this house has all kinds of really interesting stories that go with it. We'll tell them to you at dinner. This is the dining room table. My

Dad and I set it together, because I can never remember which side the silverware is supposed to go on, no matter how many mnemonic devices my Dad give me."

"MacKenzie," said Katie, "what is a mnemonic device?"

MacKenzie nodded. "Mnemonic is an adjective that means having to do with memory," she explained. "It comes from the Greek goddess Mnemosyne. She's the personification of memory. And so a mnemonic device is a memory trick that helps you remember something. 'She knew that she wrote with her left hand, so she used that as a mnemonic device to remember her left from her right.' Et cetera."

Katie laughed. "Thanks, MacKenzie," she said. "That was brilliant!"

MacKenzie beamed. "Thank you, Katie!" she said happily. "Okay, come on. I'll show you my room."

An hour or so later, Katie had received her tour of the cottage, John had built a roaring fire in the living room fireplace, and the three of them were at the dining room table finishing the last of their dinner.

"Wow, MacKenzie," Katie was saying. "Did you really make this?" She looked at John for a moment. "Did she really make dinner? MacKenzie, this food was delicious. You have a real talent."

MacKenzie grinned happily. "Thank you, Katie. Katie, tell Dad about your research on coral."

Katie looked at John. "Well," she said slowly. "If it doesn't leave this room, I can tell you that it's not exactly research. The Conservancy asked me to come here to help them solve a mystery. All the coral at the Seal Rocks are dying. Something's killing them, and I've been asked to try to figure out what it is…"

MacKenzie and her father exchanged a look. Katie spotted it right away.

"What...?" said Katie.

John nodded at MacKenzie. "It's okay, he said. "I think we can trust Katie. She certainly has trusted us."

"What is it...?" said Katie.

"I'm not here doing research, either," John explained. "Like you, I also was asked to come here to solve a mystery. And I've been asked to maintain secrecy about it, I expect for the same reasons that you have. Large clusters within the bison herd are sick. Very sick. I've been asked to try to figure out what the cause is."

"Oh, my goodness..." said Katie.

MacKenzie began to clear the table. She cleared all the dishes and silverware from the dining room table to the kitchen in several unobtrusive trips while her father and Katie talked shop and discussed with each other the various symptoms they had each found in their respective investigations so far.

"Anybody want coffee?" MacKenzie asked as she was on her way out with the final load of dishes.

"Seriously?" asked Katie. "MacKenzie, you know how to make coffee?"

John nodded. "She makes it much better than I do. I can't start the day without a cup of MacKenzie's coffee."

Katie smiled broadly, and MacKenzie beamed with pride.

"Yes," said Katie. "I'd love some coffee. Though, perhaps some more wine first, please?"

"Of course," said John, and he poured out the rest of the wine first into her glass and then the last of it into his own.

A few minutes later, MacKenzie returned to announce that coffee was underway. "We also have some vanilla chocolate chip ice cream," she added. "In case anyone wants dessert."

Katie smiled. "No thank you, MacKenzie. Coffee will be fine for me."

"No ice cream for me, thank you," said John. "But, perhaps you'd like to scoop some for yourself, Mac?"

MacKenzie grinned. "You always have the best ideas, Dad," she said.

When MacKenzie returned with her large bowl of ice cream, her father and Katie were still discussing their investigations.

"Katie," her father was saying. "It's far from my field of expertise, but what you're describing sounds to me a little bit like cyanide poisoning."

Katie stopped what she was doing and looked at John. "Oh, my goodness… John, you're right. I hadn't thought of that, but you're absolutely right. I have to test for that first thing tomorrow morning…"

"What's cyanide?" asked MacKenzie.

"It's like a kind of poison," John began. "It's not technically a poison, exactly. Technically, it's a salt of something called hydrocyanic acid. But it's very toxic, which basically means it's poison."

"But why would there be cyanide in the water at the Seal Rocks?" MacKenzie asked.

"That would be another mystery," said her father.

Katie nodded seriously. "But first," she said, "the first thing to do would be to establish that what's happening to the coral really is cyanide poisoning…"

"It sounds scary…" said MacKenzie. "Dad, is it dangerous for Katie to be diving there if there's cyanide?"

"Well…" John began. "Now that Katie knows there's a possibility of cyanide in the water there, I'm sure she'll do whatever she needs to do to make sure she stays safe."

Katie nodded. "Your dad's right," she said reassuringly. "Now that I know what might be there, I can be sure to be extra careful."

"Okay…" said MacKenzie, worried and unconvinced. "Dad, what do people use cyanide for?"

"Well..." her father began. "It's used for many different things. But, really, where it's mostly used is in gold and silver mines."

MacKenzie sat bolt upright in her seat. "Gold mining...?"

Her father nodded. "Cyanide helps to separate the precious metal, that would be the gold or the silver, from the rest of the rock that the gold or silver are in when they're mined."

"Dad!" said MacKenzie adamantly. "The weird guy in Long Beach, the treasure story, the lava tubes, the sick buffalo, the sick coral, the dolphins acting strange, and now cyanide from a gold mine? You still think these are all not connected?"

"Stay on your base, Sherlock Milles," said her father. "That ball is very high in the air, and we have no idea where it's going to come down..."

Katie looked back and forth between John and MacKenzie. "Do you mind if I ask what you two are talking about...?" she said.

John ran a confused hand through his hair. "It's complicated..." he said. "Let's shift to the living room, and we'll tell you all about it, if you really want to know..."

"I do," replied Katie, nodding. "I do very much want to know..."

Chapter 13
DISCOVERY

About half an hour later, MacKenzie and her father had shared with Katie all the various details of the chain of several seemingly-unconnected strange occurrences and surfacing information or hints of information which had manifested in their lives over the course of the past two days, details that MacKenzie remained convinced were somehow all connecting links in some as yet unrecognizable mystery. Katie and John were sitting in the two living room armchairs, and MacKenzie was reclining on the couch. The short-wave radio had been moved to one of the couch end tables, and the three of them were sitting angled so they could all see each other and also the fireplace. Katie and John were relaxing drinking their coffee, and MacKenzie was relaxing drinking hot chocolate. The ever-changing flickering light of the dancing flames, and gentle scent of slowly burning logs, and the soothing continuous soft pops and quiet crackling of the fire cast a spell of warmth and safe coziness over the living room.

"Katie," MacKenzie was saying. "Will you come back for dinner tomorrow night? Erik's going to be here, too. I mean, I haven't invited him yet, but I'm going to when I see him tomorrow."

Katie took a sip of her coffee and looked at John.

John looked at MacKenzie. "Mac," he said. "We've only just finished tonight's dinner. The evening isn't even over yet."

MacKenzie took a drink of her hot chocolate and nodded. "I'm just planning ahead," she said sensibly. "Why just let life happen to you if you can take control and make it go the way you want?"

Her father smiled at her. "I'm sure Katie has other things going on in her life." John looked over at Katie. "But, if you're not busy,

Katie, we'd of course love to have you come back for dinner tomorrow night."

Katie looked back at John. "Well," she said. "MacKenzie's a hard person to say no to."

John nodded. "After twelve years, I still haven't figured out how to say no to her."

Katie smiled. "I don't know how to do it either," she said. "So I guess I'll just say yes. Yes, I'd love to come back for dinner tomorrow night. Thank you both very much."

"Katie!" MacKenzie exclaimed joyously, bursting to life with exhilarated energy, and practically tipping over her hot chocolate as she hurriedly left it on the coffee table before dashing over and throwing her arms around Katie where she sat in one of the armchairs, nearly spilling Katie's cup of coffee in the process.

"Oh, Katie! Thank you!" she said emphatically, and buried her head in Katie's long blond hair.

Katie looked over MacKenzie's shoulder at John, who was smiling at her, and Katie reached over to place her coffee on an end table so that she could gently pat the back of MacKenzie, who wasn't letting go.

After a few more moments, Katie put her hands on MacKenzie's shoulders and carefully steered her back upright. MacKenzie was crying, and tears streaked her face.

John put his coffee down in some alarm and was ready to launch himself out of his seat over to his daughter.

"I... I'm sorry you guys..." MacKenzie managed to say. She did not seem upset, and somehow she was smiling. "I'm sorry... I'm okay, honestly..."

With gentle fingers Katie wiped away from MacKenzie's cheeks what seemed to be the last of her tears, and gently smoothed and tidied MacKenzie's glossy strawberry-blond hair to either side of her face.

"MacKenzie…" Katie said softly. "Are you sure you're okay…?"

MacKenzie nodded. "I'm okay…" she said. "I'm not sad… I'm… I'm actually really happy." An unconscious laugh escaped for a moment from her smiling mouth. She looked over at her father. "I'm fine, Dad. Honestly. It's just… This has just been a really fun and wonderful day. And… And now it seems like tomorrow might also be a fun and wonderful day, and… And I think I just got overwhelmed…"

Katie smiled gently at MacKenzie. "MacKenzie," she said, "I think you should convince your dad that you're really okay."

MacKenzie smiled back at Katie and nodded, and then made her way to standing up with Katie helping to steer. MacKenzie went over to her father's chair and sat in his lap, leaning back against him and putting her arms around his neck. "I'm okay, Dad," she said. "You know I'd tell you if I wasn't."

John nodded, putting an arm around her shoulders and smoothing her hair with his other hand. "I know, honey," he said gently.

"Because," MacKenzie went on, "if I have something to complain about, you know I'll complain about it."

MacKenzie and her father both laughed together for a moment. "That is so very true," her father said.

"For instance," MacKenzie went on, "it turns out my arms are really sore from kayaking."

Her father nodded. "That's going to get worse before it gets better," he said. "You used muscles you've never used before in that way. Bad news, you're going to be even more sore when you wake up tomorrow morning. I vote that you stretch before bed, and maybe go to sleep a little earlier than normal. Give your body a chance to rest and recover and restore itself."

MacKenzie nodded. "Dad," she said. "Would you talk some more, please? Maybe you could tell Katie about your investigation. You haven't really told her about that yet."

John looked over at Katie, whose eyes were momentarily glistening again. She was sipping her coffee, and they both smiled at each other. "It's a match made in heaven," John said to Katie. "She and I are both happier when I'm talking."

Katie laughed. "I know you're not supposed to discuss what you've been finding so far," she said.

John shook his head and continued to slowly smooth MacKenzie's hair. "I think everyone in this room can be trusted to keep in confidence anything we all discuss."

MacKenzie nodded her head firmly that he was correct.

"And actually," John went on, "there's been frustratingly little progress so far. Whatever it is, it doesn't seem to be communicable. Meaning," he added, glancing down at MacKenzie, "it doesn't seem to be a sickness they're giving to each other. It seems to be something environmental, meaning there's something around them someplace that's making them sick. And it's not all of them. Just certain clusters, meaning only certain groups of bison, not the whole herd."

Katie took another sip of her coffee and nodded thoughtfully. "And it sounds like the clusters are localized?" she asked.

John nodded. "They are. We spent today sampling air, water, and soil from those areas, but we hadn't turned up anything by the end of the day. We haven't started any blood samples yet, because we know that sort of thing will be stressful on the animals. But we're going to have to soon."

"What's 'localized'?" asked MacKenzie.

Her father smiled. "She's feeling better. That's a good sign."

A relieved smile spread across Katie's face.

"Localized," John went on. "I tend to use it as an adjective, but that's not really correct. Katie used it correctly. Really it's a verb. Gathered or collected or staying in a particular place. 'Her sore muscles were localized mostly in her hands, arms, and shoulders'."

"Et cetera," agreed MacKenzie. "Thanks, Dad."

"MacKenzie," said Katie, "this may be the best coffee I've ever had. Your father wasn't exaggerating."

MacKenzie sat up, looking and feeling much more like herself. "Can I get you some more?"

Katie nodded. "That would be lovely. Yes, please."

"How about you, Dad?" asked MacKenzie, getting to her feet.

Her father nodded. "I can never get enough of your coffee, Mac. I hope you made enough."

MacKenzie smiled. "Plenty," she said confidently. "I like to plan ahead."

MacKenzie collected their cups, ferried them off to the kitchen, poured fresh coffee into both, and brought them back to the living room, handing Katie's cup to her, and her father's cup to him.

"Thank you," said Katie.

"You are a national treasure," said her father. "For this relief, much thanks."

MacKenzie grinned at Katie. "My Dad's quoting 'Hamlet' again. It's his favorite play. I've never read it, so I have no clue what he's talking about."

Katie started to giggle and nearly spilled her coffee.

"Okay," said MacKenzie. "You two talk amongst yourselves. I'm going to use the bathroom. Excuse me, I'll be back in a minute."

MacKenzie had neither the need nor any interest in actually using the bathroom. She just wanted to leave her father and Katie a few minutes to be alone together, so she headed toward the bathroom but then took a last-minute detour into her bedroom and quietly closed the door.

She stood where she was, looking around her room. She had brought a stack of books to read, because she loved reading, but she didn't feel like reading at the moment. Her thoughts were racing and wandering through her mind along all kinds of new paths, and she absently wondered if she should actively try to untangle all of her thoughts, or just let them roam wild until they managed to sort themselves out.

She went over to her bed and flopped down onto her back. She lay there on her bed and looked toward the ceiling. But she wasn't seeing the ceiling, she was seeing a movie in her mind of everything that had happened to her during the day. She was going back to look at certain details of the movie more closely, and re-watching certain parts of the movie that she especially liked.

One of her hands found its way to the wall, and her fingers began idly and absently tracing the grooves of the wood paneling. She was thoroughly absorbed and lost in re-watching a scene in the movie of her day when something caused her to shift her focus. Her wandering fingers had accidently pulled something loose. She rolled over and looked to see what her hand had done.

A small section of the paneling had been pulled slightly away from the wall. Her first thought was guilt at having damaged the wall, and she hurriedly pushed the loose piece back into place. It slipped back to where it belonged so smoothly and completely, she couldn't even see where it had come away in the first place. Her next thought was relief that she hadn't accidentally caused any permanent damage to the Englewoods' lovely little cottage. But her next thought was one of curiosity. Why had the loose piece fit back into place so perfectly? It wasn't like a flaw or a break in the wood paneling. It was more like...

She rolled fully over onto her stomach and pulled her face right up to the wall. She still couldn't see any seam-line in the wood. She re-traced her fingers' steps, at first finding nothing but endlessly smooth and smoothly-grooved wood-paneled wall. But then her fingers found it again. There was some small little place that she couldn't see, but which was exactly right for catching the edge of a fingertip.

With a silent apology to the Englewoods, she pulled again at the wood. It resisted moving more than only the smallest bit, and then it resisted some more, and then suddenly it was open. It was a small door. It was fastened with tiny brass hinges that were dark with age, and it revealed a small compartment. Like a safe, MacKenzie thought to herself. A secret safe. The inside of the secret safe wasn't very big, but it was very dark and shadowy. From what MacKenzie could see, it looked like it was empty. But the inside dropped down, so she couldn't see the bottom, or fully see if there was anything on the bottom, wherever it was. Hoping that she wasn't about to find a handful of spiders, or disgusting biting insects, or slimy worms, or a nest of angry rats, she reached her hand down into the darkness.

Her hand touched the bottom. Or least, she thought it was the bottom at first, but it seemed too wobbly. She reached around some more and realized that it wasn't the bottom. It was something flat resting on the bottom. Her fingers found the edged of whatever it was, and grasped hold.

She lifted her find up and out from the darkness and sat up on her bed to look at what she was now holding in her hand. It was a colorful old square tin box. It was about the same dimensions and proportion as a medium-sized box of chocolate. It had very old-fashioned lettering on it, that seemed to be advertising tobacco. The lettering and the details of the advertising design were raised up slightly from the surface of the tin lid, and MacKenzie could feel them as she ran her fingers over the uneven surface. Some of the color had faded or flecked away, but most of the color was still there and surprisingly bright.

There were no hinges. The lid appeared to be simply pressed closed over the rest of the tin. There was a thin round rim running all the way around the bottom edge of the lid, and MacKenzie set her fingers to work trying to use that rim as a way to pull the lid off the top of the box. The lid at first did not want to come off, but MacKenzie found the right way to pull with the right angle of pressure, working her way repeatedly around the lid edge, and with a quick metallic sliding sound and an almost inaudible rush of air, suddenly the tin was open.

She became aware of a combination of very faint smells. There was a slight scent of something like cigarettes, a smell of long ago, a smell of wax, and a smell like paper or cardboard that somehow seemed familiar.

Whatever was inside was all wrapped carefully in wax paper. Setting the lid down on the bed, she reached gingerly into the bottom section of the tin and began to carefully unfold the wax paper to reveal what was inside. And as she saw the contents, her mouth opened and her eyes became round with amazement.

Chapter 14
CARDS

MacKenzie came hurrying into the living room, cradling the bottom section of the tin box in one hand as carefully as if it were an open carton of fresh eggs or a tray of crystal glassware, and carrying a clean towel from the kitchen and a small stack of her father's 3 x 5 index cards in the other.

"Oh my god, you guys...! Dad...! You'll never guess what we forgot to bring with us to Catalina...!"

Her father and Katie hadn't moved from where they were talking and sipping coffee in their armchairs, and they looked up at MacKenzie with curiosity and surprise as she rushed into the room. She put the towel and index cards down on the couch coffee table just long enough to move her mug of hot chocolate safely away to one of the couch end tables. Then with speed and care, she began to spread out and straighten the kitchen towel to cover part of the coffee table surface, while still cradling the bottom section of the tin box.

"What did we forget?" her father asked with a puzzled look on his face.

"My baseball card price guide! Oh my god... You guys will absolutely not believe what I just found hidden in a secret compartment in the wall of my room...!"

John and Katie had now put their coffee cups down on end tables and were sitting up and looking with mounting interest at MacKenzie.

"Honey, what are you talking about?" her father asked.

"Okay, so, you can't touch them," said MacKenzie. "I don't even want to touch them. I don't want to accidentally mess up their condition... They're in perfect condition! Like new! You guys have to see this...!"

Placing the tin box bottom down on the towel, she gently moved aside the top folds of the opened wax-paper wrapping and used an index card like a spatula to reach into the midst and gingerly lift a small card up and out. With great care, she lowered the index card and its precious cargo down onto the towel.

"Come here, you guys...!" MacKenzie insisted. "You have to see this...! Dad...! Look at this...! Do you know what this is...?! Oh my god... I know you'll know what this is the second you see it...!"

John and Katie both rose from their chairs and made their way over to where MacKenzie was standing protectively over the coffee table, her eyes bright with amazed disbelief and uncontainable excitement. Coming around from opposite sides into the space between the couch and the coffee table on either side of her, they looked down at what was lying atop the index card on the towel.

John's jaw dropped in very much the same way MacKenzie's had when she had first recognized what had been wrapped in the wax paper.

"Honus Wagner..." her father said in quiet awe.

MacKenzie nodded emphatically, grabbing on to her father's arm, barely able to keep herself from jumping up and down with giddiness.

"Dad...!!" she exclaimed. "There's nine different cards in here! And they're all like new! Just like the Honus Wagner! And there's a map of Catalina, and there's a piece of stationery that was folded around the map, and the name at the top of the stationery is Paul Cavanarro. These must belong to him. These have to be his cards. Dad, is he still alive? We have to find out. He will be so excited to get these back!"

"Mac," her father said seriously. "I know how good your

memory is. Do you remember the names of the other eight players?"

MacKenzie nodded. "Yes."

"Okay," he father went on. "The cards all should be touched or moved as little as possible. You can keep the map and the stationery out, but get that Honus Wagner carefully back into the wax paper with the others, and fold it up just the way it was when you found it. Where's the lid?"

"On my bed."

"I'll get it," Katie volunteered, already moving carefully away from the coffee table and starting toward the hall, looking completely mystified as to the meaning of anything that was happening at the moment.

"Thank you, Katie," said John.

"Dad..." MacKenzie breathed in exhilarated awe.

Her father nodded. "It's extraordinary..." he agreed.

MacKenzie replaced everything in the tin box just as she had found it, meticulously re-folding the wax paper exactly as it had been folded. She re-covered it all, with the tin lid pressed firmly back onto the box and securely into place. She kept the stationery and the map out, and decided the best safest place for the tin box was where she had found it. After showing her father and Katie the secret compartment, and describing to them how she had accidentally discovered it, she re-placed the box carefully back at the bottom of the dark shadowy compartment and re-closed the secret door in the paneled wall.

While the names were still clear in her mind, she wrote out on an index card a list of all nine players whose baseball cards she had found wrapped in the wax paper. Her father then helped her to find a letter-sized piece of paper in one of the kitchen drawers, and MacKenzie prepared to write her letter to Paul Cavanarro to tell him all about what she had found, and to ask him how she could return it all to him.

A short time later, some semblance of calm had returned to the living room. John had added new logs to the fire, and Katie and John were back in their armchairs. MacKenzie had poured them fresh coffee, and had made a fresh mug of hot chocolate for herself. The three of them were once again sitting all together and talking to each other in the soothing warmth and glow of the fireplace, and MacKenzie was leaning on one of her books to write her letter as she sat on the couch with her knees pulled up to support the book, and busily moving her pen back and forth across the page with her left hand.

"And so," Katie was saying, "Paul Cavanarro played for the Chicago Cubs?"

John nodded. "He was an all-star first baseman and outfielder, and later a Cubs manager, and he was National League MVP in 1945. And he would definitely have been here on Catalina with the team for their last Spring Training in 1951. At the moment, it certainly seems quite possible that he stayed here in this very cottage, and that that tin box is something he stashed away for safe-keeping while he was here."

"MacKenzie," said Katie. "I think you're magical. Everywhere you go, something exciting happens."

MacKenzie beamed and paused to look up from her writing for a moment. "Thanks, Katie," she said. "But I think it's because you're here. I bet I would never have found those cards if you hadn't come over for dinner tonight."

Katie smiled. "Let's just remember who invited me," she said.

"Mac," said John. "You know, Cavanarro was a southpaw too, just like you."

MacKenzie grinned. "Thanks, Dad," she said. "I'm going to add that to the letter…"

"Why is a left-handed person called a southpaw?" asked Katie.

"You can field this one, Dad," MacKenzie said distractedly, returning to her letter. "I'm writing…"

Katie laughed.

John smiled and nodded. "Okay," he said. "Well, like so many other stories of this kind, the origin is not exactly clear, but most people agree it's pretty much this. Sometime in the 1880s—"

"That's the 19th century…" MacKenzie interjected helpfully without looking up, which prompted another appreciative laugh from Katie.

John smiled and continued. "Sometime in the 1880s, a writer for the Chicago Herald began referring to left-handed pitchers as 'southpaws'. There's evidence the term had been used before that, and that the Chicago Herald was using the term based on an old idea. But it was an idea that applied to Chicago's West Side Park baseball field. This idea says that, in the early history of baseball, when a ballpark was designed, the baseball diamond was oriented so that the batters at home plate would be facing east. This supposedly was so the hitters would never have to deal with having the afternoon sun in their eyes while at the plate. And in that orientation, the pitching arm of a left-handed pitcher would be on the 'south' side of the pitching mound. And from that, supposedly, comes the term southpaw."

MacKenzie nodded. "Good job, Dad…" she said, still without looking up from her writing.

"Thank you, John," said Katie. "Okay," she went on. "I'm ready to hear more about the Honus Wagner card…"

"Still you, Dad," said MacKenzie distractedly. "Bases loaded, nobody out…"

"Mac," said her father. "You're the baseball card collector. This is your area of expertise."

MacKenzie nodded. "But you describe everything really well. And since talking is one of your areas of expertise, I think you can tell it better than me at the moment..."

Katie looked at John and smiled again, and John looked back at her and smiled helplessly.

"Okay," John began. "So, the Honus Wagner card is considered the Holy Grail of baseball cards among collectors."

MacKenzie nodded without looking up. "I know what Holy Grail means in this context..." she announced.

Katie and John shared a smiling glance again, and then John continued.

"So," he went on. "Honus Wagner played for twenty-one seasons, mostly with the Pittsburgh Pirates, from 1897 to 1917. He won eight batting titles, meaning he had the highest batting average for each of those years. That's a National League record that's never been broken. He was one of the first five players inducted into the Hall of Fame, and he's usually mentioned in the same sentence as two of those five players, Ty Cobb and Babe Ruth. Honus Wagner is considered by many to be the greatest player of the 'dead-ball' era, which is another story entirely, but basically means the period of years from about 1900 to 1919—the year that the talents of Babe Ruth introduced the world to the idea of a player being a 'power hitter'. Ty Cobb supposedly once said that Honus Wagner was the greatest player to ever set foot on a baseball field. Many people today consider Honus Wagner to be the greatest all-around baseball player of all time.

"The Honus Wagner baseball card is the most famous baseball card of all time, in large part because of how great he was, and especially because of how rare his card is. Historically, different companies have offered baseball cards for sale, often including some promotional treat with the cards, like a stick of chewing gum. Sometimes, the treat was the product, and the cards were something you got if you bought the product. That was the case with the company that produced the Honus Wagner card. It was a tobacco company.

"There's more than one version of this story, but most versions say that Honus Wagner was unhappy with which company was producing his card because he didn't want child fans to be buying packs of cigarettes just to get his card. So he forced the tobacco company to stop producing his card. So, while tens of thousands to hundreds of thousands of baseball cards of other star players from that era were produced, only between fifty and two hundred Honus Wagner cards were ever made. With the passage of time, most of those cards are gone forever. And that makes a Honus Wagner card rare. Exceptionally rare, and therefore exceptionally valuable. And every collector dreams of having one, which makes them even more sought after. All of which makes the Honus Wagner card not only uniquely famous, but also uniquely valuable.

"Now, as MacKenzie can tell you better than anyone, it's all about condition. The condition of a baseball card makes all the difference. Two years ago, in 1991, a Honus Wagner card sold for over $450,000. It was graded at 8 on a scale of 10, at Near Mint-Mint condition."

Katie gasped. "Oh my goodness…"

John nodded. "That was two years ago. And the Honus Wagner card MacKenzie just found looks to be in at least as good condition as that."

"John, that's so much money…" Katie breathed in amazement. "Do you think it's even safe to keep in the house?"

John took another sip of his coffee and ran a thoughtful hand through his hair. "Well," he said. "If it really was put there by Paul

Cavanarro, it's been there for decades. It's been safe all that time, so I don't see why it wouldn't be safe there now…"

"And that's not even counting the other eight cards," MacKenzie contributed, still writing. "But it doesn't matter, because all we have to do is figure out how to return them to Paul Cavanarro. They certainly don't belong to me. It's not finders keepers. It's finders helpers. People should help each other. My job is to help Paul Cavanarro get his cards back."

Katie's eyes were glistening again as she listened to MacKenzie. She took another sip of coffee and looked over at John. "What a remarkable person your daughter is…" she said quietly.

MacKenzie looked up for a moment, beaming. "Thank you, Katie," she said happily.

"Mac," said John. "Where are you going to send that letter?"

MacKenzie had resumed writing, but she stopped and looked up again. "Well," she said. "This is my plan. With your permission to make a long-distance call, tomorrow I'm going to get the number of the Cubs from 411 information, and then I'm going to call the Cubs and ask them if they can give me a mailing address for Paul Cavanarro. If they can't give it to me, I'll ask them for an address at the Cubs where I can send it so they can get it to him. But if he's not still alive, then I don't know what I'm going to do. But I want him to still be alive, so I'm just going to assume for now that he is."

John nodded. "I like that plan," he said. "That's a good plan. Just remember, when you call, Chicago's in a different time zone. They're two hours later than Catalina. You probably want to call them sometime after 9 am their time, which means any time after 7 am our time."

MacKenzie nodded without looking up from her writing. "That's good thinking, Dad," she said. "I would have forgotten that detail."

"Details matter," said John. "A famous person once said that."

MacKenzie laughed. "I'm not famous, Dad."

Her father smiled. "In this room, you are. You're a superstar."

"Thanks, Dad," said MacKenzie. "Katie," she went on, "it's really nice of you to be so patient about putting up with me and my Dad being ourselves."

Katie smiled. "Patience has nothing to do with it, MacKenzie," she said. "This is the most lovely evening. I'm having a wonderful time."

MacKenzie stood up, still holding the pen, the paper, and her book. Retrieving her mug of hot chocolate, she brought it all across the living room and handed everything except the hot chocolate to her father. "Finished," she announced. "Dad, will you proofread it please? Then I'll copy over my final draft."

Her father nodded. "Proofreading is something I can do," he said. "Happy to help. But you look exhausted. I vote you save transcribing your final draft for tomorrow morning."

MacKenzie nodded. "I vote the same," she said, making her way to Katie's chair and gently lowering herself into Katie's lap and leaning her head back against Katie's shoulder. "This is the most lovely evening because you're here, Katie," MacKenzie said happily.

"Please don't squash Katie," said John, leaning the paper on MacKenzie's book and making marks on her letter with the pen.

MacKenzie nodded. "I'm making myself light," she said confidently.

Katie smiled and gently smoothed MacKenzie's hair with the hand that wasn't holding her coffee.

"And I promise I won't spill your coffee," MacKenzie said to Katie.

Katie nodded, smiling. "I trust you, MacKenzie," she said.

"Just don't fall asleep on Katie," John said, still without looking up from proofreading the letter. "Because you'll spill your hot chocolate, and no matter how light you're making yourself, it will be a major project if we have to carry you to your bed."

"Ha!" MacKenzie scoffed. She tilted her head back to look at Katie's face. "He's way stronger than he looks," she said. "He can pick me up with one hand."

Katie laughed.

The logs in the fireplace settled, and the fire quietly blazed, casting calm flickering light and radiating warmth and reassurance over the two armchairs that were a harbor of safety and security, and the living room that was an island which could not be reached by sadness or loneliness or danger.

Chapter 15
SWIMMING

The next morning, as her father had forecast, MacKenzie's arms and shoulders were significantly more sore than they had been the previous evening. MacKenzie had very reluctantly gone to bed before Katie had left, but MacKenzie and her father now both agreed that MacKenzie's soreness would have been worse if she had not gotten the extra sleep.

Shortly after 7:00, MacKenzie and her father had finished breakfast, and John was contentedly sipping the coffee MacKenzie had freshly made for him. As she had planned with her father, MacKenzie got the phone number of the Cubs offices in Chicago from 411 information, and she had then called the Cubs, where she received two pieces of good news.

The first was that Paul Cavanarro was indeed still very much alive, and the second was that, after listening to MacKenzie briefly tell her story and explain why she wanted to write to Cavanarro, the person speaking with MacKenzie on the phone was cleared by a manager to give Cavanarro's address to MacKenzie.

MacKenzie was still copying over the final draft of her letter with the help of her father's proofreading notes when Davenport showed up like clockwork at 7:30 to pick up John.

At MacKenzie's request, Davenport happily provided the return-mailing address of the cottage. So as not to delay her father and Davenport any longer than necessary from heading off to their work, MacKenzie told Davenport the story of her discovery as succinctly as she could, and with characteristic good-natured cheerfulness Davenport was delighted with all aspects of the tale. He reassured

MacKenzie that, although the Conservancy were now the owners of the property, given the extraordinary nature of the circumstances, he had no hesitation in formally concurring that what MacKenzie had found seemed to clearly belong to Paul Cavanarro, and that returning it all to him was absolutely the right thing to do. Davenport also expressed how impressed he was with MacKenzie's honesty and integrity, and said he was confident that Cavanarro would be excited to learn about the remarkable find, and grateful to MacKenzie for the effort she was making to get in touch to re-unite him with his valuable possessions.

MacKenzie thanked him and said her good-byes to her father and Davenport, and the two men drove off in the Conservancy golf cart.

Shortly after she had finished transcribing the final draft of her letter, the telephone rang. It was Erik, and he and MacKenzie made their plans to meet by the trolley tour at 8:30.

After sealing and addressing the letter, with her backpack filled with all the things she wanted to have with her for the day, MacKenzie locked up the cottage and bicycled down Avalon Canyon Road and then the length of Summer Avenue to Crescent Ave and the beach, where she found Erik talking with his mother at the trolley tour waiting area.

Erik's father had left on the 7:45 ferry to Long Beach, and MacKenzie and Erik and his mother Brenda chatted and reviewed plans for the day. MacKenzie invited both of them to come over for dinner that night, and Brenda had to politely decline because she already had plans with friends for the evening. But Erik was happily given the okay from his mother to go to MacKenzie's for dinner, and MacKenzie then shared with both of them the exciting and improbable story of her extraordinary discovery from the night before. Neither Erik nor his mother quite grasped the idea of old baseball cards being valuable, but both of them thought it was wonderful that MacKenzie was so determined to re-unite the lost possessions with their rightful owner.

When it was time for Brenda to start her first tour of the day, Erik and MacKenzie said good-bye and pedaled off the to the Avalon Post Office on Metropole Street. MacKenzie had gotten permission from her father to send the letter Urgent Special Delivery, which turned out to be more expensive than she had expected, but she knew it was for a good cause.

MacKenzie then wanted to go back to Big Olaf's for ice cream, which took some persuading because Erik was insistent that it was way too early in the day for ice cream. But MacKenzie explained that it was to celebrate sending the letter off, and that sometimes it was very important to have a good dessert after breakfast. It was Erik's feeling bad about how sore MacKenzie's arms were from all the kayaking of the previous day which allowed him to give in to her wishes, and they made their way to the tasty destination and enjoyed mountainous helpings of delicious ice cream with numerous colorful toppings.

MacKenzie had worn her bathing suit under her street clothes in anticipation of further water activities, which worked out well because Erik wanted to go swimming. He took them back to the beach at Frog Rock, where they had seen the bald eagle while kayak-ing, and they spent the rest of the morning swimming and splashing in the warm surf, and playing Frisbee and lounging in the sun on beach towels Erik had brought for them in his backpack.

The day was too bright for either of them to take off their sunglasses, and MacKenzie kept putting on more sunblock, because while Erik's skin was well-tanned from uncountable hours in the summer sun, MacKenzie's skin was pale and, as she had painfully learned from past experiences, it burned easily if it wasn't sufficiently protected.

Erik reminded MacKenzie a little bit of her father, because Erik was smart and interesting and liked to talk a lot, which made MacKenzie feel very relaxed. She hated having to figure out what you were supposed to say next in a conversation. She considered herself to be really good at responding to things other people said, and not particularly interested in the seemingly never-ending stress of having to initiate a topic or sentence.

Erik had an endless supply of fascinating details about the island and its history. He seemed to relish and appreciate getting to share them all, and getting to talk about trains and movies and philosophical ideas on life with someone who seemed genuinely interested in all he had to say.

And MacKenzie was genuinely interested. She liked listening to Erik talk, and she found that what he had to say gave her exciting new information and exciting new thoughts she enjoyed having. It was a very different experience than spending time with her friends in Chicago. And Erik could listen as well as he could talk. He didn't simply wait for her to finish so that he could go on talking. MacKenzie could tell that he thought deeply about everything, and that included anything she said to him.

"I can't believe you weren't tempted to keep those valuable baseball cards for yourself," he said after MacKenzie had responded to his request to share every detail of the previous night's discovery.

MacKenzie shook her head dismissively. "They don't belong to me," she said simply.

Erik shook his head in appreciative awe. "You're a good person, Mac," he said. "I wonder if I would be as good a person as you in the same situation.

"You would," MacKenzie replied confidently. "You're a good person. You would do the right thing."

Erik nodded with hesitant uncertainty.

They looked out at the water for a moment. Some gulls were

flying past and announcing themselves triumphantly in the process, and the late morning sun glistened in shimmering sparkles across the pristine blue surface of the ocean.

"Do you miss your friends?" Erik asked.

MacKenzie thought about this. "I've only been away for three days," she said. "But it feels like so much longer than that, in a good way. I do miss them. But I like having adventures on my own sometimes. And I know we'll all be even happier to see each other again after being apart. Do you wish you were spending time with your friends right now?" she asked.

Erik shook his head. "First of all, I'm really happy to be here with you," he said firmly. "The past two days have been amazingly fun for me."

MacKenzie nodded. "Me, too," she said.

"Second," he went on, "most of my friends are away at different summer camps being camp counselors. It's kind of like an animal migration. Most of the kids who live on the island usually leave for the summer. I don't blame them. There's more to life than just life on Catalina. But, I get to travel a lot with my dad, and sometimes with both my mom and my dad together. And I've been to summer camp a few times. I liked it all right. There's a camp in Vermont that I like to go to. But I don't want to go there every summer. And I'm on a spring-season swim team in Long Beach, and we compete from April to the first week in July. And I like doing that, too. But what I really like is how relaxing it is here in the summer, having the island to myself. Which I know probably sounds ridiculous, but that's how I feel—like I have the whole island all to myself. I really like being with my friends. But I also really love getting to spend time on my own. And like you said, it will be even more fun to be with my friends again when the summer's over because we'll have been apart."

"It's funny," MacKenzie said thoughtfully. "You and I are so very different, but there are some very particular things that we really have in common."

Erik nodded. "Like ice cream," he said, grinning.

"And pizza," added MacKenzie enthusiastically.

"Should we have pizza for lunch?" Erik suggested. "We can eat it at my house. You said you wanted to watch *The Vanishing American*. We can watch the video while we're eating, if you'd like."

"You don't mind?" asked MacKenzie. "Even though you've seen it before, and it's a really sad movie?"

"It is a really sad movie," said Erik. "We'll go mountain biking on the fire roads in the wildlands afterward to cheer ourselves up. We have extra mountain bikes in the garage. You can choose whichever one you want."

"Should we buy popcorn?" asked MacKenzie. "It would feel weird to watch a movie without popcorn."

Erik nodded. "I completely agree. We have plenty of popcorn at the house. But my mom always makes it. I tried to once, and nearly burned the house down."

MacKenzie laughed. "I'm a whiz at cooking. And I love to cook. And that includes making popcorn, even though that's not really cooking, per se."

"Per what?"

"Per se," MacKenzie repeated, smiling. "It means 'in itself, of itself, by itself'. Like, 'chocolate is not bad for your teeth per se, it just matters how much sugar is in it'. Et cetera."

Erik laughed. "Got it," he said, grinning. "And by the way, we have dark chocolate at the house, too."

"Perfect!" declared MacKenzie.

Erik looked at his diving watch. "We might be able to catch my mom in time to say hi to her before her next tour starts."

"Can we go on one of her tours?" asked MacKenzie.

"Oh my god, she would get such a kick out of that. Yes, let's. Tomorrow?"

MacKenzie nodded. "Perfect," she said happily.

Hurriedly gathering and packing all they had spread out on the soft clean white sand, they stuffed it into their backpacks, got on their bikes, and pedaled off, heading back toward Crescent Ave.

They arrived at the trolley tour in time to say hi to Brenda before her next tour departed, and Erik told her about their plans for the afternoon.

"How are you getting the pizza to the house?" she asked.

"I'll just balance it on my handlebars," Erik explained.

"Hmm…" said his mother, unconvinced. "Well, try not to cause an accident or have an accident yourself, please."

"Mom," said Erik with confident reassurance. "I've done it a thousand times."

"Well, I'm glad I didn't know about it," Brenda said with motherly exasperation. "Do you know where the tape of *The Vanishing American* is? We haven't watched it in a long time."

Erik nodded. "Front hall closet, top shelf. With all the other tapes we haven't watched in ages."

Brenda nodded. "MacKenzie," she said. "Please tell me you know how to safely make popcorn. If Erik tries it, he'll burn the house down. At the very least, you'll end up with popcorn which is inedible."

MacKenzie smiled. "Don't worry, Mrs. Roebling," she said. "Erik warned me about his cooking issues. I do nearly all the cooking for me and my dad."

Erik's mother nodded and gave a grateful sigh of relief. "Thank you, MacKenzie. Truly. Erik probably doesn't even know where any cooking supplies are…"

Erik grinned and nodded. "That, unfortunately, is probably true."

Brenda nodded. "As I suspected. MacKenzie, there's butter in the fridge on the inside door, there are different kinds of oil in a cupboard under the left side of the kitchen counter, and there's salt in a spice cupboard over the counter to the left of the kitchen sink. Erik, do you think you can manage remembering where the pots and bowls are?"

Erik grinned again. "Seriously, Mom? Yes, I'm not completely useless in the kitchen."

Erik's mother rolled her eyes and smiled at MacKenzie. "Don't let him near the stove."

MacKenzie smiled at Erik and his mother. "I won't, Mrs. Roebling. I promise."

"MacKenzie," said Brenda. "What time did you say you're having dinner tonight?"

"I'm planning to be home by four," MacKenzie explained, "so my Dad and I can play catch. We may have to go shopping again, afterward. I'll probably start making dinner at around six, so Erik could come over any time after 6:30."

Erik's mother smiled. "You really are the house chef, aren't you."

"Well," said MacKenzie, "my Dad keeps me company and talks to me the whole time. I don't think I'd enjoy cooking if my Dad weren't there talking to me and keeping me company."

Brenda's smile widened. "That sounds exactly like what Erik does," she said, nodding in amusement.

"I think my Dad and Erik are going to like each other," said MacKenzie.

"It certainly sounds like," said Erik's mother.

"And," Erik added, "Mom, remember I told you and dad about that nice woman we met yesterday? Katie? She's going to be there at dinner tonight, too."

Brenda nodded. "Well that sounds quite lovely indeed," she

said. "Okay, you two. Have fun this afternoon. Erik, I'll be home before you leave to go to MacKenzie's house for dinner. Probably around 5:30."

"Thanks, Mrs. Roebling."

"Thanks, Mom. Love you."

"Love you, sweetheart," said Erik's mother.

Erik's mother headed for her trolley tour, and MacKenzie and Erik had started to ride off when MacKenzie suddenly stopped them.

"What's up?" asked Erik.

MacKenzie was looking off, over toward the Cabrillo Mole. "It's him... He's there again. That mysterious man I told you about..."

"Where...?" said Erik.

"I don't want him to see me pointing..." said MacKenzie. "He's right there, right over by the..."

"Where?" Erik repeated.

MacKenzie shook her head. "Now he's gone. He just disappeared in with the rest of the people or something..."

"Are you sure it was the same guy?"

"Positive..." said MacKenzie. "It makes me anxious... I feel like some big thing I don't know about is going to happen, and he has something to do with it..."

"I don't know, Mac..." Erik said skeptically. "It's probably just some guy..."

MacKenzie shook her head. "Maybe..." she said doubtfully.

They turned their bikes and pedaled off to get the pizza.

Chapter 16
MOVIE

At what had become MacKenzie's favorite Italian restaurant, they ordered a large pizza to go. Once it was ready, Erik balanced it expertly on the front handlebars of his mountain bike, and he and MacKenzie bicycled their way to Erik's house on the opposite side of Avalon. The trip was uphill most of the way, since Erik's family lived in a neighborhood that was slightly up in the hills at a higher elevation than the main part of central Avalon, and their house had a luxurious view of the water facing east.

After dumping their backpacks on the kitchen table, Erik gave MacKenzie a quick tour of the house, which included a stopover in the front hall closet to retrieve the VHS copy of The Vanishing American. It was a lovely home that MacKenzie liked right away. It had a nice feeling to it. And it was very much larger than the cottage, and larger than MacKenzie's home in Chicago.

Back in the kitchen, they loaded themselves up with plates, glasses, a large bottle of soda, plenty of napkins, the pizza, and the movie, and Erik led them to into the living room.

"It's an hour and fifty minutes long," reported Erik, turning on the VHS player and slotting the tape cassette into the opening at the front of the player.

MacKenzie nodded. "Running time 110 minutes," she concurred from where she sat comfortably on the large couch reading the back of the thin cardboard box-sleeve which was the cover for the videotape.

Erik nodded, picking up the remote-control unit and returning to seat himself on the couch next to MacKenzie.

"What's 'navv-uh-joe'?" she asked.

Erik shook his head as he opened the big bottle of soda, which let out a vast satisfying hissing whoosh. "No, Mac," he said, pouring loudly-fizzing soda into their glasses. "That's how it's spelled, but that's not how it's pronounced. It's a Native American Indian tribe. It's pronounced 'navv-uh-hoe'."

MacKenzie looked at it again. "Then why is there a 'j'?" she asked.

Lifting open the top cover of the large pizza box and releasing a burst of appetizing pizza fragrance into the room, Erik separated a still-steaming piece of pizza from the circular pie and dropped it onto one of the plates. "The 'j' in Navajo is pronounced like an 'h'," he said, licking pizza grease off his fingers and handing the plate to MacKenzie.

"Thanks," said MacKenzie, taking the plate and putting it down in front of her on the coffee table. "Okay, I get it. It's a transliteration."

Erik separated another pizza slice from the pie and dropped it onto the other plate. "What does that mean?" he asked, closing the pizza box and licking his fingers again.

"A translation," said MacKenzie, "is what a foreign word means. A transliteration is what a foreign word sounds like, using letters from your own language's alphabet. 'The Japanese word arigatō is translated as "thank you", and is transliterated in English as a-r-i-g-a-t-ō, with a long-vowel accent over the 'o'.' Et cetera."

"How do you know Japanese?" asked Erik.

"I don't," said MacKenzie. "I just know how to say 'thank you' in a lot of different languages. I think it's import to thank people."

Erik smiled and nodded. "Of course you do. That is so very MacKenzie Milles of you."

MacKenzie smiled. "Thank you," she said.

"Okay," he said. "So, you're saying that—for some reason—in the proper noun Navajo, the 'h' sound is transliterated as a 'j'."

MacKenzie grinned. "I like the way you said that. Very correct."

"Thanks," said Erik, taking a bite of pizza. "Should we wait to make popcorn until we've finished eating pizza?"

MacKenzie nodded. "Makes sense," she agreed. "Fresh popcorn always tastes better."

Erik nodded. "Okay," he said, wiping his fingers on a napkin and picking up the remote. "Remember, it's a silent movie, so there's no talking or sound effects. Just music, and title-cards every once in a while to show what people are saying. And they don't have title-cards for every word of dialogue. Just some of it. A lot of what the characters say, you have to just kind of figure out based on what's happening on the screen. Some of the title-cards are narration, and not what someone's saying. And in this particular movie, the first time any important character appears, the title card also tells the actor's name."

"Okay," said MacKenzie, nodding and biting hungrily into her pizza slice.

"And remember," said Erik, "this is not a happy movie."

"And also," MacKenzie added, "no scenes filmed on Catalina."

"Correct," said Erik. "They were filmed for the movie, but they never made it into the actual movie."

"But even so," said MacKenzie, "this movie is the reason why there are buffalo on Catalina."

Erik nodded, pressing the play button on the remote. "Without this movie, Catalina would have no buffalo."

About thirty minutes into the movie, MacKenzie put her hand on Erik's arm. "Can we please pause the movie?"

"Sure…"

"Can we please go back to that last title-card?"

"Okay…"

Erik backed the movie up to the previous title card.

MacKenzie studied it for a moment, then read it aloud. "*NOTE: The character of Nasja is played by Man Hammer's Oldest Boy, who has no name of his own. Nor will he have until he does something to distinguish himself among the people of his tribe.*"

Erik nodded. "I know," he said. "I was really drawn to that title card, too, the first time I saw it…"

"It's like a whole moment of real-life story, just in that one card…" said MacKenzie.

Erik nodded again. "And that moment really is Real Life. Most of the people in this movie were not professional actors, they were Navajo tribal people."

"What year did you say this movie was made?" asked MacKenzie.

"1925."

"In the movie, how old would you guess Nasja is?"

"Maybe, eight or nine?" suggested Erik.

"So," said MacKenzie, "if Man Hammer's Oldest Boy was still alive today, he would be…"

"Very old," said Erik.

MacKenzie shook her head. "Not so old. Only about seventy-seven. I wonder what ever happened to him. I wonder if he ever did something important so that he could have his own name…"

"My dad is a big movie buff," said Erik. "My mom, too. But my dad's the real expert. I'm going to talk with him on the phone later, before I come over for dinner, and I can ask if he knows anything about this, or he if might know someone who does."

"That would be really cool," said MacKenzie. "Thanks."

"Time to make the popcorn?" suggested Erik.

MacKenzie nodded enthusiastically and stood up. "Absolutely. And I can already tell from the way the movie story's going, we're probably going to want to watch the rest straight through without stopping."

About twenty minutes later, MacKenzie had used Brenda's directions to successfully navigate her way around the Roeblings' kitchen, and had worked her magic at the stove so that she and Erik were now once again back on the couch with two large heaping bowls of freshly-made popcorn, ready to resume the movie.

"Mac," Erik was saying. "This is delicious. No exaggeration, this is absolutely the best popcorn I have ever had…"

"Thanks," said MacKenzie. "Your mom has really good-quality popcorn kernels. It makes a big difference. My Mom taught me everything I know about cooking. I think about her all the time, but I'm also always thinking about her whenever I'm cooking. It's one of the reasons I love to cook."

"Here's to awesome moms," said Erik, raising his popcorn bowl in the air toward MacKenzie, who raised her bowl to meet his. They clinked bowls like champagne glasses, and then settled in to resume watching the movie.

About an hour and twenty minutes later, the movie ended. MacKenzie and Erik sat still on the couch in contemplative silence, wrapped in their own thoughts. In the VHS player, the tape reached its end. The television screen went dark, and the automatic-rewind function of the player engaged. The tape rewound with a soft muffled rattle and whir that quickly built in speed and raced on at a leisurely rapid pace, before finally audibly slowing, and at last settling to a complete stop with a click of finality. After some more noises from somewhere deep within the player, the tape cassette was ejected, the length of its black plastic shell pushed partially forward out of the front slot, where it then sat motionless.

It was several minutes before anyone said anything.

"You're a really good person to watch movies with," MacKenzie said, still managing her emotions from experiencing the movie. "You don't talk during the really serious parts, and you're like me—you like to be quiet and not talk at the end of the movie. No one knows how to do that. But you do."

"Thanks, Mac..." Erik said quietly. "I get really affected by certain movies... It's a little overwhelming sometimes... But, I guess I'd rather feel all those emotions, even if they're so strong, than not have them..."

MacKenzie nodded. She knew exactly what he meant.

They cleaned up everything from the living room and the kitchen, and Erik shut down the VHS player and the television, and put the movie back in its place in the front hall closet. MacKenzie and Erik were both emotionally wrung out, and Erik's earlier suggestion of a bike ride was the right plan. MacKenzie picked a mountain bike for herself from the several in Erik's family's garage, and she and Erik pedaled eagerly out into the fresh air and life and sunlight of the early afternoon day.

With Erik as guide, they rode on the seldom-used fire roads of the island interior, high up in the wildlands where the wind was stronger, and where there were numerous simultaneous views of the ocean on both the north and south sides of the island.

MacKenzie saw her first Catalina buffalo, and she decided it must not be one of the sick ones because it looked perfectly healthy. It was idly grazing with noble nonchalance in the company of three other bison, all of whom seemed as unaffected by any sort of health issue as they were unbothered by MacKenzie and Erik stopping to observe them.

MacKenzie and Erik were standing, straddling their bikes, contemplating the placid bison, and standing close together because the periodic wind gusts were strong and trying to blow their words away.

"You still thinking about the movie?" asked Erik.

MacKenzie nodded.

"Me too…" said Erik.

"Erik, who was the actor who played Nophaie the Warrior?"

"Richard Dix," said Erik.

"Can we watch another movie that has him in it?"

Erik nodded. "We can go to the video store tomorrow and see what other movies they have that he's in."

"Would you mind?" asked MacKenzie.

Erik smiled. "Totally not. I like him too. It's just never occurred to me to try to find another movie he's in. I like your idea a lot."

"Thanks," said MacKenzie. "Do you remember, early in the movie, after all the history part, when Nophaie the Warrior first appears?"

Erik nodded. "The young Nophaie was played by a different actor. The part is so small, he doesn't even get his name in the credits."

"But," said MacKenzie, "they showed his name at the very bottom of the first Nophaie the Warrior title card…"

"Yes, they did," said Erik. "But even though it was a small part, I think they should have also put his name in the credits."

"I don't remember that actor's name," said MacKenzie, "but the narration on that title card is something I don't think I'll ever forget. It said, *In every generation, a Nophaie the Warrior dared to do what no other would attempt.*"

"You have a really good memory," said Erik.

"For some things…" MacKenzie replied. "But… But, that's what I want to do. That's who I want to be. I want to be a Nophaie the Warrior. I want to do something important. Something brave and noble and heroic. Something that matters. I want to be a Nophaie the Warrior…"

"Mac," Erik said. "Even though we haven't known each other

that long, part of me feels like I've known you forever. And I'll tell something I know about you. Anything you decide you're going to do, you will find a way to make it happen. That's who you are."

MacKenzie smiled. "I feel like I've known you for forever, too," she said. "In a good way."

"Do you think," Erik went on, "that you might stay on the island a little while, even after your dad solves the buffalo mystery?"

"It makes me feel a little guilty," said MacKenzie. "Because every day he doesn't solve it is another day to get to stay. And that's not right. It's not the right way to think..." She gazed at the buffalo, still in front of them. It hadn't moved from its spot, and was contentedly browsing on grass, and periodically looking interested in the sounds of MacKenzie's and Erik's voices.

"I want my dad to succeed as soon as possible," MacKenzie went on. "I want the sick buffalo to get healthy as soon as possible. I just don't want to have to leave Catalina. Not yet. It would be too soon..."

"What do you think would happen," said Erik, "if you asked him if you two could stay on the island a little longer?"

MacKenzie laughed. "Well, first he would laugh at me. Because I so badly did not want to leave Chicago, or come here. I was a real brat about it. But I feel like such a different person than I was, even just a few days ago. I guess it just goes to show, sometimes you're upset when some curveball from out-of-the-blue comes in and interrupts your life, and then later you look back and say, 'thank god for that interruption because my life is so much better now.' I don't even want to imagine how not-as-good my life would be if that interruption hadn't happened. So, there's only one way to find out how my dad will answer, after he's done laughing at me. And that's to just ask him, and find out."

Chapter 17
CONFIDENCE

By 4:00, MacKenzie was back at the cottage. She had not passed Davenport on her way this time, but her father was home when she got there. She and Erik had finished their ride in the wildlands, and had made their way back to his house, where Erik had offered to let her keep the mountain bike she had been riding, for as long as she was in Catalina. This had made MacKenzie happy and grateful, because she now very much preferred the ride of the mountain bike over either the bike from the cottage or even her own bike at home in Chicago. Erik had said he was going to ask his mother to pick him up at the cottage around ten, and he was sure she would be willing to put MacKenzie's regular bicycle on their golf cart bike rack to ferry it back to the cottage, the same rack that would be used to ferry Erik's own mountain bike back from the cottage when his mother would drive him home at the end of the evening.

MacKenzie and her father headed down to the ball field to play catch, and to catch each other up on how the day had gone for each of them. John still did not feel as though he was any closer to solving the buffalo mystery, and it was during that part of their conversation that MacKenzie asked him about the possibility of their staying longer on the island. To her surprise, he did not laugh at her. But he also could not give her an answer because he said they would not be able to make any kinds of decisions about anything like that until both his mystery and Katie's mystery had been successfully solved. But he hadn't said no about the possibility of extending their stay, and to MacKenzie, that seemed like good news.

After catch, they took a ride in Bertie to the Vons to make

sure they had plenty of supplies for the evening's dinner-for-four, and they dutifully plugged Bertie back in to charge as soon as they returned to the cottage.

At around 5:30, Katie telephoned. She was on the mainland, in Long Beach, and intended to catch the 5:45 ferry back to Avalon, but she wanted John and MacKenzie to know that that meant she would arrive late, probably closer to seven.

After showering and getting themselves and the cottage cleaned up for guests, MacKenzie began to cook dinner, while her father paced the small kitchen, talking with her and keeping her company, and trying to stay out of her way.

MacKenzie had just finished all the cooking and preparations she had planned, when Erik arrived at around 6:35. MacKenzie introduced him and her father to each other, and as she had privately suspected, they both instantly connected. She had not really been that worried about whether or not they would like each other, but seeing how quickly and easily and eagerly they got along made her happier than she had dared hope for.

"Okay," John said at last. "I don't want to hog Erik all to myself. Mac, why don't you give Erik a tour of the cottage while we're waiting for Katie."

MacKenzie nodded and took hold of Erik's hand. "C'mon," she said enthusiastically. "I want to show you the secret compartment...!"

"But I don't think you should re-open the tin box, Mac," her father recommended as she was leading Erik out of the living room.

"Agreed, Dad," she called back over her shoulder.

When they got to her room, she re-told Erik the entire story of her discovery, and showed him the secret compartment. She even reached in to pull out the tin box to show him, but she then quickly and carefully put it back in its place and re-closed the hidden door.

As part of her re-enactment of her discovery, she handed Erik the piece of stationery and the map that she had kept out of the box.

Erik was fascinated with every aspect of her story, and he was studying with avid interest the two pieces of paper she had just handed him.

"Look at this cool logo on the stationery," he said, marveling. "It must be a really old Cubs logo. I've never seen one like this before…"

MacKenzie nodded. "Amazing, right?" she said happily.

"Hey, Detective," said Erik. "Did you happen to notice there's an 'x' on this map? Somebody's marked it in pen…"

MacKenzie nodded. "I did notice. Details matter. I mentioned it in the letter I wrote to Paul Cavanarro, and asked him what it meant."

"It's so old…" mused Erik. "And with this 'x' on it, it kind of looks like a treasure map…"

MacKenzie laughed. "I definitely doubt it's a treasure map. Paul Cavanarro already had his treasure. A treasure in baseball cards. And it wasn't buried there…" she said, pointing to the 'x' on the map. "It's buried there…" she said, pointing to where the secret compartment could not be seen in the wall. "But," she went on, "if he writes me back, and if he says anything about the map, maybe then we'll learn for sure why there's an 'x' marked on it…"

A little before seven, the doorbell rang, and MacKenzie bolted through the cottage joyfully calling out Katie's name, racing to be the first to the front door, and throwing her arms around Katie's waist the moment the door was opened.

"MacKenzie Milles," said Katie, grinning. "You are always so full of happy energy, you remind me of the dolphins playing in the water with the boat as the ferry was leaving Long Beach."

MacKenzie politely untangled herself from Katie and nodded emphatically. "That's me," she agreed exuberantly. "I'm a dolphin!" She grabbed Katie by the hand and led her into the living room, where Erik was patiently standing and John was just coming in from the kitchen.

"Hi, Erik," said Katie. "I'm so glad you're here. It's so nice to see you again."

"It's nice to see you, too, Katie," Erik replied, smiling.

Katie and John greeted each other by casually and lightly kissing each other on the cheek, and MacKenzie immediately stole a quick shared secret glance with Erik, MacKenzie's mouth open so wide in delighted amazement that she had to cover it with her hand to stop herself from saying anything out loud.

Katie was holding a larger paper bag than she had had the previous night, and she handed it to John.

"There's two bottles of red in there," she said.

"Thank you," said John. "Between this and what MacKenzie and I bought when we were shopping today, we can start our own wine cellar…"

Katie grinned. "There's also a bit of a present in there," she went on. "But it's a surprise for the four of us, so don't peek…!"

John smiled and nodded. "Understood," he said. "I promise to just take the bottles out without looking inside," and he turned and headed with the bag into the kitchen.

"Did you two have a fun day together today?" Katie asked MacKenzie and Erik.

Erik nodded.

"We went swimming at Frog Rock," said MacKenzie excitedly. "And we had pizza and watched a movie and went mountain biking."

Katie smiled. "No ice cream?"

"Oh, we had ice cream," Erik reassured her.

MacKenzie nodded. "To celebrate mailing the letter to Paul Cavanarro."

"And also," Erik added, "because MacKenzie had a really

convincing argument for why it's important to have dessert after breakfast."

Katie laughed, and John returned from the kitchen and stood contemplating everyone for a moment.

"So," he began, "why don't we all have a seat in the living room for a minute…"

MacKenzie stole another secret significant shared glance with Erik. She knew from experience that they were all about to have 'a talk'. And she was right.

Katie sat in her armchair, and John waited until MacKenzie and Erik had seated themselves on the couch before sitting down himself in his armchair.

There was an uncomfortable pause where no one said anything, and then MacKenzie's father spoke. "Katie," he said. "Do you want me to say it?"

"Say what…?" asked MacKenzie.

"MacKenzie," Katie began. "Your father and I thought this evening would be more relaxed for everyone if we told Erik."

"Told me what…?" asked Erik.

MacKenzie nodded. "The real reasons why my Dad and Katie are here on the island," she said.

"MacKenzie speaks very highly of you, Erik," said John. "I'm afraid that, because we all trust you, we're going to burden you with a secret."

Erik looked confused and turned toward MacKenzie. "Mac…?"

"Can he tell his parents?" asked MacKenzie.

"That will be his decision," said John. "No child should ever hide from a parent anything she or he wants to tell them."

"But Erik," said Katie. "You would have to ask them to not discuss it with anyone. Not until it's all been resolved."

Erik looked more puzzled than ever. "Is this about the mysterious man…?" he asked.

John and Katie looked at MacKenzie.

"We saw the mysterious man again today," said MacKenzie. "He was down by the Cabrillo Mole again, watching passengers get off the ferry."

"Well," said Erik, "MacKenzie saw him. He disappeared before I could see him…"

"Okay," said John. "So, that is a completely different conversation, which we will not have at the moment, if that's okay with you, MacKenzie."

MacKenzie nodded. "Fine with me," she said. "I don't want to talk about him anyway. He makes me anxious…"

"Erik," said Katie. "Something is killing coral under the water at the Seal Rocks. I'm here on the island because the Conservancy asked me to find the cause."

"And," John added, "something is making many of the island buffalo very sick. I'm here on the island because the Conservancy asked me to find the cause."

"Oh…" said Erik quietly. "Okay… Wow…"

"Erik," said Katie. "I'm sure you understand why we and the Conservancy want to keep this quiet for now."

Erik nodded. "Yes…" he said slowly. "Yes, of course… That's information that would be harmful to the island if it got out…"

Both Katie and John nodded solemnly.

"Well…" Erik went on uncertainly. "Thank you for trusting me. And you can trust me. I love Catalina. I would do anything to protect the island. I won't say anything to anyone. And I don't feel like I need to tell my parents right away. But, can I tell them eventually?"

John nodded emphatically. "Yes, of course. Absolutely."

"And Erik," said Katie. "Our hope is that when you do tell them, by then the story will have a happy ending, and we'll have successfully solved both mysteries."

Erik nodded. "I understand," he said. "Is there anything I can do to help? I know a lot about the island."

Katie nodded. "MacKenzie has very proudly told us how knowledgeable you are," she said.

John smiled at Erik. "Thank you for offering to help, Erik," he said. "At the moment, I don't think there is anything you can help with directly. But indirectly, you are already helping greatly. Knowing that you and MacKenzie are spending so much time together is a huge help for me. She is, of course, quite well able to take care of herself…"

Erik smiled. "Oh, yes. I know," he said, glancing at MacKenzie. "She really is."

"But," John went on, "knowing she's with you means I have no nagging thoughts in the back of my mind about being away from her all day long. I know that when she's with you, she's happy, and having fun, and safe. That peace of mind frees me to fully focus on the work I need to do."

Erik was looking a bit overwhelmed. "That's a huge compliment, Mr. Milles," he said. "It means more to me than I can say… Thank you… I would do anything for MacKenzie."

John smiled and nodded. "I can tell," he said. "Thank you, Erik."

"Your parents must be very proud of you, Erik," said Katie.

Erik smiled modestly and shook his head. "They love me, because they're great parents," he said. "But mostly I think I just drive them crazy. I don't do it on purpose. But, thank you, Katie."

John nodded in recognition and then turned toward MacKenzie. "Mac," he said earnestly, "you really have found a kindred spirit."

"What's a kindred spirit?" asked Erik.

"A kindred spirit," MacKenzie recited, "is a person who likes what you like, feels the way you feel, sees the world the way you see it. 'The moment she met him, she could tell how much they were alike, and she knew she had found a kindred spirt.' Et cetera."

All four of them laughed, and Katie exhaled a great puff of air and shook her hands out for a moment. "Okay," she said with some finality. "That's better. Let's all relax a little bit and talk about less serious things, at least for now."

MacKenzie looked at her father. "Dad, can we have another fire?"

John raised an eyebrow theatrically. "Two nights in a row?"

MacKenzie nodded reassuringly. "It's okay to do things you like over again," she explained helpfully. "Erik and I had ice cream two days in a row, and look at us. We're perfectly okay."

Katie smiled at MacKenzie's father. "Not to gang-up on you John," she said. "But, I also would love another fire," and she winked at MacKenzie.

MacKenzie grinned and winked back.

John turned toward Erik. "Erik, would you like to weigh-in on this...?"

Erik quickly put his hands up into the air in a defensive posture. "I'm staying out of this one..." he said sensibly.

John smiled. "You're a good lad, Erik. And very wise, too. Okay, fine. Mac, why don't you and Erik go haul in some more firewood for another fire."

"Yes!" exclaimed MacKenzie, pumping a fist into the air with triumphant jubilation, and she leapt to her feet and grabbed Erik's hand. "C'mon," she said. "I'll show you where the wood is."

"Okay," said Erik. "But I'll haul it. Your arms are still sore."

MacKenzie shook her head dismissively. "They're not as bad, since we went swimming. And anyway, they're never too sore for carrying firewood."

MacKenzie led Erik out, and the two of them headed toward the backyard.

Chapter 18
CURSE

A short time later, with the new fire blazing in the living room fireplace, the four of them were seated together at the dining room table, contentedly enjoying the dinner MacKenzie had prepared for everyone.

"Simply delicious," Katie was saying, adding some more food from one of the serving bowls to her plate. "Truly, MacKenzie, your cooking talents are extraordinary."

"Thank you," said MacKenzie, brimming with happiness.

John raised his wine glass slightly in the air. "To the chef," he said.

Katie raised her wine glass, and MacKenzie and Erik raised their glasses of soda.

"Am I allowed to toast myself?" asked MacKenzie.

Everyone else nodded and practically at the same time said, "Yes!" They all carefully and lightly clinked glasses, and took a ceremonial sip to celebrate MacKenzie's cooking, before resuming their dining and conversation.

"So," Erik was saying, "my mom and dad both said to say hi to everyone, and my mom says thank you for the dinner invitation, and she's sorry she couldn't make it tonight. Mr. Milles, my mom says she's looking forward to meeting MacKenzie's father, and my dad is hoping to meet all three of you when he gets back from his trip. And Mr. Milles, my dad also said that, since you and MacKenzie are such strong Cubs fans, he says to say he's sorry your team is under a curse. I asked him what he meant, and he said he didn't know that much about it, but he was sure you guys would…"

"Curse...?" asked Katie.

MacKenzie and her father both grimaced.

"The Curse of the Billy Goat," said John, frowning.

"The Goat Curse," said MacKenzie, her face wrinkling as if the words themselves had a bad taste.

"No way..." Erik remarked incredulously.

"What's the Goat Curse?" asked Katie with great interest.

"It's the reason we haven't won a world series in the last forty-seven years," MacKenzie explained ruefully.

Katie raised her eyebrows. "Because of a curse?"

"MacKenzie, do you want to tell the story?" her father offered. "It's too painful for me to tell it."

MacKenzie frowned and nodded. "Ugh..." she said unhappily. "I'll tell it..." She took a long drink of soda to steel herself for the ordeal, then wiped her mouth resolutely with a napkin.

"Okay," she began. "So, in 1945, there was a guy named William Sianis. He owned a place called 'The Billy Goat Tavern'. He came to a Cubs game at Wrigley Field with his pet goat."

"Seriously?" asked Erik.

MacKenzie nodded. "I guess that's the sort of thing that happened in 1945. They let you bring your pet goat to a baseball game."

"That's nuts," said Erik.

MacKenzie nodded. "It gets worse. So, the goat's name was Murphy. And Murphy smelled bad. Because he was a goat! So, a bunch of people at the game complained that Murphy's bad smell was bothering them. And so the Cubs people told William Sianis that he and Murphy had to leave the ballpark. And William Sianis got so angry, he put a curse on the whole team. What did he say exactly, Dad?"

"'Them Cubs, they ain't gonna win no more,' is what he said," John reported. "I don't think anyone took it seriously or literally at the time. But then the Cubs lost the 1945 World Series to the Detroit Tigers. And since then, they still haven't won a World Series. So, while they technically have won plenty of games since 1945, they have not won a World Series."

"And then," said MacKenzie, "about twenty-five years later, William Sianis tried to take away his curse. But it didn't work. And then he died."

"Well," said John, "I don't think he died because he tried to take away the curse. He tried to take away the curse once he realized he didn't have much longer to live. It just didn't work."

"And then," MacKenzie went on, "there was the guy who was the nephew of William Sianis. He tried to take away the curse, too."

John nodded. "William Sianis had a nephew, named Sam Sianis. He tried to break the curse several times by bringing a goat to Opening Day at Wrigley. And twice, it almost worked. The Cubs ended up winning the division in 1984, and again four years ago in 1989. And both times, Sam Sianis had brought a goat to Opening Day that year."

"Not Murphy, though," explained MacKenzie. "Murphy the goat was dead by then. Sam Sianis brought some random goat."

"And here we are," said John. "Forty-seven years after the curse, and still no World Series."

"That is a crazy story..." said Erik.

"My goodness..." said Katie sympathetically. "What a peculiar story. I'm so sorry the Cubs haven't won a World Series since then, goat or no goat."

"Well," said Erik. "Anyway, I'll tell that story to my dad. He'll be happy to hear it. I mean, he'll still feel bad for you and MacKenzie, Mr. Milles, that the Cubs keep not winning any World Series games. But he'll be glad to know the story. He likes stories like that. That's the sort of weird and interesting story he tells me all the time. Oh, that reminds me... Mac, I asked my dad about that

Navajo actor from the movie, and he said he'll try to find out for us."

"What movie did you two watch?" asked Katie.

"*The Vanishing American*," said MacKenzie. "It was really emotional…"

"Hmm…" said John thoughtfully. "You know, I saw some sort of memo about that movie on Ed's desk at the Conservancy. I meant to ask him about it. I assumed it was just something routine having to do with buffalo, but maybe there's something more… I'll ask him tomorrow."

"Erik, what did you ask your dad about?" said Katie.

"Well," said Erik, "MacKenzie was really interested in the little boy character named Nasja in the movie."

MacKenzie nodded. "The title card said that he didn't have his own name yet. The Real Life little boy, not the character. And it said he wouldn't get his own name until he had done something important."

"And MacKenzie asked a really good question," Erik went on. "She wondered if the boy had ever gotten his own name. So my dad is going to try to see if he can find out anything. He's a real movie buff, and he has some friends who know a lot of movie information."

"Oh," said Katie, "and that reminds me. Speaking of getting answers to MacKenzie's questions, I found something while I was in Long Beach today…"

"Is it okay to ask why you went to Long Beach?" said MacKenzie.

Katie nodded. "Your father's idea about cyanide poisoning being a possible cause of what's killing the Seal Rocks coral really seemed to fit a lot of my observations at the site. So, I went for an early dive this morning, to get some samples specifically with that in mind. I didn't want to have to wait for the test results, so I took the samples myself to the lab in Long Beach. That's why I went. I was hoping they could process the samples for me right away, so I stayed in Long Beach as long as I could, hoping they would get all the testing done."

"And did they?" asked MacKenzie.

Katie nodded. "They did. And John, you were right. All the samples tested positive for cyanide…"

"Does that mean," asked Erik, "that there's cyanide in the water at the Seal Rocks?"

"Unfortunately," said Katie, "yes, that is what it means."

"But," said MacKenzie, "how would cyanide get into the water all the way down by where the coral are?"

Katie nodded. "That's the next part of the mystery to be solved…" she said. "I have a meeting with Ed Davenport from the Conservancy tomorrow to discuss it."

"Oh!" said MacKenzie. "Mr. Davenport. He's really nice."

"Yes," agreed Katie. "He's a nice person, and he works really hard for the Conservancy."

"Katie," said John. "I haven't yet mentioned to Ed that you and I know about each other's work here on the island."

Katie nodded. "Nor have I," she said. "I think it's time to tell him. Especially since you're the one who's solved the first part of my mystery for me. I'm going to ask him if the three of us can have lunch together tomorrow. If you think that's a good idea…"

John nodded. "I don't know that I deserve any credit for all the work you've been doing," said John, "but I do agree that everyone could benefit from all three of us meeting together."

"I'll call him first thing in the morning," said Katie.

"You'll have to do that early," said MacKenzie, "because Mr. Davenport always picks my Dad up here at 7:30."

"That's helpful MacKenzie," said Katie, smiling. "Thanks. That's what I'll do."

"Is the cyanide dangerous for divers or kayakers?" asked Erik with some concern. "Or the fish or the seals?"

"At the moment," said Katie, "it looks as though it's pretty localized. What I mean is, is seems to be in very strong amounts right by the coral. But with so much ocean water, it spreads out quickly. So, while it's horrible, and we have to find the source, and we have to stop it, at the moment I don't believe it's a health threat to anyone. And that includes the other marine life. The fish and the seals I've observed in the area look and act perfectly healthy. The coral are really sensitive to this kind of poisoning, and they obviously can't move themselves to other water. And those coral in particular are apparently very close to whatever the source of the cyanide is. So, they're really getting the worst of it..."

"Mr. Milles," said Erik. "What is cyanide used for? I mean, besides killing victims in murder-mystery movies."

John nodded. "MacKenzie asked about that last night. As I told her, it's used for many different things, but it's mostly used in gold and silver mines."

"Why is it used in gold and silver mining?" asked Erik.

John nodded again. "As we talked about last night, because of the chemical properties of cyanide, it's commonly used to separate precious metals, like gold or the silver, from the rest of the rock that the gold or silver are in when they're mined."

MacKenzie nodded. "And I keep trying to tell everyone," she said adamantly, "that all these mysteries are connected. I mean, seriously. Gold mining? How is that not connected to everything? Everybody wants gold."

"Well..." said Katie slowly. "So, speaking of gold, and mines, and everything being connected, while I was in Long Beach waiting for the lab results, I stopped in at a store I know there. Like Catalina, this store seems to be someplace from another time. It's a lovely old book store called Acres of Books, and they have the most unusual and large collection of used books I've ever seen. And everyone who works there seems to love books, and love old things, and love information about the past. So, I asked one of them if there was a book I could buy that would tell the story of the Catalina Island treasure. After a bit of searching, she was able to help me. I don't know which I was more surprised by—that there was only one book on the subject, or that there actually was a book on the subject. But, there was. And I bought it, and I brought it with me tonight."

Chapter 19
GOLD

Everyone finished the delicious dinner, and MacKenzie and Erik cleared everything away to the kitchen and washed all the dishes together while John and Katie sat in the living room and sipped their wine in front of the fireplace. MacKenzie and Erik had ice cream for dessert, and MacKenzie made hot chocolate for herself and Erik, and brewed fresh coffee for her father and Katie, who were very appreciative and said they were looking forward to drinking it, but that it was a bit too early for them to start on coffee, and they were happy with their wine for the time being.

John retrieved Katie's large brown paper bag from the kitchen, and true to his promise never once looked inside at the contents. He brought it to her in the living room, and with everybody in their places—MacKenzie and Erik on the couch with their hot chocolate, and John and Katie in their armchairs sipping wine— everyone was ready to see what Katie had brought for them.

"Okay," she said, reaching into the bag and taking out what appeared to be a very old paperback book with no front cover. "So, this is the book. It's not in very good shape, but all the pages are here. It's not very long. I have no idea how much of it is accurate, but it's all pretty fascinating. And so, if you all would like, I thought I would just read it aloud."

MacKenzie nearly burst with joy. "Oh, Katie!" she exclaimed ecstatically. "You're perfect. I love being read to!"

And so with the fire placidly blazing, and everyone comfortable and ready to listen, Katie turned to the start of the book and began to read.

The Treasure of Santa Catalina Island

CHAPTER ONE

A Brief History of 20th Century Mining on Catalina Island

In 1923, Catalina's most famous owner William Wrigley, Jr. started a mining operation at the west end of the island on Black Jack Mountain. It was called the Black Jack Mountain Mine.

Primarily from the sales of mined zinc and silver, the mine was productive and profitable for four years. In 1927, international prices for metals dropped, and many mines suddenly could no longer be profitable. As a result of those dropping prices, all Black Jack mining operations stopped. The mines were all closed and abandoned. But as Wrigley's son Philip K. Wrigley would later say about the wealth of minerals on Catalina, "When the time comes that we need them, we know where they are."

Also in 1927, William Wrigley, Jr. and Malcolm Renton started a commercial tile, brick, and earthen-pipe products shop on Pebbly Beach, selling building materials such as roof tiles and enamel tiles. It was so successful, that a year later it expanded at the same site with factory operation. The business was named Catalina Clay Products. They began producing dinner pottery, garden pottery, and decorative artware pottery products in addition to the tile. Until it was closed ten years later in 1937, it was the source of what has since become world famous Catalina Pottery and Catalina Tile. That pottery used various clays it removed from the ground in different places throughout the island, but the removal of those clays was never formally categorized as mining or quarrying.

CHAPTER TWO
Tongva Gold

It has often been believed that Catalina is an island with great mineral wealth. There have always been stories that Catalina Island is rich with natural deposits of such metals as lead, zinc, copper, silver, and gold. In modern times, no mining company has ever either received permission to mine there, or felt that mining there would or could be profitable. The only private or industrial digging that currently takes place on the island is the now-famous stone quarry, Pebbly Beach Quarry, which has been in operation since the 1930s.

Evidence exists which suggests that, while Catalina may or may not still have significant deposits of other metals, it may once have been rich with deposits of gold. The two most famous mines, the Black Jack Mine toward the west end of the island, and the Renton Mine, toward the east end of the island, were closed and sealed up years ago. Countless other mines exist scattered throughout the island, from numerous claims staked by individuals hoping to find gold and silver on the island during the 1800s.

But for this story, we start a bit farther back in time. The indigenous Tongva people lived on Catalina Island for nearly 8,000 years. During those thousands of years, the Tongva people expanded existing caves and caverns on the island that had been formed by nature, and they tunneled countless new tunnels and new caves.

Whatever the Tongva people's purposes were for making use of all those tunnels and caves, there was at least one purpose that is known: to find gold.

Whenever it was that the Tongva first discovered gold in underground passages of Catalina, once they knew it was there they actively went about finding more. The Tongva may have been getting gold from deep inside the island for thousands of years, long before the seven years of the great California Gold Rush in the mid-1800s.

The California Gold Rushed peaked in 1849. That year is why the hundreds of thousands of gold-seekers flocking to California at that time came to be known as 'forty-niners'.

Most of the gold collected by the Tongva people on Catalina Island was made into special ceremonial and religious objects, all of which were kept in a sacred cavern called The Temple of the Sun. During the 1700s, when whalers first discovered the existence of Catalina, and began to invade and overtake the island, the whalers learned of the Tongva gold, and they wanted to take it for themselves.

At first, the Tongva were able to repel the whalers. But the Tongva were an ancient culture, and the invading whalers had the advantages of modern technology, especially superior weapons.

The Tongva eventually were forced to flee the island for their own safety and survival. They ended up living in various places along the southern California coast, many of them in Spanish missions. As time went on, their numbers became smaller, and their culture as a people began to become lost.

But before they had left Catalina Island, they had moved their gold. To protect it from the greedy whalers, the Tongva moved all the Tongva gold out of the Temple of the Sun, and into a hidden cavern, one they either knew of, or that they themselves had dug out. Wherever that cavern was, the Tongva believed it would be undiscoverable by the whalers, and that their gold would be safe, even if they themselves would never see it again.

Of the Tongva who knew the location of the cavern, none ever spoke of it to anyone, even to their own people, for fear that greed and the poverty of their new lives might cause someone to reveal its existence and its whereabouts for some profit to a stranger.

CHAPTER THREE
Turei

As the years went on, more of the original island Tongva people died.

A Tongva chieftain named Turei had been living for many years in the San Gabriel Mission in Los Angeles County. In 1828, realizing he was nearing the end of his life, Turei believed he was the last living soul who knew of the gold. Whether he was or not, he believed that he was.

He struggled with the idea that the knowledge would die with him. But he struggled more with the pain and discomfort and loneliness of what he knew were the final days of his life.

A man visiting the mission came upon Turei and saw how he was suffering. This man changed all his plans and stayed with Turei, taking care of him, trying to help ease Turei's pain, being a friend and companion for Turei, trying to help the old chieftain have a less difficult passage into the afterlife.

The man had no reason to expect anything from Turei in return. He just wanted to help someone who was suffering. But Turei was desperately grateful for the kindness, and he wanted a way to thank the man. The man had transformed the loneliness and gloom of Turei's final days into a time of peacefulness and companionship for the old chieftain.

On his final day on this earth, as Turei lay dying, with his new friend at his side caring for him, Turei asked for a pencil and paper. With a shaking hand and his last effort, he drew a rough picture of the Island of Santa Catalina. He made a mark on one part of the picture, and handed it to the man.

Turei told the man the picture was Catalina, and the mark showed where a vast amount of gold was hidden beneath the ground. With his last breath, Turei thanked the man for his great kindness. And with his new and most precious companion caring for him at his side, Turei passed from this world to the next.

The man was deeply saddened by the death of Turei. He sat by the lifeless body of the chieftain and looked at the scrawled picture of Catalina Island. And he made a decision.

That man's name was Samuel Prentiss. Prentiss had little money of his own. But he resolved to go to Catalina Island and find the gold that Turei had told him about.

CHAPTER FOUR
Samuel Prentiss

Prentiss was from Massachusetts. He had many skills, such as being a carpenter, a fisherman, and a seaman. It was in his capacity as a seaman that Prentiss had been earning a living as a crewmember aboard a ship called the Danube.

In 1828, the Danube was wrecked during a storm off the coast of San Pedro. After the wreck, Prentiss managed to walk to the San Gabriel Mission, where he was taken in and cared for as he recovered from his injuries. It was there, at the San Gabriel Mission, that Prentiss had met Turei.

After the death of Turei, Prentiss had now set his mind on going to Catalina. But he had no money and no possessions. So he borrowed some carpentry tools, and returned to the San Pedro beach where parts of the wreck of the Danube had washed ashore. Using salvaged parts of the Danube, Prentiss used his carpentry skills to cobble together a small boat, which he planned to use to get himself to Catalina Island.

He returned the borrowed tools, and set out on his boat to row and sail his way across the twenty-two miles of Pacific Ocean to get to Catalina. He was heading for the west end of the island. From what he understood of the drawing Turei had given him, that was the part of the island which was represented by the mark Turei had put on the picture.

Prentiss was less than a mile from the shore of the island when a sudden Pacific storm hit. The waves were high, the wind and rain were terrible, and Prentiss's small makeshift boat was capsized. Desperate for his life, Prentiss swam toward Catalina.

Exhausted and losing body heat and near death, Prentiss at last made it to the island. He was lucky enough to be washed ashore by the wind and high waves onto a sandy beach. He crawled up the beach as far as he could and at last ran out of strength and will, and fell unconscious where he was.

When he awoke, it was the next morning. The storm was gone, the sky was cloudless, the sun shone warm and bright. Prentiss had somehow lived through his ordeal. He had lost his boat, and he had lost all of the few things he had had on board. And as he was being thankful just for being alive, he realized he had lost one other thing. He had lost Turei's picture of Catalina.

Prentiss's only way to find the buried gold was now gone forever. Prentiss tried to burn into his mind the picture Turei had drawn, and the location of the mark Turei made.

Prentiss spent the next thirty years of his life living on Catalina Island. At first, he raised money and sustained himself by hunting otter and fishing. Eventually, he raised enough money to buy a small plot of land, where he built a small house for himself.

And once he was settled in, he began secretly looking for the gold Turei had told him about. His searching was done by digging near where he believed Turei's mark had been on the picture. Some of Prentiss's searching led him to finding some silver, and he was able to make a modest living off of the money he made from the silver he sold.

Content to be a loner, Prentiss mostly kept to himself. He had few friends or acquaintances during the time he lived on Catalina. Over the years, Prentiss continued to expand his search for the gold, and continued to use the profits from the silver he found to buy more mining tools and equipment for himself.

Prentiss never did find the gold Turei had told him about. In 1854, at age 72, after searching for the gold for nearly thirty years, Prentiss died on Catalina. He was buried in a simple grave near the part of the island now known as Two Harbors. To this day, at the west end of Catalina, a small headstone grave marker still sits on the place where Prentiss was buried after his death. Prentiss was Catalina's first non-native permanent resident, and he was the first non-indigenous person to ever be buried on the island. But before he died, Prentiss told the secret of Turei's gold to one person.

That person was Santos Louis Bouchette.

CHAPTER FIVE
Santos Bouchette

Bouchette was the son of man Prentiss had known during his time as a crewmember aboard the Danube. In 1854, Bouchette had come to Catalina looking for opportunities to try to mine for silver and gold. Bouchette sought out and befriended Prentiss, who had been friends with his father.

After nearly thirty years of unsuccessful searching, as Prentiss found himself near death, he decided to share with Bouchette all of what he had been told by Turei.

After Prentiss's death, Bouchette took action. Bouchette was more of a business man than Prentiss had been. Using some of the silver from Prentiss's mining as evidence of why money could be made doing more mining on Catalina, Bouchette was able to find backers for a mining investment. On the mainland, he found investors willing to give him a lot of money to start his own mining operations on Catalina, in exchange for a percentage of the money that would come from the sale of any silver that was found. Bouchette believed that in this way, he could use the money to secretly search for the gold, while still satisfying his backers with the profits from any silver he found while he was searching.

This went on for many years. Bouchette continued to secretly search for the gold, while being sure to also mine any silver he found to satisfy his backers and to make money for himself. Over time, he had made so much money from his successful silver mining, that he had become modestly wealthy.

Now as someone with money, Bouchette began to spend more time on the mainland, especially in Los Angeles, where he could go to fancy parties and enjoy a fancy lifestyle. During one of his trips to Los Angeles to enjoy spending his money, Bouchette met and fell in love with a French dancer. They got married, and Bouchette brought her to live with him on Catalina.

But she was unhappy with how isolated and unglamorous the island was. To try to make her happy, Bouchette built her a large fancy house, and filled it with furniture imported from her French homeland. For a while, this made her less unhappy, and they continued to live on the island. Over time, however, she grew unhappy again, and decided she wanted to end the marriage and move back to France.

At about this same time, Bouchette found a very large deposit of silver in one of his mines. It was the largest silver deposit he had ever found. Without telling his backers, or anyone else except his wife, Bouchette collected as much of the silver as he could safely hide. He then sealed up the tunnels he had dug which led to that large deposit of silver.

A short time later, very early one morning, Bouchette and his wife loaded some of their possessions onto a boat, along with all the silver the boat could safely hold. The two of them sailed away from the island, and neither of them was ever seen again. To this day, one of the old closed mines on the west end of Catalina still bears his name, the Bouchette Mine.

Some say Bouchette and his wife were caught in a storm and sank with their boat and their silver. Some say they secretly landed on the mainland, and changed their names and identities so that they could start new lives with more money than they had ever had before. One old newspaper article tells of how someone in France later recognized Bouchette's wife as living there. Another old newspaper article tells of someone in Las Vegas recognizing Bouchette and accusing him of being a thief.

The only thing known for sure about Bouchette is that, like Prentiss, he too was never able to find the gold that Turei had told Prentiss about.

CHAPTER SIX
Where is the Treasure?

The mystery of Turei's gold is still a mystery today. Some historians and archeologists who have studied this story have come up with a theory about why, after all those years of calculated searching, neither Prentiss nor Bouchette was ever able to find the right location of the gold.

This theory suggests that Turei did not successfully communicate to Prentiss that the gold was in an underground cave. It is possible that when Turei was trying to describe 'underground cave', Prentiss may have understood Turei to simply mean 'buried'. If that is the case, it would explain why Prentiss, and then Bouchette, spent all that time looking for something buried, when in fact they should have been looking for something in an underground cave.

There is a further interesting theory, which is perhaps the most intriguing explanation for why Prentiss and Bouchette could not find the hidden cavern of Tongva gold.

Although Catalina Island is not precisely symmetrical in shape, in a hastily created and roughly drawn picture with no compass indications, it would be possible to mistake the orientation of the picture, and confuse the west end of the island with the east end. So a theory has been proposed that Prentiss, with only his memory of Turei's picture to rely on, confused the orientation of the picture.

That would place the mark made by Turei on the picture not at the west end of the island, but rather on the east end. This would place Prentiss and Bouchette at the opposite end of the island from where the subterranean gold is actually located. This would mean that Prentiss may have spent thirty years digging at the wrong end of Catalina.

Corresponding to the digging efforts of thirty years that Prentiss did at the west end of the island, if the orientation is flipped, the Pebbly Beach Quarry would be not too far from where Turei's mark may have been on the picture.

There are currently no mineral-mining activities on Catalina Island. Large scale digging is done regularly now only by the Pebbly Beach Quarry & Mill. The quarry is a rock, sand, and gravel construction mine. It is a profitable and successful business that has been operating since the 1930s. They are digging for stone, not gold. But they do a lot of digging in that area.

So who knows, perhaps we will one day be reading about how the activities at the quarry have accidentally unearthed the ancient Tongva gold.

The question then will be, who owns the gold? Does the quarry company have the rights to whatever they find? Does the Catalina

Island Conservancy own whatever is found there? Does ancient Tongva gold belong to modern day Tongva people currently living in California?

It would seem the answer to the last question is 'yes'. The gold was originally found and fashioned by the Tongva people. It seems clear that any Tongva gold recovered on Catalina should be restored to the Tongva people.

The process and manner of specifically how to 'give them back their own gold' in today's modern complicated world might initially be a challenge. But certainly, Tongva gold should be returned to the Tongva people. If the gold is ever found, a way should be found for restoring to the Tongva people what rightfully belongs to them and their culture and their heritage.

However, the question of what to do with Turei's gold seems to be a question that may never need to be asked. After all this time, the treasure of Tongva gold in its hidden cavern has never been found, and there is little to suggest it ever will be.

Chapter 20
BOATS

"**Y**ou're a really good reader, Katie," said MacKenzie. "You did such a good job reading, I feel like I just watched a movie. I need some time to think about it all and sort it out in my head…"

Erik nodded in silent contemplative agreement.

"And," added MacKenzie, "you're so wonderful for finding that book, Katie. What an amazing story…"

"It really is quite an extraordinary story…" said John. "I wonder how much of it is true…"

"Well," said Erik slowly. "I can tell you one thing that's definitely true. There really is a grave marker for Prentiss. It's at Emerald Bay, west of Two Harbors."

"Oh, Erik, can we go see it?" asked MacKenzie.

Erik nodded. "That will be fun. I haven't been to Two Harbors in ages. And I sure never knew about the story that goes with that grave marker…"

"Erik," said Katie. "Your mom must know this story. Or at least parts of it, right?"

Erik shook his head. "I've never asked her. I will now, though. No one knows more about the island than my mom."

"MacKenzie," said Katie. "I would never have looked for or found this book if it weren't for you, so I hope you'll accept it as a present from me. But, maybe we could lend it to Erik, so that he could show it to his mom, if she's interested in reading it."

"Oh, I'm sure she'll be interested," said Erik. "Though, I'll bet my dad will be even more interested. He loves stories like this."

"Thank you, Katie," said MacKenzie. "It's the most special present ever. I love it because you got it for me. And I think it's a really nice idea for Erik to borrow it. Maybe his mom might even be able to let us know if anything else in the story is for sure true."

"Erik," said Katie. "How are you planning to get to Emerald Bay?"

"Well," said Erik. "I was going to talk about options with MacKenzie. It's too long for a bike ride. It would take us more than two hours each way. I was thinking I would borrow my parents' boat. Then we could probably make it from Avalon Bay to Two Harbors in a little over half an hour…"

"That's my daily commute," said Katie with a smile. "I'm staying in Avalon, but the Marine Center is out by Two Harbors. They've given me the use of one of their electric-powered speed-boats while I'm here."

"Not *Ada*?" asked MacKenzie.

Katie shook her head. "*Ada*'s great for going back and forth from Avalon Bay to the Seal Rocks. But her little outboard motor doesn't have enough speed or battery-life to make the trip back and forth between Avalon and Two Harbors."

"The speedboat's electric?" asked Erik.

Katie nodded. "She uses a large array of batteries. They're big, and they charge fast, and they drain slowly, and they can power the engine of the onboard motor, which is a bit of a monster. And, of course, the batteries take up a lot of space. There are almost more batteries on that boat than there is boat. But battery technology keeps improving. Batteries will keep getting smaller, and will hold more energy, and will last longer between charges. And the Marine Center makes a serious effort to use fuels like diesel and gasoline as little as possible."

"That's awesome," said Erik, clearly impressed.

"What's the speedboat's name?" asked MacKenzie.

"P. K.," said Katie.

"Like the son of William Wrigley, Jr.?" MacKenzie asked.

Katie nodded. "But, the boat is still referred to as 'she'. Boats are always called she. I don't know why."

"Dad?" asked MacKenzie.

Her father nodded. "Well," he began, "it's a centuries-old tradition to refer to a ship as 'she', whether the boat's actual name is female or not. Like so many of these kinds of traditions, there are many different explanations for it. One explanation comes from languages with nouns that are grammatically male or female. The Latin word for ship is 'navis', and in Latin, 'navis' is 'feminine'. Another explanation is that there is a centuries-old tradition of male boat-owners naming their vessels after important women in their lives, like a wife or a sweetheart or a mother. A similar explanation is that, long ago, ships were once dedicated to goddesses. Sea-going vessels were named after female divinities not only out of respect, but also as a way of asking for divine protection. And that kind of female-naming persisted, even as people over time began to have different kinds of religious beliefs. Another explanation is that sailors once thought of their ship as a kind of mother-figure, carrying them safely in the same way a mother carries a baby before it's born.

"Whatever the reason or reasons might be, it's an age-old tradition that doesn't only apply to boats. Things like cars and countries have often been traditionally referred to as "she". Of course, a boat can be any gender it wants to be. But historically, boats have been traditionally thought of as 'she'. So, the short answer is, I don't actually know why."

Erik nodded. "Mr. Milles," he said, "I think you and my dad are going to like each other. You're both really smart."

John smiled. "Thank you, Erik. I'm looking forward to meeting both of your parents."

"Erik," asked MacKenzie, "what's the name of your parents' boat?"

"*Brenda,*" said Erik.

"That's your mom's name."

Erik nodded. "My dad got the boat for my mom as a present, about a year before I was born. He named it. My mom loved the boat, but she wasn't so crazy about it being named after her. But she got used to it. So, my mom is called 'Brenda', and the boat is called '*The Brenda*'. I've grown up with it, so it seems normal to me."

Katie smiled at Erik. "That's very sweet," she said.

MacKenzie nodded in agreement, and then thought for a moment.

"Dad," she said, "I've been thinking. If the story Katie read us really is true, doesn't it seem like the gold should be left undiscovered? I mean, if someone finds it, there's no way to be sure it will get returned to the Tongva people where it belongs, right?"

John took a sip of his wine. "Well," he said. "Think about the baseball cards you found, Mac. There has been no complication. You found them, but you felt strongly they should be returned to Cavanarro. The Conservancy owns the house, but thanks to Ed, they feel as you do, that the cards should be returned to Cavanarro. And so far, it seems you'll be able to track down Cavanarro and return the cards to him. All not too complicated. But I think you're right, it might be very different with the Tongva gold, if it ever is found. As the book Katie read to us suggests, whoever finds the gold may claim it should go to the finder. The Conservancy, as primary owners and caretakers of the island, may feel that anything with that kind of money-value and historical-value belongs to them. Museum people may feel the gold should belong to no one, and should be put in a museum. Representatives of the Tongva people may very rightly believe the gold belongs to them, but then that creates a problem of how does the gold or its value get restored to living Tongva tribal people who are related to the island's original Tongva tribal people. It's not that it couldn't be done. But no matter what happens, it would all be extremely complex and complicated. It could become a real mess…"

With questions about the Tongva gold left unresolved, the evening proceeded onward. MacKenzie had earlier persuaded her father while they were shopping to let her buy ingredients for chocolate chip cookies. So as John and Katie sat by the fire chatting and drinking their wine, Erik kept MacKenzie company in the kitchen while she baked fresh cookies from scratch. Soon the enticing smells of baking cookies filled the cottage with homey sugary sweetness, the familiar aromas of doughy chocolate goodness mingling with the cozy redolence of the fireplace fire, transforming the inside of the cottage into a fragrant beguiling oasis of summer holiday warmth and festiveness.

Because MacKenzie had insisted on being extra-prepared, just in case, there remained an additional unused package of semi-sweet chocolate chips. MacKenzie decided that everyone should play poker, and use the extra chocolate chips to take the place of the poker chips they didn't have. So while they were all enjoying the scrumptious results of MacKenzie's baking, the four of them happily lost themselves in spirited rounds of poker, John and Katie now sipping coffee instead of wine, animatedly discussing betting tactics and the comparative rankings of different poker hands, while MacKenzie and Erik faced the formidable challenge of trying to stop themselves from eating their own winnings.

Erik's mother rang the doorbell shortly after ten. Erik and MacKenzie introduced her to MacKenzie's father, and Brenda agreed to stay for a few minutes and play some hands of poker with everyone. At around 10:30, Erik and MacKenzie went out to Erik's mother's golf cart and took MacKenzie's cottage-bike off the rack and put Erik's mountain bike on the rack in its place. They put MacKenzie's cottage-bike into the garage with the mountain bike she was now borrowing from Erik, and the two of them then went back into the cottage so everyone could say good-night.

Erik and his mother left for home with the borrowed book about the treasure story, and MacKenzie cleaned up from poker, and washed her and Erik's hot chocolate mugs, and adamantly refused to let John or Katie help with clean-up in any way.

"Okay," MacKenzie finally announced. "I'm going to bed."

"'Tis now struck eleven," said her father. "Get thee to bed, MacKenzie."

MacKenzie and Katie exchanged a glance.

"'Hamlet'?" asked Katie.

MacKenzie nodded. "Only, I think my Dad's changed a couple of words."

"Only two," her father protested.

MacKenzie put her hands on her hips. "A couple is two, Dad," she explained patiently.

"Completely correct," agreed her father. "Per usual."

MacKenzie smiled at her father and Katie. "Do you guys have enough coffee?" she asked.

"You take very good care of everyone, MacKenzie," said Katie.

MacKenzie beamed. "Thanks, Katie," she said. "I like helping people."

"We're all set for coffee, thank you," her father said appreciatively. "No one is a better helper than you, MacKenzie."

"Thanks, Dad," she said. "Dad, can Katie tuck me in after I brush my teeth?"

Her father smiled broadly. "Mac, you haven't been tucked-in in years."

MacKenzie nodded. "Yes, but Katie's never tucked me in."

John looked at Katie and smiled, then turned back to MacKenzie. "Only if you're in bed in three minutes," he said, glancing at his watch. "I'm timing you."

"Thanks, Dad!" said MacKenzie's voice as the rest of her disappeared hurriedly down the hall.

Less than three minutes later, MacKenzie's voice made its way to the living room again.

"Katie, come tuck me in, please," she called out from the hall.

A few moments later, Katie came in and sat down on the side of the bed next to where MacKenzie was lying comfortably and expectantly.

"All ready for some delicious sleep?" asked Katie.

MacKenzie nodded. "Very ready," she said. "Today was another wonderful day. I can't wait to wake up tomorrow and start another one. My Dad told me that dolphins sleep with one eye open."

Katie nodded. "He's right," she said. "They do."

"Well," said MacKenzie thoughtfully, "even though I'm a dolphin, I think I'll sleep better if I have both eyes closed."

"Dolphins are very intelligent," said Katie. "They're allowed to do things in whatever way works best for them."

"Katie," said MacKenzie, "would you mind if I asked you why you're not married? You're so pretty, and you always smell so good, and you're smart, and you're really fun to be with."

Katie laughed kindly for a moment. "Oh, MacKenzie," she said. "That is a very big question."

MacKenzie nodded. "Okay," she said respectfully. "So, then I won't ask."

Katie laughed quietly again. "That's very polite of you," she said. "But, I'll try to explain a little. MacKenzie, I like to be independent. I enjoy being on my own. I am... I have been very happy having my life to myself."

MacKenzie nodded. "That sounds like me," she said. "I totally get that."

Katie smiled. "I knew you would understand how that is," she went on. "And I have lots of great friends. Any time I want, I'm around lots of wonderful loving people who care about me, who I care about very much."

MacKenzie nodded again in recognition. "That's like me, too."

Katie smiled again. "I know. You and I have a lot in common. And there's one other important thing, MacKenzie. It will probably make more sense when you're older. But, I have... I had never met the right person. For me, it was never that I wanted to get married and was searching for the best person. It was the flipped version of that for me. If I ever met the right person, then I would happily get married. I simply had never met the right person. And that's been fine. I love life, I love living, and I love my life."

MacKenzie nodded. "I love life," she said with deep enthusiasm.

"I know you do," said Katie. "You do the best job enjoying life of anyone I've ever known."

"I love my life more now that you're in it," said MacKenzie.

Katie's eyes glistened for a moment. "That's how I feel about you, too," she said.

MacKenzie reached under her pillow and pulled something out.

"Look..." said MacKenzie, showing it to Katie. "It's the 1951 penny you gave me. I keep it in my pocket in the daytime, and I keep it under my pillow when I'm asleep."

"I'm glad you like it," said Katie.

MacKenzie nodded. "I love it," she said, turning it over in her hands and looking at it fondly as she held it in the air just over her head.

"Okay, little dolphin," said Katie, gently brushing some of MacKenzie's hair away from her face. "Have lovely sweet dreams."

MacKenzie nodded and reached behind her head to carefully put her penny back under her pillow.

"Thanks, Katie. Thanks for tucking me in. Would you please ask my Dad to come in and say good-night to me?"

Katie nodded. "Good-night, MacKenzie."

"Good-night, Katie. Thank you for coming over again, and for reading the story, and for giving me the book."

Katie smiled. "It all makes me very happy, MacKenzie. Truly."

As Katie left the room, MacKenzie reached over for the knurled brass knob on the base of the side-table lamp and turned it until the light went out.

A few moments later, her father came in alone and sat down next to her on the side of where she was lying in bed. "Mac…" he began slowly.

"Dad," MacKenzie said before he could continue. "I love Mom. She was the best Mom in the world. No one will ever have a better Mom than I did. I'll always love Mom. She's part of me forever. She's part of you and me, Dad. No one will ever take her place. No one ever could. Mom made us the best family, and she always wanted what was best for us. For all of us. And she wouldn't want us to stay in place. She would want us to move forward. She always said, 'Keep moving forward. The farther—'"

"'The farther you go,'" John recited, "'the better you get,'" he finished for her.

MacKenzie nodded. "Mom was smart. She made us better. She helped us make ourselves better. She's still helping us make ourselves better. We're like boats, Dad. We shouldn't just sit in the harbor. We should go to new places, and see new things, and meet new people, and have new fun adventures. That's what Mom would want. She would want us to keep moving forward."

John looked lovingly at his daughter and gently smoothed her hair with one hand. "Your mother brought so much beauty and light and goodness into this world," he said quietly. "And the greatest gift she ever gave me was you, Mac."

"You and Mom will always be my parents," said MacKenzie. "Nothing will ever change that. You and Mom will always be why I'm me."

Her father nodded. "I love you very much, Mac," he said.

"I love you, Dad," said MacKenzie, sitting up to hug her father.

After a moment, she lay back down and John stood up, each of them slightly different than they had been minutes earlier, both of them slightly better than before.

"Door open or closed, honey?" her father asked.

"Closed, please," said MacKenzie. "If I hear the fireplace, I'll want to stay up and be in front of it."

Her father nodded. "Okay, honey. Good-night."

"Dad?"

"Mac?"

"I'm really glad we came to Catalina."

Her father nodded. "That makes me happy, Mac."

"Are you happy we came to Catalina?"

"If I'm with you, Mac, I'm happy."

MacKenzie smiled in the darkness and the light from the hall. "Erik said something just like that to me. It's a really nice thing to say. It's really nice of both of you."

"You have good taste in friends, Mac."

MacKenzie nodded. "So do you, Dad," she said.

"Good-night, honey," said her father, turning to leave.

"Dad?"

"Honey?" he said, turning back around.

"If I'm with you, Dad, I'm happy."

Her father came back over to her for a moment. "You are a gift from Heaven, Mac," he said quietly. He kissed his daughter good-night lightly on her forehead, and then went out, closing the door softly behind him.

Chapter 21
INFORMATION

The next morning, MacKenzie and her father settled in to what had become their new start-of-the-day routine. They got up early, MacKenzie made breakfast for both of them and fresh coffee for her father, and after breakfast John sat in the kitchen sipping coffee and keeping MacKenzie company while she cleaned up and washed dishes from breakfast.

As they had planned during the previous day's game of catch, with half an hour of time before Davenport would show up, MacKenzie and her father went about setting up the short-wave radio in front of the television in the living room. Twenty minutes of testing and experimenting ended with the two of them triumphantly high-five-ing each other as they discovered they could indeed successfully get a reasonably strong and clear signal from WGN 720 AM, the Chicago flagship-radio-station home of the Cubs, freeing both MacKenzie and her father to enjoy looking forward to that afternoon's game without intrusive concerns about possible technical difficulties.

Davenport showed up with characteristic promptness at 7:30 to pick up John, and the two of them drove off together. MacKenzie left the cottage on her borrowed mountain bike directly after her father left, on an impulse deciding to do some exploring entirely by herself before meeting up with Erik. It was a bit of irony that here she was on Catalina, farther away from the rest of the world than she had ever felt in her life, and yet in the time she had been on the island so far, she had spent less time on her own by herself than she could ever remember.

She pedaled her way down Avalon Canyon Road as she always

did. But when she got to the edge of town, instead of heading as usual straight down Summer Ave all the way to the Catalina Tile Fountain circle at the top edge of the beach, she turned onto Tremont and then onto Clarissa. This still took her ultimately to one end of Crescent Ave, but on a route which connected with Pebbly Beach Road, the drive that led past the Cabrillo Mole and then on along the northern shoreline toward the east. That was just what she wanted, she realized as she pedaled past the Mole—a few minutes of the morning to herself, biking alone along the coastline.

She rode until she saw a large towering rock that rose from the beach on her left, extending high above the already-elevated shoreline drive. She pulled over into a paving-stone surfaced turnout to check her map and see where she was, which turned out to be Abalone Point. Looking west back toward Avalon, she had a spectacular postcard view of the distant Casino building, with the glistening early-morning harbor in the foreground and the sloping low-mountain points of the Avalon hills framing the scenery behind it.

In the opposite direction, several feet away from her toward the east, was another rock formation, smaller only by comparison to the craggy mass of rock next to her, extending up from the beach and rising like a statue above the level of the roadway. MacKenzie stood straddling her bike and gazing at this other angular cluster of rock. There was something about it she liked. It seemed to have a face, possibly wearing a battle helmet, and a raised right arm. It looked to MacKenzie like some fantastic ancient boulder god, or a benevolent rock monster, or a stone warrior sentry keeping watch over the island. It made her smile, and she raised an arm of her own to wave back to it in respectful reverent greeting.

Encountering the rock-warrior sentry had made her happy, and she felt like she had accomplished what she had set out to. Getting back on her bike, she reversed direction and pedaled her way back, eventually past the Mole now on her right, and at last onto Crescent Ave along the paving-stone top edge of the beach until she saw Erik up ahead.

It was only 8:00, but MacKenzie and Erik wanted to talk with Erik's mother together, and they had agreed to meet early so she would have time to talk with them before heading out on her first tour of the day. They walked their bikes over to Erik's mother who was waiting for them by the trolley stop.

"MacKenzie!" said Brenda, bubbling with enthusiasm and affable energy, and cordially kissing MacKenzie lightly on first one cheek then the other in friendly greeting. "It was so nice of you to lend me that book Katie gave you. I read it last night. It's quite interesting. I've heard different versions of the treasure story, but I've never seen so many different details all tied together in a single narrative like that. It makes a great story."

Brenda's opal earrings caught the early morning sunlight as she spoke, dancing about and reflecting glittering rainbow iridescence with every movement of her head. Her chic sunglasses with glossy black frames and large lenses were pushed up fashionably over her dark auburn hair arranged neatly beneath a stylish white headband, and her perfectly-fitting flower-patterned dress was a flowing landscape of cheery summertime.

"Mac," said Erik. "Is it okay if we keep it until my dad gets back?"

"Oh, yes, MacKenzie," added Brenda. "Erik's father will love it. Would you mind?"

MacKenzie smiled. "No, of course not. I'm so glad you enjoyed reading it, Mrs. Roebling. And I know from what Erik's told me that Mr. Roebling will probably really enjoy reading it, too."

Brenda nodded. "Oh, he will. That story is his kind of thing."

"Mom," Erik asked. "Is there anything in that story that's for sure true?"

"Well," said Brenda. "I can tell you that the details having to do with the island itself are all pretty accurate. All the history of mining on the island is accurate, and there are absolutely countless old sealed-up silver mines all over the island, especially at the west end near Two Harbors. Bouchette certainly was a real person. Some people believe his first name was Stephen, but that may just have been a more familiar name than Santos Louis for people to say back then. And there is a mine named after Bouchette. There's even a road named after him."

"There is?" Erik asked with surprise.

Brenda nodded. "Boushey Canyon Road, way out on the west end. It's past Two Harbors. Both Prentiss and Bouchette really did live on the island. And as you know, Erik, Prentiss really is buried at a place near Emerald Bay. What I will tell you, that's not in the book, is that Prentiss's original grave marker no longer exists. It was originally wood. It was replaced in 1900 with a grave stone, the one that's still there today."

"Who put it there?" asked Erik.

"Before William Wrigley, Jr. bought most of Catalina," said Brenda, "the island was owned by the Banning Family. They were the ones who replaced the old wooden marker with an engraved headstone. But as for the parts of the book about Bouchette, I believe there is actually quite a bit of historical evidence which matches the details in the story of Bouchette's life on the island as a silver miner. And the part about Bouchette and his wife leaving in a boat and never being seen again is also true. There were actually people who saw them leave the island for the last time together in their boat."

"Mrs. Roebling," asked MacKenzie, "how is Boushey Canyon Road named after him?"

"Well," said Brenda. "You likely can hear the similarity. Boushey is just another name that people called Bouchette by. Bouchette is a French name. So, even though it's properly pronounced

'Boo-shet', people at the time who didn't know how to say French names pronounced it 'Boo-shay'. It's been spelled differently in different places on the island, sometimes B-o-u-c-h-e-t, sometimes B-o-u-s-h-e-y."

"It's different transliterations," Erik realized with excited recognition.

Brenda smiled broadly. "MacKenzie," she said. "I assume I have you to thank for expanding the size of Erik's mind?"

MacKenzie shook her head politely. "He was way smart long before I ever showed up, Mrs. Roebling. I've learned way more from him than he has from me."

Erik shook his head. "So not true," he said to MacKenzie. "I've learned way more from you."

Brenda laughed in good-natured amusement. "Oh," she said, grinning, "you two are really kindred spirits."

MacKenzie and Erik looked at each other.

Erik's mother looked momentarily surprised. "Do you two really not know what kindred spirts are?" she asked.

MacKenzie and Erik together both shook their heads.

"Oh, we know, mom," said Erik. "It's just funny that you happened to say it. That phrase is like one of the clues in MacKenzie's island mystery. Everywhere we go, it keeps showing up."

"MacKenzie," Brenda asked with interest. "Are you solving an island mystery?"

"Well," said MacKenzie. "Right now, I'm still trying to figure out what the mystery is. Solving it is going to be a whole other mystery."

Brenda laughed. "Well," she said, "I certainly hope you'll be staying on the island for a while. I love Erik dearly. But who he's become since he has been spending time with you makes a mother quite happy and proud."

"Thank you, Mrs. Roebling," said MacKenzie. "That's a really nice thing to say. Thank you."

Brenda slowly shook her head in impressed appreciation. "So remarkably polite," she said. "That's certainly another thing you both have in common. Well," she went on, "I understand that you two are going to brighten my morning tour by coming along for the ride?"

MacKenzie and Erik nodded.

"But mom," said Erik, "MacKenzie was hoping to go on one of the tours where she can listen to you narrate."

Brenda nodded. "Well," she said. "MacKenzie, I always start my tour day here, as the operator of the trolley tour. However, there's no narration. I just drive people from point to point, and drop them off or pick them up. Then, depending upon the day, for my next tour I switch to either the open-air tram tour, or the Inland Expedition bus tour. The trolley and the tram tours are each about an hour, but the Inland Expedition bus tour is over three hours. There are several of us tour operators, and we have a rotation for who does which tour when. But I do especially like the tram and the bus tours, because I get to narrate the whole time."

Erik glanced at MacKenzie. "You see where I get it from…?" he asked, grinning.

Brenda smiled. "Oh, yes," she agreed heartily. "The Roeblings are a family of talkers. There's no denying it or changing it. So we just embrace it and celebrate it."

Erik nodded. "You should see us at meals together," he said to MacKenzie. "No one can get a word in edgewise."

MacKenzie giggled and smiled at Erik's mother.

"And so as I was saying," Brenda went on, "I like the open air of the tram, but I also really like the lovely old 1951 bus that's used on the Inland Expedition tour."

MacKenzie and Erik both looked at each other.

"What?" asked Brenda, looking momentarily puzzled again.

Erik shook his head. "It's nothing, mom. It's just that Katie gave MacKenzie a really cool present, a penny she found while diving that she knew MacKenzie would like because the date on the penny is the same as the Cub's last year of Spring Training on the island."

"1951?" asked Brenda.

MacKenzie and Erik both nodded.

"Well," said Brenda. "My goodness gracious, that certainly is another coincidence, isn't it."

"Erik and I were going to take your trolley tour, Mrs. Roebling," said MacKenzie. "But I'd really like to take a tour where I can hear you narrate."

"Well," Brenda went on, "as I said, the bus tour's wonderful fun, but it is over three hours. Now, MacKenzie, since today's Thursday, the tour I'm doing after this trolley tour will be the open-air tram tour. Why don't you and Erik come back at around ten, and take the tram tour with me. It's not three hours. But even in only an hour, I do manage to get in plenty of talking! And then afterward, if you two would like, I'll take you both out to lunch."

"Oh, that sounds perfect!" said MacKenzie enthusiastically.

Erik nodded. "That's great. Thanks mom."

"Fabulous," said Brenda. "Oh, and I know you two want to take the boat out to Two Harbors and Emerald Bay, and that's fine. But I called the yacht club this morning, and apparently Erik's father is having some maintenance work done on her. So, she won't be ready in time for today, but she will be ready tomorrow. That is, if you two can wait that long," she added with a smile.

Erik glanced at MacKenzie. "I told my mom that you're as impulsive and impatient as I am. Once I think of something, I always want to do it right away."

MacKenzie nodded. "Yes," she agreed. "That's me, too."

"Thanks, mom," said Erik. "We'll try to manage waiting until tomorrow," he added, smiling first at MacKenzie and then at his mother.

"Oh," said Brenda suddenly. "Speaking of your father and coincidences, that reminds me. You were talking with him on the phone last night about *The Vanishing American*."

Erik nodded. "He's going to try to find out about one of the actors MacKenzie and I want to know about."

Brenda nodded. "Well, you two may be interested in something we were all told this morning at the tour office. And you'll be able to see for yourselves if you stop by the bulletin board over at the Casino. But there's a newly-restored print of *The Vanishing American* that's going to be released soon. And before it's officially released, it's going to have a premiere screening right here on the island. At the Casino, of course. I'm sure the leaflets telling about it are already up along Crescent and Metropole, and over at the Mole."

Erik shook his head and absently adjusted the position of his shark-tooth bracelet on his wrist. "Wow, mom,' he said. "That definitely is kind of another coincidence all right..."

"And it's really exciting information, Mrs. Roebling," said MacKenzie. "Thank you for telling us."

"It might be really fun to go to that premiere," mused Erik.

"Although," said MacKenzie, "I'm not sure I could see it again so soon. It's really emotional..."

Erik nodded in thoughtful agreement.

"Well," said Brenda, "I thought you might be interested. But I wouldn't get your hopes too high about going to the premiere. Catalina may not be the celebrity glamour destination it was back in Hollywood's Golden Age. But for an event like this, the rich and famous tend to appear out of nowhere, so tickets to that premiere will likely be quite difficult if not utterly impossible to get a hold of. In fact, I'm pretty sure all tickets were already spoken for by people of means with influence and connections before the premiere date was even announced. The leaflets around town are likely just for publicity, and mostly to alert us locals that things may get suddenly busy around here for a day or so next week."

"Wow," said Erik. "Next week? That's really soon."

Brenda nodded. "It's now been moved up to the 20th, this coming Tuesday."

"That's in five days...!" Erik said with astonishment.

Brenda nodded. "Apparently it was originally scheduled for the end of August. But there's going to be a live orchestra performing the music, and there was some complication with their schedule. So, someone in charge of something decided to move up the date of the Catalina premiere. It's possible the Conservancy had something to do with that. They're so protective of the island, as they should be. They may have done something behind-the-scenes to make it so that, with such suddenly short advance-notice, there will be fewer people able to plan to come to the island for the event. We were told this morning the film's formal theatrical re-release isn't actually happening until September, and that's been the plan all along. It's only the Catalina premiere event that's had its date changed."

"I like it when the Conservancy gets tricky with how they protect the island," said Erik approvingly.

Brenda nodded. "We do very much count on them to do whatever it takes, and they usually do," she agreed.

"It does all sound very exciting," said MacKenzie.

"Yes, even with the sudden short notice, it's certainly likely to be the island's biggest event of the summer," said Brenda, checking her watch. "Very well, you two," she went on efficiently. "Speaking of short notice, it's time for me to go to work."

"Have a good tour, Mrs. Roebling," said MacKenzie.

"Love you, mom," said Erik, giving his mother a kiss good-bye. "We'll see you back here by ten."

Chapter 22
NECKLACE

"Okay," Erik said to MacKenzie. "Time for after-breakfast dessert at Big Olaf's?"

"Really?" she said with happy surprise. "Are you sure?"

"Totally. After-breakfast dessert is one of my favorite MacKenzie-isms," Erik said with deep enthusiasm. "And besides, we're celebrating."

"Celebrating what?"

"That it's another day, and you're still in Catalina."

MacKenzie grinned. "Oh," she said with eager delight. "I could get used to this!"

"Me too," Erik agreed, smiling. "I already have."

They locked their bikes to a rack and made their way to Big Olaf's, where they selected and customized their desserts, and then strolled back to sit at the top of the beach and enjoy the colorful extravagance of their towering servings of creamy-cool deliciousness in the morning's warm welcoming Pacific sunlight and the idyllic view of the shimmering tranquil water of the bay stretching majestically into the ocean and on toward the horizon.

MacKenzie glanced with concern for a moment in the direction of the Cabrillo Mole. The second ferry of the day would not arrive for at least another thirty minutes, and there weren't many people gathered on or near the Mole.

"Looking for the mysterious man…?" asked Erik between mouthfuls of ice cream.

MacKenzie nodded and turned back to resume eating her own ice cream. "It's annoying that he makes me anxious even when I don't see him…" she said with some frustration, and she forced her mind to move on to less-troubling other thoughts.

"I like your backpack," she said. "It's nice and small and cool-looking. You can hold all the stuff you want with you, but your pack takes up such little space on your back. Plus, it just looks really cool and comfortable."

Erik nodded and ate some more ice cream. "Thanks," he said. "I like your Cubs backpack. But I can see how it would sometimes be too big. I have another pack exactly like the one I'm wearing. I can lend it to you if you want. It doesn't have cool Cubs logos, though…"

MacKenzie laughed. "That's okay," she said. "I still have my Cubs hat, and my Cubs watch, and like, everything else I own. So, yes, I'd really love to borrow your extra pack. Thanks. Mine's just too big to wear around all the time. Especially for things like bike-riding."

"We just have to make sure," said Erik, "to get everything from your Cubs pack into it, so you don't end up missing something you want or need."

A sound like the tolling of church bells rang somewhere in the distance, rising and falling as it was gently buffeted by sea breezes.

"What is that…?" asked MacKenzie turning her head and looking around. "I feel like I've been hearing it ever since my Dad and I got here… I've never been to London, but it sounds like something you'd hear there…"

Erik nodded. "That's the Chimes Tower," he said, pointing up in the direction of the hills somewhere behind them. "We'll see it up close on my mom's tour. She does a good job of telling the history. The tower was built by William Wrigley, Jr. It was his wife Ada's idea. She wanted there to be a nice sound that would make people who heard it feel happy. I think the chimes first started ringing in 1926. They've been chiming every fifteen minutes ever since.

Because of the wind, you can't always hear them. But sometimes you can hear them really clearly. I like them."

MacKenzie nodded. "I really like them, too," she said. "What a wonderful idea, to have chimes that ring to make people feel happy. I love that…"

They went on eating their ice cream, and MacKenzie absently put her hand on the outside of her jeans pocket to make sure her penny was still there. As usual, she couldn't feel it, and she went through what had recently become a new ritual, which was momentary panic at thinking she had lost her penny, hurriedly shoving a hand into her pocket, discovering the coin was still there, and then relaxing with welcome relief.

"Everything okay?" asked Erik.

MacKenzie nodded. "I keep randomly panicking about losing the penny that Katie gave me. I like it so much. I always want to have it with me. I keep it in my pocket, but I wish there was some way to make it into a necklace or something…"

"There is," said Erik.

"How?"

"There's a guy I'm friends with named Jake who makes Catalina jewelry to sell to tourists. He's got a little shop over on Summer Ave. He's a really nice guy. He could probably take the penny Katie gave you and make it into a necklace."

"But," said MacKenzie, "I don't want a hole drilled through it. I mean, I really like your shark-tooth bracelet. A lot. I think it's really cool. But I just don't want a hole in my coin. I like it just the way it is."

Erik nodded in understanding. "Jake knows all sorts of ways to make all different kinds of jewelry," he said. "He can wrap a metal jewelry band around the edge of the coin to hold it, and the band will have a place for the necklace chain to go through. I've seen ones like that that he's made before. He's really good at what he does. He doesn't spend too much time on the tourist jewelry, but for anything that's important, he knows how to do a really good job."

"Can he make it strong?" asked MacKenzie. "I want to be able to wear it all the time, and I don't want it to ever break."

"Sure," said Erik. "We'll just tell Jake what you want. He'll know how to do it."

"Do you think it will be expensive?" MacKenzie asked with some apprehension.

"Nope."

"But, it sounds like it would be."

"But I'm friends with Jake," said Erik. "So he'll give me a good deal. And also, you're not paying for it. I am."

"No. Erik, I won't let you."

"Why not?"

"Because..." she began. "Because you shouldn't have to be spending any of your money on me."

"Mac," said Erik. "That coin is a special present from Katie, and Katie is really important to you, and you're really important to me."

"You're really important to me, too."

"Okay, then," said Erik. "And so, it's really important to me to be able to do this for you. And it would be really nice if you would just say okay and let me."

MacKenzie exhaled resignation. "Okay, fine. Thank you. Really. It's so generous and so nice. And it means a lot to me. Thank you."

Erik had been about to finish the last of his ice cream, but he paused and looked closely at MacKenzie. "MacKenzie Milles..." he said sternly.

"What...?"

"I know you," said Erik. "And I know exactly what you're thinking. You're plotting to get me some kind of present to make up for it."

MacKenzie left her large paper bowl of ice cream in her lap and threw up her hands in frustration. "It's not fair if you can read my mind, Erik Roebling."

"Listen," said Erik. "I don't want you to get me a present just because I'm giving you a gift. That's not how it works."

"Fine," said MacKenzie. "If I ever give you something, and I'm not saying I ever will, I promise it will not to be to thank you for helping me with my necklace. It will be because I want to give you something special, that I would have given you anyway, even if there had never been a necklace. Deal?"

"Deal."

They finished their ice cream and made their way back to Big Olaf's to put their trash into the recycling bins.

Erik checked his watch. "Plenty of time," he said. "Video store?"

"Video store," confirmed MacKenzie.

They chatted and strolled their way together along the sidewalk amidst the slowly growing crowd of tourist visitors and local residents, and soon Erik had led them to their video store destination.

"Speaking of things I want or need..." MacKenzie said, unshouldering her backpack for a moment and unzipping a pocket on the outside. Reaching in and pulling out a fat pack of Wrigley's Spearmint gum, she extended it politely toward Erik.

"Want some?" she asked.

Erik nodded and slid a stick for himself out of the pack. "Thanks," he said.

"Sure," said MacKenzie, pulling out a piece for herself and returning the rest to where it had come from, zipping the pocket closed. She slung her pack back over a shoulder with one hand, and with the other neatly slid the foil-wrapped stick out from its paper sleeve, unfolded the foil to reveal the gum without any of the wrappings falling, popped the stick of gum into her mouth, and crumpled the wrappers, all in a single smooth one-handed motion.

"Hey," said Erik in impressed surprise. "That's pretty nifty. You did that like a magic card trick. I've never seen anyone do that with one hand. That was awesome."

MacKenzie grinned happily as she stuffed the wadded ball of crumpled wrappers into a jeans pocket. "I ought to be good at it," she said with a laugh, "considering how many millions of times I've done it."

Erik shook his head. "That's not just practice or experience. That's real skill and talent. You did that like a magician."

"Thanks," she said, smiling broadly.

Erik needed two hands to open his own stick of gum, and after popping it into his mouth and stuffing the wrappers into his own pocket, he and MacKenzie headed inside the video store.

Shelves of videotapes on every wall reached from the carpeted floor to the height of the low ceiling. Closely-stacked uniform rows of shelving cabinets rose from foot-level to slightly higher than eye-level in aisles like a market, stretching from one end of the video store to the other, all with seemingly endless arrays of boxed videocassettes sandwiched together like innumerable identically-sized library books and arranged variously by genre or alphabetically by title.

An action movie was playing on a video screen mounted at an angle for easily-seen viewing in one corner of the ceiling over the check-out counter, while the sound effects and periodic dialogue and urgent music of the soundtrack played at a courteously low volume and came from ceiling speakers mounted at opposite ends of the store.

Erik knew the owner, and told him what they were looking for. After getting directions for which aisle would be most likely to have what they had in mind, Erik thanked him, and MacKenzie and Erik browsed their way through the racks and displays of videotape selections toward their objective.

In the oldies and classics section of silent movies, other than the several copies of *The Vanishing American*, there was only one other Richard Dix film. It was titled *Trans-Atlantic Tunnel*.

"1935," said Erik, as he and MacKenzie stood close together so they could both read the blurb description on the back of the box. "So, this is a 'talkie', not a silent movie. Is that okay?"

MacKenzie nodded. "It has Richard Dix, so that's fine with me. It will be cool to hear what his voice sounds like."

Erik was still reading. "It's a British science fiction movie. It says the story's about building a train tunnel under the ground, under the Atlantic Ocean, from England to America. Oh, and at one point they apparently have to try to drill through an underwater volcano…"

"That sounds awesome!" said MacKenzie eagerly. "A train, an underground tunnel, an underwater volcano, *and* Richard Dix. This is the perfect movie for us!"

Erik grinned in agreement. "Okay, then," he said happily. "Let's go rent it."

"Oh, Erik, look…" said MacKenzie, lightly grabbing his arm for a moment and pointing toward a shelf closer to the floor. "That's the Buster Keaton movie you told me about, *The General*. Should we rent that too?"

"Are you sure you really want to see it?" asked Erik.

MacKenzie nodded. "From the way you described it, it sounds really cool. I would definitely like to see it. But, I feel bad that it will be the second movie we watch that you've already seen…"

Erik shook his head. "I love that movie," he said. "And it's very uplifting, and not the slightest bit depressing or too emotional. I love it so much, we own a copy. So, if you're sure you really want to see it, I'd be very happy to see it again and get to watch it with you."

MacKenzie smiled. "Okay, then," she said contentedly.

They proceeded back to the counter, where the store owner

aimed the red light of a handheld scanner at the barcode on the videocassette box and put the rental on Erik's family's account. He slid the videotape into a bag for them, which Erik zipped into his streamlined backpack. The store owner thanked them both for coming by, and MacKenzie and Erik left the store and walked the several blocks to where Jake's shop was located on Summer Ave.

Jake's shop window had countless pieces of displayed jewelry, many of them themed with ocean and island and Catalina motifs, and the inside of the shop had a fascinating combination of smells with distinct traces of machinery and machine oil, and metal and metal polish.

As Erik had described, Jake was very nice. He was thin and tall, and had very long straight black hair with a circle of folded bandana wrapped around it just above his ears and across his forehead. There were several earrings decorating both his ears, tattoos on his arms, layers of different-sized metal bracelets on both wrists, rings on every finger, and he wore several necklaces. He gave Erik a big friendly smile, and seemed genuinely pleased to meet MacKenzie. Jake reminded MacKenzie of a doctor, with the matter-of-fact confidence possessed by someone who knows what they're doing, knows how good they are at what they do, and has no interest in boasting about it.

MacKenzie took out her penny and handed it to Jake, and she and Erik carefully explained exactly what MacKenzie was hoping to have done to it. Jake listened with attentive patience, turning the penny over in his hands as MacKenzie and Erik spoke, and nodding knowingly with each detail they described. His agreeable clear grasp of her wishes gave MacKenzie that uniquely comforting feeling that can only come from someone who is an expert, and who understands what is wanted, and who is completely able and willing to accomplish it in exactly the right way.

There were several different-sized free-standing mirrors perched in various places atop the glass counter, as well as two large full-length wall-mirrors mounted at either side of the shop. Jake handed MacKenzie a coin-necklace he had already made and asked her to hold it by the chain, look in a mirror, and adjust the level of the coin until it was hanging exactly where she wanted her penny to hang. After some brief experimentation, she had it where she wanted it. Jake nodded and made several notes to himself on a small pad of paper, and MacKenzie handed the demonstration necklace back to him.

Jake told them he would have it all finished and ready to pick up by the next day, and they could come back to get it any time after his shop opened in the morning. MacKenzie thanked him with enthusiastic appreciation, and Jake thanked them earnestly for trusting him with something which was so clearly important to both of them.

They all said good-bye, and MacKenzie and Erik left the shop and headed back toward the trolley stop, chatting together at length first about how nice Jake was, with MacKenzie thanking Erik for helping her so much with her necklace, and then discussing the open-air tram, with Erik describing the kinds of things they were about to see and hear about on Brenda's tour of Avalon.

Chapter 23

HORSES

MacKenzie wasn't sure which she enjoyed more about the tram tour, seeing and learning about more of Avalon, or listening to Erik's mother narrating it all. Brenda was tirelessly cheerful and energetic. She reminded MacKenzie of her father and Erik. She seemed to know so much about so many things, she had a pleasant, fun, and clever sense of humor, she never ran out of things to say, and she seemed to be happiest when she was talking.

Stopping every five minutes or so at different landmark attractions along the way, the tour made its way at a leisurely pace through the heart of Avalon and up along the foothills above town, stopping at sites like the Hermit's Gulch campground, the Catalina Conservancy Nature Center at Avalon Canyon, the Catalina Island Golf Course, and the Joe Machado Baseball Park near the cottage.

MacKenzie particularly enjoyed the parts they visited of the 38-acre Wrigley Botanical Gardens, especially the elegant tranquil solemnity of the Wrigley Memorial tower which, as Brenda explained over the tram's speakers, was the original burial site of William Wrigley, Jr. One of the tram passengers asked if Wrigley was still buried there, and Brenda explained that sometime in the 1940s after the United States entered World War II, due to wartime security concerns over a possible attack or invasion of Catalina, Wrigley's remains were secretly removed from the island and brought to a new permanent location on the California mainland, in the Sanctuary of Gratitude at Forest Lawn Memorial Park Cemetery in Glendale.

As the tram headed west on Pebbly Beach Road, Brenda directed everyone's attention to the steep hill above. "The second most eye-catching architectural sight when you first come to

Avalon," she said, "after the Casino, is this beautiful Queen Anne architectural style cottage now named Holly Hill House, built into the steep incline of this hill by the Cabrillo Mole, overlooking Avalon Bay. One of oldest structures in Avalon, it was completed in 1890. The builder was also its owner, Paul Gano, a civil engineer and craftsman from Ohio who came to Catalina to help create the island's first fresh water system, and ended up staying when he fell in love with the island. Gano ferried his building materials from the mainland to Avalon using his sailboat, and designed and constructed his own pulley-and-slide system to move those materials from the beach up the steep hill. Originally named Lookout Cottage, the house was built in two years by Gano with the assistance of only one helper: Mercury, a large white horse adopted by Gano when Mercury was forced to retire from the circus due to failing eyesight. It was Mercury who helped move every beam of timber used to construct the house on its precarious but spectacular site. To honor Mercury, Gano topped the now-famous pointed cupola of the towering uppermost floor with a weather vane made to look like his beloved horse. That weather vane is still there today."

This story drew spontaneous applause from all the tram passengers, and Brenda smiled and blew a kiss of thank you to all of them as the tour continued on its way.

On the west side of Avalon harbor, the tour paused at the Catalina Yacht Club and then the Descanso Beach Country Club, but MacKenzie's favorite stop of the tour was the Chimes Tower. Hidden away below the edge of a winding narrow road on the downslope of a high hill, the tower was small and unassuming, but its aged eccentric charm was enchanting. Brenda explained to the tour that William Wrigley, Jr. had purchased the bronze tubular-bell Westminster chimes from the J.C. Deagan Company of Chicago in 1925, after his wife Ada had come up with the idea of bringing a unique musical sound to Avalon that would express and enhance the magical quality of the island. The distinctive Spanish-style tower, with its landscape-terraced base and colorful Catalina-tile roof was built as the permanent home for the chimes and completed in 1926. Since then, the chimes had been ringing every quarter hour, from 8 AM to 8 PM, with the same original chimes and the same original tolling mechanism.

The chimes sounded just as the quiet electric tram pulled to the side of the road near the top of the tower at 10:45. Hearing the melodious notes so clear and distinct from so close was entrancing for MacKenzie, and for a moment the sounds transported her to a beautiful previously-undiscovered place in her mind.

The tour ended back on Crescent Ave where it had begun, and many exiting passengers were effusively complimentary of Brenda as they climbed from the tram, thanking her and appreciatively describing in detail why they had so enjoyed her narration of the tour.

Brenda, meanwhile, was just getting warmed up, and she chatted cheerfully to MacKenzie and Erik all the way to the outdoor café where she brought them for lunch, and through much of the lunch itself as well.

MacKenzie was delighted and content. Erik's mother made her feel relaxed. Brenda's unending flow of casual chatting conversation and interesting information created exactly the kind of social setting MacKenzie enjoyed being in the midst of—being with people she liked, with talk flowing like a clear fresh bubbling spring, and not feeling any pressure to have to speak or decide what should be talked about next.

Before dessert arrived, Brenda spotted some of her friends walking by, and she excused herself from the table for a moment.

"Your mom is awesome," said MacKenzie.

Erik smiled. "Thanks, Mac," he said. "I think so, too. Listen, do you want to go horseback riding after lunch?"

MacKenzie nodded eagerly. "Yes, please," she said. "I love horses. That sounds wonderful."

"And," Erik went on, "you and your dad are listening to your first Catalina Cubs game on the short-wave radio this afternoon, right?"

MacKenzie nodded. "At 5:06. It's the start of a home-stand against the Rockies. Do you want to come over?"

Brenda had not ordered dessert, but MacKenzie and Erik had. Their plates of freshly-baked chocolate cake arrived with forks and spoons and mouth-watering allure, and the two of them dug into the delectable slices with unrestrained zeal.

"Well," said Erik a few moments later. "I was thinking. This is the first short-wave game for you guys, and it seems like a you-and-your-dad kind of thing, and I think the two of you should get to be just the two of you. And I don't want you to get sick of me, and also I thought it might be nice for me and my mom to have dinner at home together."

MacKenzie smiled warmly at him. "First of all," she said, "I could never possibly get sick of you. You're the most fun person to spend time with. Second, I think your idea is really very especially thoughtful and nice. Thank you for thinking of it. That is so like you, Erik Roebling. When you're not busy reading my mind, you're busy understanding not-obvious really important things about people."

"And talking," he added with a grin.

MacKenzie laughed. "Well, I like your talking. And I like your idea very much. That all sounds like a very good plan."

"How long do you suppose the game will be?"

"They're usually a little over two hours," said MacKenzie. "Unless it goes to extra innings."

"Do you want to come over afterward, and we can watch the Richard Dix movie?" he asked.

MacKenzie nodded emphatically. "Yes, please," she said. "I'll ask my Dad if he wouldn't mind driving me over and picking me up after."

Erik smiled. "That sounds perfect," he said.

The chocolate cake had been nearly devoured by the time Brenda returned, but Erik had saved a forkful of his to share with his mother. Erik explained to her what he and MacKenzie were hoping the afternoon and evening would look like, and Brenda cheerfully agreed that it all sounded lovely, and she hoped MacKenzie and her father would have plenty of fun listening to their game. She and Erik briefly discussed what the two of them would have for dinner, and then it was time to go.

MacKenzie and Erik thanked Brenda for taking them to lunch, and MacKenzie complimented her again on the truly wonderful job she had done conducting the tour. The three of them walked back toward the beach, where they said good-bye and Brenda headed off to prepare for her afternoon three-hour tour of the island on the 1951 bus. MacKenzie and Erik unlocked their bikes and pedaled off to Erik's house to get ready for horseback riding.

When they got to his house, Erik found the slim streamlined pack which was the extra twin to the one he had been wearing, and he and MacKenzie transferred everything from her Cubs pack into the slim pack, making sure nothing was overlooked in the process.

"There's a stable where I've ridden before, out on Middle Ranch Road," Erik was saying. "There are some great trails out there, but it's kind of far from here. I really like the people at the Catalina Stables. That's much closer, on Avalon Canyon Road just over by the golf course. They do tours, but they know me, and if we wanted, instead of going on another tour today, we could ask if they would let us just take a couple of horses out for trail riding on our own. They've let me do that before. How much riding have you done?"

"I have a friend who competes," said MacKenzie. "She's really good. I go with her to where her horses are stabled sometimes, and we just do casual riding. She rides English, but I can only ride Western. So, if I can use Western tack, and as long as my horse doesn't expect me to hang on while it does a galloping jump over something, I sort of pretty much know what I'm doing."

They went into the kitchen to use the phone. Erik called the stables and spoke with someone he knew there, and asked if there were two horses who wanted some casual extra exercise. All the arrangements were made, and MacKenzie and Erik prepared to leave. They were just about to head out when the phone rang.

Erik thought it might be the stables calling back with a question or a change of plans, but it was his father. MacKenzie could tell from Erik's voice and his face that there was nothing wrong, and that this unexpected call was not for any sudden bad reason. Erik was nodding a lot, and asking a lot of questions, and soon MacKenzie realized that Erik's father had found out for them something about Man Hammer's Oldest Boy.

MacKenzie watched and listened, her interest and curiosity mounting with each passing minute. Out of habit, MacKenzie absently put her hand on the outside of her jeans pocket to make sure her penny was still there. As usual, she couldn't feel it, and she hurriedly shoved a hand into her pocket. Upon discovering the coin wasn't there, she had an awful moment of sheer panic before at last remembering they had left it with Jake.

Erik finished his conversation with his father. He hung up the phone and turned toward MacKenzie, his eyes glittering with excitement.

"Okay," he began. "So, my dad's going to call back later at his usual time. But he knows how impatient I am, and I've told him how much you're like me in that way, and so because he's an awesome dad, he wanted to see if I was home so he could tell me what he just found out."

"And so what did he find out...?"

"Well," Erik went on, "first of all, apparently a lot of people my dad knows who are film people are talking about the restored print of *The Vanishing American*. There's also a lot of talk about how the date of the screening at the Casino was suddenly changed to so much earlier. My dad knew right away that the Conservancy had to be behind that. I think what he said was, 'The Conservancy's fingerprints are all over this. I'm glad they're on our side.'"

MacKenzie and Erik both laughed at that, and Erik went on with his explanation.

"So, Man Hammer's Oldest Boy is still alive. In fact, he's the only actor from the film who's still living. And he's going to be a guest of honor at the Casino screening. Or, at least he was. That may change now that the date has changed. But he does now have a name of his own..."

MacKenzie gasped with excitement. "What is it...?!"

"Okay," Erik went on. "Listen to this. He was eight years old when he acted in T*he Vanishing American*. When he was twelve, there was some kind of terrible fire in one of the homes on the reservation where he lived. There was a Navajo family of seven people trapped inside. Man Hammer's Oldest Boy ran in, literally through the flames, and started carrying people out."

"How could he do that?" said MacKenzie incredulously. "I mean, apart from the danger, he was only twelve. How could he carry people?"

Erik nodded. "My dad said that he apparently was big for his age, and also very strong. And, my dad said, on that day, in addition to being so brave, according to the story he seemed to suddenly have even more strength. My dad said that sometimes happens to people in an emergency. They can suddenly do things they couldn't do in a regular situation."

MacKenzie nodded. "I've heard of that happening..."

"So," Erik continued, "he went back into the burning house seven times, and he carried each person out, one by one. Six of them were actually children. And he got burned pretty badly, but everyone was saved, and everyone was okay. And because of what he did, the Navajo elders declared that he had done something that distinguished him among the people of his tribe, and they gave him a name. They named him Fire-Walker."

MacKenzie grabbed both of Erik's hands and squeezed them tight with excitement. "Oh my god...! That's the most amazing story ever...!!"

Erik squeezed her hands as well, and nodded vigorously. "So incredibly cool," he marveled. "Not just that he got a name, but what it was he did that earned him his name... It's absolutely incredible..."

They let go of each other's hands, and MacKenzie lifted her cap long enough to run a hand through her hair the way her father always ran his hand through his hair, before settling her cap back into place. "That's so heroic..." she breathed in admiring awe. "I don't even know him, and I'm so proud of him...!"

Erik nodded. "What an amazing way to get your own name, by single-handedly saving an entire family from an awful fire..."

They stood silently together for a moment, letting their minds contemplate the extraordinary story they had just experienced.

"Okay," Erik said at last. "We can talk about this more while we're riding. The people at the stables are so nice, I don't want us to be accidentally rude by showing up late."

MacKenzie nodded in agreement, while Erik opened a cupboard door over one of the counters and took out the one thing in the kitchen he knew the location of—the dark chocolate. Grasping the large flat bar and opening the boxed-covering, he peeled back some of the silver foil and broke off a big piece, handing it to MacKenzie. She took it with appreciative thanks and began to eat it, while Erik broke off an equally large-sized piece for himself and held it in his mouth as he re-closed the box and stuffed it back where it had come from. He swung the cupboard door closed, and the two of them headed outside to bike their way to the stables.

Two horses were all tacked up for them by the time they arrived. After thanking the people from the stables who were helping them, and chatting with them all for a few incidental minutes, MacKenzie and Erik mounted their horses and set out on their ride.

They rode together for nearly two hours, Erik and his horse in the lead on the narrower paths, and on the wider paths both MacKenzie's and Erik's horses walking side-by-side, periodically snorting contentedly and nuzzling noses. MacKenzie loved the smell of horses. She loved the rhythmic ride and the high view from her saddle of the wildlands all around them as she and Erik talked, and as the two of them savored the beauty of the island and getting to be together doing something they both loved in such a magical setting.

Chapter 24
GAME

"**N**ice backpack," said MacKenzie's father, nodding with approval as MacKenzie came in through the front door of the cottage shortly after 4:00.

"Thanks," she said happily. "Erik let me borrow it. It's the same as the one he uses."

"Very hi-tech and streamlined."

MacKenzie nodded. "It holds all my stuff, and doesn't flop around or have too much extra space. And it fits nice and snug on my back."

"Oh…" her father said, grinning. "Someone's been horseback riding."

"Oh, that would be me," MacKenzie said brightly. "It was so much fun. How did you know?"

"You smell like horses," said her father.

"Is it okay if I don't shower right now?" she asked. "I really like the smell."

Her father smiled. "Doesn't bother me," he said. "I also like the smell of horses."

"Awesome," said MacKenzie. "Thanks. Dad, I have six thousand things to tell you about…"

Her father nodded. "Added to what I want to tell you about, that makes twelve thousand. Grab your glove and let's head down to the ball field for a few minutes of catch. We don't want to miss the start of the game."

"We definitely do not want to be late for that," she said, dashing off to her room.

MacKenzie and her father were only able to begin discussing

each other's events of the day during their necessarily-shortened game of catch because they had too much to do before 5:06, and some of the rest of their catching-up had to be done while riding Bertie into town.

John started with explaining that Katie would be having dinner with friends from the Marine Center because she wanted MacKenzie and her father to be able to have their first Catalina Cubs game just the two of them. MacKenzie laughed because it was exactly what Erik had said to her, and she and her father both agreed they were glad to be able to listen to their first short-wave game with just the two of them together, and that both Erik and Katie were uncommonly thoughtful and nice.

They next agreed that the most sensible thing to do for dinner would be to order take-out from the Italian restaurant, so that MacKenzie could get a night off from cooking and dishwashing.

Next, they agreed that John would drive MacKenzie to Erik's in Bertie after the game to watch the Richard Dix movie, and John and Katie would go see a movie themselves at the Casino, and they would pick MacKenzie up at Erik's afterward.

MacKenzie and her father stopped at the Italian restaurant only long enough to order what they wanted, before heading over to the Vons to buy boxes of Cracker Jack for the game. When they returned to pick up their food, MacKenzie noticed a leaflet about the premiere for the re-release of *The Vanishing American* posted outside, and she and her father said they both had various *The Vanishing American* topics to share with each other.

It was almost 5:00 when they got back to the cottage. They plugged Bertie back in to charge, and brought all their food goods into the living room. They moved the couch coffee table to in front of the armchairs, and spread all the food out on it. MacKenzie grabbed her favorite paper towels from the kitchen and brought the select-a-size roll to the coffee table along with her father's glove, her own glove, one of their baseballs, one of the scorecards she had brought from home, and her scoring pencil, while John turned on the short-wave radio and the familiar sounds of announcer Harry Caray and the Wrigley crowd noise began to fill the living room.

MacKenzie and her father stood holding their caps over their chests for the National Anthem and sang along with the more than 38,700 fans at Wrigley Field. John then seated himself in his armchair, MacKenzie settled herself in Katie's armchair, and they both put their caps back on and donned their sunglasses, John's up on his cap, MacKenzie's on her face with the lenses flipped up. They sat facing the radio without exactly looking at it, letting the WGN 720 broadcast of the series opener against the Rockies create the game as if they were actually seeing it before them and not only their minds' eye.

By the end of the fourth inning, the Cubs were ahead 1-0, and MacKenzie and her father had easily slipped into their ballpark habits of MacKenzie effortlessly keeping meticulous track of every play on her scorecard while she and her father alternately talked about details of the game and talked with each other about whatever they wanted to talk about while the game proceeded. They had finished their dinner, and had intentionally left the remains strewn about the coffee table because MacKenzie had insisted they were having fun and the look of the table should reflect that.

Between innings they caught each other up on all they hadn't had time to talk about while playing catch at the ball field or driving around in Bertie. John shared with her the highlights of his day and his lunch with Davenport and Katie. John and the small Conservancy team now working with him were still trying to avoid traumatizing any of the affected buffalo with the process of tranquilizing them to sleep in order to get blood samples for testing. So for now, they were instead running lab analyses of buffalo droppings to try to get more clues that way. MacKenzie was unrestrained in expressing both how gross that sounded, and how glad she would be if the buffalo could be spared having to be tranquilized.

Katie had talked about possible methods of cyanide neutralization, which John explained to MacKenzie meant adding something to the water that would cancel out or at least reduce the effects of the cyanide on the coral, without harming any of the other nearby marine life. Katie had also said she had unfortunately discovered during her most recent dive that tiny life forms which depended on the coral for survival were now also dying.

Katie had also described her worry about a new realization. Now that she knew she was looking for a source of cyanide, she had discovered that whatever it was, it was not constant. It was only intermittent, which John explained to McKenzie meant that the flow of cyanide into the water was not continuous. It would be happening, and then it wouldn't be happening, without any kind of pattern, and that kind of random on-and-off starting-and-stopping was making trying to find where it was coming from more difficult.

John confirmed that Davenport had told him, although it was not to be discussed publicly, that the Conservancy had indeed managed to force a change in the date for the premiere of *The Vanishing American* in the hopes that having it suddenly re-scheduled to a date much sooner might reduce the amount of media and film-related crowd traffic to the island.

MacKenzie told her father the exciting story from Erik's father about how Man Hammer's Oldest Boy had earned his own name, Fire-Walker. MacKenzie's father was as moved by the story as MacKenzie and Erik had been when they first heard it. John went on to say that Davenport had mentioned Fire-Walker by that name, but had not seemed to know anything about the story behind it. But Davenport had said that because of the sudden change of date, Fire-Walker now would not be able to attend Tuesday's premiere. Davenport had also said that he had a feeling Fire-Walker had never wanted to attend in the first place, since he apparently did not like public attention.

By halfway through the seventh inning, the score was still 1-0, and it was time for the seventh-inning stretch. MacKenzie and her father stood and stretched, and sang "Take Me Out to the Ball Game" along with the Wrigley crowd. The traditional close-up audio of Harry Caray's endearing gravelly voice singing the lyrics loudest of all filled the living room with his colorful personality and unique pronunciations and spirited energy.

The game resumed, and as they always did at this time, MacKenzie and her father opened their boxes of Cracker Jack. John rarely ate anything with sugar. But it was part of his Cubs game ritual with MacKenzie that he always had the first few handfuls of Cracker Jack from his box, before handing it over to MacKenzie to add to the quantity of her happy feasting.

By the bottom of the eighth inning the score still hadn't changed, and MacKenzie and her father were allowing themselves to start daring to have hope that the Cubs might actually win. MacKenzie had finished all her Cracker Jack as well as her father's, and the she had opened the two Cracker Jack prizes inside, which had been a small plastic magnifying glass the size of nickel, and a book of jokes which MacKenzie had read to her father and they had laughed themselves giddy because the jokes were so bad.

When the game ended, the score still hadn't changed, and the Cubs had won, 1-0. MacKenzie and her father high-fived and celebrated, and congratulated themselves on the success of their first short-wave Cubs game.

MacKenzie was starting to clean up the living room when the doorbell rang, and she dropped everything and ran to the front of the cottage, joyfully singing Katie's name, and throwing her arms around Katie's waist the moment the door was opened.

"Hello, little dolphin," Katie said happily. "How was the game?"

"We won!" exclaimed MacKenzie jubilantly, politely untangling herself from Katie and high-fiving her.

"Oh, and apparently someone's been horseback riding," said Katie with a smile.

MacKenzie nodded. "Erik and I went trail riding. It was really fun," she said exuberantly, grabbing Katie by the hand and leading her into the living room. "Dad," she went on, "should I shower and change my clothes before going over to Erik's?"

"Is that a trick question...?" asked her father.

MacKenzie nodded. "Okay, I'll be quick..."

"Do I have your permission to finish cleaning up the living room without you?" asked her father grinning.

"Yes, please," said MacKenzie's voice as she dashed off down the hall.

A short time later, the living room had been cleaned and tidied and restored, except for the empty Cracker Jack boxes and their prizes and prize-wrappers, which remained decorating the couch coffee table, and MacKenzie was refreshed and ready for the next part of her evening.

"Katie, I'm sorry your chair smells horsey," MacKenzie said apologetically. "I sat there for the game."

Katie laughed. "I don't mind the least bit," she said. "I like the smell of horses."

"Me too!" said MacKenzie happily. "Are you guys going to see a movie at the Casino?"

Katie nodded. "After we drop you at Erik's."

"What movie are you seeing?'

"We don't actually know yet," said John. "We're going to see whatever's playing there tonight."

"We're going to live dangerously," Katie explained with a smile.

"That sounds fun," said MacKenzie.

"I see you two had some Cracker Jacks at the game," observed Katie.

MacKenzie nodded. "You have to eat Cracker Jack because it's sticky-crunchy delicious, and it's in the seventh-inning stretch song. Dad, tell Katie about the song. There's a girl named Katie in it! And then I'll tell her about the Cracker Jack box."

John looked at his watch. "It's nearly 8:00 now. What time does the-movie-we-don't-know-the-title-of start?'

"I got the showtimes from Ed," said Katie, "but I forgot to ask him the name of the movie. I think he thought I already knew what was playing. The last showing was at 7:00, and the next show starts at 9:00."

John nodded. "So whatever it is, it must be less than two hours long. Mac, how long is the Richard Dix movie you and Erik are watching?"

"One hour and thirty-four minutes."

"Okay…" said her father. "This is starting to turn into a late night. Listen, Mac. Early bedtime tomorrow night, no matter what, understand?"

"Works fine for me, Dad," said MacKenzie, and she turned to Katie. "My dad is always saying that I make too many 'unauthorized withdrawals' from my sleep bank. So, tomorrow night, I'll be making an 'authorized deposit' in my sleep bank account."

Her father nodded. "You should have more interest in that account."

MacKenzie rolled her eyes. "He always makes that joke," she said, smiling.

Katie laughed.

"Mac," said her father. "Go call Erik, please. Make sure it's okay if we pick you up as late as 11:30. We can tell Katie all about Cracker Jacks while we're riding in Bertie."

"Bertie!" MacKenzie sang joyfully, and headed to the kitchen to make her call.

Chapter 25

SIGNAL

The sun had set, but the early twilight was still bright, and it was easy for MacKenzie to point out details on the cover of the empty Cracker Jack box she had brought along to show Katie, as John drove the three of them in Bertie toward Erik's house. They all bounced smoothly along at the casual leisurely pace of all golf carts on the island.

"So," MacKenzie was explaining to Katie, "the slogan for Cracker Jack is 'The more you eat, the more you want', and I can tell you from experience, that slogan is what my Dad calls 'Truth In Advertising', because it's totally true. And this adorable patriotic little boy," she went on, pointing, "is named 'Sailor Jack'. The picture is based on the grandson of one of the guys who invented Cracker Jacks. And this cute little fellow is Sailor Jack's dog, Bingo. Bingo is based on a stray dog named Russell who was adopted by the guy who invented the special wax-paper inside-wrapping for the Cracker Jacks, and who said that he wanted Russell to be on the cover of the box."

John nodded. "Those two mascots were trademarked in 1919. The first Cracker Jacks and the Cracker Jack name were trademarked in 1896, but the first Cracker Jack prototype was introduced at Chicago's first World's Fair in 1893."

"And," MacKenzie added excitedly, "not only is 1893 in the 19th century, it's also exactly 100 years ago, and they just had a big 100-year celebration of Cracker Jack at Wrigley Field last month! And we were there! As part of the ceremony, someone who was dressed up in a Sailor Jack costume threw out the first pitch of the game!"

John smiled. "MacKenzie ate even more Cracker Jack at the park that day than usual…"

MacKenzie nodded proudly. "I almost got sick afterward. But it was so worth it! And also, we beat the Marlins in that game, 6-to-4. That was an awesome day!"

MacKenzie handed the empty box of Cracker Jack reverently to Katie so that Katie could fully enjoy the meaningful experience of holding a Cracker Jack box.

John smiled. "We had a lot of fun at that game," he said, remembering. "And of course," he went on, "there's a lyric about Cracker Jack in the 1908 song 'Take Me Out to the Ball Game'."

MacKenzie nodded vigorously. "Everybody sang the 'Cracker Jack' part really loud at the seventh-inning stretch of the 100-year celebration game. It was amazing."

"As I'm sure you're already well aware, Katie," said John, "it's become a baseball tradition to sing 'Take Me Out to the Ball Game' during the seventh-inning stretch."

"Dad and I sang it during seventh-inning stretch today in the living room," MacKenzie added helpfully.

John nodded. "It was a good thing Harry Caray was singing so loudly, so we didn't sound as bad."

"Harry Caray is the announcer for the Cubs," explained MacKenzie. "He has a really interesting voice that makes you like him a lot."

Katie smiled and laughed.

"Dad, tell Katie about the song," MacKenzie reminded her father.

John nodded, keeping his eyes on the road and being sure he was following the driving directions MacKenzie had given him. "Well," John began. "The song 'Take Me Out to the Ball Game' has always been popular, and of course has always been associated with baseball. Singing it specifically during the seventh-inning stretch seems to have happened as early as 1934. But in 1971, it became more popular after Harry Caray started singing it from the broadcast booth into the ballpark public-address system while he was the announcer for the Chicago White Sox. Eleven years later, Harry Caray brought the tradition with him to Wrigley Field when he became the voice of the Cubs in 1982. From there, it went on to become increasingly popular, to the point of becoming a nation-wide tradition."

MacKenzie nodded. "And tell Katie what the song's about," she prompted.

"Well," John went on. "People only sing the chorus. But there are two other verses to the song, and they tell a little story about a girl named Katie."

MacKenzie grinned at Katie. "See? I told you your name was in the song!"

Katie laughed again.

"In the song," John went on, "Katie Casey loves baseball more than anything. Her boyfriend invites her to go to a show, but all she wants is for him to take her to a baseball game."

MacKenzie nodded enthusiastically. "Katie Casey is obsessed with baseball," she explained. "Katie Casey loves baseball more than anything."

John nodded. "The character of Katie Casey is one of the most famous fictitious baseball fans in history."

"And in the song," MacKenzie added admiringly, "she even corrects an umpire who makes a bad call!"

"And just for context," John added, "the first known record of fans taking a seventh-inning stretch at a baseball game was in 1869. President Taft made it more popular when he did it during an Opening Day baseball game in Washington in 1910. The tradition was called 'Lucky Seventh' until 1920, when it was given the name we all call it today, the 'seventh-inning stretch'."

MacKenzie grinned at Katie. "Now he's just showing off how smart he is," she said proudly.

The three of them laughed, and they pulled up into Erik's driveway. MacKenzie grabbed her borrowed backpack, kissed her father and Katie good-bye, and affectionately patted Bertie's hood before heading to the front door and ringing the bell. John and Katie waited until Erik opened the front door. Erik greeted MacKenzie and waved hello to John and Katie, who waved back and then backed out and drove off toward the Casino building's Avalon Theater.

MacKenzie and Erik caught each other up on all that had happened since they had last seen each other earlier that afternoon. MacKenzie told him all about how much fun she and her father had had listening to the Cubs win, although MacKenzie kept describing it as 'watching' the Cubs win because it had felt so much like actually seeing the game. MacKenzie also told Erik about how Katie had chosen to have dinner with friends during the game because she was as thoughtful and nice as Erik was, and about how her father and Katie were now off to see a movie at the Casino.

Erik told MacKenzie about the dinner he had enjoyed with his mother, and about getting to talk more with his dad when he had called back at his usual time. And after MacKenzie had called to ask if it would be all right to stay until 11:30, Erik's mother had first okay-ed that plan, and had then headed out for the evening to spend time with some of her friends.

MacKenzie now knew her way around Erik's kitchen, so making popcorn took much less time, and soon they were settled with fresh salty buttery popcorn comfortably on Erik's living room couch watching *Trans-Atlantic Tunnel*.

At the video store, MacKenzie had said the movie was perfect for them. But it turned out she hadn't been exactly right about that.

The movie's ingredients were perfect for them. But the movie itself was not as good as they had hoped, although that did not reduce the amount of fun they had watching it together.

The subject matter, and the mood and feeling of the movie, though at times heavy, were far less weighty and significant than that of *The Vanishing American*. So unlike the intently serious and silent experience they had both preferred while watching *The Vanishing American*, without ever formally discussing it or agreeing to it they both seemed content to talk their way through *Trans-Atlantic Tunnel*.

"My dad," Erik was saying, "told me about what he called 'something of interest' for us to watch for in the backstory of one of the characters."

"What's 'backstory' exactly..." asked MacKenzie.

"Well," said Erik. "The word is used in lots of different contexts, but especially in describing movies and books. It could have to do with the plot, but it's often about a character. It's the information about the character's personal history that helps us understand who they are, or why they do things, or what they've done in their past."

"So what's the 'something of interest' we're watching for?"

Erik nodded. "We just saw it. That guy who they want as part of the tunnel-team? They just mentioned they want him because, in this movie, his character successfully completed an underground, underwater tunnel for trains to travel through under the English Channel, connecting France and England. Well, in real life, that tunnel actually exists. It's named the Channel Tunnel, but everyone calls it the 'Chunnel'. But this movie was made in 1935. Digging on the real life 'Chunnel' started five years ago in 1988, and it's scheduled to start operating next year."

"Wow..." said MacKenzie. "Your dad was right. That's crazy. It's like this movie sort of made a true prediction about the future..."

"Although," Erik added, "I don't think there will ever need to be a real life trans-Atlantic tunnel like what they're trying to drill in this movie, because, well, now we have airplanes."

MacKenzie thanked Erik for explaining 'backstory', and she proceeded to spend the rest of the movie using the word as often as possible to help make it part of her own vocabulary.

As much as they were dissatisfied with the movie, there were aspects of it they very much liked. They liked the way the film looked visually, and they liked the science fiction trains and the fictitious 'radium drill' used to dig the trans-Atlantic tunnel. Richard Dix was very nearly their favorite part of the movie, especially because of how—as he had in *The Vanishing American*—he so nobly brought a kind of heroic dignity to his role. MacKenzie and Erik also very much liked Leslie Banks, the actor who played his best friend. But their absolute favorite element of the whole movie was the signal. From the moment they first saw it, MacKenzie and Erik immediately fell in love with the special personal hand-signal of friendship, agreement, and success exchanged between the two best friends, the Richard Dix character and the Leslie Banks character.

The signal was a simple hand-sign gesture that one of the two characters would do, directed at the other, and the other character would respond by doing it back, usually accompanied by a knowing smile and an understanding nod of the head. It was a fast finger-snap that bounced tightly into a thumbs-up. Snap, bounce, thumbs-up. One fist, three quick steps, all in a single smooth one-handed motion.

MacKenzie and Erik liked it so much, that after the first time they saw it, they kept backing up the tape and re-watching it until they had perfected it themselves. And then it was theirs. They named it 'the tunnel-signal', and they adopted it and made it their own private signal to each other. For the rest of the movie, they kept finding opportunities to use the tunnel-signal with each other while they were talking, anytime they wanted to agree with each other. They used it far more often than they needed to, and so often that at last they laughed at themselves for what they were doing. But as MacKenzie pointed out, it was like when you learn a new word and you start using it all the time, even though you don't need to, so you can get used to it and make it a natural part of how you talk. To illustrate her point, MacKenzie referred to how many times during the movie she had used the word 'backstory' after Erik had taught it to her, even though she probably had only needed to use it once, or maybe twice.

One of the very last scenes of the movie was of the two best friends giving each other their personal signal, deep under the ground below the Atlantic ocean, as the American part of the tunnel at last connected with the European part of the tunnel to successfully complete the tunnel of the movie's title. It was that image which stayed most vividly afterward with MacKenzie and Erik, and they celebrated the success of the two on-screen friends by triumphantly exchanging the tunnel-signal with each other in Real Life.

Shortly after 11:30, Brenda came home, bringing with her into the house John and Katie, who had arrived at the same time. The five of them conversed cheerfully in the kitchen together. Erik and MacKenzie talked about the movie they had just watched. John and Katie first complimented Brenda and Erik on how lovely their house was and how nice the location and views were, and then talked about the movie they had just seen.

At the Casino they had watched *The Sandlot*, a new coming-of-age kids' baseball comedy set thirty years in the past. John liked the whimsically nostalgic and hyperbolically improbable small-town baseball escapades. Katie liked the idiosyncratic characters and the dialogue. Both of them thought the story ought to have had more female characters. But they had enjoyed the film. They both had found it charming and entertaining.

John's favorite part of their experience was the Avalon Theater itself, which he had never been in before. Everyone agreed that the art and architecture and Art Deco of the Avalon theater were uniquely beautiful, and Brenda couldn't resist launching herself for a few minutes into tour-narration mode.

The entire Casino building, she explained, now was at last scheduled to undergo a complete restoration next year, which she personally felt was long-overdue. The Casino had been a gift to the island from William Wrigley Jr., and it had first opened in 1929 to mark the 10-year anniversary of Wrigley's 1919 purchase of Catalina Island.

Brenda went on to explain that the dance hall on the top-level of the Casino was the largest circular ballroom in the world, and the Avalon Theater was first theater in the United States to be built specifically for "talkies" or 'talking pictures', meaning movies with sound. With its 50-foot-high domed ceiling, and all the other design choices made to get the highest possible sound quality from the space, the Avalon Theater was famous not only for how beautiful it looked, but also for the extraordinary quality of its sound, and its design was later copied by the builders of Radio City Music Hall in New York to try to achieve that same high level of sound quality.

Everyone appreciatively applauded for Brenda's spontaneous presentation, and she playfully blew them all grateful kisses of thanks. Erik glowed with pride for his mother, and also decided to mention that, speaking of talkies, he wanted to share that he and MacKenzie had both found it interesting that the two of them had ended up wanting to remain silent during the silent movie *The Vanishing American*, but had seemed to want to talk their way through the talkie *Trans-Atlantic Tunnel*, an observation which everyone agreed was indeed ironically noteworthy.

They all went together out to the driveway to say good-night as John and Katie and MacKenzie with her borrowed backpack settled themselves into Bertie for the ride home to the cottage. At the last minute, Erik dashed back into the house and returned moments later to hand MacKenzie her now empty Cubs backpack. Everyone said good-night again, and that part of the evening came to an end.

When MacKenzie and John and Katie arrived back to the cottage, John pulled Bertie up next to Katie's golf cart, and MacKenzie plugged Bertie back in to charge. The three of them then made their way inside to the living room, and MacKenzie asked if they wanted her to make them some coffee. John and Katie appreciatively thanked her, but said they were just going to have a glass of wine before Katie headed home.

MacKenzie went over to smell Katie's armchair, and after a moment made the reassuring announcement that everything was fine, it still smelled horsey. Then she hugged her father, and kissed him and Katie good-night. She brushed her teeth, and got ready for bed, and within moments of lying down for the night she was fast asleep.

Chapter 26
ALLOY

MacKenzie had not seen the mysterious man on Thursday, but she did see him again on Friday. It was while she was biking, after her father had left for the day with Davenport. She was indulging herself in her new ritual of leaving the cottage early before she went to meet up with Erik, so that she could go for a ride all by herself at the coastline, and she had once again pedaled along Pebbly Beach Road as far as Abalone Point until she arrived at her rock-warrior sentry. She had stepped down from her bicycle seat and stood straddling her bike, just long enough to smile at her rock-warrior sentry and wave back to him, before getting back up on her bike and turning to head back on Pebbly Beach Road toward the Avalon Bay beach to meet Erik. And that route took her past the Cabrillo Mole.

It was right as MacKenzie was peddling past the Cabrillo Mole that she saw the mysterious man. She got a good clear look at him this time. He was an even larger man than she had first thought, and there was something about the way he was standing. It was the posture and stance of someone who would do whatever was necessary to get what they wanted. It gave MacKenzie a chill.

And as if he could feel her looking at him, he suddenly turned around and looked directly at her. It was so sudden, she nearly crashed her bike and she almost screamed, although MacKenzie couldn't remember ever actually screaming at anything. She wasn't the screaming type. She didn't even scream at the startling moments in scary movies. But right now she very definitely was scared, and she looked away and pedaled as fast as she could past him and all the way to the Crescent Avenue shops, where she hurriedly biked around a corner onto Clarissa Ave, leapt from her bike, and peered back around the corner of a clothing and souvenir store in cautious fear, desperate to see if he had run after her or followed her.

He was gone. She couldn't see him anywhere.

Not knowing where he was was nearly as awful as seeing him. It was like being in water with a shark but not seeing the shark's dorsal fin anywhere above the surface.

After waiting a few more minutes without seeing him, she finally got back onto her bike and pedaled the rest of the way to meet Erik. As if the bike itself had somehow been affected by passing so close to the mysterious man, one of the gears had now developed a strange slip-clicking sound, and MacKenzie resolved to ask Erik about it.

Erik was just saying good-bye to his mother as MacKenzie approached, and Brenda waved cheerily at MacKenzie before heading off toward her first tour of the day.

MacKenzie had waved back, and now she got off her bike and greeted Erik.

"So, I just saw the mysterious man again..." she was saying unhappily.

Erik could apparently tell that MacKenzie was still shaken by the experience. "You okay...?" he asked with concern.

MacKenzie nodded. "It just creeps me out, that's all... I saw him really close up..."

"At the Mole?" he asked.

She nodded again. "I was coming back from visiting my rock-warrior sentry that I told you about. And suddenly I was biking right past the mysterious man, and he turned around and looked right at me..."

"Should we head over to the Conservancy, and you can try to get in touch with your Dad?" Erik suggested.

MacKenzie shook her head. "No, I'll be okay..." she said. "I'm with you, so everything will be fine."

Erik smiled. "Plus," he said, "we're getting out of town for the day. Or at least, for the first half of the day. Two Harbors is a long way from here."

MacKenzie nodded. "Okay... Thanks..."

"Maybe you'll feel better after some after-breakfast dessert..." Erik suggested hopefully.

This reminder did work to brighten MacKenzie's mood, and she started to make her way in her thoughts back toward normal.

"Oh...!" she remembered. "My bike—I mean, your bike that I'm borrowing, one of the gears just started making this weird clicking sound..."

Erik nodded. "I know what it is," he said, slipping off his pack and reaching inside. "I keep thinking I've fixed it, but it keeps not wanting to stay fixed..."

He pulled out a small can of WD-40.

"What's that...?" MacKenzie asked.

"After duct-tape, it's the greatest invention ever made," said Erik. "Technically, it's 'a penetrating oil and water-displacing spray lubricant'. Actually, it's just something you spray on whatever you need to be fixed, and it fixes it..."

MacKenzie laughed. "Sounds like a good thing to have around..."

"I keep a can of it with me everywhere I go," agreed Erik.

He uncapped the can, and sprayed it across the rear gears and the entire chain of MacKenzie's bike. Re-capping the can and setting it on the sidewalk, he lifted the bike by the seat to raise the back wheel partially into the air, and used a hand to pedal the bike. The rear wheel began to spin, and the gears snap-clicked again for a moment then suddenly began to behave smoothly and quietly.

Erik nodded, and stilled the spinning wheel by setting the rear of the bike back on the ground. "See?" he said. "All fixed."

"That's awesome..." said MacKenzie appreciatively. "Like magic... Thank you."

"Sure," said Erik, putting the can back into his pack.

The two of them locked their bikes to a rack, and put their matching twin backpacks back on.

"Okay," said Erik. "Big Olaf's for ice cream, then Jake's to pick up your necklace?"

MacKenzie smiled and gave him their tunnel-signal, snap-bounce-thumbs-up.

Erik grinned and gave her the sign back, and they headed off toward Big Olaf's.

Because of how much they had planned for their day, they did not linger long over their ice cream, but they did make sure to thoroughly enjoy every bite. And after contentedly finishing their after-breakfast dessert, they began making their way toward Jake's shop.

"Today's Cubs game starts at 12:21 Catalina time," MacKenzie was saying. "You and I don't need to be back by then if we don't want," she said. "I feel bad that my Dad can't see it—I mean listen to it, because he'll be working. But if we are back in time, do you want to come over to the cottage and we can watch it together?"

Erik nodded. "That sounds fun. And also," he went on, "my mom wants to take us out to lunch if we get back before she has to go back to work. I told her we wouldn't be spending too much time at the Isthmus. A lot people who've lived on the island for a long time still call Two Harbors by its old name, the Isthmus. Whatever you want to call it, it's beautiful there, but I told her that for today we're mostly going just to see Prentiss's grave marker, so we could be back in time for her lunch break."

"Should we wait and get the necklace later...?" asked MacKenzie.

Erik shook his head. "I think you should start wearing it as soon as possible."

They stopped off briefly at the video store just long enough to return the *Trans-Atlantic Tunnel* videocassette, and then proceeded toward Summer Ave.

The small bell on the door jingled as they entered Jake's shop, and Jake seemed happy to see them. He took out the necklace he had crafted for MacKenzie. It was wrapped in tissue paper, which he carefully removed. He held it up and described to MacKenzie and Erik what he had done.

Jake explained that the band now wrapped around the outer edge of the coin to hold it was called a bezel, and the loop attached to the bezel—the loop that the necklace chain passed through—was called a ring. He said he had made everything in her necklace using a titanium yellow-gold alloy, which was a light metal, and was also the strongest metal he had. The bezel and the ring were made of this alloy, and the ring was attached to the bezel with a titanium weld. As MacKenzie had requested, he hadn't cleaned or polished the coin in any way, with the exception of the edge and part of the rim, which he had cleaned to make sure the bezel would always hold the coin securely.

The necklace chain was made with the same alloy. Jake said it would have been strong enough with just a single strand, but he had used a triple-braided chain for extra durability. The chain was still thin and light, and fit easily through the ring, but it was very strong. The braided chain was joined to itself with titanium welds, so there was no clasp, which he had done to ensure the strength of the chain—because there was no clasp, there was no clasp to break. To take the necklace on and off, MacKenzie would have to slip it over her head. The titanium welds had been precisely micro-polished, so she not only wouldn't feel them, but she might not even be able to see where they were.

He also explained that since it was a titanium yellow-gold alloy, it would never rust, so she could swim with it, even in salt water, or do anything else she wanted while wearing it. She would never have to take it off if she didn't want to.

He handed the necklace to MacKenzie. She gazed at it as if she had been handed long-lost treasure. Her 1951 penny was nearly entirely visible, but clearly was also held solidly by the bezel. She slipped the necklace on over her head and into place around her neck. She looked in one of the mirrors, and felt like she had been transformed into a princess in a fairy tale. It was perfect. It was more than perfect. It was more perfect than she had imagined or dreamed.

She was nearly crying when she thanked Jake for his craftsmanship, and for all the care he had put into helping her. Then she thanked Erik, and somehow managed to resist her impulse to hug him in gratitude and happiness.

Erik blushed and smiled, and asked her to please wait for him outside while he paid for it. MacKenzie was too entranced with her necklace to protest, and she silently nodded and went outside of the shop to wait for him.

I'm never going to take it off ever, she was thinking to herself with ardent determination as Erik came out of the shop a few moments later. She was holding the coin part of the necklace in both hands and letting her fingers feel all the new surfaces of the coin and its bezel, and all the new textures of the ring and the braided chain. Everything about it made her feel like a different person. She already couldn't remember what it felt like to not be wearing it, to not have it on and around her neck.

MacKenzie was overwhelmed. "Oh, Erik..." she said in blissful appreciation as he came over to her.

Erik was beaming.

"Erik..." she said softly. "It's... It's the most wonderful gift ever... I love it so much... I..."

"It makes me really happy to see you wearing it..." he said quietly. "And now every time I look at you, I'll see it..."

She nodded and couldn't take her hands from her new necklace, and couldn't find the right words to express what she was feeling.

Chapter 27
EXCURSION

After returning to unlock their bicycles, they pedaled the short distance to the yacht club, where they walked their bikes along one of the long piers to the front of an office. Erik spoke with someone inside, then came back out and pointed toward the end of the pier.

"There she is," he said to MacKenzie, gesturing toward a large fancy power-yacht tied up in the near distance. "That's *The Brenda*. 1978, 58-foot Bertram Convertible. Thanks to my mom and the yacht club, she's all ready for us to take her on a little trip west."

"Wow..." said MacKenzie. "Erik! That's such a nice boat...!"

Erik nodded. "My dad always says, 'don't buy a lot of things, buy things you like, and the few things you buy should be the best'."

MacKenzie giggled. "What a luxuriously lovely way to think!" she said delightedly. "And another Bertie...! I keep being transported to wonderful places in some kind of Bertie...!"

Erik laughed, and they walked their bikes over the deck-boards toward *The Brenda*, past several tall unconcerned brown pelicans sauntering and strolling and loitering along the pier.

"The pelicans are so casual and cool..." MacKenzie marveled. "Do they bite...?"

Erik shook his head. "They're pretty used to people here," he said. "Some like to be fed or petted, but I think the best thing to do is just enjoy that they're here."

At the end of the pier, they made their way down an inclined ramp to the large floating dock where the yacht club had tied up *The Brenda*. Erik and MacKenzie lifted their bikes and then lowered them on board, down into the open stern-section of the first deck. Erik started to handle the ropes, and showed MacKenzie how to help him undo the lines that were keeping the boat tied to the dock-cleats.

"So," Erik was saying, "she's a convertible. Which means we can take the roof cover off the flybridge on the top deck, if you want. It gets a little windy, but today's a nice day. Do you have your sunblock?"

MacKenzie nodded and patted the side of her borrowed backpack. "Always. I'll put more on once we get going. So yes, may we please take the top down? That seems like it would be really nice."

Erik gave her the tunnel-signal. MacKenzie returned it, and they laughed.

"Hey," said Erik. "Would you please do your magic-gum-trick again?"

MacKenzie grinned. Taking out her fat pack of Wrigley's Spearmint gum, she one-handedly opened a piece for Erik, which she had to put into his mouth for him because his hands were busy with some of the boat lines, then opened a piece for herself.

The tolling of the Chimes Tower reached their ears, and MacKenzie smiled.

Erik glanced down at his watch. "9:00," he said, nodding. "Somehow, Mac, we're right on schedule."

They climbed the ladder to the flybridge, and Erik showed MacKenzie how to help him take down the overhead covering. Then Erik started the engines, while MacKenzie climbed back down to the first deck and clambered back onto the pier. She freed the last line from its deck-cleat and jumped with the rope back onto the boat as Erik had showed her.

Up on the flybridge, Erik powered the boat in reverse to back away from the pier, as MacKenzie climbed back up the ladder to join him. Erik brought *The Brenda* about and slowly guided her forward until they had left the harbor.

"You're a really good boat driver," said MacKenzie, finishing putting on more sunblock and flipping her sunglasses back down.

Erik grinned from behind his own sunglasses. "Thanks," he said as he began to throttle the engines up and the boat began to pick up speed. "Thanks to my dad, I've had a lifetime of experience learning how to do it. It's just like driving a train, only it's a boat!"

The trip west to Two Harbors took just over half an hour, and as they arrived, line-handlers from the Isthmus yacht club helped them tie up *The Brenda* at one of the long docks. MacKenzie and Erik offloaded their bikes, and pedaled off to explore. The west end of the island was very different from Avalon. There were far fewer people or man-made structures, and no landmark buildings. The area seemed mostly populated with tourist visitors there for hiking, camping, diving, boating, or other closer-to-the-natural-world recreational experiences.

Erik led them first to Emerald Bay so they could see the Samuel Prentiss grave marker. They stayed there a long time, sitting together on the ground in front of the headstone, drinking bottled water they had brought along, talking about the treasure story that Katie had read to them, and contemplating the small monument which had for them taken on so much new significance.

Eventually they traveled on, with Erik leading them up a steep trail to a wildland vista overlooking the Isthmus, so that MacKenzie could see from the high vantage point how narrow the land became in between the west end and the rest of the island.

They had allotted themselves an hour to explore, and by shortly after 10:30, they had wended their way eventually back down to the Isthmus and the yacht club docks. For both of them, the most exciting part of the trip had been seeing Prentiss's grave marker, knowing what they now knew about his role in the history of the island and in the extraordinary tale of the Tongva gold.

Their second most enjoyable part of the morning's explorations had been incidentally coming across a foraging family of island foxes, waving their large bushy tails as if in friendly greeting. Two of the smallest cubs had pranced with playful curiosity over to investigate MacKenzie and Erik, and the mother had watchfully let them indulge their bold impulsiveness for several minutes, before finally making a sound that her offspring evidently recognized, and the fox family had all turned as one and scampered off, bounding and frolicking and disappearing into the landscape.

The return ride to Avalon on *The Brenda* featured more wildlife spectacles, as a school of flying fish broke through the surface of the water and for several minutes repeatedly propelled themselves airborne in low-soaring acrobatics to rival those of the dolphins. Gulls gliding nonchalantly on currents of air had accompanied *The Brenda* for various parts of the trip, and at one point, Erik spotted two whale spouts in the distance, though too far off for the whales themselves to be seen. And as the boat neared Avalon and passed by Frog Rock, MacKenzie, who was successfully learning from Erik not only how to look but also how to see, spotted atop a rocky ledge at the shoreline what she was sure was the exact same bald eagle they had seen together while kayaking on the first day they had met.

MacKenzie was still compulsively and regularly checking her necklace, delighting in the new feeling of always finding it still there, and thrilled at the new permanence of knowing it now was always going to be there. And she kept turning over in her mind a strange new thought which had occurred to her at Two Harbors. The story of the Tongva gold had seemed like just that—a story. But seeing Prentiss's grave marker had changed something. It was like an anchor point, or a connecting link between story and Real Life. MacKenzie had begun to wonder if making contact with an actual element from a story somehow moved your own life closer to other things in the story. She wondered if seeing Prentiss's grave marker herself, in person, had somehow edged her closer to something else, something still unknown that she didn't yet understand.

Chapter 28
ENGINEER

It was 11:30, and the tubular bells of the Chimes Tower were tolling from the height of the nearby hill as MacKenzie and Erik walked their bikes back along the now pelican-less yacht club pier to head toward meeting Erik's mother for lunch. They had put the fabric roof back up and into place atop the flybridge of *The Brenda* after securing her to the dock, and Erik had briefly stopped in at the yacht club office to let them know he was finished using the boat for the day.

Brenda was cheerfully waiting for MacKenzie and Erik when they pedaled up to greet her at the trolley stop. The three of them walked together toward Brenda's favorite café, stopping only long enough for MacKenzie and Erik to lock their bikes to a rack.

At lunch, Brenda gushed over how beautiful MacKenzie's new necklace was. She said that after Erik had first told her about how he planned to help MacKenzie with it, she couldn't wait to see it. It had turned out even lovelier than what she had pictured in her mind when Erik had described what they had asked Jake to do for them, and for the next few minutes everyone talked about Jake's extraordinary artistry and craftsmanship, and how his personality was as delightful as his talents were remarkable.

MacKenzie thanked Erik's mother for helping them with arrangements for using *The Brenda*, and complimented in detail all the different aspects of the luxurious boat she had found especially amazing. MacKenzie and Erik together described all they had seen and done during their excursion to Two Harbors, and Brenda shifted momentarily into tour-narration-mode to describe how the

Catalina Island fox was a mammal that had been living on the island for over 5,400 years.

From there, Brenda's talking swept over the rest of lunch like a refreshing spring breeze. For MacKenzie, being around Erik's mother was always like being on a vacation. Brenda's sunny tireless chatting and seemingly limitless flow of interesting information and casual conversation was reassuring and soothing, like a slow pleasant boat ride that you didn't want to end, that you knew would go on for a long time.

MacKenzie and Erik politely declined Brenda's offer of dessert, explaining that they needed to reserve some sugar-space for all the Cracker Jack they were going to eat during the Cubs game. Brenda laughed cheerily and paid the bill, and MacKenzie and Erik thanked her for taking them to such an enjoyable lunch. Erik told his mother that after the game, he and MacKenzie planned to come back to the house to watch *The General*, which put a big smile on Brenda's face because, as she explained, it was her favorite movie of all time. MacKenzie said that she had promised her father she would go to bed early, and Erik commented that that seemed like a good idea, suggesting that he too probably ought to go to sleep early himself, so that they would both get a good night's sleep and be all rested for a bigger day tomorrow.

Before the three of them said good-bye, Brenda and Erik made plans to have dinner at home together after MacKenzie and Erik were done watching *The General*. MacKenzie and Erik wished Brenda good-luck on her next tour of the day, then went to unlock their bikes and pedal over to the Vons to buy Cracker Jacks.

By 12:20, the two of them were at the cottage, re-arranging the couch coffee table so it would be in front of the armchairs, and spreading out across its surface the provisions of soda, select-a-size paper towels, and newly-purchased Cracker Jacks, as well as MacKenzie's left-handed baseball glove, her scoring pencil, a blank game-scorecard, and a baseball. MacKenzie powered-up the short-wave radio just in time for the 12:21 start-time, and she and Erik stood with their caps over their chests, singing along with the National Anthem, Erik in front of John's armchair, and MacKenzie in front of Katie's.

By the end of the seventh-inning stretch, all the Cracker Jacks had been eaten, and small plastic prizes were spread out and scattered across the coffee table. The Cubs were ahead of the Rockies by a score of 7-to-1, and MacKenzie was in elated high spirits.

She shared with Erik all the discussion she had had the night before with her father and Katie in Bertie about Cracker Jacks, the seventh-inning-stretch, and the song 'Take Me Out to the Ball Game', which both MacKenzie and Erik had sung along with the Wrigley Crowd at a zealously loud enthusiastic volume that nearly drowned out the singing of Harry Caray coming in over the short-wave.

By 3:00, the game was over and the Cubs had won by a final score of 8-to-2. MacKenzie and Erik high-fived, and then together cleaned up the living room and restored the coffee table to its proper place in front of the couch. MacKenzie wrote a note to her father on a 3 x 5 index card telling him she would be home for playing catch by 5:15, and she and Erik headed out.

After all the Cracker Jacks they had just eaten, MacKenzie and Erik needed a break from popcorn products, but they didn't want to watch a movie without something to munch on the whole time, so on the way to Erik's house, they stopped off at the Vons and stocked up on chips and salsa, which MacKenzie transformed into a stylish gourmet presentation in Erik's kitchen shortly after they arrived at his house.

"You really are outstanding at food preparation," Erik was saying to her in appreciative admiration. "Somehow you find ways to either make delicious food, or make delicious food taste better because of the way you arrange it."

MacKenzie beamed. "Thank you," she said. "You're the most fun person to eat delicious food with. You and I have the exact same taste in food."

They gave each other the tunnel-signal, and laughed at themselves for doing it, and then laughed some more at MacKenzie's unintentional joke, before carrying all components of the vast chips-and-salsa presentation to the living room, along with a healthy supply of soda and napkins. Erik had found his family's copy of the Buster Keaton movie earlier that morning before he had left to meet MacKenzie, and it was already slotted into the VHS player and all ready to go.

They watched *The General*, and MacKenzie was in an ecstasy of enjoyment and awe. It was the greatest movie she had ever seen. She and Erik repeatedly rewound and re-watched some of their favorite parts, and after the movie ended, they got so involved in talking together about what they liked and all the ways in which Buster Keaton was a movie genius, and about how his stunts were incomprehensibly amazing, that MacKenzie now was going to be late getting home.

They agreed on a meeting time for Saturday morning, and MacKenzie wished Erik a fun dinner with his mother, and Erik wished MacKenzie a fun dinner with her father and Katie. They both wished each a good extra-long night's sleep, gave each other the tunnel-signal, and MacKenzie biked off toward the cottage with the now soundlessly-smooth click-free gear that Erik had fixed for her, while she savored the exhilarating feeling of her new necklace gently bouncing below her neck as she pedaled home.

The first thing she did when she came into the cottage after hugging her father hello was to breathlessly show John her new necklace, explaining in detail and at great length all the backstory of how she had come to think of the idea, and how much Erik had wanted to her help, and how nice Jake was, and how perfectly Jake had done everything she had wished for. Her father glowed with happiness to see MacKenzie so radiantly excited about something which had come from Katie and now from Erik as well, that was so full of significance and joy for her.

"It was my wish, Dad," MacKenzie was saying. "And Erik made it come true. And my necklace is made of a titanium and gold alloy, and I know what an alloy is because Erik and Jake explained it to me. It's two different metals blended together, which makes my perfect necklace even more perfect, because it's just like a mix of Katie and Erik that I get to have with me all the time forever."

At MacKenzie's enthusiastic insistence, John carefully inspected every inch and aspect of the necklace, and he told her how impressed he was with how simply and exquisitely it had been crafted and assembled, how beautifully it had turned out, and how most beautiful of all was the part of her that had dreamed of the necklace and the reasons why she had wished for it to exist.

MacKenzie hugged her father again, and the two of them got their ball and gloves and headed down to the ball field for their game of catch and to catch each other up on all their other events of the day.

It was almost 6:30 by the time they had returned to the cottage. Katie was just pulling up in her golf cart, with the stowage shelf at the rear of the little vehicle fully loaded with grocery bags from Vons strapped in with bungy cord like paper passengers.

MacKenzie jubilantly sang out Katie's name and dashed over to throw her arms around her as Katie was getting out of the golf cart. MacKenzie immediately showed her necklace to Katie, and insisted on telling Katie every detail of the necklace story right there outside before anyone could go into the cottage.

John stood with his arms folded contentedly, listening to MacKenzie re-tell her beautiful tale, while Katie became enraptured with the necklace and with hearing the story for the first time. MacKenzie and Katie beamed at each other and luxuriated in the glow of radiant happiness they both were so ardently engendering in each other.

Katie had shopped for dinner, which launched MacKenzie into another animated and vocal ecstasy of jubilation that Katie had been so thoughtful, and that the two of them were going to get to make dinner together. Everyone helped carry the cache of groceries into the kitchen, and MacKenzie and Katie set about preparing everything and starting to cook.

After pouring wine for himself and Katie, and soda for MacKenzie, John said that he didn't want to be completely useless, so he would set the dining room table. MacKenzie thanked him because she knew that way the silverware wouldn't get put on the wrong sides, and she added that if he really wanted to help with dinner, he could stay in the kitchen and talk to her and Katie while they cooked.

When dinner was nearly ready, MacKenzie quickly went to put all the laundry into the washing machine, because she had promised that she would. When she came back to the kitchen, she remembered that on Wednesday her father had let them buy ingredients for brownies at Vons when they were buying ingredients for the cookies, and MacKenzie now asked her father if it would be okay if she baked brownies for dessert after tonight's dinner.

John said that sounded like a fine idea, and Katie said it sounded delicious, and so the issue of dessert was settled.

Dinner was served, and was twice as delicious as it usually was. Neither John nor Katie talked shop about anything having to do with work, and the three of them simply chatted and conversed and enjoyed the food and each other's company.

MacKenzie wanted to be inspired by Brenda, and so she made an effort which she hoped wasn't obvious to keep having interesting things to say.

She described all the exciting things she most liked about Erik's family's amazing boat, and how much fun she had had with Erik watching the ocean speed past from the lofty height of *The Brenda*'s flybridge. And she talked about what an extraordinary experience it had been to have part of the treasure story come to life by actually seeing Prentiss's grave marker.

And she shared what she thought were some of the most important details of the Cubs win, while trying to not make it sound so exciting that her father would feel bad that he had missed getting to watch the game. MacKenzie had completely abandoned referring to short-wave Cubs games as something she listened to, because it seemed to her so much like watching, that there seemed no point in describing the experience in any other way.

She hit a home run with her father when she started telling about how much fun she had had with Erik watching *The General*, because it was one of John's favorite movies and it seemed as though he had memorized every scene.

"That is a brilliant movie-masterpiece," John was saying, brimming with enthusiastic conviction. "I have so many favorite moments. But one of my favorites is when the train-track switch is broken, and there are a half-dozen professional railroad guys standing around looking at it and scratching their heads, discussing and trying to figure out how it could be fixed. And finally, Buster Keaton, the train engineer, comes over, looks at it for about a second, whacks it in the just the right place once with a sledge hammer, and then it's fixed. It's not only humorous, it's brilliant. A bunch of so-called experts standing around and wasting time and discussing, and the one guy who actually knows what he's doing solves the problem in an instant with a simple solution. So many valuable life-lesson truths embedded in that entertaining moment."

Katie laughed and said she really wanted to see the movie, and John and MacKenzie both assured her it would be one the greatest movie-watching experiences she would ever have.

Chapter 29
COPPER

After dinner, John and Katie cleared the table and loaded the dishwasher while MacKenzie got started on the brownies. MacKenzie usually preferred to wash the dishes herself by hand. But there was so much more clean-up than usual tonight because of all the different delectable courses Katie had prepared, that MacKenzie and her father agreed this would be a good night to use the dishwasher.

At MacKenzie's request, once the butter and chocolate had melted, Katie helped get the mixture underway with the rest of the ingredients because, as MacKenzie said, that was the part where the flour always accidentally started flying all over the place.

Once the brownies were at last in the oven to bake, MacKenzie made coffee for her father and Katie, and asked them if anyone besides her would be having vanilla chocolate chip ice cream with their brownies, but apparently the brownies alone would be enough sugar for them for one evening. MacKenzie had rolled her eyes and said that honestly she didn't even understand how they could get through the day on so little sugar. Then she told them it was time for the two of them to go to their armchairs in the living room, and she would come to join them as soon as the brownies and the coffee were done.

About an hour later, the dessert had all been enjoyed and eaten, and John and Katie were relaxing in their armchairs with their mugs of MacKenzie's coffee, and MacKenzie was lying comfortably on her stomach in the middle of the living room rug, browsing through her Cubs schedule and sipping her mug of hot chocolate, her knees bent and her feet crossed in the air behind her.

"Mac," her father was saying. "What time is tomorrow's game?"

"I was just looking at that," said MacKenzie. "It's another afternoon game. 1:08 Catalina time. Sorry, Dad…"

"Well," her father said. "Since tomorrow's Saturday, Ed suggested we start a bit later in the morning, but I still won't be home until four. So, yes, unfortunately I'll be missing that game."

"I was looking at data from the Marine Center's weather radar," said Katie. "There's the possibility of a fairly serious storm system passing through tomorrow afternoon."

"Mac…" he father began."

MacKenzie nodded. "Don't worry Dad," she said. "If Erik and I are outside, we'll be sure to find a safe place somewhere till it passes, if it does show up. And if there's lightning, don't worry, we won't go under a tree."

Katie smiled and finished the rest of her coffee.

"MacKenzie Milles," her father said. "As I'm sure Erik can tell you, you do not want to mess with a Channel Islands Pacific storm. It's not the same thing as a Chicago storm."

"I seriously promise I'll be careful, Dad," said MacKenzie. "And I can take care of myself. And Erik would never let anything happen to me."

Her father nodded. "Mac, if you wouldn't mind, could you please get some more coffee for KC?"

MacKenzie turned to look up at her father. "Who's KC?" she asked.

John shook his head. "I mean Katie."

There was a pause.

Katie grinned. "John…" she said. "You have to tell her."

"Tell me what?"

"Sorry…" said John. "That's my bad…"

MacKenzie stood up and put her hands on her hips and looked at them both. Inside, she was secretly smiling, but outwardly she was trying her best to seem annoyed. "Okay, what are you guys up to...?"

"It's your fault, Mac..." John said defensively.

MacKenzie nodded. "It's always my fault. That's nothing new. I'm used to it..."

"Okay..." said Katie. "Your father's too embarrassed. MacKenzie, after you and your dad told me about the song 'Take Me Out to the Ball Game', you got me interested in the song's main character. So on the way to the movie last night, I asked your dad to sing all three verses to me."

MacKenzie was having a harder time keeping herself from smiling with excited happiness. "Well that's awkward..." she said. "Dad's a terrible singer."

Both Katie and John nodded at the same time.

"Well," said Katie smiling. "That's true. But it was very sweet. And as you told me, MacKenzie, the name of the girl in the song is Katie Casey. And my name is Katie Coleridge, and my initials are KC, and—"

"Oh my god...!" said MacKenzie, realizing. "Dad gave you a nickname...! It's your initials, and it sounds like 'Casey', which is Katie Casey's last name, and your name is Katie, and your initials are KC...!"

Katie grinned and nodded, and John looked sheepish and embarrassed.

"Oh my god..." said MacKenzie. "The cuteness is too much...! Okay, I'm leaving for the kitchen now, to get Katie more coffee. I hope it's okay that I still call you Katie, Katie."

"Yes," said Katie, still grinning, "I would prefer it if you would, actually."

"Oh my god..." said MacKenzie shaking her head and taking Katie's coffee cup as she walked out. But in the privacy of her thoughts she was throwing a party of celebration.

A few moments later, MacKenzie returned and went over to Katie's armchair and handed Katie her now-filled cup of coffee.

"Thank you very much, MacKenzie," said Katie gratefully.

MacKenzie knelt down on the rug in front of Katie and lifted her chin slightly so that Katie could look at the penny again. "See how beautiful my necklace is?" MacKenzie said happily.

Katie smiled and nodded. "I think what's beautiful is what you chose to do with the penny..." she said, lifting the coin gently off MacKenzie's neck and holding it carefully in her hand. "MacKenzie, this is so..."

Katie paused. She was looking at the penny, and MacKenzie could see that Katie's thoughts had suddenly raced off to another place.

"John..." Katie said slowly. Her face had become deadly serious.

"Katie...?" asked MacKenzie's father with sudden concern.

"John, you haven't done any blood tests on the buffalo yet, have you..."

John shook his head. "No, we haven't..."

"I think you need to," she said. "First thing tomorrow..."

'Katie," said John. "What—"

"Something's been nagging at my brain ever since you first described to me the symptoms of the sick bison," she said. "It's just broken through to the surface of my thoughts. John, I think the bison are suffering from a copper deficiency..."

"What's a deficiency?" asked MacKenzie.

"It's when there's not enough of something..." John explained distractedly. "Katie," he went on, "I... I think you may be exactly right... And if the bison do test positive for copper deficiency, the likelihood is that they're suffering from—"

"Molybdenosis," said Katie and John at the same time.

John nodded, and ran a hand through his hair in sudden intense thought.

"What's muh-lib— Whatever you just said?" MacKenzie asked.

"Muh-lib-duh-NOH-sis," said Katie, pronouncing it the way it sounded. "It's a sickness that cattle and buffalo get if they have too much molybdenum in their bodies. The molybdenum causes them to not get enough copper from their diet, which makes them very sick."

"How do they get too much…"

"Molybdenum," said Katie.

MacKenzie nodded. "How do they get too much of that in their bodies…?"

"That will be the next mystery…" said Katie. "But it's likely going to have to do with something they're eating. However, the first thing to do is find out for sure if the buffalo have a copper deficiency…"

John nodded. "That's extraordinary, Katie…" he said quietly. "It never occurred to me. I suspect you are exactly right…"

Katie looked back at MacKenzie's 1951 copper penny now suspended in her elegant new necklace. "Everywhere you are, MacKenzie…" she said in appreciative amazement. "Everything you do, wherever you are, you make things better. I would never have thought of this without you…"

MacKenzie looked intently at Katie, her eyes bright with emotion.

"And," said MacKenzie, "every time I think about you giving me this penny you brought up from the bottom of the Catalina ocean, I think about when Erik and I met you. And for a second I get really scared, because what if you hadn't surfaced right when you did, and we had paddled away just like we were about to. And then we would never have met you, and you wouldn't be in our lives. And then I make that scary thought go away, because that's not the way it happened. You *did* surface before we paddled away, and you are in our lives. And when I think about that, I get really relieved and happy. And I just think about how much I love having you in our lives, and how much I love that you thought I would like this penny, because I do. I love it. I love it more than anything. And I love it even more now because now it's protected in its special necklace and I can always have it with me forever."

The alarm on John's watch beeped. MacKenzie had asked him to set it for her, so that she could keep her promise of going to bed early.

MacKenzie was still kneeling in front of Katie, and she turned toward her father. "Thanks for setting your alarm for me, Dad," she said gratefully. "Don't worry, I haven't forgotten. I'm going to bed early. You will get no argument from me. I'm exhausted..."

MacKenzie turned back toward Katie and hugged her, clinging tightly and pressing her face into Katie's hair.

"I love you, Katie," MacKenzie whispered into Katie's ear.

"I love you too, little dolphin..." Katie whispered back into MacKenzie's ear.

MacKenzie went to give her father a hug and a kiss good-night, and then went off to put the laundry from the washer into the dryer, and then brush her teeth.

When at last she got into bed, she was so tired that—as she had the previous night—she fell asleep nearly the moment she lay down.

And it was a good thing MacKenzie had gone to bed early as she had promised, because Saturday would turn out to be the longest day of MacKenzie's visit to Catalina. It would also be the most exciting and dangerous and terrifying day of her life.

Chapter 30
LETTER

The day started out extremely well. As John had alluded to the night before, even though he and Davenport would be working on a Saturday, they had planned a slightly later start time. Davenport would come to the cottage at 8:30 instead of 7:30, so MacKenzie was now getting to enjoy the bonus of having some extra morning-time with her father.

The doorbell rang too early to be Davenport, and instead it was a mailman with an Urgent Special Delivery letter for MacKenzie which had just arrived on the first ferry of the day from Long Beach. The return address showed that the letter was from Paul Cavanarro.

Beyond unable to contain her excitement, MacKenzie raced into the living room with exuberant exclamations and her hot chocolate and the letter, and her father joined her with his cup of coffee as the two of them sat together on the couch. Hurriedly placing her mug on the coffee table, MacKenzie tore through the several postal labels and seals of the envelope to get to the correspondence inside, and she and her father read the letter together.

The letter had been typed with a typewriter on several sheets of bond-paper stationery that had Cavanarro's name and home address as the letterhead, along with a full-color graphic of the Cubs' current team logo.

Cavanarro started by thanking MacKenzie for several things he was touched and impressed by. He thanked her for finding his old baseball cards, and for making the effort to contact him, and most of all he appreciated how honest and honorable she had been in wanting to return collectible objects of value which she so easily could simply have chosen to keep for herself.

He went on to explain that he had completely forgotten about the tin box of old baseball cards, although forty-two years ago those cards had been the pride of his collection. He had had them since he was young, and had re-discovered his childhood baseball-card collection in an attic during the 1950 off-season. Those nine cards had always been his favorites, and he had been excited at finding them, so much so that he had wanted to have them around to show to his teammates at their 1951 Spring Training. Neither he nor any of the other Cubs at the time had any idea that 1951 would turn out to be the team's last spring on Catalina.

Cavanarro didn't know who had originally made the secret wall-compartment, or why, but he had discovered it by accident. It was next to his bed in the room he shared with two teammates, and he had decided it would be an ideal place to store his cards. He had never been concerned about his teammates or anyone else taking the cards, he had just thought the hidden compartment would make for a fun location to keep his 'treasure' in. However, he added, his choice to keep his cards in such a hidden place was probably what had led to him forgetting to take them with him at the end of Spring Training. And of course, it also had never occurred to him that he wouldn't be back the following spring to retrieve them.

Even farther off in Cavanarro's recollection was the map MacKenzie had asked about. However, her question had brought back a long-lost memory of why he had once marked and saved the map. He had been out hiking one weekend afternoon with a few of his teammates, and they had been caught in a sudden storm. They had sought refuge, and the overgrowth they had ended up sheltering under was clustered around some large rocks, one of which they discovered had some kind of small metal door built into it. They hadn't been able to get the door open, and once the storm passed, his teammates had lost interest in investigating it any further. But Cavanarro had found it interesting, and had marked its approximate location on a map so he could come back and investigate more at another time. He never did return to the spot. But from MacKenzie's question, he now remembered thinking that the map was the kind of thing which would be fun to store in his secret compartment.

Cavanarro explained that the baseball cards had originally belonged to his father, who had given them to him for his twelfth birthday. So they had great personal and sentimental value for him, and he felt bad that the passage of time had moved them so far from his thoughts and his memory. He was looking forward to being re-united with them.

He said that because the monetary value of cards had become so much more than it had once been, he thought it would be best for MacKenzie to not send them to him through the mail. He thought a better idea would be for him to meet MacKenzie and her father in person whenever they returned from Catalina to Chicago, and she could give the cards to him at that time. Cavanarro hinted that as a way thanking her, he might be able to arrange for her and her father to meet the current Cubs team, and he had an idea that there might be a thank-you gift of free season tickets waiting for her and her father when they returned.

In his closing, Cavanarro thanked her again for everything she had done. He told MacKenzie that her honesty and goodness were rare, and he said that how honorable she was meant far more to him than the idea of being re-united with his baseball cards. He included his office phone number, and asked that MacKenzie and her father please get in touch with him once they were back in Chicago. And he said that he had always loved Catalina Island, and he hoped that MacKenzie and her father were enjoying their time there.

MacKenzie had been holding on to her father, her hands

wrapped around one of his arms in excitement the whole time they had been reading the letter together.

"Oh my god... Dad!" she exclaimed. "We're going to meet Paul Cavanarro! We're going to meet the Cubs!!"

Her father smiled broadly and nodded. "This is really exciting, Mac," he agreed.

"Dad!" she went on, brimming with giddy excitement. "And maybe even some free season tickets...!"

"It's a very generous gift," said John. "He's obviously very grateful for why you wanted to get in touch with him."

"And he found the secret compartment the same way I did!" MacKenzie exclaimed happily. "And he even explained about the map! He's so nice!"

"He seems like a very friendly and kind person," said her father. "It's nice when a famous person turns out to be as good and decent a person in real life as they seem in public life. Quite encouraging and inspirational."

"Dad," said MacKenzie, "I'm going to put this letter in a zip-lock plastic bag, and keep it in the secret compartment with the tin box!"

Her father smiled and nodded. "Seems quite appropriate," he agreed, standing up to resume getting ready to go to work. "I suggest," he added, "that you first copy Cavanarro's office phone number onto a 3 x 5 index card, and magnet it to the fridge."

"Smart, Dad..." agreed MacKenzie, taking a quick sip of her hot chocolate and collecting the letter and its envelope. "You're always thinking ahead...!"

MacKenzie followed her father's suggestion, and after sealing the letter into a plastic bag, she placed it reverently on top of the tin box inside the secret compartment which she had now become a skilled expert at finding and opening.

Her father sipped his coffee and kept MacKenzie company in the kitchen while she washed all the dishes from breakfast, and they discussed with regret how John was again going to miss the Cubs game because he would be working.

"After Katie's rather brilliant insight last night into the buffalo illness," her father was saying, "I spoke on the phone with Ed earlier this morning before you got up. We are going to be tranquilizing some of the herd today. I don't like to do it, but Ed and I agreed it's now become essential that we get those blood samples."

"I hope the poor buffalo will get through it okay..." MacKenzie said worriedly.

Her father nodded. "It is a bit traumatizing for them," he said. "But, in the end, they really are just taking an unexpected nap. There should not be any complications. But speaking of thinking ahead, it turns out this is now going to be a long work day for me. Which means I won't be home by 4:00. I won't be home in time for us to play catch, and I likely will be too late for us to have dinner together. Would you be okay with having dinner with Erik, and you and I will catch up with each other later this evening?"

MacKenzie nodded. "I'll miss you, Dad," she said. "And I'll miss watching the game with you. Are you going to be sad if Erik and I watch the game without you again?"

Her father smiled. "I'll wish I could be here listening to it with you. But I'll be glad to know that you two are getting to enjoy the game."

"So, what time do you think you'll be home?" asked MacKenzie.

"I'll probably grab a quick dinner somewhere either with Ed or Katie after whenever the day's work finally wraps up," said John. "So probably sometime around 7:30. Is it okay with you if Katie comes over then for a few hours?"

MacKenzie grinned happily. "Yes, please, Dad. That would be awesome."

Her father smiled and nodded. "Okay. Listen," he went on. "You need to remember what Katie said last night about that possible storm. I spoke with Ed about that, too. There's a tropical depression—meaning a weather system with thunderstorms and winds moving in circles—which has now has been upgraded to a tropical storm. That means the winds have become stronger. It's been named Tropical Storm Eugene, and it's coming in the general direction of Catalina from somewhere around Baja in southern California. At the moment, it's not on track to hit Catalina directly. But an outer part of it may brush by the island later this afternoon. And if it does, it could bring that sudden storm Katie was telling us about. Potentially, it might affect not only the field work I'm doing today, but it might also affect your and Erik's safety if you're outside."

MacKenzie nodded. "I see where you're going with this, Dad..." she said. "And so I just want to repeat what I said last night. I promise to be careful, and to not do anything reckless."

"Oh," her father remarked. "That's a good word. Where did you get 'reckless' from?"

"Erik," MacKenzie explained proudly. "Not thinking or caring about what might happen from something you're doing. 'The smart girl did not stay outside during the thunderstorm because that kind of behavior would be too reckless.' Et cetera."

Her father grinned.

"Erik and I were talking about how he and I are both impulsive," MacKenzie continued. "And Erik told me that sometimes impulsiveness can lead to being reckless."

John nodded. "He's right."

"Nothing reckless about me, Dad," MacKenzie said reassuringly.

Her father gave her an exasperated loving smile. "I'll believe that when you've rounded third and I see that you've made it safely home tonight," he said, lifting her baseball cap and mussing her hair affectionately, then putting her cap back in place on her head.

MacKenzie grinned happily.

Davenport arrived at 8:30, and he and John drove off in the Conservancy golf cart to begin their long day. MacKenzie readied her borrowed backpack, and headed out on her borrowed bike for her morning ride to Abalone Point. She spent a few contemplative minutes there, straddling her bicycle and standing in front of her rock-warrior sentry, before giving it a friendly wave good-bye and pedaling off to meet Erik. Her thoughts were preoccupied with details of the letter from Paul Cavanarro, and with the lovely feeling of her necklace gently bouncing below her neck as she pedaled. She forgot to be worried about seeing the mysterious man until she reached the shop storefronts along the walking mall portion of Crescent Ave, when it suddenly occurred to her that she hadn't seen him.

She met up with Erik, and after locking their bikes to a rack, they went together to Big Olaf's to get their after-breakfast dessert. Soon they were sitting with their heaping paper bowls of fabulous ice cream in their special spot at the top of the Avalon Bay beach, perched on the curb of the Crescent Ave swirl-curved paving stones, with their sneakers off and their feet planted contentedly in the warm beach sand.

Out in the bay, dozens of moored sailboats gently bobbed and were bathed in the welcoming light of the morning sun. Closer to shore, a group of eager kayakers actively paddled about in colorful crafts and bright safety-vests as a sea-kayaking tour was about to get underway.

"How are your arms doing?" Erik asked between spoonfuls of ice cream. "Kayaking-soreness all gone yet?"

MacKenzie smiled and nodded. "Good as new," she said. "Better than new, actually, because I think my muscles have healed stronger than they were."

Erik smiled. "That's excellent," he said.

"Okay," MacKenzie went on. "So, big news. I was waiting for the right moment to tell you."

"Is this the right moment?" asked Erik.

MacKenzie looked at her Cubs watch. It was nearly 9:15. She waited a bit longer, and then the tolling of the Chimes Tower reached their ears, and MacKenzie smiled.

She scooped a large shovelful of her ice cream and lifted it ceremoniously into the air. Erik did the same, and they tapped their spoonfuls together like a champagne toast, and then each downed their own colorful creamy cool deliciousness.

"Yes," MacKenzie confirmed, nodding. "It is now the right moment. Paul Cavanarro wrote me back."

Erik looked at her with bright-eyed excitement. "Get out of here!" he exclaimed. "That's awesome! What did he say?"

"Well I'll just tell you," MacKenzie began. "These are the headlines. He was happy that I wrote him, he wants me and my dad to return the cards to him in person, he's going to take us to meet the Cubs team players, and he's giving me and my Dad free season tickets."

"Mac...!" said Erik enthusiastically. "That's so cool!"

MacKenzie nodded and ate another mouthful of her ice cream. "But that's not the most interesting part..." she said significantly. "He also explained about the map...!"

"No way...!" Erik said with mounting interest. "What did he say?"

"Well," said MacKenzie. "I'll tell you all the details, but this is the part you and I are going to want to talk about first: the map marks a place in the foothills where there's a mysterious metal door…"

"How mysterious?"

"So mysterious," MacKenzie said pointedly, "that we might have to go and see it for ourselves."

"You know," said Erik, "it could just be an old sealed-up mine. There are a lot more of those at the west end of the island, but there are a few around here, too. It might just be an old mine."

MacKenzie nodded. "It certainly might…"

Erik grinned at her. "And I guess," he said deliberately, "there's only one way for us to know for sure…"

MacKenzie grinned. "And that would be…"

"For us to find it and see for ourselves," said Erik, smiling eagerly.

They put their ice cream spoons into their bowls long enough to give each other their tunnel-signal, snap-bounce-thumbs-up. They laughed together and then set about finishing the rest of their ice cream.

Chapter 31
EXPLORATION

"**O**kay," said MacKenzie. "We need a plan..."

Still in bare feet and carrying their sneakers, she and Erik had made their way back to Big Olaf 's and put their trash into the recycling bins. Erik absently adjusted the position of his shark-tooth bracelet on one wrist, then checked his diving watch on the other.

"Let's start simple..." suggested Erik. "It's 9:35. My mom is finished with her first tour in ten minutes, and her next one doesn't leave until 10:00. Let's check in with her so I can tell her what our day is going to look like. Then let's go to my house and plan our exploration. We can get any supplies we need while we're there."

MacKenzie nodded. "We can eat lunch while we're watching the game," she contributed. "After we leave your house, we should buy some Cracker Jacks and pick up a pizza on the way to the cottage."

"That sounds good," Erik agreed. "What time does the game start?"

"1:08 Catalina time," said MacKenzie. "It should be over by around 3:30."

"Okay," said Erik. "Let's leave to start exploring the foothills right after the game. We'll bring snacks and water so we can explore anything we find for as long as we want."

"My Dad's having dinner out," added MacKenzie. "So after our exploration, if you and I come back to the cottage by around 6:30, I can make us dinner. We have plenty of ingredients. My Dad always lets me buy extra whenever we're shopping. I like to plan ahead."

"It's funny," said Erik. "For two people who are so impulsive, we both like planning."

"Being impulsive means suddenly deciding to change the plan," said MacKenzie. "You can't change the plan if you don't have one."

Erik nodded. "I think a plan is like the order-of-operations in math. If you don't follow it, you won't get the right result. But if all you ever do is follow the script and never use your imagination, you'll never come up with something new and maybe even something better."

MacKenzie smiled and gave him their tunnel-signal.

Erik gave her their tunnel-signal back, and they both laughed.

"My Dad and Katie should be home by around 7:30," MacKenzie went on. "Then we can all hang out together in the living room and play poker."

Erik smiled. "That sounds like a nice way to spend the last part of our day. My mom's going to be out with friends. I'll ask her if she can come pick up me and my bike around 10:30."

"Maybe when she comes over, she'll play some poker with us again," MacKenzie suggested hopefully.

Erik smiled. "That will be fun."

"Okay, then," said MacKenzie. "We've taken care of the simple part."

"Oh…" said Erik. "Speaking of the tunnel-signal and being impulsive, I can't believe I almost forget to tell you."

"What?" asked MacKenzie.

"So, when my dad called on Thursday after you and I watched *Trans-Atlantic Tunnel*, I told him about how much we liked the original tunnel-signal in the movie. And because he's so cool, my dad dug up some information on it for us, and he told me about it when he called last night."

"What did he say…?" asked MacKenzie, brimming with eager curiosity.

"He asked one of his movie friends about it," said Erik. "And it turns out the tunnel-signal wasn't in the original script. Richard Dix and Leslie Banks became real-life friends while they were working on that movie together, and that signal was something they made up themselves for fun. The director liked it and decided to keep it in the story. My dad called it a 'signature'. He said it ended up being a symbolic 'signature move', just for those two characters in that movie's story. So, it just goes to show, it's important to always be open to unexpected new things."

MacKenzie grinned. "That's the coolest story ever!" she exclaimed excitedly. "I love that! Our favorite thing from a made-up movie is actually something really made up by new friends from their real-life friendship. That's so awesome!"

They put their sneakers back on and found Brenda, who was characteristically cheerful and positive about all they described to her, and happily agreed to her small part in their plans. Her only concern was the possibility of an afternoon pop-up storm, which had been discussed at length in the tour office earlier that morning, and Erik assured his mother that he and MacKenzie would do whatever they needed to in order to stay safe.

As soon as MacKenzie and Erik got to Erik's house, Erik found them two sturdy heavy-duty metal flashlights with nylon belt-holsters, and he put new batteries into the barrel of each light. He then came up with two compasses, and found two maps of the foothills around Avalon and the east end of the island that were more detailed than the map Davenport had given MacKenzie to use. MacKenzie and Erik agreed that, while they were listening to the Cubs game, they would as precisely as possible mark those maps with the location of the 'x' from Paul Cavanarro's map.

The two of them then stocked up on snacks and water, loaded everything into their streamlined packs, and headed out to buy food and treats for the game.

At the cottage, they re-arranged the living room into game-watching-mode, and by the third inning had already eaten most of the pizza. By the end of the fifth inning, the Cubs were leading the Rockies by a score of 2-to-0, and MacKenzie and Erik had carefully cleaned up all traces of pizza and soda from the coffee table and were working on translating the 'x' from Cavanarro's map to the two maps Erik had come up with.

By the top of the eighth inning, the maps had been marked and stowed in their packs. They had eaten all the Cracker Jacks and finished playing with the eccentric prizes which had been inside the boxes. The Cubs were leading 5-to-0, and MacKenzie and Erik had diligently restored the living room to normal-mode in early preparation for their departure.

The game ended at 3:32, and the Cubs had won by a score of 5-to-1. MacKenzie and Erik high-fived, turned off the short-wave radio, and got themselves ready to leave. On a 3 x 5 index card, MacKenzie had written a note to her father saying she and Erik were out exploring and would be home by the time he and Katie got there, and reassuring him they wouldn't be reckless if a storm showed up. *If a storm shows up*, she added at the bottom of the note, *we might be late getting home. Don't worry about me. I'll be safe, and I'm with Erik.*

When they headed out on their bikes at 3:40, the skies were beginning to cloud over but did not look too threatening. MacKenzie and Erik pedaled their way up toward the foothills in the direction of where they believed they had their best chance to find Paul Cavanarro's mysterious metal door.

Periodically consulting their maps, they biked on main roads until their intended path took them in a different direction, and then they turned off onto a dirt fire road. When they ran out of fire road, they decided it was time to go on foot, and they stashed their bikes behind some bushes and continued to hike their way forward.

Based on Cavanarro's letter, they had decided they were looking for overgrowth clustered around some rocks. However, that described features of the terrain in almost every direction, and it quickly became apparent that even with their maps detailing the approximate location of the 'x', the odds of them actually finding the same spot Cavanarro had discovered seemed slim at best.

"Process of elimination…" MacKenzie summarized after they had been searching for some time without success. "We keep checking likely suspects until we get bored or lucky…"

Erik nodded. "Or until we impulsively check an unlikely suspect," he added. "It's been forty-two years since Cavanarro last saw what he remembers about the spot. It might look very different by now…"

MacKenzie had placed a hand anxiously on Erik's arm.

"Mac, what is it…?"

"Erik…" she said slowly. "Why do I suddenly feel peculiar inside…?"

Erik looked from MacKenzie, to the surrounding foothills, and then to the sky.

"Uh-oh…" he said grimly.

And then the breeze was gone, and in its place now came the ominous gusts of a rising wind rushing ahead of something big behind it.

The storm started suddenly and seemed to come out of nowhere. One minute the sky had been overcast, the next minute it was dark and low with thick roiling clouds. Deep rumbles of thunder rolled into vast echoing blasts. Lightning flashes accompanied the thunder, and bursts of blinding electrical light streaked up and down the sky in jagged veiny forks. Rain began to fall in unrelenting torrents, and the wind was swelling into a blustering squall.

MacKenzie had grabbed her cap off her head just before the worst of the first wave of fast-moving air hit. Moments later, her clothes had been soaked through and were heavy with water. The rain came down harder, and the surging wind raged like a furious invisible monster.

"Bikes...!" MacKenzie yelled at the top of her lungs, trying to be heard over the noise of the storm, and staggering to keep from being blown over.

Erik was shaking his head. "Up in the air on metal bicycles...?" he yelled back. "We'll be fried by lighting in two seconds... And in this wind we couldn't ride ten feet... We need to find shelter..."

MacKenzie nodded and tried to blink away the rain pelting her eyes, turning her back to the wind so her face wouldn't be stung so badly. "Not under a tree...!" she yelled as loudly as she could, and could barely hear her own words.

The sky continued to blacken, and the rain kept coming. The claps of thunder grew louder, and the blasts of lightning came faster. The wind was now so strong that even Erik was barely able to stay standing. There was no point in talking. They couldn't hear each other, and they had to do something.

Erik grabbed MacKenzie's hand, and together they ran. They couldn't possibly run against the wind, so they ran with it. The howling gusts buffeted and tossed them about, and several times both of them were nearly blown off their feet. They were battered and stung by wind-whipped rain, and pounding wind slapped and shoved them first down the shallow incline of a small hill, then up the side of a larger steeper slope.

Erik looked up toward where the wind was driving their staggered stumbled running, and pointed. "Too high...!" he yelled, looking around and trying to see anything through the rain.

MacKenzie pointed in a direction off to one side. "There...?" she yelled.

It didn't really matter. They had to get under or behind something.

Erik nodded, and they ran with faltering unsteady steps in the new direction.

The wind suddenly picked up strength and changed direction, and abruptly MacKenzie and Erik started to be blown back down the slope. They fought against it, and it was a losing battle. They were about to be forcibly tumbled down the hill when they reached what they had been heading toward, which turned out to be a thick tangle of large bushes clustered closely together.

MacKenzie and Erik dropped to their hands and knees to keep from being blown away. They crawled forward, dragging themselves to an opening between the trunks of the bushes. Pulling themselves into the midst of low-growing branches, they forced their way into the sodden pocket of a small open place between the stiff gnarled trunks, as the lowermost parts of the bushes caught at their rain-drenched hair and tugged against the packs on their backs.

For a moment, they had some relief. It wasn't much. There was no space to sit up, so they lay on their stomachs and leaned on their elbows. The rain poured in on them through the thin leaves and narrow branches of the clustered bushes, and the wind was still finding them. But for the moment, they were on the downhill side of the wind and rain. They were getting some slight protection against the storm from the overgrowth around them, and they were no longer being blown across the landscape of the foothills. And they could at least hear each other speak.

"Are we going to be struck by lightning in here...?" asked MacKenzie.

Erik shook his head. "Low bushes, downhill slope... It's not perfect, but it's an improvement... I think we'll be okay here until the storm passes."

MacKenzie nodded and twisted her cap in her hands, comically wringing a thick stream of water out of it. "I guess that's why they call it a 'pop-up storm'," she mused with soggy dissatisfaction. "It really does just pop-up out of nowhere…"

Having the thickest part of the cluster of bushes uphill and shielding them from the worst of the wind at the moment was helping. But the rain was coming harder than ever and cascading heavily down onto them through the bushes. A lightning flash lit up the inside of their bush-cluster shelter like a searchlight, and was immediately followed by a shuddering release of thunder that sounded like something had exploded only a few feet away. MacKenzie could feel the pounding vibrate through her body.

"Are we going to get hit by lighting…?" she asked again.

Erik shook his head. "It always sounds closer than it really is."

"That sounded awfully close…"

Between lightning flashes, it was getting darker with each passing moment. The bushes currently sheltering MacKenzie and Erik began to tremble from the growing force of the still-rising wind, and the narrow trunks creaked and groaned under the stress of the increasing motion.

"I feel like it's getting worse…" MacKenzie said uneasily.

Erik nodded. "Unfortunately, I think that's because it is…"

"Are these bushes going to be blown away with us inside them…?"

"Let's try to crawl farther in…" Erik suggested, pushing some of his rain-drenched hair away from his eyes. He ducked his head and started to crawl forward, trying to find more space somewhere ahead between the bush trunks.

MacKenzie nodded. Still clutching her sopping crumpled cap, she started pushing aside undergrowth and thin branches, trying to either find or make a path she could crawl through to get deeper into the heart of the cluster of bushes.

The wind was still strengthening. It howled and wailed as it tore through the branches and leaves of the bushes, and by now it was almost as if MacKenzie and Erik had no protection of any kind around them.

"Dead end…" Erik announced, now almost having to yell again to be heard. "There's the side of a huge rock back here…"

MacKenzie was still rooting through the tangle of low branches looking for a way to burrow farther forward into the depth of the bushes. And then she stopped.

"Oh my god…" she said.

In the noise of the storm and all the rainwater falling in on them, Erik almost hadn't heard her.

"Mac, what is it…?" he yelled back with concern.

"Erik… I… I think I found it…"

Chapter 32
SHELTER

There was a kind of small clearing in the heart of the cluster of bushes. MacKenzie had dragged herself into it by her elbows, and suddenly there was enough overhead open space in the lowest bush branches that she was able to sit up on her knees. The rock that Erik had found the side of was larger than it first appeared. It was over a dozen feet wide, and extended upward at least several feet. The top was somewhere in the taller branches of the bushes and couldn't be seen from inside the small clearing. But fixed firmly into the face of the rock directly in front of MacKenzie was a solid piece of old metal about two feet across and three feet high.

It was almost entirely covered over with a dense tangle of vines and overgrowth. The very bottom part of the metal piece seemed to be somewhere below the ground. The metal was rusted. It had weathered to a color which blended in with the rock, and with the weeds and bushes around it. Especially in the storm-darkened dimness and the rain pouring heavily in through the bushes, it was not easy to notice. But if this really was the same spot which had once been found by Paul Cavanarro, it was easy for MacKenzie to see why he had thought this was some kind of door. A separate narrow metal frame embedded in the face of the rock went all around the outer edge of the main rectangular piece of metal. If it was a door, it was a door without any hinges or handles. But as far as MacKenzie could see, it did nevertheless very much resemble a small door.

"Mac…!" Erik was exclaiming loudly to be heard over the noise of the storm as he crawled his way into the tiny clearing. He sat up on his knees next to MacKenzie in front of the door, while the wind racing through the bushes whipped at their drenched and dripping clothes.

There was another blindingly bright lightning flash, and almost immediately it was followed by a deafening blast of thunder. Both MacKenzie and Erik were startled by the sudden light, and MacKenzie shuddered at the pounding vibration of the violent sound. But their attention stayed fixed on the door in front of them.

"Erik...!" MacKenzie yelled over the storm noise, rainwater pouring off every part of her. Did we really find it...?"

"If we found it," Erik shouted back, "it's only because you're the one who found it...!"

"If it's a door, it can be opened, right...?" yelled MacKenzie.

"If it's a door, there's something on the other side," shouted Erik, already starting to collect information by running his fingers over the seams at the door's edges. "And whatever's on the other side, it can't be worse than being stuck in the middle of this storm...!"

As the wind blew with more force, and the rain came down with more strength, MacKenzie and Erik set to work hurriedly pulling the overgrowth away from around the metal surface. They were determined to find some way to get the door open, not only to satisfy their impulsive curiosity as to what lay beyond, but also from the very real need to get to whatever better shelter might be on the other side. The discovery was exciting, but feeling the strength of the storm continuing to intensify all around them was making them work with urgency.

On the assumption the door was somehow hinged on the left and would open from the right, Erik tried to find or create a finger-hold anywhere along right edge between the door and the frame. MacKenzie was digging away the ground across the bottom, hoping to reveal the lower edge of the door. She was having better luck than Erik, mostly because her task was more easily accomplished. The unrelenting rain had softened the soil, and MacKenzie was able to loosen and move the clay and dirt without much resistance. Soon she had dug down far enough that the bottom of the door had been exposed, and she turned her efforts toward trying to help Erik.

After several minutes of neither of them being able to get a fingerhold anywhere around the edge, MacKenzie resorted to a different approach. She took her flashlight out of its soggy holster where it was attached to her waterlogged belt. Partly from desperation, partly from frustration, and partly from determination, MacKenzie started pounding at the edges of the door with the end of the heavy flashlight, using the back-end-battery-cap as a hammer head.

Aged dirt and rust now soaked with rain began to come loose between the door and the frame, washing wetly down the seams along the sides as she repeatedly hammered against the edges of the metal. Encouraged by this progress, she hammered harder, now working her way systematically around the edges. Erik continued to work at digging his fingertips into different parts of the door seams, until he suddenly had a breakthrough. MacKenzie's hammering had loosened enough of the time-encrusted grime that at last he'd been able to find a tiny gap. He dug his fingers in further until he had enough of a fingerhold that he could begin pulling.

His repeated tugs started to slowly separate and move the right-hand side of the door, and it became clear that the door did in fact open on that side. Erik slipped off his backpack and unzipped one of its compartments long enough to take out the can of WD-40.

"Does it work in the rain...?" MacKenzie yelled over the storm noise.

Erik nodded. "It works anywhere..." he shouted back, uncapping the can and spraying WD-40 all along the outside of the door's left seam-edge where the hinge would have to be, even though there was no outward sign of it.

MacKenzie and Erik now worked together, each of them forcing their fingertips around the slightly opened door-edge to get a hold of the right-hand metal side. They then both pulled at the same time, leaning back with all their weight, tugging as hard as they could.

This resulted in the stuck reluctant door giving up a few more inches of opening, which was just enough space for Erik to extend his arm inside. Once again grasping the can of WD-40, he reached his arm around the door, and without being able to see what he was doing, he sprayed the inside of the door's left seam-edge where the unseen hinges had to be hiding.

With rainwater pouring down their faces, MacKenzie and Erik worked together once more, each of them firmly gripping the partly opened door-edge on the right-hand side, and both of them pulling together as hard as they could.

And then the door opened. Not fully, but wide enough that they could fit themselves through.

Zipping the WD-40 back into his pack, and slipping his pack onto his back, Erik pulled his flashlight from its holster on his belt and powered it on.

"If it's a mine shaft," Erik yelled over the storm noise, "we don't want to fall to the bottom…"

He stuck his head and his flashlight through the partly opened door and looked around for a moment at whatever was on the other side, before pulling himself back out and reporting to MacKenzie.

"There's a floor…" he shouted. "It's about a three-foot drop down, so watch your step…"

MacKenzie nodded, and Erik turned back to the partially-opened door. He swung one leg through the opening, then ducked his head and stepped the rest of the way through. MacKenzie could see his body going lower, and when he turned back toward her, his waist was at the level of the bottom of the door.

MacKenzie clambered through after him, and Erik was shining his flashlight onto the inside floor so she could see where to place her feet as she climbed down into the new space.

As if to punctuate their exit from the clearing, another flash of lightning lit up what could be seen of the bushes from inside the new space. It was followed almost instantly by a crackling blast of thunder as MacKenzie and Erik looked back through the doorway space they had just come through.

Erik aimed the beam of his flashlight at the door they had worked so hard to release. The partially-opened metal closure now extended out into the storm-darkened clearing they had left behind. The inside of the already rain-soaked door had a simple industrial vertically-oriented pull handle mounted halfway up the length of its outer edge. At its inner edge, a long continuous single industrial hinge connected the opposite side of the door to the metal frame. The length of the hinge now glistened and dripped with fast-falling rain, and with a slow heavy slurry of WD-40 and loosened grime and rust.

Erik directed the illumination of his flashlight to the floor he and MacKenzie were now standing on. It wasn't really a floor. It was a platform constructed entirely of metal grating. The metal was old but not rusted, and seemed sufficiently sturdy to support the weight of two people.

MacKenzie tried to power on her flashlight, but it evidently hadn't survived being re-purposed as a hammer. It flickered and came dimly on, then went dark and wouldn't come back to life.

"It sacrificed itself for the sake of the greater good…" Erik concluded, as MacKenzie slipped the dead flashlight back into its holster on her belt.

"Maybe it can be fixed…" MacKenzie said hopefully.

Erik shook his head. "Some things can be fixed, but some things should simply be replaced."

Their voices sounded different in the new space. The noise of the storm was still coming through the partially-open door, but now seemed somehow far away.

Erik placed his flashlight down on the grating, aimed up to give them some interior lighting, unintentionally creating sudden giant shadows of him and MacKenzie. The space they were standing in was small. The close walls and low ceiling were stone, and appeared to have been cut into the rock long ago.

Erik shook his head rapidly from side-to-side like a dog shaking itself after a swim, sending rainwater spraying off his hair in all directions. MacKenzie checked to make sure her necklace was still around her neck, which it was. She then used both hands to twist her Cubs cap and wring water from it once again, before opening it back up to something vaguely like its normal shape and pulling in onto her head over her drenched hair. Tilting her head to one side, she reached back to bunch her hair together and then squeezed out rainwater, sliding her hands down the length of the bunch to help escort the water on its way.

MacKenzie felt the same way Erik looked—like the two of them had just climbed out of a swimming pool fully dressed. Their sodden clothing was stuck to them like a second skin.

"We forgot to pack towels…" Erik commented wryly.

MacKenzie nodded. "And also a hammer and an extra flashlight…"

"We did not, however, forget to pack water…" said Erik, opening a compartment in his pack and taking out a bottle of water.

"That seems ironic, somehow…" said MacKenzie, slipping her pack around one shoulder and unzipping one of the compartments. "Hey…" she went on. "How is everything in my pack still dry…?"

Erik took a bite of one the snacks they had brought along and nodded his head. "They're waterproof…" he said.

"This is more than waterproof," said MacKenzie, taking out a bottle of water. "This is stormproof. Wow... Seriously, everything in here's totally dry...."

Erik removed his sunglasses from where they were somehow still perched on the top of his rain-drenched head and shook water off them. After zipping them into his pack, he squeezed rainwater out of his shirt in a long steady drip. "Okay..." he said, putting his pack back on and picking up his flashlight. "So, now we have a decision to make..."

MacKenzie had finished her drink and zipped her water bottle back into its compartment along with her flip-up sunglasses. She slung her pack back over her shoulders and stood with her soggy clothes dripping. "I'm ready..." she said. "What are we deciding...?"

Erik aimed his light back toward their feet on the metal grating. He then directed the beam away from where they were standing and on to the opposite side of the platform, revealing an open place in the grating and the top of a flight of downward stairs. The steps were made of the same metal grating as the platform, and descended down into darkness.

"Oh my god..." MacKenzie gasped. "Erik...! Stairs...!"

Erik nodded, continuing to shine his flashlight beam down through different places in the grating at their feet. "And it looks like they go down a long way..." he said. "And that's the decision we have to make. Do we wait here until the storm has passed? Or do we go down the stairs to see what's there, and then come back up after the storm is over...?"

MacKenzie grinned, her eyes bright with eager excitement. "Is that a trick question?" she asked.

Erik smiled. "We go down?" he replied.

MacKenzie nodded emphatically. "We go down," she said.

They gave each other their tunnel-signal, and Erik tucked his flashlight under one arm for a moment. He adjusted the position of his shark-tooth bracelet on one wrist, then checked his diving watch on the other. "Okay..." he began. "It is now 4:34. We'll time ourselves. However long it takes to go down, it will take us longer to come back up. Because you have such an amazing natural-sense-of-direction, you're in charge of making sure we don't get lost if it turns out there's more exploring to do at the bottom of the stairs, wherever they happen to lead."

MacKenzie nodded. "And," she clarified, "you have to be in charge of making sure we can see where we're going, because I managed to ruin the flashlight you let me borrow..."

Erik illuminated the short path across the grating of the small platform to the start of the stairs. He and MacKenzie walked the two short paces needed to get there, and together they turned toward the first flight of steps and began to descend.

Chapter 33
BELOW

The stairs and landings were made with the same metal grating as the platform at the top. At every landing, the stairs reversed their direction downward, over and over, in a repeating back-and-forth zig-zag of descending stairs. The sides of the stairway-shaft were earth and stone. There was a continuous metal hand-railing against the rough-hewn walls to the right of MacKenzie and Erik as they went down. To the left, there was no middle space between the stairs, only a solid assembly of metal beams extending vertically between the zig-zags as a central stair support. There was no open place to look up or down through, and no way to see wherever the bottom was.

Erik periodically aimed the flashlight up through the stairs overhead, back the way they had come, then down through the stairs beneath their feet, in the direction of what might be below. But it was impossible to see anything clearly through all the multiple layers of grating.

They proceeded downward. Their waterlogged sneakers squished and squeaked with every step, and the stairs reverberated with muted hollow metallic clunks as they descended. The echoes seemed to be resonating very far below, and the sounds soon led MacKenzie and Erik to realize the stairs went down much farther than they had first imagined.

For a while, the seemingly endless descent became comical. At every landing, they would turn to find the same thing below—yet more stairs. Eventually, they decided to descend more quickly. Being careful not to trip or let their soaked sneakers lose their grip and slip on the metal grating, they speeded up their downward pace as much as they dared, at times racing each other and then stopping together on a landing to laugh and catch their breath. These momentary races also presented a particular challenge, since between them there was only one working flashlight.

"I can't believe we're still going down," MacKenzie mused incredulously. "It's such a long way... And, I mean, it's not that hard to do because we're, like, going down. Of course, wearing sopping wet clothes doesn't help... But I can't help thinking about the trip back up. After whenever we finally do go back up, we're going to have some seriously sore leg muscles...!"

"If our clothes ever dry out," Erik suggested optimistically, "we'll weigh less on the way up, so that should make it a little less difficult..."

Their voices echoed strangely off the endless earthen walls and the towering stair-stack of metal grating in the vast vertical space.

"Time check, please..." said MacKenzie.

Erik held out his wrist and directed the flashlight beam at his watch.

"4:46," he announced.

"Oh my god..." MacKenzie said in disbelief. "Only twelve minutes...? I feel like we've been going down these stairs for days..."

"Want to start heading back up...?" asked Erik.

MacKenzie shook her head. "I think the only thing more frustrating than never getting to the end of all these crazy stairs would be to not ever find out what's at the bottom."

"Okay then," said Erik. "Onward and downward..."

And downward they proceeded.

They arrived at the bottom a short time later. It was 4:51, and they had completed the descent in about seventeen minutes.

The first interesting aspect of their arrival at the bottom was the space itself. Three sides of the stairway-shaft were still there, but the on the fourth side it opened into a larger area. After the last landing, the final set of stairs led down into a small cave-like space with a ceiling that was over eight feet high.

MacKenzie and Erik high-fived at finally reaching the bottom, then looked around to see what they ought to do next. On an impulse, MacKenzie took her dead flashlight out of its still-soggy holster and tried to turn it on, but without success. She shook it several times, and hit the side of the top with the heel of her hand, and it suddenly flickered to life. The light was dim and unsteady, but at least it was on. The first thing it showed was the bottom of the stairway-shaft directly under the last flight of stairs they had just come down. There were several different-sized openings in the side of the earthen wall at the level of the dirt ground, hidden beyond the metal beams of the central stair support. The largest of the openings was nearly three feet high, the smallest no higher than a foot-and-a-half.

MacKenzie crouched down and aimed the flashlight's wavering beam into each of the openings. They all seemed to be passages, each leading off to someplace dark and unknown. Then her flashlight died again, and repeatedly hitting it only hurt her hand, so she abandoned the effort and returned the flashlight to its holster.

"Anything interesting…?" asked Erik, who was still exploring the small cave with the bright beam of his fully-functioning flashlight.

"Secret passages for very small people or very large mice…" reported MacKenzie. "And also, my dead flashlight died again. How about you…?"

"A passage for larger-sized people," he said. "Want to explore it?"

"Definitely," said MacKenzie. "My legs aren't emotionally ready for the trip back up all those stairs."

Erik led her to the opening he had found in the side of the cave-space. They still had to bend down to go through it, but they didn't have to crawl. It was a long winding passage with sharp turns and a curving path. After several feet, however, the roof of the passage started to get lower, and the sides were getting closer together.

"Well," said MacKenzie, "if it turns into a complete dead-end, that's probably a sign that it's time for us to head back up…"

Erik suddenly clicked off his flashlight.

"Erik, what—" MacKenzie began.

"Shhh…" Erik said in a hurried whisper.

"What's going on…?" MacKenzie whispered quietly.

"Look…" whispered Erik. If he was pointing, MacKenzie couldn't see what he was pointing at, but after a moment it didn't matter. She knew what he was talking about.

There was a light. The passage they were in apparently continued to get smaller, but through a small opening near the ground somewhere ahead of them, some kind of illumination could clearly be seen.

"Light…?" whispered MacKenzie. "Down here…? That's impossible…"

"It certainly should be impossible…" Erik whispered back. "Let's go see what it is…"

MacKenzie took hold of one of Erik's hands, and together they made their way cautiously forward through the darkness toward the source of the light. They had to keep bending lower as they went, and several times their heads bumped or scraped against the top of the diminishing passage.

By the time they reached the end, they had been forced to crawl. On their hands and knees, they made their way through the last of the passage and out into the place where the light was coming from, and at last they were able to stand up easily.

They were standing at one side of a long tunnel that seemed to go on forever in either direction. The walls of the tunnel appeared to be formed from some kind of naturally-occurring dark rock, but the general shape of the tunnel was that of a giant circular tube more than twelve feet high. Along the ceiling at regular intervals were electric bulbs, all functioning and illuminated, each giving off a steady yellow-white light, all connected by continuous lengths of electrical conduit pipe. On the floor of the tunnel was a single set of train tracks. A railway bed of gravel supported intermittent wooden railroad ties, and the dark oily wood of the ties supported an unending length of parallel train tracks. The polished tops of the rails reflected the overhead lights, and the tracks extended in both directions of the tunnel as far as could be seen.

"What the…" Erik struggled to say, gazing around at the tunnel in speechless astonishment.

"Erik…" MacKenzie said slowly. "I'm feeling peculiar inside again…"

The unmoving still air of the tunnel had turned into a breeze. Multiple quick fleeting clanks of resettling iron and shifting steel came from the metal plates bolting the rails to the ties. Vibration was racing through the tracks from something large and heavy approaching fast. And then the breeze was gone, and in its place now came the growing forceful push of a rising wind rushing ahead of something big behind it.

"Back into the passage…!" Erik said hurriedly, grabbing MacKenzie's hand and pulling her with him back the way they had come. "Quick…!"

They ducked down and lowered themselves onto their hands and knees to crawl with urgent haste back into the small passage. Once they were safely inside, they quickly re-oriented themselves. Crouching low, they peered together back out to see what was happening in the tunnel.

The still-intensifying wind was now accompanied by a high-pitched electrical whirring-whine and the approaching rumbling roar of some large machine in rapid motion. A moment later, with a buffeting shove of fast-moving air, a train rocketed past, so fast that MacKenzie and Erik barely had time to see it.

The train was not multiple connected cars. It was a single long streamlined silver train-car with identical sloping-glass windshields at both ends. It was traveling far too fast for MacKenzie and Erik to see who may have been at the front controls, and there was no one at the controls behind the windshield at the back. The train had a single bright nose-cone light at the front, casting white brightness ahead of the train. The same nose-cone light at the back had been glowing with steady red illumination as the train had speeded by.

MacKenzie and Erik dashed forward out of the passage and stood up again in the tunnel the moment the train had passed. In the direction it had come from, the tunnel was gradually sloping down. In the direction the train had been headed, the tunnel had first levelled off and then sloped back down out of sight. If the train had stopped over the rise somewhere up ahead, there was no way for them to see it from where they were.

"Are you kidding me...?!" MacKenzie whispered in hushed disbelief. "Erik...! That was a *train*...! A train just went by...! Down here...! A secret underground train...!"

Erik glanced back in the direction the train had come from. "Not just an underground train..." he whispered. "I think we may have solved the mystery of the invisible boat..."

"What do you mean...?"

"That must be what the dolphins have been playing the chasing-game with," he said, still whispering. "Their hearing is amazing, and their sonar can 'see' vibration. This tunnel must be under the ground *under the water*. That train must be what the dolphins have been chasing..."

"Are we really that far down...?"

"Based on the elevation of where we were in the foothills," Erik whispered, "and how far we came down all those stairs, we're probably right now just about at sea level. And the tunnel slopes down going back that way, which would put it below the ground under the water…"

"Erik… What's going on here…? What is all this…?"

"We can go try to find out…" Erik whispered. "But we have to be careful. Whatever's going on down here, I'm guessing it's some kind of secret government operation, or some kind of secret illegal operation. Either way, they're not going to be happy to see us. And we're not going to be happy if they see us…"

"So let's just make sure they *don't* see us…" MacKenzie whispered.

Erik nodded. "Okay then," he whispered. "Let's go see what we can find out…"

Chapter 34
ENCOUNTER

MacKenzie and Erik made their way along the tracks as quietly and quickly as they dared. They kept to the right, the same side of the tunnel they had entered on, following the direction the train had been going.

"Will we get electrocuted walking near these tracks?" MacKenzie whispered with concern. "Our clothes are still soaking wet…"

"There's no electricity in these rails," Erik whispered back. "They're just wheel-rails. But there's no smoke or fuel smell in this tunnel, so that train probably is electric-powered. But, there's also no electricity-source for the train in here anywhere…"

"What about those lights up there…" MacKenzie asked in a whisper and pointing overhead to the top of the tunnel's curved ceiling.

Erik shook his head. "Powering light bulbs is easy," he whispered. "Powering a train is a very different story…"

"What about those wires over there…?"

MacKenzie was pointing at two cables, one significantly thicker than the other, running along the opposite wall about halfway up the side of the tunnel. They were suspended at intervals by large hooks, and the cables appeared to extend the length of the tunnel in both directions.

"Well," Erik whispered, "the train's not getting any power directly from those, either. But it does look like that larger cable is probably a power line, so that's a good thing for us to stay away from. The smaller one's probably for something like telephone communication…"

"So," MacKenzie whispered, "then, is the train battery-powered...?"

Erik nodded. "That's my guess..." he whispered. "That train probably has on-board electric batteries. Trains like that are called 'battery locomotives', but they're pretty specialized. You'd find them either in the 1800s, or during World War II, or as part of a mining railway. Any situation where you don't want to deal with fuel or direct-contact high-power electrical systems..."

"Like third rails..." MacKenzie contributed in a whisper.

Erik nodded again. "But battery locomotives are pretty unusual..." he whispered.

"Everything about this is pretty unusual..." MacKenzie whispered back.

As they approached the top of the rise, they slowed their pace and began to crouch down. The tunnel ahead descended on a slight slope, then levelled out. The back end of the train was in plain sight. It had come to a stop and was sitting motionless, the red illumination from its rear nose-cone light still glowing, and the cabin lights inside the sloped rear-facing windshield were all still on.

"If anyone inside the train comes near that rear windshield glass, they'll be able to look out and see us in a second..." Erik whispered in an even quieter voice and with more concerned caution.

"If we get spotted," MacKenzie whispered quietly, "we run back the way we came...?"

Erik nodded. "All the way back," he whispered, "including all the way back up the stairs..."

MacKenzie nodded. "If the train's battery-powered, what's all that steam...?"

They were now close enough to have a clearer look at the train. There was a slow steady wet hissing sound, and lazy clouds of steam vapor coming from somewhere near the wheels were slowly drifting upward and evaporating as they rose toward the top of the tunnel.

"Probably steam-brakes…" Erik whispered. "Electric-fired mini-boilers are pretty efficient…"

There was an abrupt final hiss of purging steam from beneath the train, and then the vapor stopped. The rear red light went off, and the lights inside the rear-facing windshield went dark.

Now keeping as far as possible to the right-hand wall of the tunnel, and trying to move with increased stealth, MacKenzie and Erik gradually continued their approach. They arrived at the back of the train, and there was now no place to go any farther forward.

Erik gazed in evident fascinated interest at the train, visually inspecting every detail. MacKenzie looked around to see what they might do next. To their right, cut into the side of the tunnel, a small flight of stone steps led up to a slightly higher level. Wordlessly getting Erik's attention, MacKenzie pointed at it. She and Erik crouched down and made their way up the steps, looking with wary caution to make sure no one was at the top.

The steps led up to a small cave-room with several door-sized openings connecting to other cave-passages. The room was piled with different-sized wooden crates, all with different kinds of numbers and lettering stenciled on the sides. Like the tunnel, the room and connecting passages all were illuminated by simple light bulbs attached to the cave-ceiling.

Neither MacKenzie nor Erik dared even to whisper. The loudest noise they made came from their wet sneakers, which were squeaking more quietly now that so much rainwater had been squished out of them. Different kinds of sounds were now reaching their ears from the different connecting passages. There were voices and activity taking place somewhere, along with the faint steady thrum of different kinds of machines.

MacKenzie and Erik proceeded through one of the passages to another cave-room. Like the previous room, this cave-room had several openings connecting to other passages. The passage on the left had a view of the train. Through that passage and the cave-room it led to could be seen a small part of the side of the train. A large sliding door on the train was open, revealing a dim glimpse of a large inner storage compartment area which was currently dark.

MacKenzie and Erik glanced back at each other, then turned to cautiously make their way toward the train. And then they were both grabbed by strong powerful hands from somewhere behind them. Their arms were pulled behind their backs and held forcefully together. They struggled, but couldn't get free or see who was holding them.

Two large men dressed in black military-style clothing entered the cave-room from another entrance, pointing large long black guns directly at MacKenzie and Erik. Without lowering their weapons, the two severe-looking men came closer. One of them reached up a hand to a small square microphone attached to a heavy strap over his shoulder and connected by a coiled cable to a walkie-talkie on his belt.

"We've got a breach," the man said into the mic.

A voice came from the speaker of the walkie-talkie. "Explain," it said.

"Two kids," the man said into the mic, still aiming his gun steadily.

"Bring them to me here," said the voice from the walkie-talkie.

"We're on our way," the man said into the mic. He nodded over MacKenzie and Erik to whoever was behind them and holding them, who they still couldn't see.

MacKenzie and Erik were shoved roughly forward, out of the small cave-room and along a cave passageway. They passed through several other cave-rooms as they went, and eventually they were pushed from a cave-passage out into a large brightly illuminated cavern. Powerful white lights hung from the high ceiling. Racks of guns and equipment lined the walls. There were consoles of control panels, and stacks of wooden crates piled everywhere. And standing everywhere were men dressed in black military-style clothing, looking serious and holding large long automatic guns. All of the guns were aimed at MacKenzie and Erik as they were prodded and shoved from behind into the space.

From another cave passageway at one side of the cavern, a man entered accompanied by two more-heavily armed companions. The man strode forward and came to a stop in front of MacKenzie and Erik.

MacKenzie looked at him. Their eyes locked, recognition flashing between them, and MacKenzie let out an exclamation of shock.

"Mr. Trelain…!"

The echo of her voice resounded throughout the cavernous space.

"You know him…?" Erik asked with baffled confusion likely shared by all the men surrounding them.

MacKenzie nodded. "This is the guy I told you about. The one who talked with me and my Dad on the dock in Long Beach…"

"Hello, MacKenzie," said Trelain. "Isn't this an interesting turn of events." He made a gesture in the air, and most of the men in the cavern lowered their weapons. The two men standing nearest to Trelain continued to keep their guns aimed at MacKenzie and Erik.

"What's going on here…?" asked Erik. "What's happening…? What is all this?"

"This is an illegal smuggling operation," Trelain said simply. "And you two are in a lot of trouble. You shouldn't be here, and now you've been captured by my men, who are very good at their jobs."

"Let go of us…!" said Erik angrily, struggling against the too powerful hands that were holding him.

"Young man," said Trelain. "Stop struggling. That is not a request."

For a moment, Erik stopped.

Trelain studied them for a moment, his bright sea-blue eyes piercing and inscrutable. "Did you swim here?" he asked MacKenzie.

MacKenzie couldn't tell if he was being serious. "We were caught in a pop-up storm..." she said.

Trelain nodded. "Well," he went on. "Unfortunately, you two have now been caught in something much more serious. I'm sorry for your parents, but they will not be seeing you again any time soon. There's nothing which can be done about that right now."

"Someone will come to rescue us," MacKenzie insisted adamantly. "I've already told everyone I know, about that man you sent to spy on me. Everyone knows, and they'll look and look for us until they find this place."

Trelain looked at her intently. "Well aren't you impulsive," he said. "It's a bit egocentric of you, MacKenzie, to think I would send any of my men to spy on you. And somewhat amusing. And also quite incorrect. When my men are not here, they're on the mainland. They do not go above to the surface of the island. As you suggest, that would be foolishly obvious and a needless risk. I do, however, find it interesting, MacKenzie, that our paths have crossed again. If I believed in such things, I would say it's some kind of sign."

"You have no right to keep us here," Erik said fiercely.

Trelain shook his head. "I disagree. You two are trespassing. I can do with you whatever I please. And I do need you both to now stop speaking. I would find it barbaric to have to tape your mouths shut, but if you persist in speaking, that is what I will have to do. I would prefer it if you would both simply stop talking."

The two men still aiming their weapons both took a menacing step toward MacKenzie and Erik.

"Hands up over your heads," instructed Trelain.

MacKenzie and Erik had their arms raised for them by whoever was standing behind them, still holding them firmly.

"Lose the backpacks," instructed Trelain. "On the floor, over there."

MacKenzie and Erik had their packs taken off by the hands behind them, and the backpacks were tossed together to the ground against a wall.

"Young man," Trelain said to Erik. "You will now put your hands behind your back again. And though I have some patience, it often goes away quite unexpectedly. So follow instructions, and do not resist. That will be better for everyone."

Erik's hands were put behind his back by whoever was holding him. Another of Trelain's men now approached carrying a coil of white cord-rope, and he tied Erik's hands together behind his back.

"Oh, don't worry, MacKenzie," Trelain said reassuringly. "You will also be tied up and re-joining your friend soon enough. But you and I are going to have a brief conversation first."

MacKenzie's hands were lowered for her, and once again held tightly behind her.

Erik opened his mouth to protest, but Trelain pointed a harsh finger at him. "Do not forget what I said. You are not permitted to speak. You will be silent willingly, or against your will. Choose carefully."

For a moment, no one said anything.

There was something deeply scary about Trelain. He seemed as though his mood could change to deadly dangerous in an instant. He seemed impulsive, which made MacKenzie inwardly shudder at the thought that she might have something in common with him.

Trelain looked at his watch. It was a large diving watch with lots of buttons around the edge and a wide ridged band made of thick black rubber. He nodded, and looked at Erik again. "Sit down over there," he said, pointing.

Erik was made to sit down, and his captor at last left him and stepped aside.

"Block H," Trelain said over MacKenzie's head to the man still holding her.

Most of the other men now returned to what they had been doing, and four of them left the cavern heading back in the direction of the passage which led to the train and the tunnel.

Trelain left the cavern from the direction he had entered, and MacKenzie was forced to follow after him by the captor who was still firmly holding her hands together behind her.

She was pushed into a cave-room that had a door frame and a door. At one end was a large desk with a big chair behind it, in a set-up that looked to MacKenzie like something from a rich business-man's office. There was another chair facing the front of the desk, and MacKenzie was forced to sit down into it. Trelain came around and seated himself behind the desk in what was obviously his chair, and nodded to the man still holding MacKenzie.

MacKenzie's captor at last released her. The man left the room, closing the door after himself, and MacKenzie heard the door lock turn and click into place.

"Well," said Trelain, settling back into his chair. "Welcome to my little smuggling operation, MacKenzie."

To MacKenzie, Trelain looked like a spy or a secret agent. He was dressed all in black, with a dark shoulder holster holding a large-handled gun at the side of his chest. Out in the cavern, she had seen he was also armed with three other guns of different sizes in different shaped holsters attached by straps to his waist and both his upper legs, as well as a large knife in some kind of holder attached around one of his legs below his knee.

Trelain looked at his watch again, then looked back at MacKenzie. "Plenty of time," he said reassuringly.

"For what?" asked MacKenzie.

"For me to tell you about myself and my operation here."

"Why?"

"Because it amuses me," said Trelain. "And because I think it's a fascinating story."

"What if I'm not interested?" said MacKenzie trying to sound brave and defiant, though she felt neither. She just felt confused and worried and scared.

Trelain smiled.

"Oh, I think you'll find it interesting," he said. "And I don't believe you're not interested."

"What if I run out of here screaming?"

"The door is locked," said Trelain. "And I don't think you're the screaming type. But listen to me carefully. I'm not a good person, and I've done bad things, and I do bad things. Now, I don't kill people, and I certainly don't kill children. But I warn you. Don't do anything stupid. It won't turn out well for you, or your friend."

MacKenzie said nothing.

"And now," said Trelain, "I'm going to tell you about who I am and how I got to where I am now. I've never before been in a situation suitable for me to tell this story. It's a good story. I like it."

MacKenzie sat motionless and uncomfortable, thinking about Erik, and desperately trying to figure out how the two of them would ever escape from their current horrible circumstance.

Chapter 35
CHRONICLE

"I was born the year after World War II ended," Trelain was saying. "I've always been very patriotic, and I joined the military right out of college. I moved up the ranks, and ended up working directly for the government, in one of the many secret unofficial departments.

"Most of our work focused on issues related to the Cold War, but we ended up dealing with a wide range of international-crime issues. I was there for eleven years. During that time, I earned a moderately high security clearance, and ended up with access to some interesting things.

"One day I came across a file about some money that had been seized during an operation. The file had been mis-filed. There was a case-number associated with it, and I knew that number was wrong. Because it was the same number as a completely different case, a different operation that I myself had worked on.

"At first, I thought I'd just report the incorrect file-number duplication. But the government doesn't like to admit mistakes. And they don't like anything that could make them look bad. They often arrange to make serious trouble for the person who found the mistake, and the mistake itself usually ends up getting buried deep and hidden away. So, I knew simply reporting it would fix nothing, and would likely get me fired, if not something even worse.

"But I wanted to make my point. I wanted to reveal the dangers of the flaws in how they did things. So, I decided I might be able to do that more effectively—and more safely for myself—by dramatically demonstrating the flaws in their record-keeping. I thought I could be noble, and heroic, and patriotic by dramatically revealing a crucial failing in how they mis-handled important information.

"So, to prove my point, I went to the evidence archives, and accessed the material with the duplicate case-number. There, along with all the boxes of material from the case I had actually worked on, were two boxes that also had the same file number. But those two boxes weren't from the case I had worked on. They were from the case associated with the mis-filed file I had found. So, I opened them up to see what was inside.

"Well, inside of those boxes was some money. A lot of money. All in cash. There were too many bills to take all at once. I took it gradually, bit by bit, over the course of several months. Then, at the bottom of the second box, I found information about a Swiss bank account. I used the information to access the account, and discovered there was even more money there. A lot more money.

"So, I opened a Swiss bank account of my own, and transferred all the money from the account I had found into the account I had just created. I was sure that would be noticed by someone. But it wasn't. I waited for any of the missing money to be discovered, so I could dramatically make my big point. But no one discovered it was missing.

"Nobody noticed, because no one knew it was there. Because their filing system had a flaw. If they'd had a better records system, someone besides me would have caught on to it at some point. But they didn't, and no one caught on. No one had any idea there was a problem.

"And I realized my plan had a flaw too. I had assumed the government would have some safeguards in place somewhere to alert them when an unknown problem started to show signs of being a real problem. But they didn't. The government was too big, and too disorganized, and too inefficient. And since they had never kept track of that money properly in the first place, they no longer knew it was there, and so they were never going to realize it was missing.

"I would never be able to make my big dramatic point. My plan had failed, and all I had to show for my efforts was the money. I had all that money in cash, and all that money in the Swiss bank account where I would have access to it, but it would never be traced to me. But what to do with it all.

"So, I made a decision. I loved my country too much to endure working any longer in a government that ran itself so incompetently. So, I retired from my government job. That was ten years ago. But before I retired, I came across one other peculiar file. It wasn't filed incorrectly. But there was only one copy of it. So, when I retired, I took that file with me. You see, this file truly fascinated me. It was an old file with all the records of an underground, underwater tunnel between the Los Angeles mainland and the Island of Catalina.

"The history in the file started with an immensely long lava tube, discovered by accident, by soldiers on Catalina during the Civil War. Union Army forces took over the island during the Civil War. They were concerned that Confederate soldiers might come to the island and use the position against the North. The lava tube was discovered while Union Army soldiers were making tactical explorations of all the tunnels, caves, and caverns on the island.

"There was a break in the top of the lava tube. The Union soldiers thought the break just led to another cave tunnel. It did lead to a tunnel, but it was a tunnel much bigger and longer than anything they had ever seen. Union Army geologists examined it. They concluded it was a lava tube which had been formed millions of years ago, and that it was a tunnel of extraordinary length. They also reported finding inside of it what they described as 'ancient primitive tools' and 'ancient cave paintings'.

"The Union Army field officers made a record of the find, and went on about their business. Then the Civil War ended, and the Union military left the island. When World War II started, the military took over Catalina again.

"This time, the government was concerned the island would be invaded by the Japanese and used as a base to launch an attack on the US mainland. When the US entered the war in 1941, someone in our government found the old file about the lava tube, and a team was secretly sent to inspect it. They discovered the truly extraordinary scope of the tunnel. It was over twenty-four miles long. It was a dream come true for them. A millions-of-years-old naturally-occurring secret tunnel running all the way from Catalina to the mainland.

"It was a deep tunnel that ran under the ground, under the water. It started somewhere in the Los Angeles area and ran under the city of Long Beach on the mainland side. It ran under the ground, under the ocean to Catalina Island, where it entered Catalina under the south-east end of the island, and actually extended past Catalina to the west.

"The distance between Catalina and the mainland is only twenty-two miles. But the lava-tube tunnel wasn't a straight line. Its curving winding route was whatever path Mother Nature had dreamed up over the course of millions of years of tectonic plate shift and magma flow. And its location was deep. Most of the lava-tube tunnel was located well below the surface of the ocean floor.

"But over the millions of years, land shift had raised the ends of the tunnel at the land masses—at the Catalina end, and at the Long Angeles end. But it still would require considerable digging to open large enough access points into the tunnel at each end. But the military decided it was worth doing, and they put together a top-secret corps of engineers and workers.

"Access points needed to be dug out, and a railway bed needed to be laid for train track that would run the length of the tunnel. The center of operations for the new lava-tube tunnel infrastructure was going to be based at the Long Beach end. San Pedro Bay, the

Port of Los Angeles, and Port of Long Beach—these areas had already become centers of military activity because of the war. But as many bases of operations as there were in the Los Angeles area, none of them was near the mainland-end of the lava-tube tunnel.

"They decided to access the tunnel in Long Beach, and they had to build a special facility around where the access point was going to be, and then disguise it as just another industrial building complex. This actually worked to their security advantage, making it less likely anyone without a need-to-know would find out about the military activities involving the tunnel.

"On the Catalina end, keeping the operation secret was much easier. The tunnel was not near any existing military bases on the island, and the tunnel itself actually extended slightly beyond the island. But where it passed through the island, it was near a vast network of old mine shafts and mining tunnels and caves, which had led to its discovery in the first place.

"There at the Catalina end, they would be able to create a hidden base in an underground cavern, and then from there do more digging to widen the access point. This would give them a conveniently large staging area, and it was all underground, so no one who didn't need to know about it would know about it. And most importantly, the underground base would be a naturally protected place of military operations, in the event the Japanese did try to invade the island. So, they set up the secret bases of operations, and broke open the access points, and laid the railway bed, and laid train track for the entire length of the tube.

"On-board batteries are the oldest means of supplying electric power to a train car. You don't need a third rail, you don't need overhead wires. You just need an electric engine, and you need a massively large array of batteries, and you need to keep them charged. And that was how the Catalina-tunnel train was powered. They modified a railroad locomotive, making it longer and putting a big electric engine and a huge battery array in the middle of the car.

"It used a steam-braking system, using electric-fired mini-boilers to heat water for steam. Everything about the train was designed to be quiet so it wouldn't be noticed, and efficient because it was wartime. And it had to run clean, since a twenty-four-mile-long tunnel has no ventilation other than the air being moved through it by the motion of the train.

"The train consisted of only one car, intended for specialized transport. There was open space for troops and cargo, and identical driving controls at both ends. Because this train was designed for only one thing: going back and forth, over and over, on a single set of rails. The idea was, the Catalina military operations could be supported secretly, and here was military transport that could not be seen or attacked by Japanese submarines, boats, or planes.

"A well to get water is usually drilled down, but the cavern was already 'down', so they drilled up from the cavern to access an aquifer for the water supply. It was a complicated matter to get the underground base, the tunnel, and the train all in place, and all up and running effectively. But after a few years of work, they had done it. It had only been operating for a few weeks when the war ended in 1945. And now what to do with the tunnel.

"Well, the military sealed it up at both ends, and saved it for a rainy day. The few who knew about it lost interest in it, and it was never de-classified, so no one was ever allowed to speak of it. And over the decades, it's become a lost footnote in a poorly-filed set of government records.

"As you might imagine, I was fascinated by all this. Which is why I took the file with me when I left. And I did some secret investigating of my own. I located the mainland building that had housed the tunnel-access during World War II. It had become an abandoned storage warehouse in the industrial area of Long Beach. So I bought it.

"The warehouse had a hidden lower level that you'd have to know was there to go looking for it. I hired some contractors to break open the floor, to give me access to the lower level. I hired some different contractors to break open the lower floor's sealed access to the tunnel. They did their job, and I paid them well, and they never knew what was down below.

"And then I did some exploring. The tunnel was a long way down, but there it was. And guess what was sitting there after all those years. The modified railroad locomotive. Just sitting there. Like a train in a station. It had a name painted on it, in old World War II lettering, like the side of a Hellcat fighter aircraft. It said, *Torpedo Express*. And then I had a realization.

"I could still force my government to wake up and recognize its flaws. I just needed to do it on a larger scale. So, I decided to start a smuggling operation. I put together a team of people I could trust, who wanted to make a lot money, and who would do whatever was necessary to earn it. I paid them well. I still pay them well. We all share in the profits.

"We got the *Torpedo Express* functional and running. We broke through the sealed Catalina end of the tunnel, and set up our own base of operations in the old Catalina underground cavern military base. That's where we are now. That's where you are now.

"We are smugglers. We import and export high value goods. To whoever pays the most. Whatever their business. Wherever they're from. Whatever country they're from. We move goods back and forth on the *Torpedo Express*. Whatever people want, we get it for them. Whatever people have that they want to get in or out of the country, we move it for them. And they pay us well for the service. Very well. Goods come and go from the Long Beach warehouse. Goods come and go from here, on the island. Mostly, goods go out from here. But at both ends, we sell our goods to our high-paying customers.

"During World War II, the military had created a water under-pass into the cavern of the underground base. Most of the cavern is just above sea level, but there was a low-area which was below sea level. About a quarter mile west of the Seal Rocks, there was a small underwater cave, directly beneath the low area of the cavern. The military cut into the low area, breaking through the top of the underwater cave, intentionally flooding the low area of the cavern.

"The flooding created a sea-lake inside the cavern at its lowest point, and established a water-connection between the cavern and the ocean. There was still no direct way into the cavern, but now there was passage underwater. So it now was possible to enter the cavern from below, through the water. The military had once planned to move small submarines in and out from there, but they never did.

"But the water underpass is still there. The military had it listed in their files as Ocean Hole 1. Now we use it for our customers. Customers in small submarines and submersibles come and go through there. Sometimes customers scuba dive through there. The military had installed a mechanical underwater gate inside Ocean Hole 1, for obvious security reasons. That gate hadn't been operational for decades, so it needed some work. But my crew got it working. Now it stays closed to keep out curious scuba divers, and at night when we've got a known customer on the way, we open it.

"We keep the batteries of the *Torpedo Express* charged, and we're always ready to move. When they were first establishing this base during World War II, the US military set up a power-trans-mission cable that runs through the tunnel alongside the tracks. It carried electric power from a Long Beach power station, to supply electricity to this base. My team and I restored the operation of that cable, and 'adjusted' the metering system. So, the city of Long Beach now provides us unlimited free electricity, although they are unaware that they're doing so.

"Big operations that are run badly either don't know how or don't care to keep track of details. Their waste and inefficiency and willful ignorance are too deeply embedded. And whether it's a power utility or the government, if they don't want to be fixed, you can't fix them. All you can do is try to not to get hurt by them. Or in my case, you can take advantage of their incompetence. And that is what I have done. That is what I do.

"And that's my life, and that is my operation, and that is how I got to where I am today."

In spite of herself, MacKenzie was genuinely puzzled. "But if you already had all that money," she couldn't stop herself from asking, "why bother smuggling? Why did you do all this?"

"Because I could," said Trelain. "And because you can never have too much money. And because I was angry at the incompetence of my country's government. And because I was bored."

"I think those are terrible reasons," said MacKenzie.

Trelain nodded. "They are," he said. "But they are the reasons, nevertheless."

"It all seems so wrong and so unnecessary," said MacKenzie.

"But," said Trelain, "at least it's not boring."

Chapter 36
ADVERSARIES

"**I** don't understand you…" said MacKenzie.

Trelain smiled. "You don't need to understand me. You just need to listen to my story patiently and politely. Which you have done. Admirably well, given the circumstances, I might add."

He paused, then leaned forward, putting his elbows on the surface of the desk. "But now you need to tell me something."

"What am I supposed to tell you?" she asked.

"The man you saw," said Trelain. "The one who was watching you. The one who was watching passengers at Avalon Bay. I need you to describe him to me."

"Why should I help you?"

"Don't think of it as helping. Think of it as politely avoiding unpleasant difficulty."

"What are you going to do with me and my friend?"

"Hmm…" Trelain said thoughtfully. "I have an idea. Describe the man you saw, and I'll tell you what's going to happen to you and your friend."

MacKenzie didn't say anything.

"Oh," Trelain added. "And there's one more thing. I need you to tell me how you got in here. You need to tell me how you found this base. I've been running this operation undetected for more than eight years. Any of our machinery that makes noise or vibrates is located beneath the quarry. Far beneath the quarry, but close enough that quarry operations mask any noise and vibration from our machinery. And the only way in or out of here is either by the ocean-hole, or the railway tunnel."

"Are you doing something to make the buffalo sick?" asked MacKenzie.

Trelain shook his head. "No. There is no connectivity between here and the surface, except for air shafts. They're narrow, and they all open in rock outcroppings, and they're all near the water at the southeast coastline. The bison groups never roam that close to the east end of the island."

"Are you doing something to make the coral sick at the Seal Rocks?"

Trelain was about to shake his head no, and then paused.

"Oh..." he said, and a look of regret crossed his face. "Oh, that would be the gold mine. There's a lot of gold ore down here. It's not the famous buried gold of Catalina. As I said to you and your father in Long Beach, I don't know the details of that story. But I know it's not a tale about an undiscovered gold mine. I suspect there are other underground deposits of gold on the island, just waiting to be found and mined. This one simply happened to be discovered by one of my men, and just happened to be conveniently connected to our tunnel network here. So, we mine it. We make almost as much money selling gold we've mined as we do on sales of all other goods put together."

"Oh my god..." said MacKenzie, realization spilling over her. "You're using cyanide to get the gold out of the rock..."

Trelain looked at her. "Well, aren't you clever..." he said. "Yes, we use cyanide to separate out the gold ore. The tailings—the waste from that process—get pumped into the ocean. The output for that waste is an underwater exhaust vent. It's located right by the Seal Rocks."

"Well, it's killing all the coral there," said MacKenzie. "And also all the tiny water animals that use the coral to survive."

"That is unfortunate," said Trelain. "I genuinely regret that. The

Seal Rocks just happen to be close to where our mining operation is. It was convenient. I hadn't thought that through…"

He paused for a moment before continuing.

"And now your turn," he went on. "We'll start with the easy part. How did you and your friend get down here?"

MacKenzie hesitated. Then she answered. "There are metal stairs," she said. "We found them by accident."

Trelain nodded with immediate recognition and regret.

"Near the old Renton Mine," he said. "Yes. They're listed in the military file as the Renton Stairs. It's amazing what years of weather and salt air can do to exposed metal. When I first inspected that staircase years ago, the door at the top seemed well sealed. I should have had it re-welded anyway. That was a mistake not to…"

Trelain pressed something under his desk, and almost instantly the door was unlocked and opened. A heavily-armed muscular man dressed in the same all-black military-style uniform as the others entered the room. Trelain beckoned the man over and whispered something into his ear. The man nodded in acknowledgement and understanding, then left the room as swiftly as he had entered, locking the door behind him.

"And now," Trelain went on, turning his focus back to MacKenzie. "Your turn again. Describe the man you thought was working for me."

"Tall," said MacKenzie. "He looked like a football player. Bigger than the guy who was just in here. He was wearing sunglasses. He had a scar on his face."

"What color hair?" said Trelain with interest.

"Black," said MacKenzie.

"What color skin?"

"Like he had a sun tan."

"Describe the scar."

"Like this," said MacKenzie, and she ran an index finger from one side of her forehead down to the bone of her jaw.

An ironic smile took over Trelain's face. "So," he said thoughtfully. "I've finally gotten his attention…"

"Who is he…?" asked MacKenzie.

"An old acquaintance," said Trelain. "Reilly Berrigan. Berrigan and I go way back…"

"Is he a good guy or a bad guy?" asked MacKenzie.

Trelain laughed. "Well," he said. "If I'm a bad guy, Berrigan's a good guy. He's a G-man. That's a government man. He works for the government. We used to work in the same department. He's moved on to more top-secret military responsibilities. If he's here, that's why. You thought he was spying on you. That amuses me about you, MacKenzie. You think the world revolves around you. But it doesn't. Only your world revolves around you. The real world doesn't care."

Trelain leaned back in his chair and folded his arms. For a moment he was lost in thought.

"Berrigan…" Trelain repeated at last, unfolding his arms and returning himself to the conversation. "Berrigan's likely been watching everyone getting on or off the ferry. And if he's anything like he used to be, he's been pretty obvious about it. Of course, he may be obvious in his spying, but he's deadly accurate with everything else he does. And he's smart. If he's here, that's why. He's looking for me."

"Why would he think you're here?"

"After eight years," said Trelain, "with an operation as successful as mine, it gets harder and harder to not be noticed by the wrong people. I'm guessing I made some kind of mistake. I may have been identified by someone in Long Beach. I try to be careful. But after so much success, one can become careless. I may have gotten careless. But I think I know the real reason…"

"Is he going to arrest you?"

Trelain laughed again. "He's going to have to catch me first," he said with a grin.

Then his face became serious.

"Well," he said. "That certainly does change things. Changes things quite significantly, actually. Berrigan is like an obsessed dog. Once he has your scent, he's not going to stop until he finds you."

"Now you have to tell me what you're going to do with me and my friend," said MacKenzie.

"Well," Trelain began vaguely. "I don't plan on killing either of you. I wouldn't kill a child. But don't kid yourself. I would use anyone as a hostage, if I needed to."

Trelain paused for moment, lost in thought again.

"I hate to give up this operation..." he mused with a strange hint of nostalgia. "I've spent a lot of time getting it running the way I want. It's not only profitable, it is very enjoyable. But I suppose all things, good and bad, have to end sometime..."

"What are you going to do with me and my friend?" MacKenzie repeated.

Trelain nodded. "Yes, MacKenzie," he said. "I'm well aware you're trying protect your friend by not telling me his name. Quite admirable of you. I will let you have your protection. I'm not interested in his name. But as to what is going to happen to the two of you... Well, I could just take my crew and escape now, and just leave you two to your own devices. You'd figure a way out of here. Of course, not by going back up the Renton staircase. I've already sent a team up those stairs to weld that old door back into place, and reinforce the interior closure. It will be permanently sealed the way it was supposed to be. But you're young and clever. You'd figure something out. Or, you two could just wait for Berrigan to show up. Now that you've alerted me that he's on the island, I'm quite confident he'll find his way down here eventually, one way or another.

But I've got a big buyer coming in tonight. In just a few hours. I want to close that sale. My crew and I will make our escape afterward. On the last train out of town."

He chuckled slightly at his own joke.

"So," he went on. "You, MacKenzie, and your friend are going to sit tight and wait, until that sale is completed. After that, you two will be on your own."

Trelain leaned back in his chair again.

"I don't blame you, MacKenzie, for bringing an end to things," he continued. "In fact, if not for you, I wouldn't know Berrigan was here. That's information I need, to be able to get myself and my crew safely away before he shows up down here. Of course, Berrigan won't be showing up by coming down the way you did, since that access to the top of the Renton Stairs is now being properly re-sealed."

"How do you know he won't just break through it?" asked MacKenzie.

Trelain smiled. "He could. It's a very Berrigan thing to do. He'd bulldoze a house if it would lead him to a guilty cockroach. But he would have to know those stairs exist and where they're located, for one thing. And the skill of my men should not be underestimated. Once they seal something up, it would take explosives to get through. Or perhaps a powerful blow-torch. But that would all take time. I plan to be gone with my crew before Berrigan gets in here, however he does it. And when he does, he'll find you and your friend, and you two will be safe. Unless of course, something unplanned happens too early. Then you two will have to be used as hostages. But I don't expect that to happen, so you shouldn't worry about it."

"You said you've always been patriotic," said MacKenzie. "So why are you in a business that goes against the laws of your own country?"

"I love my country," said Trelain. "I wouldn't want to live anywhere else. But this country's government is run by people who cheat, who lie, who are stupid, and who make decisions based on what is best for them personally and not for the good of the country."

"But, isn't that what you do?" asked MacKenzie. "Things that are only good for you and no one else?"

Trelain nodded. "Yes," he said. "That is exactly what I do."

"I don't understand..."

"If you don't know where the flaws are," Trelain explained, "the flaws don't get fixed. If you don't care about the flaws, they don't get fixed. And if you don't care about something you should care about, then you need something to force you to care about it. That's me. I'm that force. Just because I'm good at what I do, just because I enjoy what I do, that doesn't mean I should be allowed to do it. Why do I always get away with everything? Because there are flaws in the system. Flaws in the government. I'm fairly sure I know the real reason Berrigan's here. You know why he's here? Because I've finally forced him to care about something he wasn't interested in caring about. You know how I finally got his attention? Plutonium. Plutonium is scary. Plutonium means nuclear weapons. Nuclear weapons are dangerous. Very dangerous. And now I've got some stolen bomb-grade plutonium. And I've auctioned it off. I've sold it to the highest bidder for more than what I paid for it. A lot more. And that sale will be completed here, tonight. Plutonium from this country being sold to another country is scary. Very scary. And I suspect Berrigan has somehow found out about it, as I expected he would. When plutonium is stolen, everyone starts paying attention. And now Berrigan finally cares. If he cares enough, he'll be able to stop me. We'll have to wait and see how smart he is. But if people don't do something, things don't change. So, I'm doing something."

"It doesn't seem like the right way to try to change something that needs to be fixed…" said MacKenzie.

"One has to do what one is good at," said Trelain. "I'm very good at what I do. And I enjoy what I do. It's the right way for me."

"I hope you get caught."

Trelain smiled. "You're very honest. And you genuinely care about right and wrong. Try to keep both of those qualities as you get older, MacKenzie. Most people can't. Maybe you will be able to."

"You're very smart," said MacKenzie. "I don't understand why you do bad things. People should help people. Think how much you could help people if you wanted."

"I don't want to help anyone," said Trelain. "No one's ever helped me."

MacKenzie shook her head. "That's no reason," she said. "You shouldn't do the right thing because you owe someone, and you shouldn't do the right thing because it might help you. You should do the right thing because it's the right thing to do."

"I do what's right for me," said Trelain.

Trelain and MacKenzie sat and looked at each other, separated by so much more than Trelain's desk.

"What about the *Queen Mary?*" asked MacKenzie.

"What about her?"

"What's the connection?"

Trelain for the first time looked genuinely surprised. "I find you quite amusing, MacKenzie," he said. "And I'm curious enough to want to know what made you ask me that question."

"You like to talk," said MacKenzie.

Trelain chuckled and nodded. "Ah…" he said with realization. "Our little chat in Long Beach… Well, aren't you clever… What an unusual young lady you are, MacKenzie. Very astute of you. I have a suite of rooms on the *Queen Mary* that I lease year-round. I sometimes stay there. I often use it for meetings…"

Trelain checked his watch. "And speaking of meetings," he went on, "I regret this meeting is at an end. It turns out there's more to do than simply wait for our buyer. We apparently have to start packing. I will be sorry to leave this place," he said earnestly. "These years have been good years…"

He appeared to be lost in thought again for a moment, before returning his focus to the current situation.

"I won't say good-bye to you, MacKenzie," he said. "Because you seem to keep turning up. So perhaps you'll turn up again sometime in my future. But let me tell you how I don't want to see you. I don't want to see you separated from your friend. But I will be forced to move you both to separate areas if you two do anything other than sit still. And I don't want to have to tape over your mouths, because I find it uncivilized. But if either of you speak, that is what will happen. I give clear directions, MacKenzie. All you and your friend need to do is follow them. You're going to have your hands tied now. Just like your friend. Do not resist. You've been very polite under unusual and difficult circumstances. I strongly recommend you continue that attitude. This is not a good time for you to be clever. This is a good time for you to be smart enough to follow directions."

Trelain pressed the button under his desk again and stood up.

The sound of the door unlocking was followed by one of Trelain's men entering.

"She's ready to join her friend," Trelain said to the man.

The man nodded and stepped out for a moment, before returning with a length of the same white cord-rope which had been used to bind Erik.

"Stand up, please," Trelain said to MacKenzie. "Hands behind your back."

MacKenzie stood. She put her hands behind her back, and she could feel them being tied together behind her.

"She can remain with her friend," Trelain said over MacKenzie's head, instructing the man behind her. "Back to back, so they won't be tempted to speak. If they talk, tape their mouths. If they do anything else they shouldn't, move one of them to Block D. Wherever they are, they are to be watched at all times. And there's been a complication," he said, checking his watch again. "After the sale, we leave. All of us. The two children will be left here when we go, unless there are further complications. Everyone should pack up, and gear-up for uninvited visitors. If we have company, it's going to be the big boys and their big toys. Full crew-meeting at the lake in ten minutes, but I want someone keeping an eye on this young lady and her friend."

"Understood," said the voice of the man behind MacKenzie.

Chapter 37

RISK

Trelain left the cave-office and headed off in a direction which MacKenzie decided led to the cave-section that had the sea-lake. Her brain was already memorizing the layout of the cavern complex. She didn't have to ask her brain to do it. It simply was the sort of thing her brain just always did on its own.

The man Trelain had been talking to drew a gun from a side holster and gestured with it at MacKenzie.

"This way," he said to her impatiently. "Let's go."

MacKenzie walked out of the cave-office, the man with gun right behind her.

Another of Trelain's men was waiting for them with a gun drawn.

"Back this way," the other man said to her.

The two men and their guns directed MacKenzie in a direction she recognized as being back the way the she had first been brought, and she hoped it would lead to Erik.

It did. He was sitting on the floor of a cave-section with his hands still tied behind his back, one side of his body next to a cave wall. He was facing away from MacKenzie as she was led over to him, so she couldn't see his face to judge how he was doing. Another of Trelain's men was there apparently in charge of keeping watch, and was standing several feet away holding a gun aimed at Erik.

MacKenzie pretended she didn't know where she was supposed to be going. She intentionally went too far and walked just past Erik. It was far enough that he could see her hands were now tied.

"Hey!" one of the men said harshly. "Back here."

MacKenzie turned around at the command, and stole a moment to look at Erik. They were able to see each other's faces and look at each other's eyes for an instant.

Erik mouthed 'You okay?' at her, and she hurriedly mouthed 'I'm fine' back at him.

"Over here," one of the three men ordered her. "Sit down. No, not like that. Back-to-back. Move!"

MacKenzie sat down, her back against Erik's, both of them surrounded by a cave wall on one side, and three of Trelain's men on the other.

"Eyes up here," one of the men ordered.

MacKenzie and Erik both turned to look up at the three men.

"No warnings," the man said, aiming a gun at them to emphasize his point. "One of you speaks, you both get taped."

The three men then stood close together and began discussing something in low voices that MacKenzie couldn't hear. But she was fairly certain they were talking about the meeting Trelain had ordered. After several minutes of talking, the three men nodded to each other, and two of them left, both walking back in a direction that MacKenzie was increasingly sure led to the sea-lake.

The one man remaining was apparently now their new guard. The meeting about to take place by the sea-lake seemed to be of interest and concern to him, and he didn't seem particularly enthusiastic about having been assigned the job of being left to keep watch over two kids. Even though he was stuck where he was, his attention and focus kept being pulled toward the direction of the meeting, which allowed MacKenzie and Erik the intermittent benefits of slightly less than full-time scrutiny.

They were desperate to not be caught disobeying instructions to stay silent, but MacKenzie and Erik were more desperate to communicate with each other. They took turns, each momentarily turning their head slightly toward the wall next to them, knowing it might bounce-echo their voices, but hoping that was less of a danger than risking the guard seeing their mouths move when they whispered to each other.

"...try to shift facing front slightly, to hide our hands..." was the first thing Eric dared to whisper to MacKenzie.

There was a steady echo of various kinds of sounds coming from different places throughout the cavern, and the combined noises provided enough steady ongoing background sound that, if MacKenzie and Erik were going to get caught whispering, at least they might not be heard right away.

MacKenzie didn't waste any of their luck by asking Erik why he wanted her to move. She just did what he had asked. Moving ever so gradually, scooting her body millimeters at time, she steadily re-oriented herself so that she was facing slightly farther away from the wall, and no longer exactly back-to-back with Erik. She could feel his fingers looking for hers as she sneaked herself slowly into her new orientation.

"...just a bit closer..." whispered Erik in a volume so soft that MacKenzie could hardly hear it, even with her ear right next to him.

Millimeters at a time, she sneaked herself slightly closer to Erik, and right away she could feel he was doing something with the ropes on her hands.

"...what are you doing...?" she dared to whisper, turning her head away from the guard for an instant and trying to be as nearly silent as Erik had been.

"...cutting your ropes..."

"...with what...?"

"...shark tooth..."

MacKenzie tried to adjust her feet and start making her body fidget slightly, hoping the guard would get used to her body making random, small, innocent, harmless movements so that he might be less likely to notice any other movements she or Erik might make.

"...pull your hands apart more..." whispered Erik. "...if I cut you by accident, don't scream..."

"...I never scream..." MacKenzie whispered back.

MacKenzie could feel him sawing away in small strong strokes. He must have been using just his fingers, because she couldn't feel his arms or shoulders moving at all.

After what felt to MacKenzie like hours, but was actually closer to several long minutes, she suddenly felt her ropes loosen, and Erik's fingers stopped what they had been doing.

The two men who had left now returned, and they rejoined the man currently in charge of guarding MacKenzie and Erik. Once again the three men stood close together, conversing with each other in low voices. They were completely focused on the importance and details of whatever they were discussing, and MacKenzie and Erik had some brief moments to whisper to each other with slightly less caution.

"...Okay..." Erik whispered nearly silently while turning his head slightly toward the cave-wall. "...I've cut through... I'm using what I can of my fingers to unwind the rest..."

MacKenzie felt the loose bonds of the ropes falling away from around her wrists.

"...What happens now...?" whispered MacKenzie.

"...You escape out of here and get help..." whispered Erik.

"...How...?"

"...Up the metal stairs, the same way we came..."

"...Trelain's men have sealed it closed..."

"...Oh my god..." Erik whispered in shock and frustration.

"...There's no way out..." whispered MacKenzie. "...And I'm not leaving you..."

"...There's always a way out..." Erik whispered firmly. "...And we can't just wait for them to do whatever they're going to do..."

"...Trelain said he's not going to kill us..." whispered MacKenzie.

"...I don't care what Trelain said..." Erik whispered. "...We know where this place is—they're not going to let us live..."

"...They're going to leave..." whispered MacKenzie. "...All of them—after their big sale..."

"...We can't just sit here and do nothing..." whispered Erik.

"...Can I try to use the shark-tooth to cut you lose...?" MacKenzie whispered.

"...You can try..."

But she couldn't. The three men were done talking, and they all turned toward MacKenzie and Erik.

"Okay, you two," one of the men ordered. "Up. You're being moved."

"...I've got your rope..." Erik dared to whisper hurriedly.

"Shut it," ordered the man. "Up. Now. Move!"

They stood. MacKenzie held her hands closely behind her back as if they were still tied together. Erik had had the presence of mind to grasp her rope inside his closed hands, so at least it wouldn't be there on the ground in plain sight when they stood up.

"Okay," the man ordered, waving his gun. "Turn around. That way. Walk."

And that was that. There would be no hiding her untied hands now.

MacKenzie and Erik turned as they were told. In an instant, the men saw that MacKenzie's hands were no longer tied.

"Hey!!" one of them shouted.

"Mac, run!!!" yelled Erik.

MacKenzie ran. Behind her, she could hear the voice of one of the men talking into the mic of his walkie-talkie. "I've got a runner," his voice was reporting. "The girl's loose. She's heading toward Block A."

A response from the walkie-talkie squawked back immediately. "We're here. We'll get her."

MacKenzie kept running. She didn't know where she was headed, but she knew what route she didn't want to take—the same one she and Erik had been taken on after they first had been captured. She was sure that was what Trelain's men would be expecting her to do.

She had looked at all the cave-rooms and cave-passages they had passed when she and Erik were being brought to Trelain. Now she had to trust that her mind had made a map of what connected to what.

On an impulse, she ran down a passage she had never been through. It led to another cave-room she had never been in. She kept running. She made turns when her impulse told her to, she ran straight when she had a feeling she should run straight. She could hear heavy fast footsteps and angry voices echoing everywhere.

Ahead of her, she suddenly saw a familiar sight—the cave-room with all the stacked crates that connected to the steps down to the tunnel. She was running toward it from a different passage, but she recognized it. She dashed through the small cave-room and leapt down the small flight of stone steps to the rear of the train. She was back in the tunnel.

She turned left toward the direction she and Erik had first come from and kept running. As fast as she could, she raced back the way they had come in the narrow path between the curved tunnel wall and the gravel supporting the railroad ties. Across the tracks, the side of the tunnel with the power and communication cables was now on her right as she ran.

She had just reached the top of the small rise in the slope of the tunnel when she heard voices behind her.

"She's heading down the tunnel!" someone shouted.

MacKenzie ran up over the rise, and then the tunnel began to slope down steeply.

I cannot run twenty-two miles through this tunnel to Long Beach she heard her thoughts saying.

She knew the door at the top of the Renton Stairs was now sealed up, but for some reason she was running back to the metal stairs anyway. The sounds of heavy-booted footsteps got louder and closer behind her.

As she reached the passage she and Erik had first come through to get into the tunnel, she threw herself down onto all fours and crawled through the opening as fast as she could. She was prepared for the passage being dark. She knew it started low, and there were curves and turns. She crawled as fast as she could. As soon as she knew the ceiling was higher, she got to her feet and ran with her head down. Her speed was slowed by having to keep lightly touching the walls in the dark so she wouldn't run into them.

She was expecting the passage to be black with darkness all the way to the stairs as it had been before, but it wasn't. There was now light coming from somewhere ahead of her. She knew that wasn't good. But for the moment it was allowing her to see where she was going, and she began to run at top speed.

When she ran out of the passage into the cave at the bottom of the Renton Stairs, she saw where the light was coming from. Battery-operated work-lights had been set up in the cave and all around the bottom of the staircase. The door-sealing team, she realized. If their lights were still here, they were still on the stairs somewhere.

As if to confirm her fears, she heard voices squawking from walkie-talkies less than two flights up.

"She's heading for the stairs," a squawking voice reported from the staircase just above her.

Then she heard the descending heavy footsteps and actual voices of the men coming down the stairs. "On our way down now."

Behind MacKenzie, waving flashlight beams were now coming toward her fast from the passage she had just run out of.

I must have run here for a reason she thought frantically. But her body didn't have time to listen to what her mind was thinking. It had already made an impulsive decision.

MacKenzie dashed under the staircase. There at the bottom of the stairway-shaft, directly beneath the last flight of stairs she and Erik had come down, were the several different-sized openings in the side of the earthen wall at the level of the dirt ground, hidden beyond the metal beams of the central stair support. The smallest was no higher than a foot-and-a-half. Like a very large mouse, MacKenzie dove forward into it and began crawling forward as fast as she possibly could

Chapter 38

DARKNESS

Crawling wasn't easy. The passage was like a drainage pipe in how small it was. MacKenzie definitely couldn't stand, and she could barely raise herself high enough to crawl on her hands and knees.

She was crawling forward in complete darkness. The small size and close sides of the passage had a benefit, in that MacKenzie didn't have to try to figure out where to go. There was nowhere to go except forward, and that path was tightly limited.

The passage seemed to be going upwards, which made crawling more difficult. It also had many twists and turns, which MacKenzie was actually grateful for because that might make it harder for her pursuers to either see her or make their way closer to catching her.

She didn't have time to be scared of the dark or of what might be in the passage ahead of her. MacKenzie had two fears that were making all her other fears seem small. She was afraid that at any moment her feet would be grabbed from behind by one of Trelain's men. Her other fear was that the passage would either suddenly end, or simply become so small and narrow that she wouldn't be able to crawl any farther.

Out of breath and exhausted, at last she had to stop crawling. She paused for a moment and listened. She couldn't hear anything behind her. She could only hear the sound of her own breathing echoing shallowly off the tight closeness of the passage. The racing of her heart was making the blood pound in her ears. She could feel herself sweating, from exertion and from fear.

The passage smelled like old rock and old dirt, and she could smell how close the top and sides of the passage were. She had never before imagined what it would be like to be inside a closed coffin, but that thought now came darkly into her mind.

On her hands and knees in black darkness, she tried to catch her breath. She tried not to think about where she was or how much earth there was all around her. And she tried to figure out what she should do next.

MacKenzie could feel her necklace swaying idly as she let her legs fold back onto her heels to rest. She reached up for a moment with one hand to hold her 1951 penny for comfort and strength.

Then she thought about Erik. She had to somehow find a way out of the situation she was in so that she could get help to him. Erik would never have left her, and she despised herself for leaving him. She turned her frustration and anger at herself into forward motion and resumed crawling, as fast as she possibly could.

And while she was crawling and trying to find something hopeful anywhere in her thoughts, something came to her. From somewhere in front of her was a smell she recognized. It was the scent of fresh air. It was only faint. But it was definite. Somewhere ahead of her was fresh air.

But now the passage was getting smaller. It was still sloping upward, but it had become so low that she now had to crawl on her stomach and move herself forward with the motion of her elbows and her toes. Only the fear of who might be behind her, and the faint but persistent smell of fresh air coming from somewhere in front of her kept her moving onward, even as she was squeezed by the appalling closeness of the rock and dirt pressing her on all sides.

Soon she had a new fear. The passage was now sloping so steeply upward, she was afraid she was going to start sliding backward. But the horrible tightness of the passage now was actually helping her. Moving any part of her body pressed her against rock and dirt, enough to stop her from falling if the passage kept getting steeper.

And then some of her worst fears were realized. The passage suddenly sloped nearly straight up, and at the same time had become too narrow for her to move any father forward.

Forced to finally stop, she lay motionless where she was, earth pressing in all around her in total darkness. She felt tears and despair and cold panic about to overwhelm and crush her.

On an impulse, she unbent her elbows and stretched her arms out, up into the black unknown ahead of her. Her fingertips found an edge. Grasping onto it, she held on firmly and pulled herself upward, forcing herself through tight surrounding earth that didn't want to let go of her. After a moment, her elbows were free of the passage. She rested her weight on them, and then used the leverage of her arms to pull herself the rest of the way out.

She no longer was in any kind of passage. She still couldn't see anything, but she could feel how much she now was in a very different space. There was vast openness all around her, and she was able to stand up. And in this new space, the scent of fresh air was stronger than ever.

MacKenzie extended both arms out protectively in front of her and began to walk forward toward the smell of fresh air. After several successful steps, she began walking faster, keeping her hands spread wide, ready to feel for anything in the darkness that might block her path.

Then she tripped over something and fell. There was a loud clattering, and suddenly she was covered. Something was all over her. She thrashed about in a frantic wild panic, rolling and trying to push off of herself all that was suddenly covering her. She waved her arms and fought blindly. She didn't know what she fighting, but she felt as though somehow she was defeating whatever it was, and she could feel the pieces of weight on top of her falling away.

At last she rolled herself free, and kept rolling. Something in her pocket was pressing into the side of her leg, and her flashlight was digging into her hip, but she kept rolling. She rolled until she was stopped by what felt like a wall of rock.

She desperately found her dead flashlight with her fingers and slid it out of its holster. She was terrified of revealing her location to her pursuers if she could get the light to work, and more terrified that she wouldn't be able to get the light to go on. She was terrified most of all by whatever had attacked her—what was there in the space with her right now that she couldn't see.

Gasping in terror and sweating cold shivering fear, she pressed the button on the flashlight barrel. Nothing happened. Her panic mounting, she shook it hard several times and desperately hammered with the heel of her hand against the side of the top. At last it flickered to life, shining a dim weak beam, throwing its fading light out across the space in front of her. And then she saw what had attacked her.

In the dark, she had run right into it. It was a pile of objects. They were all different sizes and shapes. And the pile was immense. She had to aim her dying flashlight high to see the top. The pile towered more than 30 feet upward. It was a mountain of piled-up objects. She had run into the bottom of it, and one side of the pile had cascaded down on top of her. She could see, scattered across the dirt and rock of the floor, all the objects which had fallen on top of her, that she had flung about in all directions as she had fought to escape from them in the dark.

It was all gold. The objects she had accidentally kicked and tripped over in the dark were gold. The objects that had fallen on top of her were gold. Towering up toward a ceiling so high that the dim light of her dying flashlight wouldn't reach it, the mountainous pile was entirely objects made of gold.

Her momentary astonishment and awe did not have time to linger. She had to keep going. She had to escape. She had to not get caught. She had to somehow get back to the surface and outside so that she could get help to save Erik.

Her Cubs baseball cap had come off in the skirmish. She spotted it on the floor of the cavern, amidst all the gold objects she had disturbed and scattered in her frantic struggle.

She knelt down and crawled her way back along the path where she had rolled, quickly pushing or tossing the strewn gold objects back into the giant pile where they belonged. Gingerly aiming the flickering beam of her flashlight, she hurriedly tidied up the mess she had made until she arrived at her cap. Several small gold objects and pieces of gold jewelry had fallen into it. She carefully dumped them out, back onto the base of the pile. After shaking the cap to be sure none of the smallest gold objects had gotten stuck, she hastily put it back on her head.

MacKenzie took a fast look around to determine where to go—how to exit the cavern and pursue the smell of fresh air. Spotting a small opening at the level of the floor several feet away, she hurriedly made her way toward it. And then her flashlight failed again. No amount of shaking would bring it back to life. She put it back into its holster at her waist by touch, got back down on her hands and knees, and crawled toward where she had last glimpsed the small opening. She could smell the faint cool promise of fresh air as she moved forward.

The opening was so small, it was nearly impossible for her to squeeze through. But once her shoulders had been forced through, she was able to pull the rest of herself past the tight opening.

The passage on the other side was hardly larger than the hole she had just crammed herself through. But the smell of fresh air was stronger, and it spurred her onward.

Like the previous passage she had pulled herself out of, this passage was almost too narrow to move through. And like the previous passage, it suddenly was sloping steeply upward the farther along she crawled.

Soon the slope was completely vertical, and crawling became impossible. But this passage was wider than the one where she had previously gotten stuck, and the closeness of the passage sides now worked to her advantage in a very particular way. With her feet pushing on opposite sides, and her hands pushing on opposite sides, she was able to work her way up the now fully-vertical path in quick scooting jumps.

She had climbed between two walls like this before. It was a game she had played with her friends. She would press with her feet against opposite walls, and press against opposite walls with her hands. By holding herself in place with her hands, she could scoot her feet a little higher, and by holding herself with her feet, she could then scoot her hands a little higher. It only took a few repetitions of this to get to the top of a doorway or the ceiling of a narrow corridor. She had done this once by herself at her home, back in Chicago, in the one narrow hallway of the house. She had been a rising splayed air-bridge across the hallway, scooting herself in quick alternating repeating pushes up toward the ceiling until her father had discovered her, and had made her get down and promise not to do it again.

But now it was saving her. It was a strangely efficient way to climb. She scooted herself upward, covering numerous inches with every scoot.

As she neared the top, a new fear took hold of her. She had been scooting upward for some time. That meant there was now a long distance of empty nothingness directly below her. If she slipped, it would be a fall no one could survive. She desperately wished the thought of all that straight-down space had never occurred to her. At least she couldn't see how far down the frightening emptiness extended below. She was still in total darkness.

Or she thought she was. But something made her tilt her head to look up. A calm glow of red-blue light from the sky of the fading day was visible though a small hole somewhere not much farther above her. It may have been the most beautiful and wonderful sight she had ever seen in her life.

She continued her crablike vertical scooting upward until she was right at the top. The opening was significantly smaller than the passage, and she realized that getting herself through it was going to be an extremely tight fit.

Holding herself in place with the wall-to-wall pressure of her feet, she reached her hands and arms through the small opening just above her. Once again, getting her shoulders through was the hardest part. After squirming and shifting and stretching, at last she was able to haul the first part of herself through. Supporting her weight with her elbows over the outer edge of the narrow hole, she then pulled and lifted the rest of her body. And suddenly she had squeezed herself out and was sitting on the rim of an opening barely wide enough for her body to have forced itself through.

She was outside. The realization and the sudden vast openness and fresh air all around her momentarily filled her with overpowering exhilarated relief.

The storm had passed, and the lucent pre-twilight sky was tranquil and clear. The sun had not yet set, and there still was plenty of light left in the day.

MacKenzie looked around. She was sitting atop a small outcrop of rock extending upward near several other similar rock formations, the bottoms of which were all hidden amidst expansive tangles of overgrowth and bushes. She was perched about ten feet up from wherever the ground was.

Quickly swinging her legs the rest of the way out of the small hole, she climbed down the unremarkable-looking rocky tower into the heart of the bushes. She forced and fought her way through the dense overgrowth and out into the more open space of the surrounding foothills.

She stood for a moment, re-living in her head as fast as she could the complex elaborate route of passages she had taken to get out, memorizing all of it.

Hurriedly putting a hand below the front of her neck, she checked to see if her necklace was still in place, which it was. She lifted her right arm to look at her Cubs wristwatch. The band was filthy and scuffed, and the glass covering was badly scratched. But beneath the scratched glass, the second-hand was moving and seemed to be proceeding at the proper speed. Which meant she could trust what time it said, which was 6:52.

That gave her just over an hour before sunset. She looked around to get her bearings for where she now was. The landscape looked familiar, in that it was the foothills. It looked completely unfamiliar, in that she had never been to this part of the foothills before. But she had a feeling that where she now stood was a long way from the top of the Renton Stairs, and even farther from where she and Erik had left their bikes.

She turned around a last time and memorized where she was, and what the small rocky tower with the entrance back into the passages looked like. It was utterly unremarkable. It looked identical to countless other nearby random rock outcrops surrounded with wildland clusters of plants and weeds and brush. But she memorized it anyway.

MacKenzie often followed her impulses, no matter how rash, but she didn't always trust her instincts. But there was one instinct she knew she could trust, and that was her sense of direction. Accurate maps seemed to form as if by magic in her head, and seemed to always be there for her to refer to and rely on. Even in a new place, she seemed to instinctively always know the right way to go.

As she had when she was fleeing Trelain's men in the cavern, she depended on that instinct now. She simply trusted herself to head in the right direction, and she took off running, faster than she had ever run in her life.

Chapter 39
ASSISTANCE

It wasn't long before the path of MacKenzie's running took her past the tangle of bushes and overgrowth where she and Erik had found the metal door, which connected to what MacKenzie now knew was the top of the Renton Stairs. And then she fully had her bearings, and all the maps in her head aligned and locked into place.

MacKenzie kept running, now toward where she knew she and Erik had left their bikes. She had to get there as fast as she could, and then pedal back to the cottage as quickly as possible. Her father would know what to do then.

Somewhere in the back of her awareness, she started hearing the sound of a gas-powered vehicle somewhere behind her. It occurred to her that, except for the *Torpedo Express*, it had been a long time since she had heard an engine which wasn't a boat-motor or an electric-powered golf cart. She had now been running and breathing so hard, that she hadn't heard the gas-powered vehicle approaching. She also didn't realize until it was too late that someone had been running behind her.

Just as MacKenzie was about to reach the bushes where she and Erik had stashed their bicycles, she was grabbed from behind. Strong hands wrapped around her arms and shoulders in a powerful grip, and all of her forward motion was abruptly halted. A deep terrifying voice in her ear commanded her to stop. She had been captured again.

With a roar of engine-acceleration, a large black four-wheel-drive vehicle with dark windows raced around from somewhere behind her and skidded to a stop right in front of her. The doors rapidly opened, and half-a-dozen men in suits and sunglasses leapt from the vehicle and quickly surrounded MacKenzie and whoever was holding her.

"Ms. Milles…" said the voice of whoever was holding her. It was a vast powerful voice, like the voice of a giant who had briefly decided not to crush the little fairy-tale town with one footstep, but might change his mind at any moment.

The circle of men in suits closed in, seemingly to ensure that MacKenzie could not run off. The large hands holding her shoulders let go, and MacKenzie was released. She whirled around to face her new captor.

"Ms. Milles…" the man with the deep voice said again, and he reached into an inside pocket of his suit jacket and took out what looked like a wallet. He flipped it open, revealing a United States Government identification and a large gold badge. But MacKenzie didn't need to read it to know what it said. The man standing in front of her holding out his ID was an extremely big man, built like a large football player. A long scar ran down the right side of his face all the way to his jaw.

"You're Berrigan!" MacKenzie yelled. "You have to help me! Trelain's got my friend Erik! We have to save him! We have to save Erik!"

Berrigan's men all exchanged fast puzzled glances at hearing MacKenzie say the names of both Berrigan and Trelain.

Berrigan put his ID wallet away and took off his sunglasses. His eyes were piercing like Trelain's, but less blue and more grey. Trelain's eyes had seemed mischievous and dangerous and unpredictable. Berrigan's eyes seemed icy and deadly and determined.

"Listen to me!" MacKenzie implored. "Trelain has a secret underground base, and he has the stolen plutonium you're looking

for, and the buyer is coming to the base any minute now in a minia-
ture submarine! You have to do something! You have to help me
save Erik!"

Even with their sunglasses still on, Berrigan's men appeared
genuinely astonished to hear what MacKenzie was saying.

A strange expression had instantly taken over Berrigan's face. It
was like the look of a hungry wild animal who has just smelled fresh
meat that might vanish any moment.

Berrigan pointed to the car. "Get in," he said to MacKenzie.
"Quick. Tell me what you know. All of it. As quickly as you can."

MacKenzie looked up at Berrigan and made a split-second
impulsive decision. "Okay," she said hurriedly. "I'll tell you. But you
have to listen really fast. Because you have to save Erik right away.
And you have to promise that no matter what happens, Erik won't
get hurt..."

Berrigan nodded his agreement to MacKenzie, then nodded to
his men who all climbed swiftly back into the large black vehicle,
which MacKenzie now realized had several large antennas sticking
out from it in various places, including a large wide antenna attached
to the roof.

"Front seat, Ms. Milles..." Berrigan instructed her quickly,
taking large rapid strides toward the vehicle.

MacKenzie hurried to the passenger-side front seat. The door
was already open.

Berrigan was about to climb into the driver's seat.

Before either of them got in, MacKenzie stopped and pointed
toward the nearby foothills in the direction of the bushes that hid
the door to the Renton Stairs. "And we need to drive that way right
now," she said urgently. "I'll show you where..."

As they drove off, two of Berrigan's man in the seats
behind MacKenzie already had on radio headsets with mics and

headphones, and were busily giving orders and instructions to someone somewhere.

MacKenzie had already started telling Berrigan everything she knew about Trelain's underground base and the buyer coming to get the stolen plutonium. "I didn't see the ocean lake inside the cavern," she was saying. "But I know where it is."

The vehicle was bouncing over the uneven terrain of the foothills as they approached the cluster of bushes that was hiding the metal door. With one hand on the wheel, Berrigan snapped the fingers of his other hand toward the seats behind him, and moments later a pad of paper and a pen had been handed to him. He passed them over to MacKenzie as he drove.

"Draw the layout of the cavern, please, Ms. Milles," he instructed.

MacKenzie took the pen and paper. "Does that mean—" she began.

"Make a picture of where everything is," Berrigan said briskly. "Try to make it clear what size things are, compared to other things in the picture."

MacKenzie started drawing, but then looked up and pointed. "No, not there," she said to Berrigan. "Go that way. It's that bunch of bushes over there…"

Moments later, they had pulled up next to the correct spot.

"If you crawl through those bushes," MacKenzie was saying, "there's a metal door in the side of a big rock. Trelain sealed it back up, and he said you'd need explosives or some kind of torch to get through. But those stairs lead down to the base…" She held up her picture for Berrigan and his men to see. "They go to right here. There's a lot of stairs. It's a long way down. It took me and Erik seventeen minutes to get to the bottom."

Berrigan snapped his fingers again and pointed toward the

bushes. Two of his men hurried out of the vehicle and quickly crawled into the cluster of bushes.

One of the men still in the vehicle was already giving someone somewhere instructions over the radio headset about the location of the Renton Stairs and how to get the metal door open.

MacKenzie had turned to a new page on the pad of paper and was drawing another picture showing part of the underground layout. "At the bottom of the stairs," she said as she drew, "there's a kind of cave. You have to go through this passage here, which kind of curves and has a bunch of turns, and keeps getting smaller. But at the end, you come out here, in the train tunnel…"

"Excuse, me, sir…" one of the men said to Berrigan. "Train tunnel…?"

"Ms. Milles…?" said Berrigan.

"There's a train that goes under the ground under the water," MacKenzie said hurriedly. She finished her drawing and held it up to show Berrigan and the men sitting behind him. "You go along the train tracks this way, and at the back of the train, there are some steps over here that go from the tunnel into this room here. That leads to all the other parts of the base that I drew on the first page."

She handed the pad and the pen back to Berrigan.

Berrigan studied both pages of layout for a few moments, then nodded and lifted the pad and the pen up in the air, where they were retrieved by one of the men sitting behind him.

"Remember," MacKenzie said to Berrigan. "You promised that Erik won't get hurt when you send everyone in to get Trelain and his men."

Berrigan nodded. "Ms. Milles," he went on, his deep voice filling the inside of the vehicle. "This is possibly the most important piece of information I need from you. What exactly did Trelain say about the location of the ocean-water underpass into the cavern?"

"He said it was about a quarter mile west of the Seal Rocks," said MacKenzie.

Berrigan lifted a hand and snapped his fingers again.

"Understood, sir," acknowledged one of the men on radio headsets, and he began speaking rapidly to someone over his microphone.

"Trelain said there's a 'mechanical underwater gate' that blocks the entrance," said MacKenzie. "He said that at night, when they've got a 'known customer' on the way, they open it."

Berrigan lifted a hand and snapped his fingers again.

"Understood, sir," one of the men on a headset acknowledged again.

"But," MacKenzie began, "how will you—"

"There are US Navy ships," Berrigan said briskly, "already positioned several miles out, all around the island. We knew Trelain was making the sale tonight. But we didn't know how or where. Because of you, we now know. I don't think you fully understand how valuable this information is, Ms. Milles. We must prevent that plutonium from leaving the country. Because of you, we now have a way to do that."

"Thank you…" said MacKenzie politely. "But what's the plan to protect and rescue Erik?"

"That's being factored into the operation," said Berrigan.

"I have no clue what that means…" said MacKenzie.

"We understand there's an innocent civilian boy held hostage in the cavern," said Berrigan. "Everything possible will be done to ensure his safety."

"Why have you been watching me ever since I came to Catalina?" asked MacKenzie.

"You were seen talking with Trelain at a dock in Long Beach," said Berrigan.

"He was talking with my father, too," said MacKenzie.

Berrigan nodded. "We've been watching your father, as well," he said. "But your father's whereabouts have been easy to follow. Your whereabouts, however, have been more of a challenge."

The two men now crawled out from the bushes and stood up. Their suits were smeared with mud. They jogged hurriedly to the vehicle and quickly climbed back inside.

"Just as she described, sir," one of the men reported.

"How long to cut through?" asked Berrigan.

"Ten to fifteen minutes," the man replied.

"How soon will the land-assault team be here?" asked Berrigan.

One of the other men on a radio headset answered. "Forty minutes, sir," he said.

"How soon can the naval-assault team be ready?" asked Berrigan.

"They're in position now, sir," reported one of the men on a headset. "They're prepared to take action as soon as the foreign mini-sub shows up on sonar. If you give authorization, sir."

Berrigan lifted a hand and snapped his fingers again, and one of the microphone-headsets was handed to him.

Berrigan put the headset on and spoke into the mic. "This is Berrigan. Put the commander on, please." There was a brief pause, and then Berrigan went on. "Commander," he said. "No SEAL Team on this. Just the armored mini-subs. I don't want to jeopardize the safety of the divers. The land-assault team will move-in on your green-light... Yes, Commander, that's a correct number—minimum of fifty-five minutes before that team will be in position. I authorize you to take immediate action as necessary to intercept the foreign sub. But your armored mini-sub assault must be coordinated with the land-assault team. Very good. Thank you, Commander."

Berrigan took off the headset and held it in the air, where it was retrieved by one the men sitting behind him.

"Ms. Milles," said Berrigan. "How did you get from the base back up here to the foothills?"

There were so many aspects of MacKenzie's escape that she hadn't had time to think about. But her mind had been thinking about them for her, while she had been busy with other things, so part of her already knew why she now wasn't going to tell the whole truth.

"I got lucky," MacKenzie began honestly. "I accidentally found a tiny passage that led to a bunch of other even smaller passages, and one of them ended up going all the way up to the foothills. They were all too small for full-sized people. I could hardly fit through."

"Where is the place where you finally came out?"

MacKenzie shook her head. "I was so scared and confused, I don't remember where I came out," she lied.

She couldn't tell if Berrigan believed her or not. But one thing seemed clear—he didn't seem especially interested in her escape route. All the other information she had given Berrigan was valuable to him, and that was what he seemed to be focused on.

The engine of the four-wheel-drive vehicle had been running the entire time, and Berrigan now put the vehicle into gear. "Ms. Milles," he said. "You have been extraordinarily helpful. Now it's time to take you home."

It was still half-an-hour before sunset when Berrigan's black vehicle pulled up in front of the cottage at 7:30. John and Katie were just arriving in Bertie, and there was a sudden flurry of alarm and concern and mostly confusion as everyone got out of their vehicles. MacKenzie ran into her father's arms, and Berrigan briskly suggested that everyone head inside the cottage to discuss what had happened, and what was about to happen.

Berrigan had brought only two of his men with him into the cottage, but Berrigan was large enough that he occupied a lot of space just on his own. Everyone in the living room was standing except MacKenzie. She had unrolled layers of paper towels onto the couch coffee table so she could sit without getting all her of her mud and grime and dirt on everything. In the light of the living room, she could really see how disgusting and filthy her clothes were. She silently promised herself to not look in a mirror because she was sure she must look worse than dreadful. And that thought caused her a sharp pang of guilt, as she realized that how she looked must be filling her father with terrible worry and distress.

"Mr. Milles," Berrigan was saying. "Thanks to information from your daughter, we now may be able to stop an illegal sale of stolen bomb-grade plutonium to some very bad people from a foreign country. And we may be able to finally bring to an end a dangerous smuggling operation the United States Government has been trying to find for years."

There was a lot of explaining to do, and there was a lot of emotion involved in the things MacKenzie was describing and how her father was dealing with processing all of it. With some of the more harrowing details, John's and Katie's hands found each other to hold on tightly for a fleeting moment of shared emotion and reassurance, before quickly letting go.

There were a lot of questions, and most of the answers needed a lot of clarification.

Under Berrigan's watchful eye, an attempt was made to contact Brenda by telephone, but no one answered. MacKenzie explained that Brenda was out someplace with some of her friends and had planned with Erik to pick him up at the cottage at 10:30. Katie suggested she could head into town and try to find Brenda, who she was sure would need and want to know what was happening with Erik. But Berrigan would not allow that, and increasingly it seemed to MacKenzie that, even though she and her father and Katie were the good guys, they were going to be kept in the cottage and watched as if they were under arrest.

As if to prove MacKenzie's suspicions, Berrigan went on to explain that two of his men would now remain at the cottage until the two assault-missions had been completed. For reasons of National Security, John and Katie and MacKenzie were not to have any telephone contact with anyone until further notice. Berrigan assured everyone he would be maintaining radio-contact with the men now assigned to the cottage, and they would pass along any information of importance.

The two men receiving their new assignment reminded MacKenzie of the man in the cavern who had been guarding her and Erik. He had been forced to miss the important lake-meeting because he was stuck baby-sitting two kids. Berrigan's men seemed like they wanted to be back in the vehicle and working to help the mission succeed, and instead they now were stuck keeping an eye on three ordinary people in a little cottage while all the real action was going to happen without them.

Berrigan meanwhile seemed as preoccupied with the two assault-missions he had authorized, as MacKenzie was preoccupied with worry about Erik. MacKenzie could tell that Berrigan needed to get out of the cottage and back to work, and MacKenzie understood the feeling. She needed to get back to Erik and help him. It was now clear to her that on Berrigan's list of what was most important, saving Erik was not near the top. Berrigan wanted to rescue the dangerous plutonium, and he wanted to finally catch Trelain. MacKenzie did not really blame Berrigan. But she also now realized it was up to her to save Erik.

Chapter 40
RETURN

Less than fifteen minutes had passed before Berrigan left and drove off, but it had felt to MacKenzie more like several complicated frustrating hours. A large portable communications radio had been brought from Berrigan's vehicle into the living room. Its large size and complex controls made the short-wave radio in front of the television seem like a toy by comparison. The two men from Berrigan's team who remained in the cottage had quickly made the device operational, setting it up on the couch coffee table and plugging it in, before connecting microphone headsets to it with long cables.

Further adding to the awkward uncomfortable tension and stress which had taken over the living room, Berrigan's men refused to sit. They stood with their headsets over their ears, microphones on small boom-arms positioned in front of their mouths, periodically speaking in low voices, and mostly simply standing and watching like restless museum guards.

MacKenzie had been forced to move her layered paper-towel dirt-shield from the coffee table to the rug, where she now sat grappling with a storm of emotions and trying to collect her racing thoughts.

John and Katie sat unhappily in their armchairs and looked concerned and worried and confused, and filled with anxiety. With Berrigan's men watching and listening to everything, it was impossible for anyone to feel free to speak, yet everyone's face revealed they all very much wanted and needed to be speaking with each other.

MacKenzie was dimly aware that the mud and grime now smeared across the front of her father's clothing was her own fault, having transferred some of the outermost residue of her ordeal onto her father from her filthy clothing when she had hugged him.

Various forms of earthen dust and dirt seemed to have found their way onto and into every part of MacKenzie's clothing, which had never fully dried out from the storm. However uncomfortable she felt on the outside, it was nothing compared to the discomfort she was experiencing in her mind. She felt guilty for the anxiety she was causing in her father and Katie, and immediately felt even worse at the thought that she at least got to be with her family, while Erik was abandoned and stranded far below the ground in a horrible and dangerous circumstance, far from his family or anyone who might help or comfort him.

"Mac," her father said quietly, "I don't know when you last had any water, but you should have some water now..."

"Erik can't have any water..." she said miserably. "I don't see why I should be able to..."

"The people from the Government are going to make sure he's safely rescued..." said John.

MacKenzie and her father and Katie all glanced apprehensively for a moment toward Berrigan's two men who were pretending they weren't listening, or genuinely weren't listening, or were listening and didn't care.

"I left him there..." MacKenzie said softly, turning back toward her father and Katie, and fighting back tears. I left Erik... He would never have left me..."

"It sounds like he did everything he could to help you escape..." said Katie.

"So that I could get help," replied MacKenzie, "but nobody's helping him...!"

She stood up abruptly. "I have to go..." she said with sudden adamant resolve.

"Mac..." her father said warningly.

Berrigan's men both took a step forward. "Ms. Milles," one of them said with stern firmness. "You're not going anywhere. You're staying put, right here. It's being handled. It will all be taken care of."

"To the bathroom," MacKenzie clarified. "I have to go to the bathroom."

She walked purposefully out of the living room. At the edge of her peripheral vision, she could see one of Berrigan's men starting to remove his headset so that he could follow her.

The familiar hallways of the cottage were very much easier to navigate than unknown underground passages. There were two turns to get to the bathroom. The instant she reached the foot-sound safety of the hallway carpeting, she sprinted forward, dashing to the bathroom and turning on the light and the ceiling fan. Then she locked the door from the inside, and closed it from the outside. Turning swiftly, she hurried to her bedroom and ducked inside, closing the door most of the way, but leaving it slightly ajar and leaving all the lights off.

Instants later, she heard the heavy steps of one of Berrigan's men coming down the hall. MacKenzie stood motionless against the wall of her room next to where the door was hinged. She heard the man walk past and turn the corner toward the bathroom. A moment later, she heard him walking back. The door of her room was momentarily swung open, and after a pause it was returned to its previous nearly-closed position. The sound of the man's footsteps continued back down the hall, but stopped before going all the way back to the living room.

MacKenzie tip-toed to her bedroom window. It was always wide open, because she liked to have lots of fresh clean air while she was sleeping. She glanced down at her bed.

For a moment she wanted nothing more than to climb into her bed and snuggle safely and comfortably under the covers. She wanted to disappear from everything into sweet sleep, and then wake up in the sunlight of a new day where everyone was saved and happy, and everything had been solved and taken care of, and trouble was just a dark distant memory.

Then the mounting urgent panic of reality pulled with heavy coldness at her stomach, and she turned back toward the window. Silently lifting away the screen, she climbed with rapid stealth through the window frame and then pulled the screen soundlessly back into place after her.

Even though the garage usually stayed locked, there was an outside door at the back of the cottage that connected with the garage. That door had never been locked. MacKenzie noiselessly opened it and hurried to retrieved her cottage-bike from where it was leaning against a garage wall. Rolling it backwards so the rear wheel wouldn't tick, she made sure to not let the moving pedals knock into anything as she backed it out and re-closed the backdoor to the garage.

Still rolling the bicycle backward, she walked with her bike in a wide arc through the trees on the opposite side of the cottage from the living room until she had reached a large area of grass away from the cottage. Hurrying herself up onto the seat of her bicycle, she pedaled bumpily over the grass and down to the road by the ball field. She stole a quick final glance in the direction of the cottage. No one seemed to be chasing after her, and she turned and pedaled off as fast she could back toward the foothills.

When she got as far as the fire roads, she deliberately took a different path than the one she and Erik had ridden earlier in the day, making sure her route kept her far away from the top of the Renton Stairs. She knew that if Berrigan's men weren't already there, they would be soon, working on breaking through the door and getting ready to carry out their operation.

By the time she finally reached the small unremarkable towers of rock outcropping where she had exited from the last passage, the sun had already set, and MacKenzie was already hot and sweating and exhausted from the fast frantic bike ride. The sky still glowed with early twilight, and the rock towers reached like strange fingers toward the heavens from their clustered dense tangles of overgrowth and bushes.

MacKenzie let her bike fall to the ground and ran toward the finger which was the tower she needed to climb. She crawled and shoved and fought her way through the thick overgrowth at the bottom until she reached the base of the finger. Then she shimmied and climbed her way back to the top. Climbing up was frustratingly more slow and difficult than climbing down had been.

When at last she reached the top, she sat on the rim and had to pause to catch her breath. Then she hurriedly swung her legs into the darkness of the too-small opening and began to lower herself back down into the vertical passage. Gravity was on her side now. The downward pull of her body-weight helped her to squeeze her shoulders past the tight closeness of the rim as her feet pressed securely against the narrow rocky sides below. She pulled her arms and hands the rest of the way through the opening, and then she was back inside the passage. Reversing the pattern of her crab-wall-climbing, she began to descend straight down through the vertical darkness in quick alternating downward scoots as rapidly as she dared without putting herself at risk for falling.

It was easier going down. The whole return trip was easier. She didn't have to figure anything out. She didn't have to wonder about the path. She knew exactly how to get to where she wanted to go. Her mind had a clear map of what the route was, and a clear idea of how long the trip would take. Only now it was faster, because she knew what she was doing, she knew where she was going, and perhaps most important of all, it now was all downhill.

In a strange way, she was glad she didn't have a working

flashlight. Her mind had memorized the route in total darkness, and if she could see where she was going, it might confuse the route in her mind.

When she got to the gold cavern, she kept to the outside edge so she wouldn't again run into the pile of gold objects. She didn't want to trip again, but mostly she thought it was disrespectful to kick sacred objects, even if it was by accident. She was still unhappy with herself for having disturbed them when she had come through the first time.

She found the too-small passage that connected to the floor of gold cavern, and lowered herself into it head-first. And then it was time for her to really start crawling.

For some reason, she thought to herself, crawling is easier if you know ahead of time that you'll be crawling the entire trip. She crawled and crawled, faster and faster as the downhill slope helped her along, as she increasingly knew how much closer she was getting to the end, and as she thought in growing dread about what might be happening to Erik.

And then suddenly she was at the bottom of the Renton Stairs. She had come out through the large-mouse hole at the end of the smallest passage, and was once again at the bottom of the stairway-shaft, directly beneath the last flight of stairs and behind the metal beams of the central stair support.

Now she had to go slowly and silently and cautiously. It seemed too soon for anyone from Berrigan's stairway-mission to be there yet, but she had to be fully alert for any of Trelain's men who might be patrolling around.

MacKenzie's entire return trip so far had taken place in total black darkness. And here, too, at the bottom of the Renton Stairs, it was entirely dark. The battery-operated work-lights were gone.

But MacKenzie not only remembered clearly in her mind's map where she was, she could also tell where she now was because of the sound. As the unending darkness had left her continually unable to see, her sense of hearing had become steadily smarter. Not unlike a dolphin, it was almost as if she now had her own kind of sonar. She could now hear how much vertical space there was, and it was almost as though she could hear the shape of the cavern and everything around her. She put her hand where she knew the central stair support would be, and her fingers immediately found the cold metal surface they were seeking. With that tangible physical point of reference, MacKenzie's internal maps updated and re-aligned, and she was ready to move forward.

She headed into the low passage that connected off the stairway-shaft cave and followed its turns and winding path in the darkness, lowering her head as she went and eventually getting down on all fours to crawl out at the end into the lighted lava-tube path of the train-tunnel.

In a low crouch, she ran as fast as she dared along the curved right-hand wall, up the rise toward the main part of the underground base, keeping low and staying in the clear path to the right of the railway gravel. Dropping back to a crawl as she approached the top of the rise, she peered over the top and saw the back of the *Torpedo Express*. The rear nose-cone light was off, and the cabin inside the sloping rear-windshield glass was dark.

MacKenzie stayed low and continued to make her way with alert stealth to the back of the train. She turned there and started to crawl up the access-steps on the right-hand side, ascending with care and slowness, one step at a time.

She peered furtively into the wooden-crates cave-room. No one was there. But she had been caught off-guard by surprise too many times already today, and she continued to make her way with deliberate wary caution.

She crept through a passage and entered another familiar cave-room. The passage on the left had a view of the *Torpedo Express*. She glanced down the length of the passage and the cave-room it led to, toward the train. The sliding side door was still open, but now part of the train's inner cargo area was stacked with over two-dozen large black canvas duffel bags. It certainly did look as though Trelain's crew were all packed and ready to leave. But none of Trelain's men seemed to be anywhere around. The cave-complex was eerily quiet. Most of the noises and sound MacKenzie remembered being there were now missing.

She proceeded onward, through cave-rooms and passages, increasingly convinced she was not going to encounter any of Trelain's men. She made her way to the place where she and Erik had been held captive, sitting back-to-back. No one was there. For a strange moment, she spotted on the ground off to one side her and Erik's backpacks, lying where they had been tossed in a small heap. MacKenzie was tempted to pick them up and carry them with her, but she right away realized that baggage would only hamper her mission, and she left them where they were.

Feeling more bold, MacKenzie dared to make her way to the cavern where she and Erik had been held when Trelain had first come out to see who the two intruders were. She peered around the edge of a cave-wall into the large brightly-illuminated space. There was no one there either, and the lights on most of the equipment were dark.

And now she began to realize that she had been hearing voices and new sounds. They were coming from somewhere ahead. MacKenzie knew what direction it was. And then she pieced together what was happening. Trelain himself had told her his plan. He and his crew had packed and were ready to leave, but they weren't going to make their escape until after the big sale. They were now waiting for the arrival of the buyer. And it became clear to MacKenzie that the whole team must be waiting together.

She and Erik had talked about the importance of having a plan.

And MacKenzie usually never did anything without having planned ahead. She liked to plan. And she liked to follow her impulses to then do something different from the plan, whenever an impulse occurred to her. But this time she didn't have plan. All she had was a mission. Her mission was to find Erik and somehow rescue him. She had no idea how she was going to do it. But she knew that if she didn't try to do it, it for sure would not happen.

So far, she hadn't found Erik anywhere. But now at least she knew where her next destination was. As soundlessly and invisibly as she could, she followed her mind's map and began to make her way toward the sea-lake.

Chapter 41
COMPLICATIONS

The sounds of activity and voices grew steadily louder as MacKenzie made her way forward. She kept ducking into side passages or smaller cave-rooms along the way, trying to do everything she could to not be seen or taken by surprise from behind.

And now all her instincts told her she was nearly at her destination. But she could feel and tell by the nature of the sound that the space ahead was very large. It seemed to her unlikely that she would be able to remain unseen at the verge of such a large open space, especially if, as she suspected, Trelain and every member of his crew were in that space. That was a lot of eyes to try to stay hidden from, and a lot of peripheral vision she could too easily be noticed within.

Against a cave-wall to her left, several labeled wooden crates were piled together in stacks of three or four. Because of the irregular-shaped sides of the cave-rock, the crates had been necessarily positioned slightly away from the wall. MacKenzie, who already felt as though she had spent her entire day squeezing in and out of tight situations, quickly recognized that this was the best option she was going to be able to find.

There was less of a gap toward the tops of the crates, but lower toward the bottom there was just enough space for MacKenzie to make herself thin and slip in between the crates and cave-wall. With her back to the rough uneven wall, and her face pressed up against the wood of the crates, she began to inch herself sideways.

She slid herself with careful effort past the first two stacks, and cautiously inched her way to the thin space between the wall and the third stack of crates. The third stack was the last. As MacKenzie reached the gap at the end-corner edge of the stack, from her hidden vantage-point she suddenly had a view of the entire space before her.

Like the other large cavern, this space was brightly illuminated by powerful white lights hanging from above. The ceiling of this cavern was not as high, but the space was larger and sunken down at a lower level than the rest of the cave-complex. A ledge running the length of one side of the cavern had a drop of several feet, and numerous sloping ramps and short sets of stone steps connected the floor of the cavern space to the higher level.

At the center of the space was the sea-lake. Its irregular edge formed a water perimeter that was vaguely rectangular, and looked to be more than forty feet across and over thirty feet wide. The water was so dark it appeared black. The water's surface was not motion-lessly flat, but there was little movement and no waves. It seemed to be slowly swelling in some places, and gently dipping in others, and the perimeter edge was damp-looking and green with algae, as though water from the sea-lake often spilled above its stone rim-edges.

Trelain and what appeared to be his entire crew were there, looking like they were outfitted for combat. Each man now had an automatic long-gun rifle hanging by a strap over one shoulder, automatic side-arms on both hips, and a submachine gun carried in one hand. They all had strapped on heavy black body-armor vests that looked bullet-proof, and all had heavy armored gloves protecting their hands. All of them wore heavy black helmets with boom-microphones in front of their mouths. A coiled-cord cable connected each helmet to a walkie-talkie that each man had attached to one of his waist-belts. Each man wore at least one extra waist-belt which was heavy with various supplies of ammunition to re-load the various guns.

An assembly of massive machinery was arrayed against a far wall. Huge pulleys and counter-weights hung suspended at the sides. Giant gears with big thick chains that were covered with algae and dripping with water stretched from the highest part of the cavern down into dark holes in the floor that glistened with wet seaweed around the edges. Long levers with wide handles jutted from one end, and at the middle of the enormous mechanism was a tall control-panel console with mechanical buttons and switches, and illuminated dials. A light was steadily flashing next to a readout where the word 'OPEN' was lit up on a display. MacKenzie surmised that this was all for raising or lowering the sea-gate across the underwater ocean-passage, and for a moment she imagined a vast metal grate like the portcullis of a medieval fortress that was now raised up to permit entrance into the castle.

Some of the men were attending to other equipment around the edges of the cavern-space. Some were inspecting and adjusting their armaments and body-armor. Most of them were looking with patient expectance toward the water of the sea-lake. Trelain's back was to MacKenzie, but she could see him lift one arm to check his watch. Atop a small wooden crate next to him was an ominous-looking black metal case the size of a small piece of luggage. There were thick handles on two sides, and the case was fastened with heavy bolts. MacKenzie didn't recognize the circular fan-like black and yellow-orange symbols that were stenciled on all the sides, but she could read the words below them: CAUTION - IONIZED RADIATION HAZARD. There was little doubt in MacKenzie's mind that inside that case was probably the stolen plutonium.

But of greater concern to her was what she didn't see. She didn't see Erik anywhere, and her stomach started to sink with cold heavy terror at the thought of what might have happened to him.

The water of the sea-lake began to move, and everyone in the room snapped to alert focus. Every man now stood steady with a gun aimed toward the surface of the lake. The water was starting to heave and spill up over the stone rim-edges of the perimeter, and dense surges of deeply gurgling bubbles began to break the surface in large churning froths. Moments later, the uppermost parts of a surfacing mini-sub appeared, lifting away displaced water and rising up through the roiling foam.

"That's not the buyer...!" a voice suddenly called out in alarm.

"That's US Navy...!!" someone's voice shouted.

The cavern erupted in a storm of confusion and gunfire. Trelain's men had hardly begun shooting at the sub when the still-surfacing vessel began launching cylindrical canister grenades everywhere into the space. The grenades hissed with gaseous noise as they flew through the air, spraying fast spiraling billows of thick grey smoke in all directions. Even before the smoke-grenades had landed—bouncing crazily and rolling about the rocky space— the entire cavern was already filling with choking grey smoke. Unrelenting rounds of steady gunfire echoed and filled the sea-lake cavern with deafening noise as Trelain's men continued to fire at the sub, but increasingly it was becoming difficult to see anything.

Trelain's men started coughing badly, and MacKenzie could see within the thickening smoke hazy silhouetted images of Trelain's men falling to the ground. The first wisps of smoke began to reach MacKenzie's hiding place. Her eyes and nose started to sting and burn from a sickening chemical smell, and she knew she had to get away fast from where she was. Sliding herself hastily out from behind the crates, she dashed quickly back down the passage she had come through.

She ran until she found a safe cave-corner sufficiently far from the chaos taking place at the sea-lake, and she dropped to the ground to hide herself behind it. She could hear the gunfire from Trelain's men slowing down, but it hadn't stopped.

Heavy swift footsteps suddenly came from the direction of the sea-lake and ran past her. It was Trelain. MacKenzie leapt to her feet and took off running after him. Trelain was her last hope to somehow discover what had become of Erik.

Moments later, MacKenzie suddenly slowed the pace of her chase as she began to realize where Trelain was headed. She waited until he was safely out of view in front of her, then she ran at top speed to where she was now sure he had gone.

She was right. Just as she got to the passage outside of Trelain's cave-office, she saw him unlock the door and head hurriedly inside. On an impulse, MacKenzie ran past the open door and continued on down the passage until she had found another safe hiding-corner. She peered around the rocky edge of the passage wall and looked back the way she had come. What she saw filled her with relief and horror. Trelain was coming hurriedly out of his office, no longer wearing the heavy armored gloves. He was holding a gun in one hand. In the other, he was holding Erik by the back of the neck. Erik's hands were still tied, and there was a piece of industrial duct tape covering his mouth.

MacKenzie snuck stealthily away from her hiding place and began to run as fast as could. She knew where she had to go now, and she knew she had to get there first.

Since all of Trelain's men were at the sea-lake, MacKenzie didn't have to worry about encountering any of any of them. She could take the most direct route, and she could run at top speed. But something else was worrying her. She knew that Berrigan's land-attack team would be coming down the Renton Stairs and arriving any moment. If they showed up now, while Trelain was holding Erik hostage, the chances of Erik getting injured or worse in that confrontation were alarmingly real.

MacKenzie made a last fast turn and raced through the passage and cave-room she had previously looked through but never entered—the access to the side of the *Torpedo Express*. She ran through the open side door and into the train. In front of her, the smugglers' stacked black bags were piled and secured in place with heavy canvas straps hooked to the wall and bulkheads.

MacKenzie turned to the left, dashing forward to the end of the train facing into the tunnel toward the mainland. The cabin lights were all dark, but illumination from the overhead lights of the tunnel was coming in through the high sloping glass of the wide curved windshield. After a quick moment of desperately looking around, MacKenzie hurried back toward the middle of the train's cargo area and hid herself behind a bulkhead in a stack of empty canvas cargo sacks. She pulled one of them over herself like a blanket, and tried to become invisible amidst the sack pile.

Seconds later, Trelain came hurrying aboard, forcibly dragging Erik along with him. Trelain hauled Erik forward to the end of the train facing into the tunnel toward the mainland, and tossed Erik to the floor into a corner near the front driving-control panel.

Hastily hitting a button on the control panel, Trelain then stepped back outside the train. From her hiding place and through a side-window of the *Torpedo Express*, MacKenzie was just able to see him swiftly yank the train's electric-charging plug from its port and toss the cable clear of the train. As he re-entered the train, Trelain activated a switch next to the door, and the side door-panel slid closed and locked itself into place.

Trelain hurried back and stood in front of the control panel, flicking switches and operating the controls. All the interior cabin lights came on, and moments later the train was in motion and moving forward.

MacKenzie could see in her mind the movement of the train that she was feeling, as the *Torpedo Express* started level and then tilted up slightly as it climbed the short rise. The train had picked up speed swiftly, but once it was over the rise its acceleration increased more dramatically. It was now going downhill, and everything felt pulled forward toward the front of the train as it angled lower and more steeply.

Trelain unstrapped his body-armor vest and took off his combat helmet, then tossed them both carelessly into a corner on floor of the train.

An electric whirring coming from some part of the *Torpedo Express* began to get higher and higher in the pitch of its sound. Soon the vibration of the train wheels on the tracks became noticeable, and though the ride remained smooth, it felt in all ways like a vehicle hurtling forward at ever-increasing speed.

Somewhere far above the fast-moving train, up beyond the tunnel and the sea floor, a pod of dolphins frolicking under the twilight in the ocean water off the Catalina coast suddenly all turned as one and raced off, leaping and diving forward through the waves, playfully chasing the familiar vibrations racing ahead from somewhere far below.

MacKenzie had been peering out from behind the covering of the canvas sack, and now she dared to crawl partway around the bulkhead to get a better look at all that was happening. Trelain was standing with his hands planted on the sides of the control panel, facing the oncoming tunnel as the overhead tunnel lights flew past faster and faster. His eyes were unseen. MacKenzie could see only the back of his head.

The inside of MacKenzie's ears had begun to ache from the pressure of how deep below the ocean and the sea floor the train now was, and she had to yawn and wiggle her jaw several times to clear the discomfort.

She still didn't have a plan, but now she truly needed one. She looked desperately around the inside of the train, searching for anything that might give her some inspiration for what to do next.

And then she looked above her. Her heart had already been

hammering inside her chest, but her blood began pulsing even faster as she suddenly saw something she recognized.

She crawled out into the car a little farther. Trelain was still facing forward, watching the tunnel ahead through the tall wide curved glass of the front windshield. But MacKenzie's motion had caught Erik's attention. His eyes widened with inexpressible thoughts and emotions as he saw her.

MacKenzie put a finger silently to her lips, though she doubted Erik needed any prompting to not give her presence away. Then she looked significantly at Erik, and then looked up toward something dangling from a bulky metal box fixed to the wall over her head. She pointed to it. It was a large red t-shaped handle hanging by a heavy wire cable. The handle was labeled in big black letters with the words 'Emergency Brake'.

By now the train had leveled off. It was no longer aiming downhill, but it was still picking up speed, and the high-pitch whirr of the electric engine was growing ever louder.

There were several long cargo straps not currently in use and hooked to the walls by heavy metal clasps in various places. Trying to move carefully and not make any noise, MacKenzie took one of the straps and wrapped it around herself, winding it across her waist and over one shoulder like a seatbelt. Then she looked back at Erik, and gave him the tunnel-signal, but silently, with a soundless finger-snap.

Erik nodded very slightly that he understood, and wriggled his body around to brace himself by putting his feet against a control console that was fixed in the train-floor between him and the front of the train.

His movement drew an immediate reaction from Trelain, who whirled around and pulled the gun from his shoulder holster, aiming it at Erik.

"I can shoot you without killing you," said Trelain coldly. "I promise you, it will not be a pleasant experience for you."

MacKenzie couldn't delay any longer. Whatever she was going to do, she was going to do it now. She stood up straight and reached for the red handle.

At the sudden sound and movement, Trelain whirled around in an instant, aiming the gun directly at MacKenzie.

MacKenzie grabbed the Emergency Brake handle with both hands and pulled down on it with all her weight.

Everything juddered and quaked and screamed with vibration. The hurtling train slammed to a halt. A gunshot rang out. The train's locked wheels shrieked in piercing protest against the steel trackrails.

The force of the sudden stop threw Trelain off his feet and hurled him headfirst backward into the train's windshield. The curved sloping glass ruptured in a burst of shards as his head smashed through it.

The *Torpedo Express* had come to a dead stop. Many of the lights inside the train had gone dark. Other lights that had been dark were now intermittently flashing, casting surreal repeating amber beams in all directions. Several urgent siren alarms were sounding, coming from unknown places throughout the train.

The weight of Trelain's slumped body now pulled him back into the train cabin. Sliding down over the control panel, dragging an avalanche of cascading shattered glass, his body dropped into a collapsed heap on the floor of the train.

Chapter 42

AFTERMATH

MacKenzie had been effectively restrained by the cargo strap, and had been helped by her body's anticipation of the abrupt braking, but she was not uninjured. The shot fired from Trelain's gun had grazed MacKenzie's arm as she had pulled down on the brake, and blood was flowing from the place where the bullet had torn open her skin before burying itself in the train wall behind her. Her neck was in an agony of pain from the jolt of the train's sudden stop. The inside of her head was swimming with dizziness and disorientation, and her ears were ringing so loudly from the gunshot, she could hardly hear anything.

In slow painful motions, she unwrapped herself from the cargo strap. Steam and smoke and loud wet hissing sounds from outside the train were pouring into the cabin through the huge opening left by the shattered windshield.

MacKenzie staggered over to Erik and dropped to her knees, peeling the tape off his mouth.

"The knife…" said Erik hurriedly. "On his leg…"

MacKenzie didn't even pause to be disgusted by having to touch Trelain. She crawled to his body and used her weight to roll it over so she could get the knife. Trelain's eyes were closed. His face was bloody. His arms and legs were as limp and lifeless as the limbs of a ragdoll.

She found the knife and pulled it out of its sheath, then crawled back over to Erik. The train car was increasingly filling with smoke and thick wet steam.

Erik had been able to sit himself up, so that his tied hands behind his back could be more accessible.

"I'm going to cut the rope..." said MacKenzie. "Don't move, please..."

"Be careful," said Erik. "Don't cut toward your hand..."

MacKenzie cut him free, and dropped the knife to the train floor, and she and Erik threw their arms around each other, neither of them caring about embarrassment or awkwardness or anything other than being more relieved and grateful than their words could possibly express.

They sat kneeling together on the floor of the cabin in a pool of shattered glass as flashing alarm-lights cast strange pulsating glows in the swirling steam and smoke around them.

"What happened to your arm...?" asked Erik with concern.

MacKenzie glanced down at her bleeding injury. "I think I may have been kind of shot..." she said uncertainly.

Erik tore off a piece off the bottom of his shirt and wrapped it around the wounded part of her arm. "Don't let this get too tight," he instructed. "Just keep pressure on it..."

MacKenzie looked over at the motionless body of Trelain.

"Erik, is he dead...?"

Erik shook his head. "I don't care if he's dead or not, we're tying him up." Erik glanced for a moment through the smoke over at the array of cargo straps where MacKenzie had created her improvised seat belt. "Go unhook some of those straps and bring them over here, please..." he said quickly.

MacKenzie nodded and stood up unsteadily, heading for the straps.

Erik crawled over to Trelain's body and started taking all the guns out of their holsters, making a pile of them off to one side.

MacKenzie came back with three straps. She and Erik wound and wrapped them around Trelain, binding his legs together, securing his arms and hands tightly to the sides of his body, and Erik tied the ends of the straps fast in bowline knots.

MacKenzie went to get one of the empty canvas sacks, and Erik filled it with the guns. He removed the knife sheath from where it was fastened around the side of Trelain's leg, and strapped it on to his own leg, picking the knife up from the floor of the train and sliding it into place back inside the sheath.

MacKenzie and Erik now both stood up next to each other and paused. It was first relatively calm moment they had had in the past several hours, hours that at the moment felt more like they had been several long harrowing days.

The siren alarms had gone silent, but most of the train's lighting system was still dark, and the emergency lights throughout the train were still flashing. Outside the train, the overhead lights on the roof of the tunnel stretched into the distance. The steady wet hiss of brake-steam and trails of smoke coming from somewhere beneath the train were still drifting into the cabin through the smashed windshield. MacKenzie and Erik stood together in the hazy dimness and the eerie endlessly repeating urgent flashing all around them.

"Mac…" said Erik. "I was so worried they were going to catch you… Have you been hiding out down here the whole time…?"

MacKenzie shook her head. And then suddenly she knew she was about to lie to Erik. It was something she had never imagined she would ever do, ever since they had met. She felt like she could tell Erik anything about anything. And she was sure he would never lie to her about anything. But she knew she wasn't going to tell him about finding the hidden gold.

She already hadn't told her father and Katie. She had thought that was because there hadn't been time, and because she didn't want to say anything while Berrigan and his men had been there. But now she realized that wasn't why. It was too overwhelming. It was too big. It seemed sacred somehow. The gold, hidden in its secret cavern, seemed like something of an importance which was far bigger than anything having to do with her. She felt that, even though she now knew the secret, it was a secret that didn't belong to her. So she had no right to give the secret away, even to the three people who meant more to her than anyone else in the world. She was sure she would tell them, all three of them, eventually. But not now. It wouldn't be lying, exactly. It would be more like just leaving out one detail of the truth.

"I found another way out..." she said truthfully.

"Mac...!" said Erik. "That's crazy... How is there another way out...?"

"You said, there's always a way out," MacKenzie recounted. "And you were right. There was."

"How?" asked Erik.

MacKenzie shook her head. "At first I was just trying to get away from Trelain's men. I went into one of those passage openings we saw under the bottom of the metal stairs. I picked the smallest one, hoping Trelain's men would be too big to follow me into it. And then I just kept crawling and crawling..."

"But I thought your flashlight was broken..."

MacKenzie nodded. "It was. I crawled the whole way in the dark..."

"Mac..." said Erik, both in awe of what she had done, and in shuddering horror at how terrifying her experience must have been.

"If I'd thought about it for two seconds," MacKenzie went on, "I probably would have realized no one could have been following me. No one bigger than me could possibly have fit. The passage was really small. That's why I had to crawl the whole time. And sometimes I even had to go on my stomach..."

Erik nodded. "That explains why your clothes look like you're a coal miner..." he said sympathetically.

MacKenzie looked at Erik's clothing and pointed guiltily. "Looks like I got some of it on you..." she said apologetically. "Oh, and some of my blood, too... I'm sorry..."

Erik shook his head. "I'm not," he said.

MacKenzie smiled for a moment and glanced down at her clothes. "Oh..." she said. "You're so right... This is worse than when I crawled out the first time. Ew... I look pretty gross..."

Erik shook his head again. "No you don't..." he said firmly. "You look like an angel from Heaven."

"Oh, Erik..." MacKenzie said softly. "I was so worried about you. That's why I was crawling so fast. I knew I had to find a way out... I had to get out, to get someone to help you... I was so worried about you..."

MacKenzie felt herself about to start crying, and she made herself stop. *This is so not the time for crying* she scolded herself silently.

"But," she went on, "the whole time, I could tell the passage was going uphill. It wasn't going straight, though. It kept winding around and turning corners. But all the time it was going up. And Erik, here's what gave me hope and strength the whole time. I could smell fresh air. It was coming from somewhere ahead of me. I'm glad I didn't know at the time just how far I'd have to go to get to it. But that was what kept me going. And I hated leaving you here, and I was desperate to get help, so I just kept crawling...."

"Mac, it sounds so awful and scary..."

She nodded. "It was. Very. And Erik, at the end, the passage suddenly was straight up, like a chimney. And the weirdest thing was, that was the easiest part. I just scooted up like climbing between two walls..."

Erik nodded. "I know exactly what you're talking about," he said. "I've done that so many times. Parents and teachers hate that..."

MacKenzie smiled and nodded. "But how else are we supposed to get good at something unless we practice doing it..."

"Exactly..." Erik agreed.

"So finally," MacKenzie went on, "six years later, I finally get out. And I figure out where I am, and I start running back to our bikes. And Erik, you are absolutely not going to believe what happened next. Out of nowhere, I was grabbed by someone behind me, and all of a sudden I was caught again. And you will not possibly guess who it was who had grabbed me. It was the mysterious man...!"

MacKenzie described to Erik all that had happened next, about discovering that the mysterious man was actually one of the good guys, and that he worked for the US Government, and his name was Berrigan. She recounted to Erik how she had told Berrigan all about everything he needed to know, so the Navy could launch an attack on the cavern and intercept the foreign miniature-submarine before it could buy the stolen plutonium from Trelain.

She told Erik that the hidden metal stairs actually had a secret real name, and they were called The Renton Stairs, and she had showed Berrigan where the entrance was, and Berrigan had ordered his men to break through so they could launch part of their attack on the cavern from there, even though they hadn't shown up yet when the *Torpedo Express* had last left the station.

She described how Berrigan had brought her to the cottage, and how he had explained everything to her father and Katie. MacKenzie told Erik about how they had tried to call Brenda, but since she was out, no one had answered and they didn't want to leave her any message because that would be too awful for her.

At which point in MacKenzie's account Erik had suddenly looked anxiously at his watch. But it turned out there was still more than an hour left before the 10:30 time he had arranged with Brenda for her to pick him up at the cottage, so Erik didn't have to be troubled that his mother was worrying about him yet.

MacKenzie explained how she had sneaked out of the cottage,

and she knew her father and Katie and Berrigan's men were going to be furious with her, but there was no way she was going to not try to do something herself to help Erik. She explained how she had snuck her cottage-bike out of the garage, and biked back to the foothills, and found the entrance to the passage, and come back down to the cavern the same way she escaped from it.

Erik was amazed and appalled that she had had to go all through the terrible length of the tiny passage in total darkness all over again. MacKenzie assured him it was easier going down and already knowing the route than it had been the first time. She told him she had decided to call it The Krazy-Straw, because that's what it was like—full of crazy twists and turns, and narrow as a straw the whole way, just like a real krazy straw, and calling it that in her mind made it less awful to be going all the way through it all over again.

And she told Erik how the Navy attack had started almost as soon as she got back down to the cavern, and about how she saw Trelain taking Erik away, and that she knew where Trelain was going to take him—to try to escape and use Erik as a hostage.

"Mac..." Erik breathed in awe after she had finished recounting it all to him. "I want you to think for a minute about what you've done. You escaped through an awful route that was way beyond difficult and terrifying. You told the government what they needed to know. Only because of you was the Navy able to come in and save the day. And then you saved me from Trelain by being brilliant and brave and clever and beautiful..."

MacKenzie felt herself blushing. "I... I don't know if that had anything to do with it..." she managed to say.

"Mac..." said Erik, looking at her intently. "I want you to think about something you said to me when we were in the wildlands, and that buffalo was keeping us company. You said you wished that you could be a Nophaie the Warrior. Mac, you have a good memory. What did it say? In the movie? What did the title card say?"

MacKenzie couldn't take her eyes away from Erik's eyes. She couldn't even look vaguely upward like she so often did when she was trying to remember something. Her mouth simply responded by itself to Erik. "*In every generation*," she heard herself saying, "*a Nophaie the Warrior dared to do what no other would attempt.*"

Erik nodded. "That's you, Mac..." he said. "You've made your wish come true. You are a Nophaie the Warrior... I bet if Fire-Walker himself were here right now, he would be able to tell you what your new Navajo name should be..."

MacKenzie felt tears about to come, and she stopped them again. "Well..." she said slowly. "I guess, like 'Man Hammer' and 'Fire-Walker', it would have to be a translation. I don't think I'd know what it meant if it was just a transliteration..."

Erik gave her their tunnel-signal.

MacKenzie gave him their tunnel-signal back, and they both smiled.

"How's your bullet wound doing...?" he said, looking at the blood-soaked shred of his shirt still wrapped around her arm.

MacKenzie looked at it as though she had forgotten about it, which she had. She held it up for a minute and shrugged. "I forgot to keep pressing on it..." she admitted guiltily, quickly putting her other hand on it and holding it there the way Erik had showed her.

"Does it hurt...?" he asked.

She nodded. "It does sort of hurt," she said. "But I'll be fine..."

MacKenzie checked her necklace to make sure it was still there, which it was. Then she looked around at the inside of the train car, and tried to not look at the body of Trelain. "Okay..." she said slowly. "So, what happens now...?"

Chapter 43
TRANSIT

Erik looked around at the inside of the train cabin for a moment, then looked back at MacKenzie and nodded. "Here's what happens now," he said. "We go to the other end of the train, and drive this thing back to Catalina."

"Do you know how to work it...?" asked MacKenzie.

Erik nodded grimly. "I saw some of what Trelain did at the control panel. And besides, this is a train. If it's a train, I know how to make it go..."

Erik and MacKenzie stood up. Erik stepped over the still motionless body of Trelain and stood over the control panel, studying it. The train was eerily still. The lights on the control panel had all gone dark. Emergency lights throughout the train continued their tireless silent flashing.

"Did I break it...?" asked MacKenzie with guilty apprehension.

Erik turned and looked at her. "Mac, seriously...?"

And then she realized, and they both laughed, and for a moment neither of them could stop laughing, and their bodies released some of the stress and pressure that had been building inside of them for the past few hours.

Brief minutes later, they had recovered themselves, and Erik returned his focus to the business of getting the train running. He turned some of the knobs on the control panel first one way, then the other. Nothing happened. There was still a steady steamy hissing sound coming from somewhere underneath the train, but there was less smoke coming into the cabin through the shattered windshield. The view ahead showed the tunnel toward the mainland extending forever, diminishing and disappearing into darkness off in the distance where the tunnel ceiling lights faded from view because they were so far away.

Erik looked around, scanning the train cabin until a large mechanical switch on a bulkhead next to the windshield caught his eye. He tried to move the switch upward from its current down position, but it wouldn't budge. A large panel box was fixed into a nearby wall, and Erik reached over and pulled open the panel door. There were tools inside, snap-locked into place. One of them was a hammer. Erik snapped the hammer out of its holder, and adjusted its position in his hand. Then he swung it in an upward arc from below the stuck switch, slamming the hammer home with a single solid stroke into the bottom of the switch. The switch immediately responded to the impact and slid suddenly from its down position into an up position.

Everything flickered. And then the emergency lights went off and the rest of the lights that had been dark all came back on. The control panel lights all blinked to life, and the sound of hissing steam stopped. Something big grumbled and clicked and thunked somewhere below the floor of the train, and at the other end of the cabin, the large red pull-handle of the Emergency Brake glided upward, as its cable cord retracted mechanically back up into the housing.

Erik glanced back down at the control panel for a moment, inspecting the illuminated knobs and buttons, and tapping some of the readout dials.

"Okay, then..." he said nodding. He snapped the hammer back into place with the other tools, and swung the door of tool panel-box closed. "Looks like we're good to go."

MacKenzie grinned at him. "Erik Roebling..." she said proudly. "You're just like Buster Keaton..."

Erik smiled. "Thanks, Mac…" he said slowly. "But mostly…" he hesitated. "Thank you for coming back to rescue me…"

She reached up and put her index finger against his lips to shush him. "No," she said. "I would do anything for you, and you would do anything for me. So we're just going to not talk about that right now…"

Erik silently nodded, and she took back her finger. "*Torpedo Express*," she said.

"Excuse me…?" asked Erik.

"*Torpedo Express*," she repeated. "That's the name of this train."

Erik nodded. "Got it," he said. "Well, it's time for us to move to the controls at the other end of the *Torpedo Express*, so we can drive her back to headquarters…"

Erik picked up the sack of guns, and he and MacKenzie made their way to the opposite end of the train. Within moments, Erik had easily worked the controls and coaxed the *Torpedo Express* into motion. Her electric engine whirred to life as she rolled and glided her way forward, beginning to pick up speed and heading in the opposite direction, toward the cavern and back the way she had come.

"Do you think it's safe to go back…" MacKenzie said hesitantly. "There was a lot going on there when we left the station…"

Erik nodded. "I don't care what kind of smugglers these guys are," he said. "If they're dealing with the US Navy, they don't stand a chance."

"My Dad was in the Navy," MacKenzie said with pride.

Erik looked at her in surprise. "Get out of here. Really…? So was *my* dad!"

"Well, finally…!" said MacKenzie. "At last we have something in common…!"

They both grinned at each other, and gave each other the tunnel-signal, snap-bounce-thumbs-up. And with ever increasing speed, the *Torpedo Express* carried them safely and successfully forward.

When the tunnel started to slope steeply upward, they knew they were getting close to the cavern, and Erik began to throttle back the engine and let the incline slow the speed of the train. They were traveling at a cautiously slow speed by the time they came over the top of the rise, and Erik let the *Torpedo Express* coast to a crawl as the train neared the end of the railway path. At the termination of the track in front of them, a steel-girder pyramid-like structure about four-feet high was bolted to the rails as a bumping-post to ensure the train went no farther, and Erik pointed out to MacKenzie the reflective black-and-white-diagonal-lines sign-marker fixed to the tunnel wall on the left that showed the exact spot for the train to stop. There was a loud long steamy hissing as Erik applied the brakes, and the *Torpedo Express* came smoothly to a full complete stop.

"Nice train-driving, Buster...!" praised MacKenzie with a wide admiring grin.

They high-fived at the successful return, and Erik picked up the sack of Trelain's guns. MacKenzie and Erik went to the sliding side door of the train to exit. Having watched Trelain do it, MacKenzie knew how to operate the switch that opened the door-panel, and she activated it. There was a shuffling electronic unlocking click, and then with a nearly soundless electric glide, the door slid sideways and opened to reveal over a dozen heavily armed men pointing long-gun automatic rifles directly at Erik and MacKenzie.

"Drop it!" a voice ordered.

Erik let go of the canvas sack containing Trelain's guns, and it fell to the floor of the train with a muted clatter.

"Hands high!" the voice ordered again.

MacKenzie and Erik raised their hands up above their heads. The blood-soaked piece of Erik's shirt that MacKenzie had been holding wrapped around the wound on her arm fell in a small sodden heap to the floor of the train.

"It's okay…" Erik said to MacKenzie. "They're US Marines…"

"Step out of the train," the voice commanded.

"Wait!" said MacKenzie. "You have to call Reilly Berrigan! My name is MacKenzie Milles! He knows who I am!"

A Marine officer in the train-access cave-room directly in front of MacKenzie and Erik took a step forward toward them.

"Where's Trelain?" he asked. It was the same voice that had been giving them orders.

"He's inside this train," Erik said, keeping his hands up and gesturing with his head in the direction of the rear driver-cabin. "He's tied up. He might be dead."

"Take two steps to your left," the officer ordered. "Both of you,"

MacKenzie and Erik did as they were told, creating a clear path of entry into the train.

Still holding his gun aimed at MacKenzie and Erik with one hand, with the other hand the officer made a gesture to the Marines around him. Four Marines came forward and entered the train, their guns aimed with alert caution ahead of them. Two of them turned and moved carefully toward one end of the train, two of them headed for the other end.

Moments later, all four had returned, their guns lowered.

"Clear," one of them reported.

The officer nodded and lowered his weapon. "Stand down," he instructed the rest of the Marines, and all guns were lowered.

"Officer…" said MacKenzie.

"You can put your hands down," said the officer.

MacKenzie and Erik gratefully lowered their hands.

"Officer," MacKenzie said again. "Please. You have to call

Berrigan. Two of his men are with my Dad. Someone has to tell my Dad that MacKenzie Milles and Erik Roebling are alive and safe. Please!"

The officer nodded. "Understood, Ms. Milles. Both of you step out of the train now, please. We need to get you up to the surface, and it's a long way from here to there.

MacKenzie nodded ruefully. "Oh, we know…" she said as she and Erik started to exit the train. Then she stopped and pointed down at the blood-soaked piece of Erik's shirt. "May I pick that up, please?" she asked.

The officer nodded. "Go ahead," he replied. "Quickly, please."

MacKenzie picked it up and re-wrapped it around her arm.

"There's a medical unit at the top of the stairs," said the officer. "They'll take care of you there."

MacKenzie nodded. "Thank you," she said.

Erik pointed to the canvas sack he had dropped. "Trelain's guns are in there," he explained to the officer.

The officer nodded. "Understood. Keep moving, please."

"What's going to happen to Trelain?" MacKenzie asked the officer.

"We'll take care of it, miss," he replied.

"Do you think you could please have someone get in touch with my Dad now?" asked MacKenzie.

The officer nodded. "Go with these men," he said, indicating some of the Marines standing next to him. "Once you're on your way up the stairs, someone will contact your father."

"Thank you," said MacKenzie. "I don't think I could ever get used to having guns pointed at me all the time," she added solemnly. "I don't know how you do it… Thank you for your service, officer. All of you. We really appreciate everything you do…"

"Thank you, miss," the Marine officer said earnestly. "Keep moving, please."

MacKenzie nodded, and she and Erik made their way with several Marines to begin the trip to the surface.

The ascent back up the Renton Stairs took more than half-an-hour. MacKenzie had been right—their leg muscles were much more sore by the time they finally got to the top. MacKenzie didn't understand how climbing stairs could make muscles more sore than crawling in the dark, but somehow apparently it could.

All twilight was gone by the time they at last were back out beneath the starry Catalina nighttime sky in the fresh clean cool Catalina air. A staging area had been set up by the Marines ground forces, and bright lights illuminated the foothills surrounding the entrance to the top of the Renton Stairs.

MacKenzie's gunshot wound was attended to by a mobile Naval medical unit brought in with the land-assault operation to assist with any causalities. MacKenzie was told that her graze-wound was 'clean', in that there were no small pieces of the bullet anywhere in her arm. One of the medics took several close-up flash photographs of her injury, and when MacKenzie asked why, the medic reassured her that he was just following orders.

MacKenzie's arm was stitched up with dissolvable sutures, which she was told would be gone within ten days. She also had an impressively wide range of superficial cuts, scrapes, and bruises on her knees, elbows, and the palms of her hands from all her crawling, but none of it was overly serious. She and Erik were both pronounced as being otherwise intact and healthy, and MacKenzie was given instructions for how to take care of her graze-wound over the course of the next two weeks. MacKenzie asked about who else besides Trelain had been injured in the assaults, and she was told that all that kind of information was classified.

The Marine officer had kept his word, and MacKenzie's father had been contacted and informed that both MacKenzie and Erik were alive and safe, and would be brought to the cottage within the hour.

MacKenzie asked one of the Marines if someone could please try to get her and Erik's backpacks for them from the cavern, and she described what they looked like and where in the cavern they were. The Marine politely promised that he would see what he could do.

By 11:30, MacKenzie and Erik were at the cottage. Brenda had been there for over an hour, after arriving to pick up Erik shortly before 10:30 as she and Erik had previously arranged. Just before she arrived, the report of MacKenzie and Erik being safe and sound had been relayed to Berrigan's two men stationed at the cottage. This fortunate timing spared Brenda having to be subjected to any traumatic period of awful uncertainty about where her son was and what might be happening to him.

Berrigan's men informed everyone in the cottage they all would be required to attend a meeting the following day, on Sunday afternoon, and the exact time and place for the meeting would be communicated to them by telephone in the morning. In the meantime, in the interest of National Security, they were forbidden to discuss with anyone any aspect of anything that had happened. Brenda clarified for them that she would be telling her husband, Erik's father, every aspect of everything that had happened, and Berrigan's men made the sensible decision to not argue the point with her.

Berrigan's men and their large portable communications radio finally left and drove off with other members of their team in the large black four-wheel drive vehicle, and everyone in the living room at the cottage could at last—for many reasons—finally exhale.

Everyone was shaken and relieved and emotional, and understandably overwhelmed by all that had happened, and trying to process it all at the moment was too daunting for any of them. Brenda said she needed to get Erik home, and they all agreed to talk more with each other in the morning.

After Brenda and Erik left, MacKenzie took a long and much-needed shower. The Navy medics had told her she needed to keep the dressing of her bandages dry, and Katie had wrapped MacKenzie's arm in kitchen plastic-wrap for her, covering her right arm from just above her elbow to her wrist, so that she could safely shower.

After she got out of the shower and into her pajamas, MacKenzie piled all her filthy clothes including her sneakers into the washer, and promised her father she would do the laundry first thing in the morning. John reassured her that he was, at the very least, going to give her a vacation for a while from things like laundry and cooking and washing dishes and making coffee. MacKenzie thanked him, but insisted that she would need to be doing normal things to help herself feel normal after such an un-normal difficult day.

MacKenzie was starving, but far too tired to eat anything. So instead, she had a big glass of water and said she was going to bed. She gave her father and Katie hugs and kisses good-night, and hugged her father extra much because she was so relieved and happy to be safe and home and with him.

Before she headed off to bed, MacKenzie asked if it would be okay if Katie stayed at the cottage a while longer before heading back to her hotel, because even though she was sure she would be fast asleep after two seconds, it still would make her feel better knowing that both Katie and her father were in the cottage. She said she just needed everything to feel normal and nice for a little while, and Katie promised that she wouldn't leave until MacKenzie had had plenty of time to start having well-deserved sweet dreams.

MacKenzie thanked her, and hugged and kissed her father and

Katie good-night again, and headed off to bed. And as she had predicted, about two seconds after she got into bed, she was fast asleep.

Chapter 44

BREAKFAST

It was past 10:30 when MacKenzie finally woke up Sunday morning. She was stiff and sore everywhere. Her hands and knees and elbows were hurting, and the wound on her arm was aching. But the Catalina sun was shining brightly outside her window, and even though her body was grumpy, the rest of her was in a light-hearted mood. Her momentary wishful waking dream from the evening of the previous day seemed to have come true: she had woken up in the sunlight of a new day where everyone was saved and happy, and everything had been solved and taken care of. The difference, however, was that she hadn't been able to simply sleep through the hard part; she'd had to actually live through it, and somehow find a way to make it all turn out the way she wanted.

She could hear classical music coming from the short-wave radio in the living room, which further cheered her mood. After she finished brushing her teeth, she came out of the bathroom to find the whole cottage filled with a luxuriously delicious familiar smell. Like a princess summoned by the enchantment of a magical spell, MacKenzie padded her way down the hall in her bare feet and Cubs flannel pajamas, following the smell until it brought her to the kitchen.

No sight could have been more wonderful to behold than what greeted her there. Her father and Katie were sitting at the kitchen table, drinking coffee and causally chatting together as if there were no other way than this for a Sunday morning to begin. MacKenzie beamed and felt as though she had never been so happy before in her life as she was at this moment. She stood where she was, just enjoying and glowing inside, and silently giving grateful thanks.

John and Katie both looked up and smiled at her.

"And stepping up to the plate," her father announced with a loving grin, "is Very Special Agent MacKenzie Milles. The crowd cheers wildly."

"You guys are baking cinnamon rolls with icing!" MacKenzie exclaimed joyfully. As quickly as her tired aching muscles would let her, she dashed over to give her father and Katie good-morning hugs and kisses.

"Cinnamon rolls with icing!" MacKenzie exclaimed again, because the great good news was worth repeating. "They are my very favorite breakfast food of all time," she explained to Katie. "Dad lets us have them every Sunday morning. I love them! We haven't had them in ages...!!"

"We had them last Sunday," John reminded her.

"That was a million years ago," MacKenzie reminded him.

"Well," said John. "You can thank Katie. She spent all morning grocery shopping at Vons so that she could make you a special breakfast."

MacKenzie threw her arms around Katie and hugged her again. "Thank you, Katie," she said ardently.

"You must be starving, you poor thing..." Katie said to her, getting up to resume making breakfast for everyone.

"I really am...!" agreed MacKenzie.

"Well, I've made lots of food for all of us," said Katie.

"Thank you for making us a special breakfast, Katie," MacKenzie said with deeply-felt appreciation.

Katie smiled and affectionately smoothed some of MacKenzie's hair away from her face. "It's the least I could do," she said. "I got everything nearly ready while you were sleeping. So it will be just a few more minutes before you can start eating. But maybe you can let me know the best time to take the cinnamon rolls out of the oven. They went in eight minutes ago."

MacKenzie nodded. "Heat oven to 400 degrees, bake 13 to 17 minutes or until golden brown," she recited. "I've memorized the directions," she added helpfully.

"She likes them slightly under-baked," John contributed.

"That's true," agreed MacKenzie. "And Katie, you remember from when you and I made dinner together, this oven is a little bit hotter than the numbers say. So, I vote we take them out after twelve minutes. They keep baking a little, even after you take them out."

Katie smiled broadly. "Sounds good to me," she said.

"But," said MacKenzie, "haven't you guys eaten breakfast already?"

Her father shook his head. "We were waiting for you to wake up. And we thought it would be unfair to start baking your cinnamon rolls until you were awake, because I knew the smell would wake you up before you were ready."

MacKenzie nodded. "That was really thoughtful of you guys," she said. "Because it definitely would have."

"All food projects were launched into action as soon as we heard the water running in your bathroom," said her father, handing her a fresh mug of hot chocolate.

"You guys are the best," MacKenzie said appreciatively. "Thanks, Dad. Who made coffee?"

"I did," said her father. "It's not as good as when you make it."

"Well, you did a great job with the hot chocolate," MacKenzie said enthusiastically. "This is the best it's ever tasted."

Her father smiled. "That's probably because Katie made it," he said.

Katie laughed. "MacKenzie, did you sleep okay?" she asked.

MacKenzie nodded. "I did," she said, sitting down in one of the chairs at the kitchen table and trying to not use any of her sore muscles, which was impossible because they all were sore. "Thank you. I made a major deposit in my sleep bank account," she explained.

"That account was seriously overdrawn..." said her father.

"What's does 'overdrawn' mean in that context?" MacKenzie asked.

John shook his head. "More than what's there has been taken away. I'll explain it later. How do you feel...?"

MacKenzie shook her head, and then wished she hadn't because her neck was so sore. "I feel like I went way past my pitch-count, and I should've been taken out of the game about eleven innings ago..." she said.

Her father smiled and Katie laughed again.

"It's good to hear you sounding like yourself, Mac..." John said earnestly.

"Thanks Dad," she said. "I feel like I should maybe go for a bike ride or a swim, but my muscles left me a message saying that if I need anything, they're not available so don't call them. Plus, I'm not allowed to go in the ocean for a week because of my arm. And also, I have no bike..."

John nodded. "Well," he said. "I think we can help with one part of that, anyway. After breakfast, you and Katie and I can take Bertie up into the foothills and collect your and Erik's bicycles from wherever you two left them."

"Bertie!" MacKenzie sang happily. "That would be awesome, you guys," she added gratefully. "Thanks, Dad."

She took another sip of her hot chocolate.

"Listen you guys..." MacKenzie said, suddenly feeling guilty. "I... I'm sorry I snuck out last night..."

John shook his head and put up his hand like a stop sign. "To quote my favorite 12-year-old Cubs fan," he said firmly, "we're just going to not talk about that right now."

MacKenzie nodded penitently, and silently sipped her hot chocolate.

"So," John went on. "Even though you were sleeping, Mac, the world kept spinning, and here are some updates for you…"

MacKenzie took another sip of her hot chocolate, and her father filled her in on what had been happening while she was sleeping. The kitchen phone had apparently been ringing all morning, and both John and Katie were relieved that it hadn't disturbed MacKenzie before she was ready to wake up.

John had first called Davenport early to let him know that he would be taking the day off from work, and Davenport had adamantly agreed this was no day for John to be away from his daughter. Someone from Berrigan's team had already been in contact with Davenport, and Davenport had been told basic details about what had taken place underground on the island on Saturday, and about how Trelain had been operating his smuggling operation for years. The details of the lava-tube train tunnel and the underground cavern-complex secret-base were both profoundly fascinating and gravely troubling for Davenport. He would be at the meeting with Berrigan later that day.

Brenda had called twice, once just to see how everyone was doing, and the second time to say that someone from Berrigan's team had called to inform her that the Berrigan meeting would take place in a conference room at the Conservancy. Brenda had been dissatisfied with the arrangement, because she felt that an already difficult situation needed a less-formal setting, so she had gotten the location of the meeting changed. It now would take place at the Roeblings' house, which Brenda felt would be less stressful for everyone except possibly Berrigan, and she wasn't concerned about whether or not he was stressed. Davenport had supported the change in venue, and the meeting was scheduled to begin at 2:00.

Someone from Berrigan's team had then called the cottage to confirm the time and new place of the meeting, and to make sure it was clear to MacKenzie and Katie and John that all three of them were expected to attend.

At this point in John's account, MacKenzie interjected that the Cubs homestand against the Rockies was still going on, and there was a game at 2:33 Catalina time. John said unfortunately they would have to miss it because they all would be at the Berrigan meeting at that time.

MacKenzie's father continued his summary, saying that Erik had called twice for MacKenzie, and John suggested to MacKenzie that she ought to call him back as soon as she was done with breakfast.

Davenport had then called back to say the first tests of blood samples from some of the buffalo had come back positive for copper deficiency. He had taken the samples himself overtown to Long Beach the day before, to help speed up the process, and the lab had just called him. Even though there were still more samples to analyze, Davenport was expecting the tests all would come back with the same result. So the mystery was moving on to its next phase, which would be trying to determine what was causing the copper deficiency in the animals' diet, when such a problem had apparently never existed before.

By now, MacKenzie and John and Katie had been eating for some time, hungrily and appreciatively enjoying all the different delicious courses Katie had prepared for their elaborate lavish breakfast. MacKenzie had already gone through three mugs of hot chocolate, as well as two glasses of grapefruit juice while she was eating. But at this point in John's account, MacKenzie had to interrupt again.

"Oh my god…" she said hurriedly, hastily swallowing a mouthful of food so she could speak clearly and politely and without choking. "You guys... I totally haven't had a chance to even tell you about half of everything that happened yesterday, but this is important. Really important. Listen. Trelain told me there wasn't anything his secret operations were doing that would hurt the buffalo. But the secret operations were accidentally hurting the coral. There's a secret gold mine down there, and they've been using cyanide to get the gold out of the rocks. There's some kind of underwater drainpipe at their gold mine, and all the cyanide leftovers—they're called tailings, in case you didn't know—all that leftover cyanide has been going into the water by the Seal Rocks. That's what's been killing the coral...!"

For a moment, the room stopped.

Katie put down her knife and fork and paused for a moment in sudden deep contemplative thought.

"Okay..." she said after moment. "You're right, MacKenzie. This new information is extremely important. This changes so many things... All of them for the better, I think... But, it seems to me that right now, this morning, at our special breakfast, this is not the right time for us to focus on this. This news is so important, it's going to require a lot of new discussion and decision-making... But right now, right here, this breakfast with the three of us is the most important thing. So, I think we should set this topic to the side for now."

For a few moments, no one said anything, and the only sounds in the kitchen were breakfast utensils resuming their muted clinking and clacking on plates, and the continuous classical music coming from the short-wave radio in the living room.

The cinnamon rolls served to bring everything back to normal. MacKenzie and Katie got to work spreading icing on the rolls. The knife-smears of thick cool icing melted to glossy softness as the warmth from the rolls heated it just enough to densely pool and start to run in small satisfying rivulets to the edges of each roll without quite spilling over the sides. It was just the way MacKenzie liked it, and the chatter and banter and dialogue of the special breakfast settled itself back to a more comfortable familiar place.

After John and Katie insisted they each only wanted to eat one cinnamon roll, MacKenzie happily ate all the rest. She also expertly licked out every last vestige of icing inside the small round white-plastic icing-container from the cinnamon-roll tube. As John explained to Katie, this was something MacKenzie did every Sunday morning with the determined zeal of someone who knew there would be a long seven-day wait before getting to have that taste experience again.

While she had been shopping, Katie had bought mountains of first aid supplies. After breakfast, while John loaded dishes into the dishwasher, Katie changed the dressing of MacKenzie's bandages, showing her how to carefully clean the skin around the stitches, and what details were most important to pay attention to if MacKenzie was ever changing the dressings on her own.

John had done all the laundry earlier in the morning, and all of MacKenzie's favorite clothes which had been so badly treated by the difficult ordeal of the previous day's events were now clean and dry and folded, and stacked for her on the dining room table. Her favorite jeans now had sizable holes in both knees, but MacKenzie thought it was a good summertime-beach look, and she was untroubled by the unintentional new alterations. And they were her favorite jeans, so there was no way she wasn't going to wear them.

As she was getting dressed, MacKenzie discovered that the shred of Erik's shirt was in one of her jeans pockets and had been washed along with everything else. It was still dark with leftover blood-stain, but it was otherwise completely clean. MacKenzie was happy and relieved to see she hadn't lost it, though she couldn't remember putting it into her pocket. She sometimes felt as though anything might somehow make its way into her pocket, and she would never even notice. This reminded her of her 1951 penny, and she reached up a hand to make sure her necklace was still on, which it was.

MacKenzie phoned Erik, who shared with her the exciting news that his father was on his way home. He wouldn't be back in time for the Berrigan meeting, but he would be back in Catalina before dinner time. MacKenzie and Erik talked and chatted eagerly with each other until John finally had to come into the kitchen, tapping his watch significantly, and reminding MacKenzie that she and Erik would be seeing each other in less than two hours, and Bertie was waiting to take them on a bike-finding expedition. MacKenzie told Erik she was going to get their bikes, and that she would bring his when she came over for the meeting.

After finally getting herself off the phone, MacKenzie was at last ready to go. She and John and Katie made their way to Bertie, and then headed up to the foothills to retrieve the three abandoned bicycles.

Chapter 45

RETRIEVAL

For MacKenzie, it was strange to be re-tracing the path of the previous day. She gave driving directions to her father as they went along, and soon they had turned off the pavement of the main road and onto the dirt of one of the fire roads. When they ran out of fire road, MacKenzie explained that it was time to go on foot, and she led Katie and John to where she and Erik had stashed their bikes behind some bushes the day before.

The two bicycles were still there. They seemed to have survived the storm and the following many hours intact and undamaged. The bikes were walked back to Bertie, and hooked onto the small bike rack over the stowage shelf at the rear of the little vehicle.

MacKenzie now insisted that her father and Katie had to see the place where the metal door was, and they agreeably let her lead them the short distance further into the foothills until they arrived at the site of the infamous cluster of bushes.

It all looked as ordinary as any other part of the foothills, and almost as if nothing had happened there. Careful inspection revealed numerous tire tracks which evidently had been impossible to fully disguise, and large areas of crushed and trampled grass from the military activity of the night before.

As she guided her father and Katie forward, MacKenzie heard herself busily narrating all the events of the storm that had led her and Erik to seek refuge within the cluster of bushes. But her own words were sounding to her like details of some fantastic tale about other people, and not about herself. Somehow, now being back where it all started was making events of the previous day seem unreal and dreamlike and far away. It was the exact opposite of how she had felt in Emerald Bay at Prentiss's grave marker, where being in the presence of something significant from someone else's story had made her feel as though by being there, she was somehow closer to being in the story herself.

"I want to go see the metal door," MacKenzie announced impulsively. "I want to see if the military people sealed it up again…"

She hastily dropped down onto her hands and knees and began to crawl forward, a series of actions which her cuts, scrapes, bruises, and sore muscles immediately and severely punished her for. But with a wince and a quiet groan, she proceeded ahead, continuing to re-trace the path of the previous day, through the bushes toward the face of the large rock hidden beyond. She could tell right away that numerous people had come through there. The ground was clear and thoroughly flattened. There was much more room on all sides as well as above her head, and she didn't have to crawl on her stomach at all to get to the rock.

But when she got to the rock, a wave of bewildered confusion washed harshly over her. The door was gone. The rock was there, but the door was gone. There wasn't even a flat place in the rock where the door should have been. There was only the rock itself, and no sign that anything other than rock had ever been there. Just a large uneven irregular surface of ordinary rock.

MacKenzie scrambled back out the way she had come, vaguely aware that she had never before exited the cluster of bushes—her only other visit through there had been a one-way trip.

"Dad…!" she exclaimed, crawling out and getting painfully to her feet as her muscles continued to reprimand her. "It's impossible…! It's gone…! The door's all gone… I don't understand… I could understand if they sealed it back up, but it's just gone… How could it be just totally gone…?!"

Like a loving father who would do anything for his daughter, John got down on his hands and knees and crawled forward, disappearing into the cluster of bushes. He wasn't gone long. Moments later he re-appeared, although he was now crawling strangely, using only one hand. In the other hand, he seemed to be holding something.

He clambered the rest of the way out and stood up in front of MacKenzie and Katie, brushing himself off with his free hand. The other hand, he extended forward and down so that MacKenzie could see it clearly.

"I don't get it..." said MacKenzie, looking at her father's fingertips and feeling more confused than ever. "You've got some gooey mud on your fingers..."

John shook his head. "It's not mud. Smell it..."

MacKenzie stuck her nose over the earth-colored substance and inhaled deeply. "Oh..." she exclaimed. "I've smelled that before... It's kind of like chemicals... It's... It's..."

"It's paint," said John. "Oil-based paint."

MacKenzie hesitated. "I'm still confused..." she said.

"They didn't just seal up your door, Mac," he explained. "They also covered it over with rock-face concrete. They made the shape and texture of the concrete seem like actual rock, and then they sponge-painted it with a mix of colors to make it look like rock. Your door's still in there somewhere, it's just been covered over with concrete. It's a buffalo job. The new false surface of rock is supposed to look like something it actually isn't."

"Wow..." MacKenzie said slowly, both displeased and impressed. "That's pretty tricky..." Reaching into a pocket of her jeans, she pulled out the clean shred of Erik's shirt and handed it to her father.

John nodded. "Thanks, Mac..." he said, using the shirt-shred to wipe the paint off his fingers. "Since when do you carry a spare rag around for random mess-emergencies?"

"Since this morning," she explained.

"Isn't that what your arm was wrapped in when you came home last night?" asked Katie.

MacKenzie nodded. "It has very special significance," she said solemnly.

John handed it back to her. "Well, I'm honored you've let me use it, honey. Thank you."

"You did a pretty good job crawling into those bushes, Dad," MacKenzie said, smiling proudly.

"Navy training never leaves you..." John said philosophically. "Okay," he went on. "What's the next stop on the tour?"

MacKenzie nodded. "Just one more bike to pick up, and we're all finished. Time check, please..."

John glanced at his watch. "1:15," he replied. "We should leave the cottage for Erik's no later than 1:40..."

MacKenzie nodded. "Okay," she said. "Listen, my cottage-bike is kind of not very near here, and there's no way Bertie can drive there. I'm going to run ahead to get it, and I'll just meet you guys back at Bertie."

"Are you sure that's a good idea?" asked Katie with some concern. "Your poor body has been through a lot recently..."

"Thanks, Katie," said MacKenzie with earnest appreciation. "I think that running today, with my body being uncomfortable but relaxed, will be easier than it was yesterday when I was full of energy but scared out of my mind."

"Don't push it too hard, super-hero," her father advised.

MacKenzie nodded. "I'll be careful. I promise."

She headed off in a slow jogging trot. Her muscles were furious with her for being so inconsiderate, but she told them to just stop making things so difficult and it would all be over soon.

She was able to pick up the pace of her running after a few minutes, and soon she had reached the place where she had left her cottage-bike. She was now realizing that the foothills seemed much more green after all the rain from the storm, and it looked almost as if weeds and wildflowers had deliberately chosen to grow up though the various parts of her bicycle where it lay on its side on the ground where she'd dropped it.

The map in her mind of this part of the foothills had been created near the light's end of the previous day. Now in bright sunlight, everything around her seemed oddly unfamiliar. She looked around and decided she didn't have time to go re-visit the site of the finger-rocks, and she hurriedly uprighted her bicycle.

A cluster of what looked like wildflowers had had the misfortune of ending up between some of the spokes in the rear wheel, and the caught-stems were unintentionally snapped and severed from their roots when MacKenzie hastily raised her bike. MacKenzie immediately felt guilty about having so carelessly harmed innocent plants, and resolved to make it right somehow. She took all the detached flower-stems with their cheery rose-colored blossoms and put them in a bunch into the small stowage bag hanging under the back of the bicycle seat.

Then she pedaled off. Whole different sets of muscles were griping about bike-riding than had been complaining about running. But biking was definitely easier than running, and soon she was back at Bertie where her father and Katie were patiently waiting for her.

Bertie's bike rack was getting crowded, but John found a way to get all three bikes securely strapped together with bungy cords. MacKenzie and Katie and John slid themselves back onto the little golf cart's comfortable bench seats, and off they all drove, heading back down out of the foothills.

There wasn't much time to linger at the cottage. Since they had eaten breakfast so late, and they had all—especially MacKenzie— eaten so much food, no one needed any lunch. Which was just as well, since there was no time for a meal. They would have to leave for Erik's house almost immediately in order to not be late for the Berrigan meeting.

Two of the bikes were swiftly moved into the garage, and Erik's bicycle was left on Bertie's bike rack, although MacKenzie insisted on clarifying that in fact both mountain bikes belonged to Erik.

John and Katie headed into the cottage to get ready to leave. MacKenzie retrieved the wildflowers from her bike's stowage bag and brought them inside, transporting them carefully into the kitchen. She arranged the bunch in a glass of water, which she then re-located to the couch coffee table to add cheer to the living room, and to remind herself to try to be more careful in the future when she was doing something hurriedly.

It was about 1:55 when MacKenzie and John and Katie arrived in Bertie and parked her at the end of the driveway to Erik's house. MacKenzie recognized Davenport's Conservancy golf cart, already parked in the driveway ahead of them. Berrigan's unmistakable large black 4-wheel-drive vehicle with its dark windows and several tall antennas was parked in the street in front of the house. John sarcastically commented that Berrigan might as well just put a big sign on the hood saying 'I'm A Secret US Government Car' and call it a day. Katie laughed and agreed it would be a conspicuous vehicle anywhere, and certainly stood-out even more obviously on Catalina Island.

MacKenzie ran ahead to ring the bell, and was greeted at the door by Erik who was wearing a smile and holding their two missing backpacks. He said that one of the Marines had found them, and the packs had then made their way to Erik's house by way of one of Berrigan's men, who hadn't seemed too thrilled with being assigned the errand. MacKenzie said she and Erik needed to try to find out the name of the Marine so they could write him a thank-you note for paying attention to something which was important only to them, on a night when he obviously had so many other genuinely important things he had to be paying attention to.

John and Katie said hello to Erik at the door, and they all headed inside.

The meeting would be taking place in Erik's big dining room, at his family's large dining room table, with a lovely view of the city of Avalon spread out in the near distance below. Already seated around the table were Berrigan and two of his men, Davenport, and Brenda. Erik took a seat next to his mother, and MacKenzie sat next to him. Katie took a seat, and John sat down in between Katie and MacKenzie.

Berrigan looked at his watch with large impatience, and then it was time for the meeting to get started.

Chapter 46
MEETING

$\mathbf{B}$errigan began by making it clear the meeting would not be long.

Berrigan's presence was large. His deep resonant no-nonsense voice filled the expansive dining room and perfectly suited his no-nonsense attitude. He was not interested in small talk, and he proceeded to briefly introduce the two members of his team, whose names he would not reveal for security purposes.

He began by referring to certain data and several reports and specific Government policies, all regarding guidelines which had to be followed without exception. If anyone at the meeting were to have any dissatisfaction with what they were about to be told, there would be nothing Berrigan could do about it. He was simply follow-ing orders and long-established Government rules for handling this kind of situation.

Berrigan went on to explain that what had happened, the Government's response so far, and their actions going forward, all affected the welfare of Catalina. Since Catalina Island was such a unique part of the United States, the actions of the Government had been taken with the special concerns of the island in mind. Of most crucial importance, of course, were the concerns and interests of National Security. But all decisions had been made with mindful consideration for the welfare of Catalina Island.

"I'm here as a representative of the United States Government in this situation," Berrigan was saying. "Mr. Davenport is here as a representative of the interests of Catalina Island. In the past twelve hours, I've already had several phone conversations and meetings with Mr. Davenport and two members of the Conservancy's legal team. We are all in full agreement about what the Government has done so far, and what will be done going forward.

"Mr. Davenport has requested that I give him an opportunity to provide certain information at the start of this meeting. And Mr. Davenport, I will again ask you to please keep it brief."

Davenport nodded. "Good afternoon, everyone," he said. "So, this is certainly an extraordinary circumstance we find ourselves in—as an island community, and as US citizens, and as individuals and family members. None of the decisions which have now been made were easy ones. But Mr. Berrigan is correct when he says the Conservancy fully supports the Government's actions so far, and supports their proposed actions going forward.

"Mr. Berrigan has been good enough to share with me information from several classified Government files, and I very much appreciate his doing so. It is information which was previously unknown to me, and unknown to the Conservancy.

"Names and history are important, and that certainly is especially true here on Catalina. So that we can all understand what we're talking about, I just want to quickly share with you some of the names that will be being used when referring to details of this extraordinary circumstance.

"Based on old documents and files unearthed in the last twelve hours by Mr. Berrigan's office in Washington DC, the US Government has records of the underground area beneath the east end of the island which was being used by the smugglers. Those caves were accessed by US military forces during both the Civil War and World War II. Sometime in the 1940s, the Government apparently designated that system of caves as the 'Renton Cavern Complex'.

"The cavern, and the network of underground caves and passages, were formed over time by naturally-occurring activity— primarily magma flow—dating back to the formation of the island.

Those same areas were later expanded—over the course of thousands of years—by periodic excavation done by the indigenous Tongva people. While there is no way to know why the Tongva were digging or adding to the underground caves and passages, the assumption is that they were doing so for religious purposes.

"Since human-made underground passageways for any religious purpose are referred to as catacombs, the underground chambers and passages created or expanded by the Tongva were designated by the US Government as 'catacombs'.

"Some of those underground areas were later expanded or added to by miners during the surge of interest in mining on the island in the 1800s, and then again in the early 1920s. The largest known mine in that area is the nearby David Malcolm Renton Mine. That mine has been closed and sealed-up for decades, and it has been commonly referred to since the 1920s simply as The Renton Mine.

"In the Government records just unearthed by Mr. Berrigan's office, all files from the 1940s seemed to have—perhaps for simplicity—labeled all features of the cave-complex as though they were somehow associated with the Renton Mine. So the Renton name was put on all of them. The Conservancy and the Government have mutually agreed to continue using these names. The names which are most relevant for the purposes of this meeting are: the 'Renton Stairs', the 'Renton Catacombs', the 'Renton Cavern', and the 'Renton Cave Sea-Lake'. Collectively, these features are named as the 'Renton Cavern Complex'. The only exception to this naming pattern in the files found by Mr. Berrigan's office is the underwater pass-through to the Renton Cave Sea-Lake. That underwater access-portal was designated as 'Ocean Hole 1' by the US military when they created it sometime in the 1940s.

"And that brings us to the tunnel. In the records found by Mr. Berrigan's office, according to reports filed by the US Army Corps of Engineers—first in the 1860s and then again in the 1940s—the tunnel is a lava tube. It was formed by magma-activity millions of years ago, and over time portions of it were shifted both in length and elevation by the movement of tectonic plates. In all documentation where it is mentioned, it is referred to simply as 'the tunnel'. The Conservancy and the Government have now mutually agreed to formally designate the tunnel specifically as 'The Catalina Train Tunnel'.

"Thank you, Mr. Davenport," said Berrigan, taking a folded piece of paper out from a pocket inside his suit and opening it in front of himself on the surface of the dining room table. "I first want to inform all of you briefly about the results of the Government's two coordinated assaults on the Renton Cavern Complex. No US military personnel were killed or injured. The stolen plutonium was securely recovered. All thirty of Trelain's men were captured and are in custody. None were killed. Seventeen of them were injured and are receiving appropriate medical treatment. Trelain is alive and in custody, and getting medical treatment for a concussion and other head-wounds. Trelain is facing a lot of charges. And he's going to be facing a lot of prison time, even if he decides to cooperate with authorities."

Berrigan looked over at MacKenzie and addressed her directly.

"Ms. Milles," Berrigan went on. "In addition to the numerous other charges the Government will be bringing against Trelain, I'm sure you'll be pleased to know he will also be facing charges for shooting you."

MacKenzie shook her head. "It was an accident," she said. "He wasn't on purpose trying to shoot me. It's not something he would do. The train stopping so all-of-a-sudden made him fire his gun by accident. And he wasn't going to shoot Erik, either. It was just a threat. Erik and I had guns pointed at us all afternoon. If Trelain had wanted, he could have shot us any time. The guns were just a threat to get us to not make trouble. Waving a loaded gun around is careless. I think he just got careless."

Berrigan scowled darkly. "Ms. Milles, you don't know what kind of a person Trelain is."

"Well," said MacKenzie, "everything he told me was true. And he said he doesn't kill people, and so I believe him."

"Don't let him fool you, Ms. Milles," Berrigan said unpleasantly. "He would kill anyone if he thought it would help him."

"Has he ever actually killed anyone?" asked MacKenzie.

There was a pause, and Berrigan looked as though he were losing the last of his short patience. "That information is classified," he said tersely.

Berrigan glanced down at his piece paper, and then looked back at MacKenzie. "Ms. Milles," he went on. "You apparently were not truthful with me when you claimed to have no memory of the access-point location for the route you took to escape the cavern-complex. You also flagrantly disobeyed my orders for you to remain in the cottage."

At this point, John interrupted.

"Excuse me, Mr. Berrigan," John began. "But it seems to me that without the information MacKenzie gave you, you would not have known about the cavern complex, you would not have been able to direct the Navy to launch assaults on the complex and capture the members of the smuggling ring, and you would not have been able to stop the stolen plutonium from illegally leaving the country. It also seems to me that if MacKenzie had not disobeyed your orders, Trelain would not have been caught, and the safety of Erik Roebling, who Trelain had taken as a hostage, might have been jeopardized quite tragically. Could you please clarify exactly what MacKenzie did that directly or indirectly led to anything other than you having complete success with everything you were hoping to accomplish?"

"Mr. Milles," replied Berrigan sternly. "The Government recognizes and appreciates the invaluable role your daughter has played in these events. But orders must be followed, and lying to the Government, or to a representative of the Government, is unacceptable. But to be clear, Mr. Milles. The Government is interested in results, no matter how those results are achieved. In this situation, the Government achieved the results we wanted. In the end, that's all that matters."

Berrigan glanced impatiently at his watch and looked down at his paper, before looking up and continuing.

"Next," he went on, "I next want to inform all of you briefly about the future of the Renton Cavern Complex.

"The top access door to Renton Stairs has been permanently sealed and covered over with rock-face concrete whose texture and color has been modified to blend with the surrounding rock."

At this, MacKenzie exchanged a quick knowing glance with her father and Katie.

"The gold mine is currently in the process of being sealed up," Berrigan was saying. "This will have the ancillary benefit of stopping the flow of cyanide into the water by the Seal Rocks, and the water-vent will be permanently sealed at the gold mine site.

"The train car is being left where it is on the tracks in the Renton Cavern Complex. All entrances to the Catalina Train Tunnel are being permanently sealed, at both ends. Today, this work is underway both at the Long Beach end of the tunnel and the Catalina end.

"Currently, the Renton Cave Sea-Lake through Ocean Hole 1 is the only access to the cavern complex. With the use of Navy submersibles, Government teams will continue to use that water-access to move work-crews in and out of the cavern complex until all their work is completed. In this way, no island residents, no tourists, and no satellite observation will be aware of the work being done in the Renton Cavern Complex. Once all the work is completed, the Ocean Hole 1 pass-through will then be permanently sealed.

"The idea of the overall approach agreed to by the Government and the Conservancy is simple. No one should ever again have access to these places. No one should ever know these places exist. No one should ever have any reason to try to access any of these places which, by their very existence, pose a wide range of different kinds of possible dangers, for a wide range of different reasons."

Berrigan checked his piece of paper again for a moment, then looked up.

"And finally," he went on, "I need to instruct all of you about the future of your role in this situation. No one is ever to know about any of this. As I have discussed with Mrs. Roebling, this circle of secrecy will be extended to include Mr. Roebling. It already includes the two members of the Conservancy legal team who are not present at this meeting. That makes nine of you. It's not a big number. But it's a big responsibility. I cannot impress upon you strongly enough how essential it is that you never share with anyone what you now know about this situation. As United States citizens, you have an obligation to your country to respect this crucial new responsibility. And it is not only for purposes of National Security. It is also for the welfare of Catalina Island. It doesn't take much imagination to recognize how this island would be changed if the curious world were to learn about these hidden places, and what had occurred there. It all must remain hidden. That is your responsibility."

Berrigan looked over at Davenport.

"We welcome the world to our beautiful island," Davenport said to everyone at the table. "That welcoming is part of what makes our island beautiful. But we must protect our island.

"The Conservancy just went to a lot of trouble to pre-emptively reduce the incoming crowds for a movie premiere. The premiere is a good thing. But the crowds would not have been good. We didn't cancel the premiere. And we didn't want to. But we had to protect the island from the crowds. We didn't solve the problem, but we did manage the problem.

"Should word of what we've discussed here today get to the public, it would not be manageable. It would be irreversible. It would change things on this island forever. And for the people who live here, and for the people who know and love our island, that change would not be good change, and it would be irreparable.

"We do no harm by keeping this secret. No one is hurt by our keeping to ourselves what we now know. In all parts of life, what we love, we must protect. At any cost. Our secrecy regarding all details of this extraordinary circumstance is vital to ensuring that we can preserve our beloved island as what it is and has always been—a magical place."

Berrigan nodded at Davenport. "Thank you, Mr. Davenport," he said.

Berrigan check his watch, and then checked his piece of paper again.

"Ms. Milles," said Berrigan, turning the force of his focus once again on MacKenzie. "Regarding the route you took to escape the cavern-complex. While the passage may be—as you've claimed—too narrow for an adult to pass through, it nevertheless remains a point of access to the Renton Cavern Complex. As such, it needs to be closed and permanently sealed. Directly following this meeting, Ms. Milles, you and your father will go with Mr. Davenport. You, Ms. Milles, will lead Mr. Davenport to the exact place where that entry-point is situated. Mr. Davenport will then record its precise location, and pass that information along to me, so that I can immediately dispatch a work-crew to close it up."

"MacKenzie," said Davenport. "I know that you understand the significance of names. You may be interested to know that I and the two members of the Conservancy legal team have persuaded Mr. Berrigan to agree that the name of the route you took to escape the cavern-complex will be formally designated as the 'Milles Passage'. You're going to be famous. However, no one will ever know about it."

"That's awesome, Mr. Davenport," said Erik. "What a cool idea."

"Thank you, Mr. Davenport..." said MacKenzie quietly. "That was a really thoughtful and nice thing for you to do. Thank you..."

Berrigan folded up his piece of paper and returned it to the inside pocket of his suit.

"Mr. Berrigan," said Erik. "I have a question.

"Go ahead," Berrigan replied briskly.

"What happened to the foreign mini-sub that was coming to buy the stolen plutonium?"

Berrigan nodded. "It was apprehended by US Naval forces prior to the assault at the sea-lake," he said. "Everyone aboard was uninjured and is now in custody. They will also all be facing charges. The country of origin for that sub is classified. As a precaution, US Naval forces will remain positioned several miles off the coast of Catalina for an indefinite period of time. Those ships will not be a conspicuous presence regarding boaters and divers and other recreational visitors to the island, as I have reassured Mr. Davenport."

Berrigan stood up. "Thank you all for coming to this meeting," he said. "If anyone has any further questions or concerns or relevant information, Mr. Davenport knows how to get in touch with me."

"Mr. Berrigan," said Brenda. "On behalf of all of us, I want to thank you for agreeing to change the location of your meeting so that we could have it here. We all appreciate it. And we all very much appreciate everything you and your team have done to protect us and protect our island. Thank you."

Berrigan nodded. "Thank you, Mrs. Roebling," he said. "We're all on the same team."

And then the meeting was over.

Everyone stood up and began talking to one another, and Berrigan and his men looked like they couldn't get out of there fast enough.

MacKenzie went with Brenda to politely walk Berrigan and his two men to the front door, where Brenda thanked Berrigan once more as he was leaving.

MacKenzie followed Berrigan outside and stopped him for a moment.

"Mr. Berrigan," she said.

Berrigan impatiently checked his watch and then looked down at MacKenzie. "Ms. Milles?" he replied.

"I wanted to say thank you," said MacKenzie

"Explain..."

"I..." MacKenzie hesitated. "Mr. Berrigan, I know you and I don't agree about a lot of things. But I know one thing. If you hadn't shown up, if you hadn't caught me while I was running, if you hadn't listened to what I had to say, I don't think any of this would have turned out the right way. No one does anything by themselves. We all need help. I needed your help. Erik needed your help. Catalina needed your help. And you helped us. And so, I just wanted to tell you that I think it's important for people to help people, and you helped us, and I'm really thankful that you did. So, I just wanted to say thank you."

"I appreciate that, Ms. Milles," said Berrigan. "It doesn't matter how we succeeded. We all achieved the results we wanted. That's all that matters."

Berrigan paused for a moment, thinking. "Ms. Milles," he finally said. "It doesn't make any difference to me, but it may to you.

Trelain said he was glad you weren't seriously injured. I don't believe him. I don't believe anything Trelain says. But you might choose to feel differently."

MacKenzie nodded. "Thank you for telling me that, Mr. Berrigan."

Berrigan nodded and went to re-join his men. The black vehicle started up, and then made a quick agile U-turn in the middle of the street before driving away.

Chapter 47

SEEING

Brenda was waiting inside the still-open front door, and she gave MacKenzie a great big hug as MacKenzie came back into the house.

"Beautiful brave heroic little MacKenzie…!" Brenda cooed fondly. She took a slight step back and put her hands affectionately on MacKenzie's shoulders. Her large glittery earrings clacked and jingled softly. "Erik told me about all you did and everything you went through to rescue him," she said.

"I would do anything for Erik," said MacKenzie quietly.

Brenda smiled broadly. "I know you would, MacKenzie," she said. "He would do anything for you."

MacKenzie nodded. "I know," she said. "That makes me really lucky…"

"Well," said Brenda cheerily, "you both make me really happy!"

Brenda closed the front door, and she and MacKenzie made their way back the dining room.

There was suddenly a lot of arranging to be done. MacKenzie needed to go for a golf cart drive with her father and Davenport into the foothills. MacKenzie also needed to get Erik's mountain bike for him off the rack at the back of Bertie. Katie needed to drive Bertie back to the cottage and make some important phone calls about the changing situation with the coral, somehow without revealing any details of the smugglers' gold-mining operations. Brenda had said that Erik's father, Brant, would be home shortly, and he wanted to take everyone out that evening to a fancy dinner. Davenport had to politely decline, since he had far too much work to do at the Conservancy for Berrigan. But Davenport and Brant Roebling were good friends, and Davenport asked that Brenda please extend a thank-you and a welcome-home to Brant, and to please assure Brant that Davenport was looking forward to getting together with him and catching up soon.

John and Katie and MacKenzie were sorry that Davenport wouldn't be able to be there, but the three of them were now eagerly looking forward to the dinner outing, and to at last getting to meet Erik's father. Brenda said she would call them at the cottage with details as soon as the reservations had been made, and MacKenzie asked if she needed to dress fancy since it was going to be a fancy dinner. Brenda laughed and said it was going to be a private room, and reassured MacKenzie that how she was dressed right now was perfectly fine, and she just needed to dress comfortably to suit herself.

MacKenzie and Erik headed outside to get Erik's mountain bike off Bertie, and then together they walked the bicycle into Erik's garage. Erik told MacKenzie he had spoken with Davenport about their backpacks, and Davenport had promised to somehow find for them the name of the Marine who had helped them.

Erik's house was large, and the return route they took from the garage back to where everyone was still congregating in the dining room ended up leading through a hallway of Erik's house that MacKenzie had never been through. A picture on one of the walls as they went past stopped her.

"Erik," she said. "What's that...?"

She was pointing to an engraved black-and-white portrait hanging on the wall within an old decorative frame that had little three-dimensional railroad tracks running around all the edges.

"That's such an amazingly cool frame..." MacKenzie went on, fascinated. "Who's that in the picture...?"

Erik smiled. "One of my distant relatives," he explained. "He was a railroad tycoon in the 1800s, and he was really successful. He wasn't Wrigley-wealthy, but he was pretty seriously wealthy. I think we're still spending his money..."

"What's a tycoon?" asked MacKenzie.

Erik paused for a tentative moment, smiling hesitantly. "Milles-method...?" he suggested.

MacKenzie grinned. "Go for it...!"

Erik took a dramatic breath. "Okay..." he began. "A tycoon is a person who's become rich and powerful from big success in a particular kind of business. 'The 19th century railroad tycoon made a lot of money because he ran all of his train businesses so well.' Et cetera."

MacKenzie nodded empathetically, smiling broadly. "You nailed it!" she said delightedly. "Nice job!"

She and Erik high-fived.

"My Dad would approve," MacKenzie added proudly. "You're now a member of the family...!"

When MacKenzie and Erik got back to the dining room, everyone had already said their thank-yous and good-byes to Brenda. John had given Katie the keys to Bertie, and she had headed out to make her way back to the cottage. Davenport was now outside in his Conservancy golf cart waiting for MacKenzie and her father.

MacKenzie said her thank-yous and good-byes to Brenda and Erik at the front door, and Brenda repeated that she would be calling the cottage with dinner-reservation information within the hour.

MacKenzie and her father headed down the driveway toward where Davenport was patiently waiting for them and talking with someone on his walkie-talkie.

"Dad," said MacKenzie as they walked. "About those classified files that Berrigan shared with Mr. Davenport..."

"What about them?"

"Well, Trelain told me about them. But he said there was only one copy, and that he had taken it..."

"Did Trelain say why he thought there was only one copy?"

"He said the government's filing system was flawed..."

"Well, then," said John. "So, that might explain it. If the system is flawed, and it seems like there's only one copy, that sounds to me like no one should be surprised when it turns out there's more than one copy..."

MacKenzie nodded. "In a weird way, Dad, that actually makes sense... Trelain said that he thought he might have been careless. If he didn't think about it the way you just did, that sure seems like he was kind of careless..."

They reached the Conservancy golf cart and slid their way onto the cushions of the bench seats, and Davenport drove them off toward the foothills.

MacKenzie's driving directions took them as far as the edge of one of the fire roads, and they had to hike on foot from there. She led them to the small unremarkable tower of rock outcropping where she had exited from—and then later re-entered—the last passage-pathway of The Krazy-Straw. The several rock-tower fingers reaching up from their dense tangles of overgrowth and bushes all looked nearly indistinguishable from each other, and MacKenzie gave Davenport a reliable visual mnemonic device he could use to remember which one was the correct entrance to the Milles Passage. Saying that new name aloud gave MacKenzie a strange feeling that she couldn't tell if she liked or not.

They hiked their way back to the golf cart, and Davenport drove them back to the cottage.

Katie greeted everyone at the front door, and Davenport asked if he could please come in and use the phone. Davenport made a quick call from the kitchen, and arranged to rendezvous with members of Berrigan's team back up in the foothills to show them precisely where they could begin their work sealing up the top opening of the Milles Passage.

Davenport thanked MacKenzie for her help, and for all she had done, and he thanked the three of them again for coming to the meeting. Wishing them an enjoyable evening out with the Roeblings, he headed back outside and drove off. MacKenzie felt bad for him that his work-day was being so extended and busy, while they would be getting to have fun out at a fancy dinner with wonderful people.

Katie had listened to the end of the Cubs game for MacKenzie and John on the short-wave radio, and she shared the good news that the Cubs had defeated the Rockies by a score of 12-to-2 in a rain-shortened game that had ended in the middle of the eighth inning. MacKenzie hugged and thanked Katie, and the three of them high-fived in elated high spirits.

As she had promised, Brenda called with details of the dinner plans. Katie headed hurriedly off in her Marine Center golf cart back to her hotel to change, and said she would meet-up with John and MacKenzie at the restaurant. MacKenzie and her father then got themselves cleaned-up and presentable, although MacKenzie decided to take Brenda at her word and chose to not change out of her favorite clothes.

The dinner was like *The Brenda*. It was a large fancy affair, and everything about it was fun and enjoyable. Erik's father was as excited to meet MacKenzie and John and Katie as they were to meet him. Like Erik and Brenda and John, Brant loved to talk. And like them, he was entertaining and good at it. Brant and John instantly recognized each other as kindred spirits. The two of them spent a great deal of gregarious time in lively discussion together, and they bonded like brothers over their shared experience of both being Navy veterans.

In the cloistered safe seclusion of the restaurant's large private room, Erik and MacKenzie were able to share with Brant all the details of their harrowing adventure. It was the first time for all of them hearing the entire tale fully told by Erik and MacKenzie together. The parents were amazed and horrified in turns at what they were hearing, and even MacKenzie and Erik at times found themselves incredulous that the extraordinary events they were recounting had actually happened to them.

By the time dessert was served, it seemed as though the six of them had all known each other for years. The full-group conversations and satellite-aside chats were flowing with an effortless ease that pulsed with a family-casual fondness and energetic familiarity they all were reveling in together.

Brant apparently had been holding in reserve a special surprise, and at last revealed that he had 'pulled some strings' and had gotten them six tickets for *The Vanishing American* premiere at the Casino on Tuesday. After joyful gasps and delighted exclamations, everyone spontaneously applauded and showered Brant with deeply appreciative kudos and gratitude.

The Bertie-ride back to the cottage was spent with MacKenzie and John and Katie all talking with animated enthusiasm about how much everyone liked Erik's father, and how amazing the dinner was, no so much for the lavish food fare, but more for how much they had enjoyed being all together with Erik's family.

"Erik was so happy to see his dad," MacKenzie said as the three of them made their way into the cottage and began to settle themselves in the living room. "He has so much energy when his dad's around."

John sat heavily down into his armchair and nodded. "That's just what you and Erik need," he said sarcastically. "More energy…"

MacKenzie and Katie laughed, and Katie relaxed her way into her armchair.

"Erik's dad is awesome…" said MacKenzie, sprawling comfortably on the couch.

"He's smart," John agreed. "And very entertaining. The Roeblings are such enjoyable people to spend time with."

"They're a really great family," said Katie.

"And that was such a lot of so much amazing delicious food," MacKenzie said contentedly. "I don't think I'm going to need to eat again for days… Anybody want me to make them some coffee?"

John shook his head. "No thanks, Mac," he said. "I'm with you—I don't think I'll need any kind food or beverage for several days…"

"No thank you, MacKenzie," Katie said distractedly. Her attention had been pulled in a different direction by the cheery rose-colored blossoms of the plants in the glass of water on the coffee table.

"MacKenzie," said Katie. "Did you put these here…?"

MacKenzie nodded. "This morning. You guys probably didn't notice. We were in a rush to get to the Berrigan meeting. It's my wildflower-reminder."

"What is it supposed to remind you?"

"To be more careful when I'm doing something in a hurry," explained MacKenzie.

"Where did they come from?" asked Katie.

"The foothills," said MacKenzie. "They were growing around the spokes in my bike wheel. Only, I didn't notice because I was hurrying, and I by accident snapped them off their roots when I lifted my bike up. It was really careless of me, and I still feel bad about it…"

Katie was now leaning forward in her chair and looking intently at the plant blossoms.

"John..." said Katie, her voice now edged with concern.

"KC...?" John replied.

"Did you see this...?" she asked.

"What do you mean?" John asked.

"Those aren't just wildflowers..." said Katie.

John leaned forward and looked. There was a long pause. "I think you're right..." he said slowly. "Oh... Oh my goodness..."

MacKenzie sat up straight. "What...?" she said quickly. "What's happening? What's going on...?"

"It's red clover..." said John, recognition and understanding flooding across his face.

"Is that bad?" asked MacKenzie.

"It's bad for cattle and buffalo..." John said slowly.

"Why?" asked MacKenzie.

"It causes molybdenosis," said Katie.

John nodded, and ran a hand through his hair in sudden intense thought. "If they eat a lot of red clover," he explained distractedly, "it affects their digestion. It makes the level of copper in their bodies drop too low..."

"Wait..." said MacKenzie. "You mean, the reason the buffalo are sick is because they've been eating red clover...?"

"As of right now," he said slowly, "I think the answer to that question is yes..."

John stood up. "Mac," he said quietly. "When we were on the dock in Long Beach, you said you wanted to help solve the mystery of the sick buffalo. Well, thanks to you and Katie, I think the mystery may have just been solved..." He looked at his watch. "Excuse me, you two," he went on quickly. "I need to call Ed about this..."

John hastened out of the living room and headed into the kitchen.

MacKenzie watched with concern as he left, then turned toward Katie.

"I don't understand…" said MacKenzie. "Why would red clover all-of-a-sudden start making the buffalo sick…?

Katie shook her head. "Red clover is not indigenous to Catalina," she said. "It's never been here before. It shouldn't be here now. It's never made the buffalo sick before because they've never eaten it before."

"So, then what's it doing here…?" asked MacKenzie.

"Well," explained Katie. "Red clover is not a 'bad' plant. It's just bad for animals like cattle and buffalo if they eat too much of it. So, at some point—most likely in the past two years—red clover seeds somehow got on the island. Clover spreads easily and quickly."

"But how did the seeds get here…?"

Katie shook her head. "There's probably no way to know. Someone could have brought potted plants from the mainland that had red clover or red-clover seeds in the soil mixture. Someone hiking on the mainland could have gotten red clover seeds in their shoes or clothing, and then worn those same clothes on a day-trip to hike in Catalina, and some of the red-clover seeds got lucky. There are so many different ways it could have happened."

"Do you think someone did it on purpose?"

Katie shook her head again. "That's unlikely. Someone may have liked the look of the red clover and brought a lot of it from the mainland for a garden. Red clover is very pretty. And I doubt that anyone who did that was thinking about how it might one day make the island bison sick."

"So, what will Dad do next?" asked MacKenzie.

"Well," said Katie. "If it turns out that red clover really is what's making the buffalo sick, that would mean there's a lot of it growing all throughout the wildlands. If that's the case, there are three things your dad and the Conservancy are going to have to deal with. One, is finding and getting rid of all the red clover. Two, is making sure that the buffalo then fully recover their health. Three, is coming up with the best way to always be on the lookout, in the future, for when the red clover might start to grow back in the wildlands."

"Is Dad going to be okay..." MacKenzie asked worriedly.

Katie got up and came over to the couch. She sat down next to MacKenzie and put her arm gently around MacKenzie's shoulders. "This is the answer your dad has been looking for ever since he got that first phone call from Ed Davenport," she said gently. "The solution to a problem doesn't always show up with a big colorful burst. Sometimes it just tip-toes in from a place you didn't see, and then it's just there. Solutions don't always come with a big celebration. Sometimes our own thoughts and feelings are caught by surprise, and they need time to catch up. You know better than anyone, little dolphin. Your dad cares deeply about his work. The answer he's been working so hard to find has just been found. That can be overwhelming. But it's a good kind of overwhelming. Your dad's going to be fine. He's going to be more than fine. The path of its arrival may be unexpected, but this solution is what he's been hoping for. Solutions so often don't come easily. Sometimes you need some good luck. Sometimes you need to have a magical daughter."

Chapter 48

WARRIOR

The next morning, MacKenzie and her father returned to their Catalina-normal start-of-the-day routine. They got up early, and MacKenzie made breakfast for both of them and fresh coffee for her father. After breakfast, John sat in the kitchen sipping his coffee. He kept MacKenzie company while she cleaned up and washed dishes from breakfast, and the two of them made plans to have lunch together at the Italian restaurant. Before MacKenzie had gone to bed Sunday night, Katie had once again changed the dressings of MacKenzie's bandages, and this morning all of MacKenzie was generally feeling much better, including her gunshot wound.

MacKenzie and her father then talked about the buffalo and the red clover until Davenport showed up like clockwork at 7:30.

Shortly after Davenport and John had driven off, Erik called to tell MacKenzie he was going to be spending the first part of the day with his father, but he wanted to get together with MacKenzie after lunch, and they agreed to meet at their usual spot on Crescent Ave at 1:00.

MacKenzie brushed her teeth, popped a piece of Wrigley's Spearmint gum into her mouth, and headed out on the mountain bike she had borrowed from Erik. It felt like years had passed since the last time she had gone for a by-herself morning bike ride. Her still-sore muscles were not fully cooperating, but they didn't give her too much of a hard time as she pedaled her way down to Pebbly Beach Road and on toward Abalone Point.

The cool breeze and warm sun of the bright new morning made her feel even better. It was nice to be able to pedal fast without being in a hurry or scared, and the swift speed of her forward motion was making her feel refreshed and exhilarated and strong.

Someone was standing on the side of the road in front MacKenzie's rock-warrior sentry as she approached. Unlike the disturbing chill she had always felt when seeing the mysterious man who had turned out to be Berrigan, this person made MacKenzie feel neither apprehensive nor fearful. But she was having a peculiar feeling inside. For no reason she could identify, she felt as though whoever was standing there was somehow waiting for her.

Flipping up her sunglasses, she biked slowly up to him and stopped. She stepped down onto the pavement, straddling her bike and holding on to the handlebars.

The man was tall. He was dressed in ordinary black clothing and a plain white shirt, with a thin black tie. His face was shaded by the broad brim of a simple black hat with a band of turquoise stones set in silver wrapped around the base of the round-crown top. The man looked to be very much older than MacKenzie's father. His skin was dark from sun and wrinkled with age. His eyes were clear and steady, and looked as though they had seen a great many things. His face was severe and strong, but his expression was calm and kind. To MacKenzie, he seemed wise and dignified, so much so that she almost wondered if she should take off her baseball cap out of respect.

"Excuse me, sir…" she said with slow cautious politeness. "I hope it's not too rude of me… But if don't mind my asking… Sir, who are you…?"

The man nodded kindly at her. "I am what I have done," he said.

His voice was deep and powerful. Not like the iron-fist power of Berrigan's voice, but a noble mightier kind of power. A power that came from a strength far greater than muscle or authority.

"My mother was a great woman," the man continued. "My

father was a great man. Any goodness I have ever brought to this world is in honor of my father and mother. Any goodness that is within me has come from my father and mother. My name comes from my father. I am the oldest son of Man Hammer."

MacKenzie gasped in amazement, and by itself her hand covered her mouth.

"You're Fire-Walker..." she said in quiet awe.

He nodded.

"Are... Are you here for the movie premiere tomorrow...?" she asked.

"I am here to see you," he said.

Somewhere far in the distance, the tubular bells of the Chimes Tower began tolling.

"I have been waiting for you," Fire-Walker said.

"Today...?" asked MacKenzie in increasing confusion.

Fire-Walker shook his head. "For many years," he said. "I knew you would come here."

"Here...? MacKenzie asked, momentarily glancing up at the steadfast motionless waving hand of the rock-formation behind Fire-Walker. "To the rock-warrior sentry...?"

"To this island," said Fire-Walker. "I did not know who you would be. But I knew what you would do."

"I... I'm MacKenzie Milles..." she said hesitantly.

Fire-Walker nodded. He gestured with a weathered hand toward the stone bench next to where he was standing. "I would ask you to sit for a short time," he said.

MacKenzie got fully off her bike and leaned it against the railing. On the far side of the railing, the rock-formation that was the body of the warrior-sentry widened where it met the narrow strip of beach below, as if underneath the surface of the sand was vastly more of the rock than what could be seen rising into the air above.

MacKenzie sat down on the flat pink stone of the bench. Fire-Walker sat on the bench not far apart from her.

It felt to MacKenzie as though time had stopped and the world was standing still.

The two of them looked at each other.

"I... I'm really honored to meet you, Mr. Fire-Walker," she said. "I... I think what you did to save those people from the fire was so brave and heroic... I haven't stopped thinking about it ever since I heard the story of what you did..."

"For some," said Fire-Walker, "when others are in need, an inner part of ourselves awakens to makes us better than we are."

"I..." MacKenzie faltered. "I... I think I know what you mean..."

"The strength to go into the fire was a gift of bravery from my father," said Fire-Walker. "The recognition that I had to go into the fire was a gift of goodness from my mother."

"Were your parents proud of you?" MacKenzie asked.

"My mother left this world before Man Hammer's oldest son became Fire-Walker."

"I... I'm sorry..." MacKenzie said quietly.

"It is the way of things," said Fire-Walker. "Man Hammer is with her now. One day, I will again be with them together."

"The Navajo people must be so very proud of you..." said MacKenzie. "I think anyone who knows your story must be so proud of you..."

"We call ourselves Diné," said Fire-Walker. "It means 'the people'. Navajo means 'place of great planted fields'. Some of us say Diné is the name of our past. Some of us say Navajo is the name of our future. You may say Navajo. It is more familiar to you. I will feel no dishonor.

"I am not Tongva. Should you meet someone of the Tongva tribal people, you must ask how they wish to be addressed. Their wishes should be respected. Some will say Tongva. Some will say Gabrieleño. Many will say Kizh. It means 'people of the willowhouse'."

Fire-Walker pronounced the third name as 'Keech', and MacKenzie etched the sound permanently into her memory.

"This is about the Tongva gold, isn't it..." said MacKenzie.

"It is always about gold, and never about gold," said Fire-Walker. "What truly is of worth has nothing to do with gold. But it is the way of the world to always be about gold. That will never be otherwise."

"Did... Did I do something wrong...?" MacKenzie asked anxiously.

"What you did not do—that has to do with the gold," said Fire-Walker. "What you did do—that has nothing to do with gold."

"Please forgive me..." said MacKenzie. "But, I don't understand..."

"There is no greater goodness than helping others," said Fire-Walker. "There is no greater harmony with the universe than saving a life. You were brave in the face of danger. Danger is not the same for all people. You faced a danger which was very real for you. You had fear, and you did not know what would be the path to success or survival. But still you went into the heart of the danger to help another."

"So did you," said MacKenzie quietly. "When you ran into that fire..."

Fire-Walker nodded. "Danger is not the same for all people," he repeated. "Fire is not the same for all people."

"Mr. Fire-Walker, how... How do you know about what happened to me underground...?"

"Many things cannot be understood or explained," said Fire-Walker. "But the longer one lives, the more one knows."

"Did I do something wrong…" MacKenzie repeated apprehensively. "In the cavern with all the Tongva gold…?"

"You found the gold," said Fire-Walker. "Yet, you told no one."

"I didn't think it was right…" said MacKenzie. "The gold doesn't belong to me. The secret doesn't belong to me. I know the secret, but it's not my secret. I don't feel right sharing a secret that doesn't belong to me. It's too important. And it would affect so many things. It would affect so many people…"

Fire-Walker didn't say anything.

"Did you know where it was?" asked MacKenzie. "Did you know where the gold was hidden?"

Fire-Walker shook his head. "No," he said. "I knew it would be found. And I knew it had been found by you. I yet do not know where it is, nor do I need to know. I am not Tongva. I am Navajo. The gold does not belong to me."

"I still haven't told anyone…" said MacKenzie. "Is that the right thing to do?"

"The bond between a child and a parent is sacred," said Fire-Walker. "No child should ever hold back anything they wish to tell their parent."

MacKenzie nodded. "I haven't told my Dad or Katie or Erik, yet," she said slowly. "But I'm going to. At least, I think I am… But I also don't know if it's fair to them, to make them have to keep such a big secret. Is it okay to tell them…?"

"What does your heart say?" said Fire-Walker.

"That it's probably okay…"

Fire-Walker nodded. "Trust your heart."

"But, should I tell anyone else…?"

"What does your heart say?"

"That I shouldn't…"

Fire-Walker nodded. "There may one day be the right time. But now is not that time."

MacKenzie nodded. "Okay…" she said quietly.

"In the cavern with the gold," said Fire-Walker. "You took nothing. You not only told no one, you took nothing."

MacKenzie shook her head. "It doesn't belong to me," she said again. "And I felt awful that I by accident disturbed some of the objects. I still feel terrible about that. I didn't mean to be disrespectful…"

"You told no one, and you took nothing," Fire-Walker said again. "By what you did not do, you did what no other would do. You sought no personal gain for yourself. You respected what is sacred. You did what was right. You sought neither recognition nor reward. To do what is right brings great honor. To do what is right when no other eyes are watching brings greater honor."

"Thank you…" MacKenzie said quietly.

"You took nothing, but something chose to leave with you," said Fire-Walker.

MacKenzie shook her head adamantly. "No," she said. "It's not possible."

"It found its way into your pocket," said Fire-Walker.

MacKenzie flashed back in her mind to that horrible moment in the dark cavern when she was sure she was being attacked. She now remembered something she had forgotten—the pain of something pressing into the side of the top of her leg as she rolled. Had something small from the pile during all her thrashing and panicked chaos somehow fallen into a pocket of her jeans? She was wearing them now. Her crawling-bruised knees were showing through the new holes. But her once-filthy jeans had been washed since then. They were now clean and free from the dirt and dust and grime and terror of all she had been through that night. Even if something small had somehow gotten trapped in one of her pockets, by now it would be long gone.

"No," said Fire-Walker. "It yet remains."

MacKenzie looked up at him. Why is everyone always able to read my mind? she asked herself with perplexed frustration. But that thought was pushed away for another time.

She stood up and put her hand on the outside of her jeans front pockets. There was a bulge in the one on the right. She reached into the pocket and pulled out the still-blood-stained shred of Erik's shirt. And now it had oil paint on it from her father's fingers. She stuffed it back into her pocket and patted the outside of her other pocket. Nothing. It just felt flat. It just felt... But there was something. Something at the bottom of her left front pocket. It was small, but it was something. She couldn't believe that in all these past few days she hadn't noticed it.

She put her hand inside and found nothing. She reached down farther, to the very bottom of the pocket. Her fingers touched something. A small, smooth, curved object. Grasping it, she pulled her hand from her pocket and opened her fingers in front of her eyes to see what it was.

It was a small gold dolphin. It was more flat than round, but it was precisely detailed. A round gold circular loop had been crafted into the top of the gold figure, on the dolphin's back in front of its dorsal fin. This had once been a piece of jewelry.

"It... It didn't want to stay with the rest..." MacKenzie said slowly.

"Sometimes there is one who chooses a different path," said Fire-Walker.

"It's beautiful..." breathed MacKenzie. "It's amazing... I... I feel like now I've helped it... I helped it to go its own way... But, I also feel like... Can I..."

Fire-Walker nodded. "You may do with it as you wish," he said. "It is yours—to keep or to give away."

"Will... Will it be mad at me if I give it to someone...?"

Fire-Walker shook his head. "It knows what is in your heart. It wants you to follow the path your heart leads you on."

Fire-Walker stood up and faced MacKenzie.

"I always will be Man Hammer's Oldest Boy," he said. "But I was given another name. Names make a difference. You will always be MacKenzie Milles. But you have distinguished yourself, and you too have been given another name."

MacKenzie looked up at him, feeling the smooth curved surface of the gold dolphin in her hand, feeling confused excitement in her heart.

"I... I don't understand..." she said.

"You are now Honor-Bringer," said Fire-Walker. "From what you did, and from what you did not do, you have brought great honor. You are a Nophaie the Warrior now. You dared to do what no other would attempt—not for your own sake, but for the sake of others. Your actions bring goodness. Nophaie the Warrior is not Tongva. Nophaie the Warrior is Navajo. You are not Navajo, but you now are a Nophaie the Warrior. And you are now Honor-Bringer. Your actions bring honor—from what you have done, and from what you have not done."

MacKenzie was trembling with excitement. She didn't understand how a name could make you a different person. But she felt suddenly different. She wasn't just MacKenzie Milles. She was Honor-Bringer. She was a Nophaie the Warrior.

"I'm a Nophaie the Warrior..." she said aloud.

She liked the way it sounded. She liked the way she felt when she said it.

"Thank you, Mr. Fire-Walker..." she said breathlessly. "Mr. Fire-Walker..." she went on. "I... I think it's amazing that you saved those people. I know you didn't save them so that you would have a name. But I think it's amazing and wonderful that by doing such an incredible and brave thing, that was how you got to have your own name. I know you're a hero to those people you saved. I just want you to know, you're a hero to me, too..."

Fire-Walker bowed his head to her.

MacKenzie bowed her head back to him. She didn't know why. But she felt it was somehow right.

The two of them stood for a moment, their heads bowed slightly to each other, and then they both stood straight.

"Now you must return to your family," said Fire-Walker. "Your family that you have always had, and your new family that you have made. You are young to have done something of such greatness. For some, early greatness becomes a burden. You must not let that be your path. Instead, aspire to future goodness, without measuring yourself by your past goodness. Permit yourself to live forward, inspired by the past, but never confined by it."

MacKenzie nodded, trying to understand and process all she was hearing, all she was thinking, all she was feeling.

"Mr. Fire-Walker," she asked. "How are you connected to all this...? The more time I've spent here on Catalina, the more I've felt like all these things are connected. I feel like you are connected. I know you're connected, because you're here, and you and I are talking with each other... But... I don't understand... How are all these things connected...?"

For the first time, the trace of a smile appeared on the face of Fire-Walker.

"Honor-Bringer," he said kindly. "Nophaie the Warrior. Do you yet not see?"

MacKenzie shook her head.

"The connection is you," said Fire-Walker. "You are what connects all these things."

MacKenzie's thoughts were shocked motionless. In a vast terrible slow-rising curl, realization loomed. And then it crashed down, flooding over her like an ocean wave.

She was so overwhelmed, she had to sit down. Her thoughts were swimming. Her mind flashed back to when she and Erik were at Emerald Bay, sitting on the ground in front of Prentiss's grave marker. She now was having a feeling like what she had experienced there. It was a strange overpowering confusion. Some boundary was suddenly gone. Some barrier wall suddenly was no longer there, and the solid definite line between story details and the real events of her own real life had abruptly become grey and blurred.

"You are trying to understand," said Fire-Walker. "But recognition and understanding do not always walk together. Often one arrives before the other. Sometimes, one never arrives at all."

MacKenzie's mind was reeling. Part of her was overwhelmed in a cloud of confusion. Part of her was overwhelmed at the thought of what she might see if the confusion cleared.

"New thoughts can bring new questions not easily answered," said Fire-Walker. "The best answer to a question can sometimes be a different question. The Navajo people believe in the goodness of harmony—the harmony of all living things and the universe. Honor-Bringer, I ask you this—it is an old Navajo question: Is the bee there for the flower, or is the flower there for the bee?"

MacKenzie had no words to express what she so much did not understand.

"There are many things we must leave to the Divine Spirits," said Fire-Walker. "Things we cannot understand, things we are not meant to understand."

In the distance, the tubular bells of the Chimes Tower once again began tolling.

"It is time, Honor-Bringer," he said.

MacKenzie forced herself to stand up. She was dizzy with all that was going on inside her heart and her thoughts.

"You and I will not speak again, young Nophaie," said Fire-Walker. "I lament that. But none can change what has been willed by the Divine Spirits. We exist at this moment in the Fourth World, The Glittering World. Perhaps you and I shall meet again, in another world.

"But not all things are heavy. You are part of the new family which you have made. There are few things in any of the four worlds which can equal the goodness of family. And you have plans for the independent spirit of the object you yet hold in your hand. You must move forward to set those plans into their proper motion."

MacKenzie struggled to find her voice. "What... What will happen to the gold in the hidden cavern?" she at last managed to say.

"What the Divine Spirits have determined to happen," said Fire-Walker, "that is what will happen. I do not know what that is, or when that will be."

MacKenzie nodded, in recognition, without understanding.

"There is one other path," said Fire-Walker. "Not all paths are connected, but some paths are parallel. The curse upon your baseball team will end. It will not end in my lifetime. But it will end in yours. And when it ends, you are to accept that as a sign—a sign that you are then free to tell what you know of the Tongva gold, if you wish. It is a long time to keep such a secret. But until that time has passed, because you are she who brings honor, you will keep the secret. And when the curse is ended, you are then released from your burden of secrecy. The curse and the Tongva gold are not connected. But the time when the curse ends, and when your burden of secrecy ends—that time is entirely connected."

"Thank you for telling me that..." MacKenzie said quietly.

She paused for a moment.

"Mr. Fire-Walker..." she said at last. "Why did you want to meet me...?"

"To give you the gift of your name," said Fire-Walker. "To give you help in understanding. To give myself the gift of meeting you."

"Thank you..." said MacKenzie softly. "I am so honored to have met you... I am so very honored to know you... I... I don't know how to say good-bye..."

Fire-Walker nodded. "Man Hammer never said with his words that he was proud of his oldest son. But he said it with his eyes. I have lived through many years, through many things. The look in Man Hammer's eyes when his oldest son became Fire-Walker is the most important moment of my life. It gives me strength and light every day I am alive. My father is no longer in this world. But he is always with me. And that moment is always with me. Yet, words do have weight and value. Names make a difference. Words make a difference. There is something I do not want left unsaid... Young Nophaie, I am proud of you."

"Thank you..." MacKenzie said quietly. "I... I know words matter so very much... But... I don't know the right words to say... I am so very grateful to you... I am so honored by you..."

"Your words are of great value to me," said Fire-Walker. "I thank you for having said them."

"May I shake your hand...?" asked MacKenzie.

"I would be honored," said Fire-Walker.

They shook hands, and for a moment MacKenzie felt as though she was connected with the universe.

"Keep your eyes forward, Nophaie," said Fire-Walker as MacKenzie put the gold dolphin back into her pocket. "The path ahead not only leads to where you've never been. It also keeps you close to all you never want to leave behind."

MacKenzie climbed onto her bike and pedaled off toward the heart of Avalon. She didn't look back. She didn't have to. Meeting Fire-Walker would be part of her forever.

Chapter 49
PRIORITY

MacKenzie pedaled her way to Crescent Ave and locked her bike to a rack. From there, she went on foot. Fire-Walker had known she had plans for the gold dolphin. MacKenzie was moving forward to set those plans into their proper motion. Fire-Walker had said the gold dolphin was hers, to do with as she wished, to keep or give away. He had told her the gold dolphin knew what was in her heart, and that it wanted her to follow the path her heart was leading her on. And it was that path she was following now.

MacKenzie walked to Summer Ave, and the little bell on the door jingled as she entered Jake's small shop. She was greeted by the now-familiar smells of metal and machine oil and metal polish, and by a cheerful smiling Jake.

She first told Jake that her penny necklace had had a really rough day on Saturday, and thanks to the amazing job he had done of creating it, it had survived everything perfectly fine—just as she had wished for, just as he had promised her it always would. She thanked him effusively again for all he had done in crafting her necklace, and Jake told her how glad he was it had turned out the way she wanted.

MacKenzie took the gold dolphin from her pocket and handed it carefully to Jake, asking him if he could do the same thing he had done with her penny. The small dolphin wouldn't need a protective bezel. It would just need the loop-ring to be made stronger, and it would need a chain as strong and reliable and sure as the one that secured her penny around her neck.

She didn't say where the dolphin had come from, and Jake didn't ask. MacKenzie explained that it was a surprise gift for Erik, and Jake promised to keep it fully secret.

Jake explained that he would use the same braided titanium and yellow-gold alloy for Erik's chain. In fact, it would actually be the exact same chain. Jake had made an extra-long length for MacKenzie's necklace, just in case any imperfections had showed up when he was assembling everything together. None had, so he had the extra.

For MacKenzie, knowing that Erik's chain would be the same chain used in her own necklace made her thrilled and extremely happy.

Jake went on to say that Erik's dolphin-necklace would be much less complicated to make than MacKenzie's penny-necklace had been. There would be no bezel to craft or fit, and he already had the chain he would be using. So he would be able to have it all finished for her in a couple of hours.

"Can you get it the right size without having Erik's neck here...?" MacKenzie was asking with some apprehension.

Jake gave a friendly laugh. "I've known Erik a long time," he said. "And I'm a pretty good judge of necks. It's part of my job. So please don't be concerned. I can easily do this without Erik's neck."

MacKenzie grinned. "Thanks, Jake," she said earnestly. "Can you please make it so that the dolphin hangs on his neck in the same place where my penny hangs on mine?"

Jake nodded. "Easily," he said.

Jake's nodding always made MacKenzie feel like everything was all going to turn out perfectly. There are few feelings as soothing as when someone who knows what they're doing is matter-of-fact about everything being fine.

"His chain is the same as yours," said Jake. "And I'll give this loop-ring the same titanium-weld reinforcement as yours. In a couple of hours, this necklace will be just as durable and secure as yours. So, as long as Erik's wearing it, he'll never lose it. But I just want to tell you, MacKenzie. I've seen this kind of gold object before. Nothing exactly like this one, but I recognize the style and the type of gold. This is very old. And more than that, it's Tongva. It was made by the people who originally lived on the island. So, I just want you to know, it's valuable. It's off-the-charts valuable. I just wanted to make sure you know."

"Thank you, Jake," said MacKenzie. "It's actually got even more value than that. It's… It's like my penny…"

Jake smiled. "I can tell," he said. "I appreciate how much you've trusted me with things that are so important to you."

MacKenzie's hand went to her penny for a moment. "I'm so grateful for you, Jake," she said. "You're so very good at what you do. It wouldn't turn out right unless you did it."

"Thanks, MacKenzie," he said, smiling. "Okay, if you come back in a couple of hours, I'll have it all ready for you."

At noon, MacKenzie met her father at their favorite Italian restaurant, and they decided to eat lunch at one of the outside tables. The day was Catalina-warm-without-being-too-hot, and there was a periodic cooling breeze carrying the freshness of clean air and the salty sweetness of the ocean. John had his sunglasses hooked and hanging from the neck of his T-shirt. MacKenzie took her flip-up sunglasses off her Cubs cap and hooked them over the front of the white tank top she was wearing under her brightly-colored ragged-edged short-sleeve sweatshirt top.

This was the first lunch out that MacKenzie had had with just her father since they had come to Catalina. The food was delicious, and MacKenzie was enjoying the time alone with her father.

She didn't tell him about meeting Fire-Walker, and she continued to not tell him about finding the gold. She knew she would tell him everything eventually, but she wasn't yet ready.

John first told MacKenzie that Katie was having a full day of diving and being at the Marine Center in Two Harbors, but the three of them would be able to have dinner together that night at the cottage.

John also caught MacKenzie up on the new status of the situation with the buffalo. It hadn't taken long to confirm the presence of red clover in the wildlands. Now that he and the Conservancy team knew to look for it, they had found it everywhere. It was growing especially thickly in the areas with the largest number of sick buffalo, and there now was little doubt that the red clover was the cause of the sickness. Plans were in progress for determining the best and fastest ways to get rid of the red clover. None of the plans would involve herbicides, which John explained were chemicals used to kill certain plants. No one was interested in introducing any kind of chemicals into the Catalina wildlands environment.

MacKenzie and her father talked more about how much they had enjoyed the previous night's dinner with the Roeblings, and how much they liked Erik's father. MacKenzie told her father that she and Erik were spending the afternoon together after lunch, but that Erik would be spending the evening with his parents.

John said he would be home in time for catch, and if Katie didn't mind, the three of them could listen to the Cubs game, which MacKenzie clarified started at about 5:36 Catalina time.

They finished eating, and John checked his watch. It was nearly time for him to head back to Clarissa Ave and meet Davenport at the Conservancy building, and MacKenzie said that she wanted to walk with him.

"Dad..." MacKenzie was saying as they strolled together. "I know I've never asked this before, but... Could I please borrow your credit card...?"

John didn't hesitate, and he took his wallet out of one of his back pockets. He slid the card out and handed it to MacKenzie.

"Thanks, Dad..." MacKenzie said with quiet earnest gratitude.

She put the card carefully into the same left front pocket of her jeans where the gold dolphin had been hiding.

John slipped his wallet back into his pocket.

"It's for Erik…" said MacKenzie. "I mean… It's for something I'm kind of getting for Erik… I can't really explain right now…"

John nodded.

"I'll pay it all back to you…" said MacKenzie. "I promise…"

"Is it going to be expensive?" her father asked.

MacKenzie nodded. "Sort of probably yes…" she said.

"Okay."

"Thanks Dad…"

Her father smiled. "I trust you, Mac," he said. "You've never asked to borrow the credit card before. So I know it's important."

MacKenzie nodded. "It is… It's important…"

"And I give you permission to forge my signature when you sign for whatever you buy," her father went on. "Frankly, you could probably just write a scribble. Nobody ever checks those things. Do you have your school ID so you can prove you're a Milles?"

MacKenzie nodded. "It's in my pack," she said, reaching behind her back and tapping her borrowed-backpack for emphasis. "With my cottage-keys, and my sun block, and my water bottle."

John nodded. "Well, just don't buy a yacht or a house, because we honestly can't afford it."

MacKenzie laughed quietly. "I promise…"

Her father nodded again. "I just want you to know, Mac," he went on. "I know there's something else. I've known you for twelve years, and I know when you're not telling me something. And that's okay. And I love you. And I know that if you're going to tell me, you'll tell me when you're ready. And if you never tell me, that's okay too. I just want you to know, you can't sneak sunrise past a rooster. And I'm the rooster."

John tilted his head back and made a surprisingly realistic cock-a-doodle-doo crowing sound as they walked.

"Oh, dear god..." said MacKenzie. "Dad... You're embarrassing..."

"'But look,'" John recited dramatically, "'the morn, in russet mantle clad, Walks o'er the dew of yon high eastward hill...'"

MacKenzie rolled her eyes. "Something from 'Hamlet' after a rooster crows...?" she surmised.

Her father nodded.

MacKenzie stopped their walking to give her father a big hug. "I love you, Dad," she said emphatically.

"I love you, too, honey," her father said. "Thanks for putting up with me."

MacKenzie shook her head. "I don't put up with you, Dad. I'm just the luckiest daughter in the world because you're my Dad, that's all."

Her father lifted her baseball cap and mussed her hair affectionately, before putting her cap back in place on her head.

MacKenzie grinned happily.

"Please just get a receipt, Mac," her father asked. "I don't need to see it. But if you're going to start using credit cards, you might as well start getting receipts."

"Money is complicated..." said MacKenzie thoughtfully.

Her father shook his head. "You have no idea..." he said.

"Am I expensive, Dad?" MacKenzie asked.

John smiled. "Nothing on earth is more valuable than you, Mac," he said seriously.

"Thank you, Dad. But I mean, do I cost a lot?"

Her father shook his head again. "You're a bargain right now," he said. "Talk to me again in six years when you go off to college. I may feel differently..."

"Dad..." MacKenzie began hesitantly. "Dad, I—"

"Mac," said her father. "Important decisions should never be based on money. They should be based on people. Money is important. And having plenty of it makes a lot of things easier. But nothing matters more than the people we love, and the people we care about, and our relationships with them. You may be more brave and heroic and noble than most adults, Mac. But you're still only twelve. I'll teach you whatever I can about money. But you're way too young to be worrying about anything having to do with money. I've never known anyone who lives life and enjoys life more than you do. You live life right. Never let money change that."

MacKenzie nodded. "Okay, Dad..." she said. "I promise. And I promise I'll tell you everything. Both you and Katie..."

John nodded. "You never have to tell us anything. But if and when you're ready, we'll be there ready to listen."

Chapter 50
TOKEN

Shortly before 1:00, MacKenzie went back to Jake's shop. Jake carefully took the finished dolphin-necklace out of the folded tissue paper wrapping so MacKenzie could see it, and he draped it gently into her hands. MacKenzie lifted it up and held it reverently in the air by the brilliant braided chain. It was almost more than MacKenzie could manage to stop herself from crying with emotion. The necklace was magical. Seeing the little gold dolphin swinging happily in the light of day on the end of the beautiful chain filled her with indescribable joy. The dolphin seemed to be smiling at her. It seemed to be saying thank you.

MacKenzie tried to express to Jake how much what he had done meant to her, but she couldn't. But from the look on Jake's face as he watched her seeing the necklace, it was clear he seemed to recognize and understand at least some of what she was feeling.

Jake said he hoped she wouldn't be offended, but he wasn't charging her for any of the work. He was only charging her for the chain, and he was charging her only what the metals in the alloy had cost him and nothing more. He said he always gave Erik a big discount because they had known each other for so long, but he was giving MacKenzie more of a discount, and with a friendly smile he asked her to please not let Erik know about that detail.

Jake processed John's credit card for the sale. He didn't ask MacKenzie for an ID or check her forgery-version of her father's signature. MacKenzie nearly forgot to get a receipt, but Jake handed it to her when he returned John's credit card. MacKenzie put the card and receipt into her front left jeans pocket, and tried once again unsuccessfully to fully express to Jake how deeply grateful and appreciative she was. Jake said that he hoped Erik liked it, and MacKenzie promised that she and Erik would both come back soon so Jake could see Erik wearing it.

At 1:00, MacKenzie met Erik at their regular spot on Crescent Ave, and she asked him if he would please go for a short bike ride with her to Abalone Point. Erik had lived all of his fourteen years on Catalina Island, but it had never occurred to him that one of the two high rock formations at Abalone Point was a rock-warrior sentry, and he told MacKenzie he was honored that she wanted to go there together with him.

They arrived at Abalone Point. As she and Erik pedaled over to the side of Pebbly Beach Road, MacKenzie smiled at the rock-warrior sentry but she didn't wave back, because that was something she only did when she was there by herself.

They leaned their bikes against the railing and looked together for a moment out at the Pacific Ocean, stretching forever into the distance toward the horizon. Several sailboats moved across the sparkling surface of the water beneath the bright sun, the closer vessels seeming larger and travelling with more speed, the vessels that were farther away seeming smaller and making their way with more leisurely gradual slowness. Periodic gulls circled or coasted on air currents, and gave occasional distinct echoing announcements of their presence as they flew overhead.

MacKenzie suggested that she and Erik sit on one of the two pink stone benches, and they settled themselves in very nearly the same spots where MacKenzie and Fire-Walker had been sitting just a few hours earlier.

"Uh-oh..." said Erik. "I've been around you and your father long enough to know what's about to happen. We're going to have 'a talk'..."

MacKenzie nodded. "There's something important I haven't told you..."

"Okay..." Erik said with cautious hesitance.

"Erik... I met Fire-Walker..."

"Wait... What...?!"

MacKenzie nodded. "This morning," she said. "When I went for my morning ride to see my rock-warrior sentry... Fire-Walker was here... He was waiting for me... Right here..."

"Mac... I don't understand..."

MacKenzie shook her head. "I didn't understand either..." she said slowly. "But he was here, and he was waiting for me, because... Because he wanted to talk with me about something..."

Erik was shaking his head in confusion. "Mac... How does he even know you...? What was he doing here...? What did he want to talk with you about...?"

"He wanted to talk with me about... About what happened..." MacKenzie faltered. "I... I don't understand how he even knew... He doesn't look so very old, and you can tell right away he's very noble and heroic, but he's also really mysterious... He seems to know things... And... And he knew what happened... I don't know how he knew, but somehow he knew... He knew about... About something I haven't told you yet... I... I haven't told anyone about it..."

"Mac... What happened...?"

"Erik... I found it..."

"Found what?"

"I... I haven't told my Dad and Katie yet, but I'm going to. But... But I wanted to tell you first. And you're sworn to secrecy. You, my Dad, Katie, you're all not allowed to tell anyone, because I'm asking you to keep it a secret."

"Mac, what—"

"It was an accident," MacKenzie said. "I found it by accident when I was in The Krazy-Straw, trying to escape out to get help to rescue you... I found the cavern. The one from the treasure story. It had all the gold things from The Temple of the Sun. I found the Tongva gold..."

"Mac...!" Erik breathed in astonished amazement.

"When I first found it," MacKenzie explained, "I didn't know I'd found it. I wasn't using my flashlight, because I thought it was broken. And anyway, I was afraid anyone chasing me might see where I was if I turned it on. So I was in the dark.

"And then I thought I was being attacked, and I had a big fight with a whole lot of things I couldn't see. I was so scared, that I had to try my dead flashlight, and I finally got it to work for a few minutes. And then I could see what I had been fighting with. It turned out to be a lot of gold things that fell on me because I tripped over the bottom of the pile in the dark. And the pile was all the gold things from the story, stacked up like a mountain of treasure. It was so high I could hardly see the top.

"And it was a huge pile, but it wasn't a huge pile of treasure. It was a huge pile of special things that were so important to the Tongva people, that they hid them in a secret place to protect them. And so of course I didn't take any of the gold, because it doesn't belong to me. At least, I thought I didn't take anything... But it turned out that this fell its way into my pocket while I was fighting with the gold objects in the dark..."

MacKenzie reached into her jeans pocket and took out the folded tissue paper, and then she carefully took out the necklace. She held it up for a moment by its new chain, the gold dolphin glittering in the afternoon sunlight and swaying slightly as if it were swimming.

"Fire-Walker told me it's because that's what was supposed to happen," said MacKenzie. "He said even though I didn't want to take anything, this dolphin was supposed to leave the cavern with me, so it secretly hitched a ride. It was like the gold somehow knew

I wasn't going to take any of it, or tell anyone that it was there, and it wanted a way of saying thank you. And I think maybe also none of the gold wanted to leave the cavern, but maybe this little guy did. And so he was the one chosen to sneak his way out with me, and turn into a thank-you gift.

"And... And Fire-Walker also told me that...that because it was mine now, I could do whatever I wanted with it, and...and that whatever I did with it would be the right thing to do... He said... He said I could even give it away if I wanted...

"So, this little gold dolphin was made by the Tongva people. Probably a very long time ago. It didn't have its own chain, though. The chain comes from Jake because I asked him to put it there secretly, because I didn't want you to know yet. But, I want you to know now..."

Her emotions were starting to get the better of her, and she felt herself becoming overwhelmed, but she kept going.

"And I just want you to know," she said, "the chain is very strong. Jake even used the exact same chain from my necklace because he had extra left over. And he put something strong on the back of the loop-ring to make sure it doesn't ever break off the dolphin. And... And... And for a lot of reasons, I want you to please have this dolphin-necklace as a present from me..."

She held the dolphin-necklace out toward Erik.

Erik was shaking his head. "Mac..." he struggled to say. "I... I can't accept this... It's too important... It's too valuable... It belongs to you... It..."

Tears were running down the side of MacKenzie's face, and she was fiercely shaking her head.

"No," she said. "You're not allowed to say anything. All you're allowed to say is you'll take it. You can't ever sell it, you can't ever give it away. It's yours forever."

"Mac, I..."

She shook her head more adamantly, more tears flowing over her cheeks

"Say it. Say you'll keep it."

Erik slowly nodded. "I'll keep it…" he said, his voice filled with emotion.

"No matter what," instructed MacKenzie tearfully. "No matter what ever happens."

Erik nodded. Tears were forming in his eyes. "I'll never let it go," he said. "Ever."

He gently took the gift she was holding out to him. Lifting the necklace by its chain, he slipped it over his head and then down around his neck. The back of the chain became hidden by the length of his sun-and-sea-bleached hair, and the dolphin hung plainly visible against his tanned skin just inside the open halves of the top of his shirt.

MacKenzie wiped her eyes and nodded, gazing at the golden dolphin. "It looks good on you," she said. "It looks right. It's where it belongs. It looks like it's swimming. It's happy to be free."

"Mac, I…"

MacKenzie shook her head. "We're going to just not say anything about it anymore right now," she said. "You're wearing it, and it's yours. That's all I need to know. But, just… Just…" she couldn't say whatever she was struggling to say.

"I love it, Mac…" Erik said, reaching up to feel it lightly where it hung around his neck. "It's the best gift ever. Because it's from you…"

MacKenzie nodded and wiped away more of her slowing tears.

"Okay," she said. "That was a nice thing to say. I give you permission to read my mind. But only for a minute."

They looked intently at each other, their eyes still glistening.

"Okay," MacKenzie said at last with some finality. "I think we both know what happens now…"

Somewhere in the distance, the tubular bells of the Chimes Tower began tolling.

Erik continued to look into her eyes, and nodded. "After-breakfast dessert at Big Olaf's...?"

MacKenzie nodded. "Even though it's after lunch," she agreed firmly.

"Because it's our dessert," Erik explained. "We get to decide when we have it."

MacKenzie nodded again and gave Erik their tunnel-signal, snap-bounce-thumbs-up.

Erik made the tunnel-signal back in response, and they both grinned happily at each other.

They climbed up onto their bikes and pedaled off, back along Pebbly Beach Road toward Crescent Ave, on their way to Big Olaf's.

Chapter 51
COMMUNICATION

MacKenzie and Erik sat near the edge of Crescent Ave in the shadow of a tall palm tree at the top of Crescent Beach, eating from their cheery paper bowls full of towering colorful ice cream from Big Olaf's. They talked and chatted together, absently watching the animated happy activity of people enjoying the Avalon sun and frolicking on the beach, and the placidly bobbing dozens of moored sailboats and powerboats farther out in the Avalon Bay harbor.

At one point, the two of them realized they each at the same time were exploring their own necklaces with their fingers—Erik touching the smooth curves of the gold dolphin, MacKenzie feeling the textured surface of her 1951 penny. They laughed at themselves when they realized how in parallel they were, and they clacked plastic spoonfuls together in a champagne-less ice cream toast to celebrate.

Erik wanted to hear more about Fire-Walker, and MacKenzie told him all about the things Fire-Walker had said to her. Listening to herself describe it, MacKenzie felt like she was re-telling a dream. It seemed so unreal. But it had changed her. She was different now. Too different for it to have been a dream. *Dreams can change you,* she heard herself thinking. *But not the way Real Life can change you.*

She told Erik nearly everything. She didn't tell him about Fire-Walker's answer to her question about what connected everything that had happened. That was too stressful and overwhelming. She still didn't know how to think about it. Every time her thoughts tried to get close to it, they would suddenly panic and scamper away in all different directions. It was like when she sometimes tried to imagine what her life would be like if she had never come to Catalina. It was too stressful and overwhelming to think about. Except that, one was anxious confusion over 'what-does-this-mean', and the other was anxious confusion over 'what-if-this-had-never-happened'.

And she didn't tell Erik that Fire-Walker had said she now was Honor-Bringer. That was a different kind of overwhelming—that was overwhelming in a wonderful way. And it was something she had decided to keep for just herself alone.

But she did tell Erik about how Fire-Walker had told her she was now a Nophaie the Warrior. That seemed to be the most exciting part of the story for Erik. He beamed and glowed with pride and excitement, and he was adamant that there was no better person to truly recognize a Nophaie the Warrior than Fire-Walker. He went on to insist that of course Fire-Walker was absolutely right, and Erik reminded MacKenzie that he himself had tried to help her recognize that same truth when they were together on the *Torpedo Express*.

MacKenzie blushed and looked down in modest happy embarrassment, and reluctantly admitted it was hard to imagine that Fire-Walker and Erik could both be wrong about the same thing.

"Oh my god, Mac," Erik said suddenly. "I can't believe I almost forgot to tell you... You would have found this interesting anyway, but now I think you're going to be really interested in this..."

"Tell me...!" said MacKenzie, looking up eagerly.

"Okay," Erik went on. "So, my dad told me there's going to be a kind of tribute to Fire-Walker tomorrow night at the premiere, before the movie starts. Fire-Walker's not scheduled to be there, but I'll bet no one but you, and now me, has any idea that he's actually in Avalon right now..."

"I don't know if he's still on the island by now, though..." said MacKenzie. "I don't know where he lives, but if he doesn't like crowds and attention, he may have left Catalina already..."

Erik nodded. "Well, only you know what he looks like. Maybe you'll be able to see if somehow he's somewhere in the theater tomorrow night..."

"Maybe..." MacKenzie said uncertainly.

"Okay, but listen," Erik continued. "My dad has seen a copy of the tribute, and it turns out that Fire-Walker was a Code-Talker...!"

"I have no clue what that means..." said MacKenzie.

Erik nodded. "Well, the Code-Talkers actually helped the United States and its allies win World War II."

"That's incredible..." said MacKenzie. "But, how...? What did they do...?"

"During the war," Erik explained, "everyone on both sides needed to communicate with their troops and leaders, who were all in lots of different kinds of places. Everyone on both sides needed to send and receive information, especially using messages sent by telegraph. But whoever they were fighting against was always spying on their messages, and stealing valuable information. So, both sides had to use secret codes to make their messages harder to understand by the enemy. But both sides also had code-breakers, and their job was to figure out whatever code the other side was using. So each side was trying to find a code that the enemy couldn't figure out.

"So meanwhile, a lot of really patriotic Native American Indians had enlisted in the US Military when the war started. And then someone got the brilliant idea to use Native American Indian languages to code secret messages, because no one in the world understood those languages except for Native American Indians.

"So, the United States and its allies started to use Navajo Code-Talkers. The Code-Talkers were Navajo soldiers who were in all different troops, and they were in charge of coding and de-coding the secret messages, using their own Navajo language. And it was such a brilliant idea, and they were so good at what they did, the enemy could never break the code.

"But the Code-Talkers were so top secret, that no one even knew about them until 23 years after the war ended. Then in 1968, the government finally told everyone about the Code-Talkers and all they had done to help win the war.

"There had been lot of other Native American Indian soldiers who had become Code-Talkers, and so other Native American Indian languages besides Navajo had been used. It turns out there had even been Cherokee and Choctaw Code-Talkers during the First World War. But the Navajo were the most successful and most famous Code-Talkers of World War II. And all the Code-Talkers get credit for helping the United States and its allies to win the war.

"And so it turns out that Fire-Walker was one of the first Navajo Code-Talkers. So he wasn't just a hero by going into the fire to save the lives of that family on the reservation where he lived. He was also a great World War II hero."

"It's amazing..." said MacKenzie in awe. "What an incredible heroic life he's led... What an amazingly good person... Erik, just think how many people he's helped. Just think how many lives he's changed for the better... Think what a better place the world is because of him..."

Erik nodded. "It's extraordinary..." he agreed. "He's even changed our lives, Mac..."

MacKenzie nodded. "It's amazing to think how much one person could make such a difference of so much goodness in the lives of so many different people..."

After their after-lunch after-breakfast dessert, MacKenzie and Erik went to a stationery store. They bought pens and two nice cards, and then sat on the sidewalk curb outside the store to write their thank-you notes to the Marine who had retrieved their backpacks for them.

Davenport had telephoned Erik earlier that morning with the

name of the Marine, and had assured Erik that if he and MacKenzie brought their letters over to the Conservancy, he would make sure their correspondence successfully made its way to where it needed to go.

After finishing their cards and addressing the front of the envelopes with the Marine's name, MacKenzie and Erik walked to the Conservancy building and left the two thank-you notes with one of the Conservancy people there, who promised she would give them to Davenport when he returned to the office.

MacKenzie and Erik then went to Jake's shop, where Jake got to see Erik wearing the dolphin-necklace, and Erik could at last see himself wearing it in one the mirrors there. Erik said he planned to tell his parents simply that the necklace was a gift MacKenzie had bought from Jake, and though that did not include all the details, it was not untrue. Jake was unconcerned and was completely comfortable with that, and no more was spoken about it.

MacKenzie and Erik both thanked Jake gratefully for the excellence and care of his craftsmanship, and Jake thanked them in return, saying that one of the greatest rewards of his job was getting to see when work that he loved doing had made people happy.

After retrieving their bicycles, MacKenzie and Erik biked on Casino Way alongside the evenly-spaced trunks of palm trees lining the road on the ocean-side, past the brightly-painted whiteness and marine-blue trim of the yacht club, and past the elegant columned-arcade and gleaming majesty of the towering round Casino building.

They made their way to Descanso Beach where they locked their bikes to a rack, took off their shoes, and walked barefoot in the warm whiteness of the beach sand down to the water's edge. Neither of them had brought a bathing suit, and MacKenzie wasn't allowed to swim anyway because of her gunshot wound. They waded into the gently-lapping surf up to their ankles, and walked the length of the pristine beach, first in one direction, then back the other way, enjoying where they were, enjoying each other's company, and talking and chatting together about anything and everything that happened to impulsively surface in their minds.

By 4:00, Erik had headed home to be with his parents, and MacKenzie was back at the cottage. MacKenzie returned the credit card to her father with a hug and further expressions of great thanks and appreciation, and additional earnest promises to pay back to him all she had spent. John reassured her that, with all her cooking and dish-washing and laundry and coffee-making, he was sure that he was the one who owed her, and they need not discuss the credit card again, at least not until the monthly bill showed up.

The two of them went to the ball field for catch and catching-up, and by the time they got back, Katie had arrived. She had bought groceries for making dinner, as well as several extra boxes of Cracker Jack for the Cubs game.

When the game started at about 5:36, the three of them were contentedly settled in their designated seats in the living room, eating the early dinner that Katie and MacKenzie had made for everyone. The three of them had stood and sung along with the National Anthem before the game, and they again stood and sang 'Take Me Out to the Ball Game' along with Harry Caray for the seventh inning stretch, faithfully changing the lyric 'home team' to 'Cubbies', following Harry Caray's long-standing Cubs tradition. John insisted on singing a zealous solo of all the song's verses, which made MacKenzie embarrassed and happy, and which put a blushing grin on Katie's face, especially each time John delivered with extra gusto the name of song's protagonist, Katie Casey.

They all eagerly broke open the Cracker Jacks, most of which ultimately were eaten by MacKenzie, and the three of them laughed together as they diverted themselves with the ephemeral entertainment of the eccentric toy prizes from inside the boxes.

By about 8:35, the game was over and the Cubs had defeated the Reds by a score of 6-to-4. MacKenzie and her father were in delighted disbelief at the team's on-going run of great good fortune with stringing together so many wins in a row, and they high-fived each other and Katie in jubilant exultation.

Everyone pitched-in to clean up the living room, and MacKenzie made coffee and hot chocolate, although John and Katie explained they were going to have more wine for now, and would make the transition to coffee later. MacKenzie was ready to wash dishes, and Katie was ready to help her, but John insisted the dishwasher was the more sensible option.

Katie had bought powdered donettes as a surprise dessert for MacKenzie, explaining that John had mentioned they were near the top of MacKenzie's favorite-foods list, and MacKenzie let out a thrilled exclamation of joy when Katie revealed them. Katie and John were treated to hugs and effusive expressions of thanks from MacKenzie, and eventually everyone made their way back to the living room.

From her place on the couch, with donettes heaped decadently on a plate in front of her, with her mug of hot chocolate in one hand, and with powdery vestiges of donette-sugar caked around her mouth and chin, MacKenzie looked purposefully and seriously at John and Katie as they sat sipping wine in their armchairs.

"Oh…" said John. "I see what's happening here. We're going to have 'a talk'…"

MacKenzie took a bite of donette and nodded.

Katie looked from John to MacKenzie, and then back to John. "Do you two know something I don't…?" she asked.

John shook his head. "No," he said. "You and I both don't know. Only MacKenzie knows..."

MacKenzie nodded again. "And so," she said, "now I'm going to tell you..."

"Do we need more wine for this...?" her father asked.

Again MacKenzie nodded. "Probably..." she said.

John got up and made a brief trip into the kitchen, returning with a freshly-opened bottle of red wine, which he put on one of the armchair end-tables, before settling himself back into his armchair.

And then MacKenzie told them. She told them all about finding the gold. She told them about her rock-warrior sentry. She told them about meeting Fire-Walker. She told them about the gold dolphin, and the necklace for Erik. She told them what Erik was going to say to his parents about where she had gotten the necklace from. She even told them about how Fire-Walker had said she was now a Nophaie the Warrior. She told them every detail she had never told them, except for the two details she also hadn't told Erik—about her other new name, and about Fire-Walker's overwhelming answer to her perilous question. It wasn't because she hadn't told Erik that she also didn't tell her father and Katie. It was just that there sometimes are some things you just decide to keep to yourself.

There was a long speechless silence in the living room when MacKenzie finished her story.

Her father finally spoke. "You are an extraordinary person, MacKenzie..." he said slowly. "It's very exciting to be part of your remarkable life. But more importantly... I admire you, and I am in awe of you. I'm proud to be your father, Mac. And I am so very proud of you..."

Katie's eyes were glistening. "Everywhere you are, MacKenzie," she said, her voice filled with emotion, "amazing things happen, and the world becomes better. You are truly magical..."

There was another long pause before MacKenzie was able to collect herself enough to say anything.

"Thank you..." MacKenzie said quietly. "You both are so wonderful... I'm so lucky... But, all of this is sort of really stressful... Can we please just put on some classical music and play poker...?"

John smiled and nodded. "I'm in..." he said enthusiastically.

"I'm in..." Katie said, smiling broadly.

MacKenzie leapt eagerly to her feet with huge relief. "You guys are the best!" she said emphatically. "I'll get the cards and chips...!"

"Plastic chips, please," said her father.

"Dad!" MacKenzie protested. "There's hardly even any sugar in the chocolate chips!"

Her father nodded. "There's no sugar at all in the plastic chips," he pointed out.

Katie laughed and stood up. "I'll find our classical music station on the radio..." she said.

MacKenzie skipped happily toward the dining room to retrieve the cards and poker chips, and she smiled as she heard—coming from the living room behind her—the sound of her father softly singing to himself.

"'Twenty-six miles across the sea, Santa Catalina is a-waitin' for me...'"

Chapter 52

APPEARANCE

The next morning was the start of what promised to be an exciting day. The restored print of *The Vanishing American* would premiere in the early evening within the old-world magnificence and Art Deco splendor of the Avalon Theater, inside the iconic Catalina Island Casino building.

Like any day with a monumental event ticking ever-closer to occurring, this particular Tuesday felt different. There was an energy of something important and big on the verge of taking place that seemed to already be galvanizing the day, and steadily growing in intensity.

Because of all the activity and preparation-commotion surrounding the premiere, the Conservancy would be directing all of its resources and focus on the movie event, and neither John nor Katie would be going to work.

Katie had come over early, and she and MacKenzie had made breakfast together. Brenda had called to ask if she could take MacKenzie dress-shopping. MacKenzie preferred jeans over dresses, but she liked shopping, and she liked dressing up, and she liked Brenda. She was eagerly willing to go along with Brenda's fun and generous suggestion, and John had very appreciatively thanked Brenda and promised that MacKenzie would be enthusiastically ready to go when Brenda came to get her.

MacKenzie and her father and Katie were still enjoying the leisurely conclusion of their breakfast when the cottage doorbell rang. It was hours too early to be Brenda, and John knew it couldn't possibly be Davenport. It turned out to be Berrigan.

He was with two of his men, and John politely ushered the three of them into the living room, where they were joined by a curious MacKenzie and Katie. John invited everyone to sit, and Berrigan sat with large stiffness on the couch. His two men remained standing where they were, without removing their sunglasses. John and Katie sat in their armchairs, and MacKenzie sat between them on an end-table.

"All of the work underground has been completed," Berrigan began. "The entire Renton Cavern Complex, which was used as a base of operations by Trelain and his fellow smugglers, is now empty and sealed closed. The Catalina Train Tunnel has been completely sealed at both ends. The Ocean Hole 1 pass-through has been permanently sealed. I will be returning to DC in a few hours."

"He means Washington, DC, our nation's capital," John explained to MacKenzie.

"Thanks, Dad," MacKenzie said appreciatively.

"But I have a few last questions for you, Ms. Milles," Berrigan went on. "Trelain's not talking, and we still haven't figured out how he financed everything. His smuggling operation made him good money. But that doesn't explain how such an elaborate operation was first paid for. Ms. Milles, did Trelain say anything to you about where he got the money to start up his operation?"

"He said he used to work for the government," said MacKenzie.

Berrigan nodded impatiently. "I can assure you, that would not be where he got all that money from. Did he say anything else to you?"

"He said the government never wants to admit when they make mistakes," said MacKenzie.

Berrigan shook his head. "That simply isn't true," he said with some irritation.

Berrigan reached into a pocket in his suit and took out a folded piece of paper.

"Ms. Milles," he continued. "Trelain asked that you be given this message. It's been analyzed. It seems harmless. And it seems, like Trelain himself, to be of no meaningful significance."

Berrigan unfolded the paper and read the message aloud.

"'MacKenzie – When the people in charge try to make the ship look better by removing lifeboats, the passengers pay the ultimate price. Don't buy the ticket. The *Queen Mary* is the smarter bet. – Trelain'"

Berrigan lowered the paper and looked at MacKenzie.

"Ms. Milles," he said. "Does this mean anything to you?"

"I can tell you what it's referring to," said John. "It's a reference to *Titanic*. Her owners, The White Star Line, thought her decks looked too cluttered with so many lifeboats. So they removed some of them. *Titanic* was designed to have 64 lifeboats. When she sailed on her maiden—and final—voyage, she had only 16 lifeboats. That was only enough to handle 53 percent of the passengers if the lifeboats were full. And many of the first lifeboats lowered from the ship weren't full. *Titanic* sailed with 2,208 people aboard. 1,503 of those people died when *Titanic* sank."

Berrigan nodded impatiently. "That's fascinating, Mr. Milles," he said briskly. "Thank you."

Berrigan re-directed his attention back to MacKenzie. "Ms. Milles," he said to her. "I ask you again, does this message mean anything to you?"

"Trelain likes to talk," she said. "I think he just wanted to have the last word."

Berrigan nodded. "Well, now you can have it," he said, standing up and handing the paper to MacKenzie.

MacKenzie and John and Katie also stood up.

"Again," Berrigan said to MacKenzie. "If you remember something which would be useful, please immediately communicate it to Mr. Davenport, and he will pass it along to me."

Berrigan turned to leave, and John politely escorted him and his two men back to the front door.

Moments later Berrigan's vehicle could be heard driving off, and John came back into the living room.

"That was odd…" said Katie.

John nodded. "Well," he said. "So everyone's out, and no one's left on base…"

He turned his focus intently to MacKenzie, who was still holding the message from Trelain. "Mac…" he began purposefully.

MacKenzie nodded. "I already know what you're going to say…"

"Listen, Mac," said her father. "I know you're impulsive. But I also know that you don't do something unless you have a good reason. I trust you, Mac. I don't have to know what your reasons are. For anything."

"Dad," said MacKenzie. "I know Trelain's the bad guy, and Berrigan's the good guy. It's just… Well, when Trelain was telling me about Berrigan, he said that Berrigan would 'bulldoze a house if it would lead him to a guilty cockroach.' And when he said it, I didn't really understand what he meant. But I think now I do…"

"Mac," said her father. "I don't know what Trelain said to you that you didn't tell Berrigan. And I don't know why you didn't tell Berrigan. And I don't need to know. But as your father who loves you, it's my job to point out that you just lied to an officer of the US Government."

"Since when is not-telling-part-of-the-truth lying?"

"Since forever," said her father.

"Listen, Dad," said MacKenzie. "Trelain likes to talk. He said a million different things to me. About his past, and who he was, and how he set up his smuggling operation, and why he did everything that he did. I haven't even had time yet to tell you and Katie half the things Trelain told me. So I'm certainly not going to tell Berrigan every last thing Trelain said. Berrigan should understand. I mean, he doesn't know, but if he did, he should understand. Berrigan was only interested in information that he could use to save the plutonium and catch Trelain. And he didn't really care about anything else. So, now he's saved the plutonium, and he's caught Trelain. So, I don't think there's really anything else that I need to tell him."

A smiled escaped to John's face. "Well," he said. "I don't entirely disagree with you about Berrigan. I'm not really a fan. At the start of that meeting at the Roebling's on Sunday, Berrigan kept 'referencing' reports and 'referencing' data. I'm always suspicious of people with authority and power who don't know how to speak accurately. You can't 'reference' something any more than you can 'inference' something. You want to do something? Try a verb. That's what they're for..."

"What's an inference?" ask MacKenzie.

"The result you get after figuring something out even though you don't have enough information," John explained. "'The brilliant woman inferred that the bison had a copper-deficiency, and her inference was correct.' Et cetera."

Katie smiled.

"KC," John said to Katie. "Do you want to pinch-hit the next one?"

Katie grinned. "Well..." she began. "I think you two are out of my league, but I'll take a swing at it..."

MacKenzie and her father laughed, and they both applauded with impressed appreciative clapping.

"Oh, the rookie is an instant fan-favorite...!" John announced.

"You're the best, Katie!" MacKenzie exclaimed with delight.

"Okay..." said Katie, taking a breath. "Here goes... 'The woman hopefully referred to a baseball expression she'd heard, and then was glad to find out she had used the reference correctly.' Et cetera."

"Brilliant!" John proclaimed happily. "And bonus points for using 'hopefully' correctly!"

"We win!" MacKenzie exclaimed. "Because Katie's on the home team!"

The three of them laughed together.

"MacKenzie," said Katie a few moments later. "What are you going to do with that message from Trelain?"

"Figure out what it means," said MacKenzie. "There's no way he just randomly sent me some random message for no reason. But as Dad would say, 'that's not a today-issue'. I'll try to solve that mystery some other time. We have to start thinking about the premiere. And right now, there are breakfast dishes to deal with, and I'm batting clean-up."

When Brenda arrived to pick up MacKenzie, she asked if it would be all right to keep MacKenzie with her until after lunch. MacKenzie nodded eagerly, and John willingly agreed, again thanking Brenda for all she was doing.

Before she left with MacKenzie, Brenda suggested that John and Katie do the same thing she and MacKenzie would be doing, which was to have a big lunch that was also a late lunch. Arrivals at the Casino would formally begin at 5:30, and that was the time they all should plan on getting there. The screening of the movie itself was scheduled for 7:00. Everything in between would be pomp and ceremony. After whatever time the evening's festivities ultimately concluded, Brant wanted to then take the six of them out to a late dinner.

By the time Brenda dropped MacKenzie off back at the cottage hours later, it was early afternoon, and MacKenzie was now wearing her new dress. Her day with Brenda had been an event all by itself, and had included more than dress-shopping and going out to a fancy lunch. Her hair had been trimmed and styled at the same salon where Brenda had had her own hair done, and MacKenzie's face had been slightly and expertly embellished by Brenda's make-up people. Brenda had also bought MacKenzie a pair of stylish glittery-golden slightly-high-heeled sandals, and had treated herself and MacKenzie to manicures and pedicures.

Brenda had dropped MacKenzie off without coming into the cottage herself, as she had to hurry home to make sure there was enough time to help Brant and Erik get themselves properly presentable.

When MacKenzie entered the cottage living room, she felt like a celebrity, and John and Katie gazed at her as though they didn't recognize her.

"Wow...!" said Katie when she saw MacKenzie.

"All right, Ms. Milles," said her father, "you're ready for your closeup...!"

"You look beautiful..." breathed Katie. "Like a princess...!"

"Thank you..." MacKenzie said with quiet thrilled pride. "I kind of actually feel sort of like a princess right now..."

Her father shook his head in awe and admiration. "Seriously, Mac..." he said. "I don't think you've ever looked lovelier in your life..."

"Thanks, Dad..." she said softly, setting the bag full of her sneakers and regular clothes down onto the couch.

Her father and Katie were themselves looking very dressed-up. John was wearing the one suit he had brought with him, but it fit him well and MacKenzie thought he looked dashing and handsome. In the time MacKenzie had been gone, Katie had efficiently managed to buy a new dress for herself, since she hadn't brought any with her to the island. She had gotten her own hair done, and she now looked the perfectly-elegant match for John.

Katie always looked so pretty to MacKenzie, and MacKenzie cold never tell if Katie was ever wearing make-up. Right now, MacKenzie still couldn't tell. But she knew how pretty Katie looked in her new dress and her newly-done hair. John commented that they all looked like they were about to head off to a very fancy wedding, and Katie and MacKenzie agreed.

Chapter 53
PREMIERE

MacKenzie and John and Katie met up with the Roeblings near the front of the Casino at 5:30. MacKenzie had made sure the penny of her necklace was hanging over the top front of her dress and was clearly visible. And though Erik was wearing a shirt buttoned to his neck and closed over with the tight knot of a smartly-tied tie, he also had put the chain of his necklace entirely outside his collar so that his gold dolphin was hanging over the top of his shirt and tie and was clearly visible.

The scene in front of the Casino was like something out of a movie. Waving beams of powerful searchlights soared upward from massive swiveling lamps and swept repeatedly across the early-evening sky. The size of the teeming crowd was impressive and daunting. The air was nearly electric with excitement and spectacle, and thick with enthusiastic voices and gauzy drifts of cigarette smoke. There was a long ceremonial red carpet, and celebrities both renowned and less known were circulating and being seen through-out the throng. From all directions, cameras flashed in continuous intermittent bursts.

Atop the platform of a large slightly-raised temporary stage, a 1920s-style jazz ensemble in tuxedos played music made famous in the big-band era. Lights from camera crews brightly illumi-nated famous and ordinary faces, spectacular hair-styles, dazzling apparel, and glamorously glittering jewelry. Correspondents, journalists, on-the-scene reporters, and media commentators were everywhere, grasping microphones with long trailing cables, conducting interviews and talking toward the polished lenses of big television cameras.

If there was this much crowd and commotion on such sudden short notice, MacKenzie thought to herself, it was no wonder the Conservancy hadn't wanted to allow another six weeks of anticipation and preparation. She spotted Davenport amidst the multitude and clamor. He was looking stressed and busy, but not unhappy.

Brant and Brenda looked so much like a movie-star couple that many people apparently thought they actually were celebrities. All around them camera-shutters clicked and flashes popped as excited onlookers eagerly snapped photos of the two of them together.

Professional photographers ranged throughout the dense congestion of animated humanity, and Brant summoned one of them over. Conducting a swift transaction-exchange of compensation and contact information, Brant nimbly paid for a picture, and a group-photo was taken of the three Roeblings and two Milleses and one Coleridge posed all together, capturing a collective moment of radiant smiles and fancy attire and thrilled excitement.

Movie posters from 1925 of *The Vanishing American* were mounted on display stands, along with large photographic portraits of William Wrigley, Jr. and Zane Grey. *The Vanishing American* souvenirs and memorabilia were being sold everywhere, and Erik bought two 8 x 10 glossy black-and-white celebrity photos of Richard Dix for himself and MacKenzie.

With the sea of people parting in front of him as though he were famous, Brant led the Roebling-Milles-Coleridge party through the throng of pageantry and into the theater, where decorative souvenir programs were being handed out to every ticket-holder as they entered.

The six of them made their way to their seats, and it quickly became clear that Brant had apparently pulled some pretty big strings. Their seats were right in the middle of the theater at the center aisle. Erik whispered to MacKenzie that his father was a big donor for the upcoming restoration of the entire Casino building, and there was lots of grateful appreciation for his generosity, which in this case had come in the form of choice seating at a momentous event which had been impossible to get tickets for.

MacKenzie had been in the Avalon Theater before, on a tour she had taken during her second day on the island. But she realized now that she hadn't at the time fully recognized and appreciated the exquisite art and architectural grandeur. As she gazed in awe with new eyes at all that was around her, MacKenzie thought to herself that it was a good thing the lights would go dark for the start of the film. The theater's splendor was so extraordinary, she couldn't imagine how anyone would ever be able to pay attention to a movie on the screen with all that distracting beauty everywhere.

As more people took their seats, it became excitingly evident that the formal proceedings would soon be starting.

Though she had been continually searching the chaos of clothes and faces in the steadily-growing audience crowd, MacKenzie hadn't been able to spot Fire-Walker anywhere. But she suddenly somehow knew he was there somewhere, and that made her relieved and glad.

Just before the ceremonies got underway, as the lights were about to go down, MacKenzie whispered to Erik and asked him to stand up and to please just turn in a circle, and pretend he was looking around at the theater and the people. Erik was not one to seek attention, but he also was comfortably confident if placed in the spotlight, and he readily complied with MacKenzie's request. When he sat back down, he whispered over to her asking why he had just done that.

"I know he's here..." she whispered. "Fire-Walker's in the audience somewhere... I wanted him to see the dolphin again. I wanted him to see you wearing it. I want him to know that I know he's here..."

The lights dimmed and everyone applauded, and the pre-movie program got underway.

Several speakers came up in turn to an illuminated lectern on the stage, and stood in the circle of a bright spotlight beamed from the back of the theater. There were thank-yous and acknowledgements, and brief speeches about the movie, the island, and the momentousness of the current evening's event.

Someone gave a speech of recognition in honor of Fire-Walker. The woman speaking began by saying that Fire-Walker was not able to attend the premiere, but he was still alive and healthy, and doing valuable community work on Navajo tribal lands in Arizona, Utah, and New Mexico. She then highlighted significant parts of his life, from his role as Nasja in *The Vanishing American*, to his going repeatedly back into the fire to save a family, to serving in the military as a Navajo Code-Talker during World War II.

She went on to talk about the power of movies, saying it was not only movies that had the power to bring about meaningful change. It was also the people who played a part in the making of a movie—whether in front of the camera, or in the hundreds of different roles that were never in front of the camera. Those people also were often the source of meaningful change, in ways which might or might not be directly connected to the making of movies. She said that when Fire-Walker had heroically saved the family from a fire, it had nothing to do with movies. And when he was fighting for his country as a Code-Talker, it had nothing to do with movies.

"But because of movies," she said, "we know who Fire-Walker is. We know that the child who began his life as Man Hammer's Oldest Boy grew up to change the lives of many people. He has brought goodness into this world in many ways, and he continues to do so, even to this day. Because of movies, we have an opportunity to thank him, to celebrate him, to give him recognition which should be given, and to be inspired by him. In our role as members of the audience, we can—each in our own way, whatever that may be—be inspired by him to strive to bring more goodness into the world. And so, we thank Fire-Walker for the role he played as a child in *The Vanishing American*; we thank him for how the story of his life uplifts and inspires us; and we thank him for his service to our country."

The audience applauded. MacKenzie and Erik and John and Katie clapped with extra enthusiasm, because Fire-Walker held such special significance for them personally. And MacKenzie found herself once again in awe of Fire-Walker, and who he had become, and how much he had changed her life from the moment she had first seen him on the screen as Nasja in the movie. She privately promised herself to try to be like him, to find ways to make the world better in any way she could.

The evening's proceedings continued. There were more speeches and tributes, and then the lights dimmed for a ten-minute new documentary on *The Vanishing American*. The feature showed details of the elaborate technical processes involved in the physical restoration of the film. It told about the making of the movie, about the movie's significance, and about the renowned author of the book the movie was based on—long ago long-time Catalina Island resident Zane Grey, whose love of Catalina was the reason why the movie's film crews had first come to the island. And of course, the feature ultimately included details of how the movie had brought about the unlikely result of the island becoming the permanent residence of the now-famous Catalina buffalo.

And then it was nearly time for the movie itself to begin. The Avalon Theater's organist sat down at the 1929 Page Organ Company 16-rank theater pipe organ, and started to play some of the original music from *The Vanishing American*. That segued into the live orchestra starting to perform the music that would be played during the movie. An orchestra pit had been set up at the foot of the stage, just for this screening, and a surprisingly large number of musicians were arrayed in front of a dimly-illuminated lectern where the conductor was busily standing.

The lights came up for a moment, and then dimmed to black as the stage curtain ceremonially closed and then re-opened to once again reveal the screen, and the movie began.

For MacKenzie, seeing the same movie a second time was like seeing a totally different movie. In the theater, there certainly was no privacy or talking or pausing the movie. But at Erik's home on the couch, there was no large open palatial space to be amidst, no larger-than-life film projection of actual film, no shared common-experience with a theater full of people. MacKenzie didn't think that one experience was necessarily better than the other. But both experiences were very different. And seeing the movie as film projected up on a big screen while having a live orchestra playing was a very different experience than watching a video copy on a television.

The new film print was immaculate and clean. MacKenzie soon forgot that the movie was silent or even black-and-white, it seemed so vibrant and alive. Everything was bigger, including the emotional impact of the film. Richard Dix looked even more noble and digni-fied than ever. But ultimately, the movie itself was the star of the show.

When the character of Nasja first appeared, and the screen filled with the title card about his being 'played by Man Hammer's Oldest Boy, who has no name of his own', MacKenzie and Erik and John and Katie all looked away from the movie for a moment to exchange quick knowing glances of significance.

MacKenzie cried silently at several points in the movie, more than when she and Erik had first watched it. But she cried the most at the first title card about Nophaie the Warrior. Not from sadness, but from pride and happiness at the life-changing gift she had received from the words of Fire-Walker. Her hand and Erik's found each other, and for a brief moment their fingers locked together in recognition and understanding.

After the conclusion of the movie, once there had been sufficient time for everyone inside to have made their way out, there was a fireworks show in celebration of the premiere. The Pacific Ocean surrounded the Casino on three sides, and the prolonged thunder-ous and sparkly-explosive display erupted high above the water in the overhead air. In perfect complement to the beauty inside the theater, the Casino building once again revealed itself to be the architectural crown-jewel of the island. MacKenzie had never seen it at night, with its brilliant illumination accentuating the columnar vertical lines of the pavilion supports, and highlighting the elegant arcade of the circular balcony. The fireworks were colorful and exciting and spectacular, but they could not match the magnificent glory and splendor of the Casino building at night, with its structural design accents brightly lit from in front and behind, and the whole of the cylindrical towering majesty of the Casino glowing with sublime radiant magnificence.

Even after the fireworks ended, the searchlights were still in action. Their crisp angled swathes of linear brightness continued to swing in repeating waving sweeps across the night sky, beaming up from the ground and widening into beacon streaks of celebratory luminance.

MacKenzie, her father, and Katie strolled with the Roeblings amidst the leisurely animated river of elated movie-goers now wending their way back toward Crescent Ave. Awaiting them there was a charter taxi service van arranged for by Erik's father, and the six of them piled in. The van conveyed them happily off through the streets of Avalon, en route to the next portion of their festive evening—good food, good company, and good enjoyment in re-living and reveling in the fun and excitement of the experience they all had just shared together.

Chapter 54

DEPARTURE

When MacKenzie woke up Wednesday morning, she knew right away something was wrong. She could smell coffee brewing. She knew she hadn't made coffee, and the cottage didn't feel like Katie was there, so Katie couldn't have made it either. That meant her father had made the coffee, which was something he rarely did.

MacKenzie finished brushing her teeth and made her way anxiously to the kitchen. John was sitting sipping coffee. He had made breakfast for both of them, and hot chocolate for MacKenzie.

"What's going on...?" MacKenzie said with growing apprehension.

Her father nodded. "We've been thrown a curveball..." he said.

"What is it...?"

"You're not going to like it..."

"I can tell..." she said.

"We're going back to Chicago today..."

MacKenzie burst into tears. She couldn't speak, and she couldn't sit down. She just stood in the middle of the kitchen in her pajamas and wept.

John got up and poured hot chocolate into her mug, and set her plate of breakfast onto the kitchen table.

"You still have to eat..." he said gently.

Like she was sleepwalking in a nightmare, MacKenzie slowly sat down at the table in front of her plate and touched nothing. All she could do was cry.

"You may remember," John said slowly, "that I have a job working for the Illinois Wildlife Conservancy. And even though they originally said it would not be a problem for me to be away working with the Catalina Island Conservancy for several weeks if necessary, that's now changed. Some of the work I was doing in Chicago now needs me to actually be back there and dealing with it. I've been on the phone most of the morning. The IWC needs me to return immediately. They've spoken with Ed, and I also have spoken with Ed. There are no other options at the moment. Except for one small choice, that you need to make. We could make some kind of arrangement for you to stay here, and I can fly back to Chicago myself."

MacKenzie instantly shook her head. "Not a chance..." she said adamantly, wiping some of the still-flowing tears from her face. "Where you go, I go... I don't want to be anywhere without you... Ever..."

Her father nodded. "Okay..." he said slowly.

"It's not fair...!" MacKenzie cried unhappily, and she began to weep harder than ever.

John nodded. "It's not..." he said quietly.

Trembling and unsteady, MacKenzie stood up and went over to where her father was sitting. She collapsed into his lap, burying her face in his shoulder and crying.

"I don't want us to go..." she sobbed softly. "I want us to stay..."

Her father set down his coffee and put one arm around MacKenzie's shoulders, gently smoothing her hair with his other hand.

"I wish I had more control over things..." he said.

MacKenzie nodded into his shoulder and couldn't stop crying.

They sat like that for a while, neither of them speaking, and MacKenzie crying, and her father trying to comfort her.

"Are we..." MacKenzie at last struggled to say. "Are we..." She forced herself to sit up. "Are we ever coming back...?" The words were so painful, she could hardly bring herself to say them.

"I honestly don't know, Mac…" said her father, wiping away some of her tears. "There's extremely important work for me to do here on the island. Work that I want to be doing. Work that Ed wants me to be in charge of. There's red-clover abatement to deal with, and there are issues with measuring and monitoring the recovery of the herd. But I don't have any control in this situation. My first responsibility has to be to the Illinois Wildlife Conservancy, and right now the IWC expects me back there immediately. I honestly don't know for how long…"

"I have no clue what 'abatement' is…" MacKenzie said, sniffling.

"It means 'the ending' of something, or 'the making less' of something."

"Perfect…" said MacKenzie miserably.

"Honey, you need to start eating your breakfast," her father said gently. "We have to start packing…"

She looked at him in wretched alarm. "Already…?"

John nodded. "And especially if you want time to say good-bye to Erik and Katie…"

MacKenzie stood up angrily and stomped on the kitchen floor. "I am NOT saying good-bye…! I hate good-byes…! I won't do it…!"

John nodded and looked at his watch. "Well, Katie's coming over in about an hour. She's not staying long. Just a few minutes. She's… She's dealing with this about as well as you are…"

"Well I'm not going to say good-bye to her!" MacKenzie insisted. "And you can just tell her that when she gets here! YOU can say good-bye to her if want. I'm not going to…"

Part of MacKenzie could see that her father was having as hard a time as she was dealing with what was happening. He just wasn't stomping and crying about it the way she was. It made her feel bad for him, and it made her feel selfish and guilty. But she couldn't help herself. She was miserable and furious, and she didn't have any room for any other feelings.

John nodded again, with slow regretful understanding. "If you want time to see Erik, whether you say good-bye to him or not, you really do need to eat your breakfast and start packing..."

MacKenzie clenched her fists with her arms locked straight at her sides and let out an angry groan of loud exasperated misery.

With forlorn resignation, she at last forced herself to sit down at the table, bitterly wiping away more tears. She poked without interest at her food, and took a sad half-hearted sip of her hot chocolate.

"You did a good job making this..." she said distractedly.

"I wish I could say the same about the coffee..." her father replied with regret.

John washed all the dishes while MacKenzie got dressed. She came back into the kitchen and said she was going to call Erik because she couldn't bear to see him. John said he was going to finish packing, and headed off to his bedroom.

MacKenzie called Erik, and the moment she heard his voice she burst into tears all over again. She was so upset, she could hardly speak. Through her uncontrollable sobbing, she tried to explain to Erik what was happening. She apologized for leaving. She apologized for not being able to stop crying. She apologized for not being strong enough to see him in person. And she told him he wasn't allowed to say good-bye, and she told him she would not say good-bye to him. She said she couldn't even think about how much she was going to miss him because it hurt too much.

Erik was having a hard time speaking, and seemed to be having an even harder time knowing what he wanted to say. He eventually managed to tell MacKenzie that Catalina would feel empty without her. That set MacKenzie off sobbing even harder. Somewhere at the far outer edges of her unhappiness, she thought about all the times she had tried to make sure she didn't cry in front of Erik, and she now bitterly thought about what an idiot she had been.

Neither of them knew how to end the conversation. Erik asked her to please promise to call him when she got to Chicago, and she tearfully promised she would. And then they both hung up.

MacKenzie finished packing, and told her father she was going out for a bike ride by herself, and wasn't coming back until Katie had left. Then she stormed with broken-hearted fury out of the cottage, and pedaled away as fast and hard as she could.

While she was pedaling, the next part of her personal nightmare overtook her. A dam that she didn't know even existed somewhere in her mind cracked and broke open, and suddenly she was flooded with last-time thoughts. This was the last time she would see the Catalina morning sun. This was the last time she would bike past Crescent Ave. This was the last time she would be going to see her rock-warrior sentry. Last night was the last time she would see Erik.

This new onslaught of sadness wasn't even a crying kind of sadness. It was an awful sadness that was knotted and cold and hard, and all it did was find new ways to get worse.

MacKenzie slammed on the brakes of her bike and skidded to an angry stop in front of her rock-warrior sentry, stepping with dejected frustration down onto the paving-stone surface of the turnout, straddling her bicycle. She flipped up her sunglasses and glowered resentfully at the sentry as if it all was somehow his fault, as though he had somehow failed to rescue her or save her. Wasn't he supposed to be watching over her? Wasn't he supposed to be looking out for her? How could he have let this happen?

"Do you even realize that this is last time I'll ever be here...?!" she yelled at him accusingly. "You're not even waving good-bye...! You're just... You're just waving... As if there's nothing wrong...! Why aren't you helping me...?! People are supposed to help each other...! Why don't you do something...?!"

Her rock-warrior did not appear concerned. He was as steadfast and motionless as ever, eyes gazing everywhere, and nowhere, and directly at her. His raised arm was poised mid-wave, as it always was. He seemed infuriatingly unwilling to recognize how bad things had become.

"Fine...!" MacKenzie yelled at him with hopeless exasperation. "That's fine... See if I care... Because I don't...! I don't even care that you're not waving good-bye... Because... Because... Because I'm not waving good-bye either... So there...!"

She got off her bike and lowered it carelessly onto the paving stones. Then she climbed over the railing, and clambered onto the base of the rock-warrior sentry. She sat down on a small ledge of stone and leaned back, letting her head rest against the chest of the sentry. Flipping down her sunglasses, she closed her eyes and let the light of the sun enwrap her.

"Please rescue me..." she said softly. "Please save me..."

When MacKenzie returned to the cottage, Katie's Marine Center golf cart was nowhere to be seen, and MacKenzie surmised that Katie had come and gone.

MacKenzie went inside, and her father was looking more upset than she had seen him look in a very long time. She felt guilty all over again about how mean she had been to him at breakfast, but not guilty enough to overcome her own anger and resentment.

"Did Katie come by...?" MacKenzie asked.

That seemed to be the wrong question to ask, because her father just looked more upset.

"She..." her father hesitated. "She said to remind you to make sure you packed the tin of baseball cards..."

MacKenzie smacked herself on the side of her head. "Oh my god..." she said incredulously. "I totally forgot..."

Her father nodded. "I forgot, too..." he said quietly.

MacKenzie headed off toward her room to get the tin box and Cavanarro's letter out of the secret compartment. But she stopped before she got there, and went back into the living room. She went over to her father and put her arms around him, resting her head against him and closing her eyes.

"I'm so sorry, MacKenzie..." he said.

"It's not your fault, Dad..." she said quietly. "You and I are just randomly being punished... We didn't even do anything wrong..."

She could feel her father nodding in confused agreement.

"I love you, Dad..." she said.

"I love you, honey..." he said.

They hugged each other a little tighter for a little longer, and then it was nearly time for them to leave.

MacKenzie hurried to her room to retrieve the tin box and the letter. She wondered vaguely if Paul Cavanarro had been mad and frustrated and upset when he left the island at the end of Spring Training in 1951, and if that was why he had forgotten about his baseball cards.

Cavanarro had thought he would be coming back to Catalina. But he never did. He even said in his letter—it never occurred to him that he wouldn't be coming back.

It had never occurred to MacKenzie that she might one day be separated from Erik and Katie and Catalina. It was completely outside the universe of anything she had ever thought about. She was utterly unprepared and unable to manage the cold dark sadness of what was now happening. MacKenzie didn't understand how feeling sad could be more awful than being terrified, but somehow it was.

MacKenzie and her father stood with their bags on the Cabrillo Mole. Waiting for the *Avalon Express* ferry that would take them to Long Beach and away from Catalina was the second worst sad-and-painful experience MacKenzie had ever had. She could remember the worst, and she didn't want to remember. So she stopped herself from thinking about it. She had had years of practice. That memory hurt inside far too much for her to ever let it be remembered.

But she did let herself think about what her mother would probably be saying to her right now. *It gets better, Mac* is what her mother used to say whenever MacKenzie had been too sad. *You can't see it from where you are right now. But I promise you, it gets better.*

MacKenzie nodded as if her mother had just spoken to her. *I love you, Mom...* she thought silently to herself. *Thank you for always taking such good care of me."*

Chapter 55

GIFTS

Being back in Chicago was a strange re-entry for MacKenzie. The ten days she had spent in Catalina had felt like a lifetime. A wonderful magical lifetime. And for that lifetime, her life in Chicago had seemed like someone else's life—a life that she knew, but a life in a world she hadn't come from and didn't belong in. Catalina had become her real life.

But after five days in Chicago, MacKenzie was gradually starting to get re-acclimated. She had re-connected with her friends, at least the ones who weren't away for the summer. There had been no Cubs home games, so she and her father hadn't gone to the ballpark. But they still had their game of catch every afternoon. During the day, John was away at work getting caught up on the things which had been neglected in his absence, and dealing with all the issues he was in charge of that the Illinois Wildlife Conservancy had been so concerned about.

John regularly talked on the phone with Katie, and MacKenzie got to talk with her as well. And MacKenzie talked with Erik on the phone every day. But talking on the phone with Katie or Erik didn't make MacKenzie feel closer to them. It just made them seem unreal and farther away.

"But talking on the phone is better than nothing," her father had said to her.

"It's not the same as actually being together in Real Life…" MacKenzie had said to him.

"Aren't phone calls Real Life?" John had asked.

"They are if you're going to be together later, after you get off the phone," MacKenzie had explained. "Otherwise, no. It's not the same thing. It's not real. Being together is what's real. A phone call is just a way of pretending. It's just a way to pretend you're not apart. It doesn't change the fact that you're not together…"

And talking on the phone with Katie or Erik made MacKenzie miss Catalina more. And that made it harder for MacKenzie to accept and get properly adjusted to being back home. It was even strange to think of her home as home. Catalina and the cottage still seemed more like home to her, and those feelings were too difficult and confusing to untangle or manage.

Whenever she felt unbearably sad and lonely for Catalina, she would hold the 1951 penny of her necklace, and it comforted her. *Part of you will never ever leave Catalina*, it seemed to whisper to her. *No matter where you go, no matter what you do, Catalina is always part of you, always waiting for you, always waiting to welcome you back with warm wonderful magic. Catalina is part of you forever, and you will always be part of Catalina.*

MacKenzie often thought about Fire-Walker, and she often remembered how he had said that she should look ahead. *Keep your eyes forward, Nophaie*, he had said to her. But she didn't see anything ahead to look forward to. And she didn't feel like she was going forward. She didn't even know where she was going.

MacKenzie was saved by the imminent arrival of Monday. That was the day she and her father would be going to Wrigley Field. And it wasn't just to see the Cubs play a night game at home. John had called the phone number that Paul Cavanarro had sent to MacKenzie in his letter, and arrangements had been made. MacKenzie and her father would be meeting Paul Cavanarro in person at Wrigley on Monday afternoon. It was the first time since she had been home that MacKenzie was feeling excited and happy and looking forward to something that genuinely was important and significant in her life.

When Monday at last arrived, MacKenzie woke up with a feeling she hadn't had since waking up in Catalina—there was a warm glimmering sparkle inside of her somewhere which seemed to be promising that today was going to be a good day.

John usually was home from work by 5:30. But today he had gotten permission from the Illinois Wildlife Conservancy to leave early, and he was home by 4:00, his normal home-from-work-time in Catalina. It seemed to MacKenzie that her father was feeling a little bit like she was—that today was somehow going to be a good day. When he first came home from work, he was looking more cheery and bright than she had seen him since their return to Chicago. He looked like himself. Like her real father. He looked the way he had looked while they were in Catalina.

Per the phone arrangements, MacKenzie and her father showed up at Wrigley Field at 4:30. John was wearing his Illinois Wildlife Conservancy baseball cap. MacKenzie was wearing her Cubs hat, with her flip-up sunglasses perched on top. Inside her Cubs backpack was Paul Cavanarro's tin box of baseball cards. While she had been loading the box into her backpack an hour earlier, MacKenzie had kissed her 1951 penny and silently thanked Katie for making sure MacKenzie hadn't—like Cavanarro himself so many years ago—unintentionally left the cards behind in the secret compartment of her room at the cottage.

When MacKenzie and her father met Cavanarro, it was in an office he had in a building with other Cubs' management offices. And the first surprise they received was that there were several people there in Cavanarro's office waiting to meet them. Cavanarro smiled as he shook hands with MacKenzie and her father, and then politely introduced the other people in the room, and promised he would explain why he had asked them to be there.

One of the people was a man from Cubs management. There was also a woman representative from the Cooperstown National

Baseball Hall of Fame and Museum. And there was a woman who Cavanarro introduced as his personal attorney.

MacKenzie and her father were mystified, but politely asked no questions. MacKenzie handed the tin box to Cavanarro and told him that everything was still in there, including the nine cards, the piece of stationery, and the map.

MacKenzie and her father had discussed and together agreed earlier—long before arriving to meet Cavanarro—that the significance of Cavanarro's map was not going to be mentioned. As much as they were sure Cavanarro would enjoy hearing about how his map had led to bringing down an illegal smuggling operation which had been dangerously harmful to the United States, they were not going to say anything about it. Telling the story of finding the Renton Stairs and the underground cavern and the train-tunnel would not only go against what they had promised to Berrigan for purposes of National Security. It would go against what they had promised to Davenport about keeping the sanctity of Catalina Island safe by never revealing any details about what had happened. Both MacKenzie and her father felt strongly that honoring their country, the island, and the promises they had made were more important than anything else. So as much as MacKenzie was aching to tell Cavanarro about how his map had positively affected so many people's lives, and had changed so many things for the better, she said nothing to him about any of it.

Before the tin box was opened, Cavanarro asked the man who was from Cubs management to please give an envelope to MacKenzie, and asked MacKenzie to open it. MacKenzie opened the envelope carefully and looked together with her father at the piece of paper inside. It was a letter of certification showing that MacKenzie and her father were now receiving season passes to all Cubs home games for the next six years.

MacKenzie was barely able to contain her excitement and

gratitude, and she and John enthusiastically and appreciatively thanked Cavanarro for such extraordinary generosity.

Cavanarro then gestured politely for the woman from Cooperstown to sit at Cavanarro's desk, which she did. She put on a pair of magnifier glasses with a small headlight mounted in the middle, and Cavanarro handed her the tin box. The woman turned on the little headlight, and carefully opened the box. She had a pair of white cotton gloves which she put on her hands, and she then slowly unfolded the wax paper in the bottom section of the tin. After first gingerly removing the old piece of folded stationery and the folded map, she held open the edges of the wax paper. Through the magnifier glasses, she studied the Honus Wagner card which sat atop the other eight cards. She didn't touch it. She only looked at. Several long moments of silence followed. At last, she carefully re-closed the wax paper and smiled. She took off the glasses, looked up at Cavanarro, and nodded.

The woman removed her cotton gloves, and carefully re-closed the tin.

Cavanarro turned to MacKenzie and smiled.

"So, MacKenzie," he began. "I've made some arrangements, and I want to briefly explain to you and your father what those arrangements are. In your letter to me, MacKenzie, you said you're twelve years old?"

MacKenzie nodded.

Cavanarro nodded back. "So," he went on. "MacKenzie, I'm going to give you the Honus Wagner card. It, and the other eight cards, for now will be taken to Cooperstown, where they will be properly put into individual archival clear plastic cases to preserve their condition. The Honus Wagner card, and possibly also the Napoleon LaJolie card, will then go on display as part of The National Baseball Hall of Fame and Museum baseball card collection.

"MacKenzie, as of today, the Honus Wagner card belongs to you. My attorney has brought papers describing the legal details of how I am giving the card to you as a gift. She also has brought certified statements of provenance, which means statements that legally say that I own the card, and that I know its entire history and how it came to be in my possession. That card is quite valuable. But it will be more valuable six years from now, when you're ready to go to college.

"The papers drawn up by my attorney say that I am giving you the card on the condition that it remains in the Cooperstown Museum until your eighteenth birthday, and that you will not sell the card until then. At that time, once you turn eighteen, you are then free to auction the card off and keep all the money you get from it. But it is my wish and my hope that you will use some of the money you get from the sale of the card to pay for your college education."

Cavanarro paused for a moment before continuing. "MacKenzie," he at last went on. "I want you and your father to know—my reasons for doing this are simple. Your honesty and integrity are extraordinary. I could tell what kind of a good and decent person you are from every word of your letter. You did what you believed was right, and you didn't do it for any kind of reward. But I believe, that kind of integrity and goodness should be rewarded. And I believe someone who so naturally possess such kindness and honesty should be helped to succeed. So, this is my way of giving you what I believe is a reward you deserve. It is my way of saying thank you for being who you are. And it is my way of wanting to be part of your success as a person, because people like you are rare. People like you can change the world, and people like you make the world better."

MacKenzie had taken hold of her father's hand and had been squeezing it in excitement and emotion. She and her father were both overwhelmed. They tried to express to Cavanarro at least some of what they were feeling about the life-changing gift he had just given them—the gift of the card and all it would bring, and the gift of the words he had just spoken to them.

Cavanarro's attorney took out various papers, which she showed to MacKenzie's father and briefly reviewed with him, and she explained that Cavanarro would also be paying for all necessary insurance on the card until MacKenzie turned eighteen. The woman from Cooperstown carefully put the tin box into a plastic bag, and then into a metal storage case she had brought that had a padded foam interior and handles and a lock on the outside.

MacKenzie and her father continued to be in something like a state of shock. Cavanarro clearly wanted to help them feel more comfortable, and wanted them to enjoy all that was happening. He had a friendly charismatic energy, and a casual easy-going intensity. He smiled and laughed and chatted, and described what the next part of the afternoon would look like, which would include meeting the Cubs players on the Wrigley playing field before they began their warm-ups for the evening's home game.

The rest of the afternoon continued to be like a dream for MacKenzie. She and her father got a tour of the Cubs clubhouse, they met the Cubs manager and the Cubs players, MacKenzie received autographs, and she and her father got to talk Cubs history and Cubs statistics with the team. She received so many gift souvenirs that she needed two large bags to carry them all.

As it got closer to game-time, they were given a tour of the radio broadcast booth, and even got to meet Harry Caray. In thrilled awe, they were able to experience in person his distinctive appealing voice and the charming idiosyncrasy of his uniquely colorful personality. Like the star-struck admirers they were, they asked for his autograph and told him how much they had always been fans of his.

MacKenzie her father got to watch the night game with

Cavanarro and his family in Cavanarro's VIP prime-view executive-suite booth at Wrigley Field. They not only got to enjoy the Cubs defeating the Padres by a score of 9-to-6 in an 11-inning game, they also were treated to a first-class Wrigley luxury dinner, which they got to eat during the game. They got to be with Cavanarro and his family, and hear Cavanarro's endless personal-treasure of stories from his years of Spring Training on Catalina. As fellow lefties, MacKenzie and Cavanarro bonded proudly over both being southpaws. Cavanarro never once asked MacKenzie about the map, or if she had tried to find the metal door, and it was a source of great relief to MacKenzie that she hadn't had to lie to him.

The day could hardly have been more perfect for MacKenzie and her father. But it turned out there were more gifts coming.

When MacKenzie and her father at last returned home, it was late by Chicago time, but not late by Catalina time. MacKenzie was happily exhausted from all the fun of the extraordinary day, but her body wasn't tired. And after what she had been through the day of the train-tunnel adventure, part of her felt like she couldn't possibly ever be as tired out by any day as much as the way that day had drained her by the time it finally had ended.

John didn't seem tired either. MacKenzie was glad that he also didn't seem particularly interested in sending her to bed at a sensible hour.

It was already after 11:00, and the cable-TV re-broadcast of the Cubs game had just started. The game duration had been more than three hours, so it seemed to MacKenzie unlikely that she would either want or get permission to stay up for the entirety of the re-broadcast. But in a way, it was perfect. She was getting to re-live something she had enjoyed, something she knew was going to have the happy right ending, it would go on for a long time, and whenever she finally went to sleep, it would still be going on.

The day's profusion of Cubs souvenirs decorated the living room, arranged in a glorious chaotic display of celebratory memento. MacKenzie had made coffee for John, and lemonade for herself. She and her father sat together on the couch across the living room from the television, enjoying the game and the air-conditioned relief from the Chicago summer humidity and heat.

Her father put his coffee cup down on the coffee table and turned to MacKenzie. They evidently were about to have 'a talk'. MacKenzie took a quick sip of lemonade, and one more time watched the liquid whip around through the wildly-looping turns of the krazy straw on its way to her mouth, before putting the tall narrow glass down on the coffee table next to her father's cup.

"So..." John began slowly. "I didn't want to say anything to you until I knew for sure... There were several phone calls last night after you went to bed... But it wasn't all made final until earlier this afternoon, just before I left work... On Wednesday, you and I are going back to Catalina."

It took a long moment for the words to fully register with MacKenzie. And then the impact hit her.

She jolted up onto her knees atop the couch cushion, and grabbed her father by his shoulders. "Oh my god..." she breathed. "Oh my god, oh my god, oh my god! DAD!!"

She was suddenly smiling and laughing and bouncing on the couch and shaking her father in uncontrollable joy and excitement.

"Dad! Dad!! DAD!!!" she cried out rapturously, bursting with exuberance.

She hugged her father, and kissed him, and hugged him some more, and bounced on her knees crazily, up and down on the couch cushion over and over with ecstatic abandon like it was a party trampoline. Her mind was bounding joyfully about on fluffy pink cotton-candy clouds, and her heart was off on a thrilling roller coaster ride.

John glowed and grinned as her couch-shock-waves bounced him around, and he happily watched her euphoric exultation.

"Okay..." she finally said breathlessly to herself. "Okay, okay, okay... Breathe, MacKenzie... Breathe..." She couldn't stop smiling, and could barely stop herself from bursting back into joyous laughter.

She cleared some of her celebrating hair out of her face, hooking half of it behind one ear, and somehow managed to settle herself back to sitting.

"Okay..." she said again. "I can do this..."

She took a long deep breath, and let out a long tremulous exhale, and then reached over to the coffee table to take a long and winding sip of lemonade.

She put the glass down and nodded emphatically, reassuring herself that she was ready to handle this calmly.

"Okay..." she repeated to herself, still trembling with exhilaration. "I'm ready..." she said to her father.

John nodded.

MacKenzie handed him his cup of coffee without spilling any of it.

"Thank you..." her father said gratefully.

MacKenzie nodded giddily, feeling herself about to explode again from an expanding happiness that kept bubbling and re-bubbling up inside her.

"So..." her father went on. "I don't quite understand what happened... But it seems like the Catalina Island Conservancy pulled some serious strings this time..."

MacKenzie grinned. "The Catalina Island Conservancy is almost like a secret society..." she said with conspiratorial delight. "They find ways to always get what they want, but without anyone getting mad at them or realizing how tricky they've been. Erik told me that

Mr. Roebling always says: he's glad the Conservancy's on our side..."

John nodded. "Funny you should mention Brant Roebling..." he said. "I don't know for sure, but I have a feeling Brant teamed-up with the Conservancy to pull this off..."

MacKenzie beamed. "Mr. Roebling is kind of like his own Conservancy," she agreed. "I think he always has a way to get what he wants, and no one ever gets mad at him because he's tricky in a really charming and nice and generous way..."

John laughed. "I don't disagree with you," he said. "Brant Roebling may be an entire secret society all by himself..."

"Will..." MacKenzie said slowly, a sudden dark spot of apprehension intruding on her brightness. "Will... Will we be staying in the cottage...?"

John nodded. "Yes," he said. "We will."

MacKenzie exhaled with relief and her mind gratefully returned to its cotton-candy clouds.

"I think," John continued, "that Ed and Brant started quietly plotting something as soon as they found out we had to return to Chicago. I have to tell you, Mac—Ed Davenport is a deeply good person. The day we left, he told me he couldn't imagine anyone other than us ever living in the cottage."

"Dad...?" MacKenzie said abruptly and cautiously, not daring, and not believing, but seeking anyway.

"No," her father said firmly. "Back to your base, MacKenzie Milles. You and I may have that conversation. But not today. That is definitely not a today-issue."

"Wait, I'm sorry, what...?" MacKenzie stammered, stunned with sudden incredulous hope. "Do you mean there really is a possibility that we might—"

"Not a today-issue," he father repeated unequivocally.

MacKenzie nodded with hasty contrition. "Okay..." she said hurriedly. "Okay, not a today-issue..."

Her father nodded again. "So, the Conservancy has selected a red-clover-abatement contractor, and their work will begin Wednesday, the day you and I return to Catalina. I'll explain more later, but basically they're going to be combing the island and manually pulling up all the red-clover."

"That sounds like an awful lot of work..." said MacKenzie.

"It will be," John agreed. "But it's necessary. And I agreed with Ed, for many reasons it's the best way to go."

MacKenzie nodded.

"Katie," her father went on, "has been asked by the Marine Center to continue to be in charge of monitoring and supporting the recovery of the coral eco-system at the Seal Rocks. The people she works for in San Diego have a bit more of an understanding approach than the Illinois Wildlife Conservancy..."

"So, she'll still be there when we get back...?"

John nodded and smiled. "She will," he said.

"How long will she be there?" asked MacKenzie.

"The same amount of time that you and I will be there: three more weeks."

MacKenzie's mouth dropped open in speechless joy. Her insides were tumbling. She couldn't believe what an incredible wonderful amazing day she was having. It was the perfect kind of overwhelming.

"So..." John went on slowly. "I've been talking with Katie a lot on the phone since we left... And I have two questions to ask you. And please don't answer until you've heard them both. Question one, how would you feel if Katie moved into the cottage and stayed with us for the rest of the time that we're in Catalina. And question two, how would you feel if, when we come back here to Chicago at the end of the summer, if Katie comes with us and stays here to live with us for a few weeks..."

MacKenzie spilled onto her father and wrapped herself around him, burying her head in his shoulder. She couldn't stop herself from crying, and suddenly she was crying more than she could ever remember crying before.

"I love you, Dad..." she managed to say through her tears, her voice muffled in his shirt. "Yes, please, Dad... I love you so much... I love Katie so much... That would be the best most wonderful gift I ever got ever in my life..."

Her father put one arm around her trembling shoulders, and slowly and gently smoothed her hair with his other hand.

"I love you so much, Mac..." he said quietly. "I just want you to be happy..."

MacKenzie sat partway up and looked at her father, tears still streaming down her face.

"Dad..." she said. "Do you and Katie make each other happy...?"

Her father smiled at her and nodded without hesitation. "Yes, we do..." he said. "It turns out there are only two things I love more than being with Katie. One is being with you, and the other is being with you and Katie together..."

MacKenzie laughed, but still couldn't stop herself from continuing to cry, and she smiled through her tears at her father. "That's how I feel about you, too, Dad..." she said.

She hugged her father again, and they stayed like that on the couch as the game continued to play on the television set across the living room.

Eventually, MacKenzie had at last managed to get some of her emotions to calm themselves down, and she sat up less unsteadily. "More coffee, Dad?" she asked helpfully, standing up and wiping her eyes and her face with the back of her sleeve.

Her father nodded. "Thank you," he said. "It's only the second inning. This game's just getting started."

MacKenzie nodded philosophically. "It's one kind of exciting fun when you don't know how the game is going to turn out," she said. "And it was amazingly fun getting to watch today's game with Paul Cavanarro in his special fancy seats and hearing all his cool stories," she went on. "But, it's also a really happy special kind of fun to get to re-live it all over again, when we know for sure that it's going to have a happy ending."

MacKenzie picked up her lemonade glass and her father's mug from the coffee table, and climbed with easy agility over the back of the couch, making her way toward the kitchen.

Chapter 56

CATALINA

Tuesday was MacKenzie and her father's last day in Chicago before heading back to Catalina. John went into work early, and was home by 2:00 so that he and MacKenzie could go to the 2:33 game at Wrigley. In the third inning, a hard-hit fly ball soared into foul territory in the right-field stands, straight toward MacKenzie. She stood up on her seat with her father steadying her and holding her scorecard and pencil. MacKenzie readied her glove for what was sure to be her first successful Wrigley catch. In the instant before it would have made its way to her glove, the hand of someone in front of her stretched up higher into the air and stopped the ball in its flight, snagging away the spinning round souvenir. Another thrilled and happy fan who wasn't MacKenzie.

"I'm still working on my convergence..." MacKenzie said to her father that evening as they were getting packed. They weren't watching the cable-TV re-broadcast of the game because the Cubs had lost to the Padres 8-to-0, and neither of them could bear to re-experience the loss.

"And how's that going?" asked her father.

"It's still really disappointing when something you want to happen comes so close to happening, and then doesn't happen..." said MacKenzie.

"The home team didn't come particularly close to winning today..." said John.

MacKenzie nodded. "Their convergence was worse than mine today..." she agreed. "But I know the Cubs are trying to win. And I'm definitely really trying to catch a foul ball. But not everything always turns out the way you want. You have to just keep trying. And sometimes, you have to just get lucky…"

"You're certainly having a positive outlook on things…" her father said.

MacKenzie nodded. "Being happy makes you see everything more clearly."

"Well, it certainly makes you see things differently, anyway…" her father replied.

"I like the way things look from Happy," MacKenzie said, smiling.

"It's definitely a nice view," agreed her father.

"And also," MacKenzie went on, "my trajectory's improving."

"Getting closer and closer to the day you catch your first foul ball?" suggested her father.

"Getting closer and closer to being back in Catalina," MacKenzie said excitedly.

John smiled.

"And besides," MacKenzie went on. "It's not really about catching a foul ball. I'll never give up trying to catch a foul ball. It's one of my life-ambitions. And, it's nice when the Cubs win, but that's not why I like seeing them play. I like seeing them play because they're the Cubs. And mostly, I like seeing the Cubs play because I'm with you. I have fun because you and I are there together. Every game, you and I win!"

Her father gave her a fond loving smile. "That certainly makes me lucky," he said, lifting her baseball cap and mussing her hair affectionately, then putting her cap back in place on her head.

MacKenzie grinned happily.

MacKenzie and her father had flown out on a red-eye flight very late Tuesday night. It was now early Wednesday morning, and they were just stepping off the *Avalon Express* after it had completed its first trip of the day from Long Beach to Avalon Bay. Both Katie and Erik had been there waiting for them, waving with animated eager enthusiasm as the ferry approached the dock, and then greeting them with happy excitement as MacKenzie and her father made their way to the top of the inclined ramp and onto the Mole.

"Welcome back to beautiful Santa Catalina," said Katie cheerfully, kissing each of them lightly on the cheek. "The island has missed you both very much! We can take Bertie back to the cottage. I drove her here with Erik so we could pick you two up in style."

"Bertie!" MacKenzie sang out joyfully.

While John and Erik were chatting together for a moment, Katie bent down to MacKenzie's ear and whispered to her. "Your dad said that you two talked, and that it was okay. I hope you don't mind that I've already moved my things into the cottage..."

MacKenzie beamed and threw her arms around Katie, and whispered into Katie's ear. "I love you, Katie..." she said softly. "I want you to always be with us, always..."

Katie squeezed MacKenzie in a gentle loving hug, her eyes glistening. "That makes me happy, little dolphin..." she whispered. "The happiest I've ever been in my life..."

John came over to see Katie, and MacKenzie made her way to where Erik was standing and smiling, waiting for her. Across the bay, the tubular bells of the Chimes Tower began tolling from the hilltop above the Casino.

MacKenzie and Erik stood for moment, beaming at each other. "It's really good to see you, Mac..." said Erik, the golden dolphin around his neck gleaming for a moment as it caught an ideal angle of morning sunlight. "I... It's... It makes me really glad that the best part of Catalina is back where she belongs..."

MacKenzie blushed and grinned. "Don't make me hug you,

Erik Roebling," she said. "Because right now I am so happy to see you, I don't even know what to do with myself…"

Erik blushed and smiled broadly back at her. "Well," he said, "then how about ice cream?"

MacKenzie nodded emphatically. "Yes, please…" she said, smiling and giddy. "That, I can handle…"

"Okay then," he said, nodding happily. "Well, I impulsively asked Katie if it would be okay to bring our bikes, and she said yes. So, both our bikes are loaded on the back of Bertie right now. If you want, while your dad and Katie drive back to the cottage, you and I could bike over to Big Olaf's for some after-breakfast dessert."

"That sounds deliciously perfect," MacKenzie said eagerly, grinning and giving Erik their tunnel-signal.

Erik grinned and gave the tunnel-signal back to her.

"Dad," said MacKenzie. "Can we please have a fire tonight? And can Erik come over for dinner?"

Her father and Katie exchanged a smile with each other, and then John turned back toward MacKenzie and Erik. "Sounds fun to me," he said, smiling. "So long as you and Erik don't mind hauling firewood…"

MacKenzie nodded, grinning. "Thanks, Dad! Thank you, Katie!"

"Listen," said Katie. "I hope it's okay with everyone—Brenda and I have planned a nice dinner for all six of us at the Roeblings' tomorrow night."

"That's awesome!" MacKenzie exclaimed happily.

Erik nodded. "That's going to be really fun," he agreed with keen enthusiasm.

"Dad," said MacKenzie. "Is it okay with you and Katie if Erik and I leave all the baggage unloading at the cottage for you guys to do, while Erik and I are busy having delicious ice cream?"

John smiled and looked at Katie.

"That seems like a perfect arrangement," said Katie, smiling.

"Thanks, you guys!" MacKenzie said happily, and she grabbed Erik's hand and led him off down the Mole toward the transportation area.

"Look," she said to him, gesturing widely with her other hand as they walked. "No mysterious man…!"

They both laughed.

"So," she went on. "Remember the other night when we were talking on the phone, and I told you all about meeting Paul Cavanarro?"

Erik nodded. "It really sounded like an amazing and incredibly fun day."

"Well…" MacKenzie went on as they approached where Bertie was parked. "I didn't exactly tell you the whole story… There was one part I wanted to wait to tell you in person. It's kind of a surprise…"

They arrived at Bertie. Erik unhooked the bungy cords holding their bikes in place, and he and MacKenzie lifted their bikes down onto the asphalt surface of the transportation area.

"I don't mind surprises," said Erik, smiling and climbing onto his bike. "As long as they're not bad ones…"

MacKenzie grinned. "Well, this one was not a bad one, and it was definitely a surprise to me…" she said, climbing onto her bike. "It was a surprise gift I got…"

"Well," said Erik, "that certainly sounds like a good kind of surprise."

MacKenzie nodded. "You're not even going to believe it when I tell you. But, it's still not the most important gift anyone's ever given me…" she said, and her fingers by themselves found their way to her penny necklace.

Erik's fingers found their way to his gold dolphin, and MacKenzie and Erik stood together, straddling their bikes for a moment.

"Erik," MacKenzie said. "Can we please just visit the rock-warrior sentry before we go to Big Olaf's...?"

Erik nodded. "Of, course. He's probably missed you very much while you've been away."

MacKenzie looked intently at Erik. "I missed him, too," she said. "I've missed everything about Catalina. It's really true, that even if you think you know how important something is to you, you don't really understand how much it means to you until you're away from it, and then at last you get to have it back."

Erik nodded earnestly. "I know just what you mean," he said.

They pedaled their way to Abalone Point, and while Erik stood straddling his bike, MacKenzie lowered her bicycle to the paving-stone surface of the turnout and went over to her rock-warrior sentry. She climbed the overlook railing and stepped from the top handrail rung up onto the small stone ledge she had once sat on at the base of the warrior. Lifting her left arm to mirror-match her sentry's waving right arm, she reached forward until her palm was pressed against the stone palm of the warrior's waving hand.

She looked up toward the sentry's head and leaned closer.

"Thank you..." she whispered. "Thank you for saving me... Thank you for rescuing me... Thank you for taking care of me... Thank you for always watching over me..."

She leaned closer and whispered more softly. "Thank you for my Dad... Thank you for Katie... Thank you for Erik and his family... Thank you for bringing me back to Catalina... This is where I belong..."

She stood where she was for a moment. The stone of her warrior's palm was warm. It pressed motionlessly back against her hand.

"See you tomorrow morning..." she whispered softly.

She climbed down from the railing and went back to Erik, picking up her bike and straddling it alongside of where Erik was still standing over his bicycle.

"So, while I was in Chicago," she reported, "I didn't catch a foul ball. Again."

Erik nodded. "Did your rock-warrior have any helpful points-of-view about that?"

MacKenzie nodded. "I think there are some things I'm supposed to keep in mind..." she began thoughtfully. "Sometimes what's important to you changes. I still desperately want to catch one. But a few weeks ago, wanting to catch a foul ball was one of the most important things in my life. I think what's important to me has changed since I came to Catalina. Catching a foul ball hasn't gotten any less important. It's just that other things have become more important.

"And also, not everything comes your way. Not everything goes the way you want. And you know what I've learned from that? Be thankful for the things you actually have. Be thankful for the things that *have* come your way. For the things that *have* gone your way. Not everything can be perfect. Not everything should be perfect. Maybe nothing could ever even *be* perfect. Things have flaws. That's just how things are. If you look at it the wrong way, all you see is the flaw. If you look at it a better way, you see all the parts without a flaw. If you really know how to see, you can look at the whole thing all at once, and you can see that the flaw is just part of what it really is. Sometimes being not-perfect is exactly what makes something really truly perfect.

"But what's most important of all is enjoying what's happening right now, while also always having fun exciting things to look forward to in your future. Normal may be boring, but in some ways, it's also the most special kind of wonderful. Normal is a luxury. Exciting is exciting, but normal is heavenly. It's important to always appreciate normal, and be thankful for it.

"And this is normal. Being in Catalina. Being with you. Knowing my Dad and Katie are doing something somewhere together having fun. Knowing the buffalo and the coral are going to be okay. Knowing the summer isn't over. Knowing we don't have to worry about a mysterious man. Knowing you and I are going to have after-breakfast dessert, but enjoying that we haven't had it yet and it's something so near in the future that I can almost taste it.

"You have to be aware of how lucky you are. You have to make sure your family and your friends always know how much you love them and appreciate them.

"Sometimes the most important things aren't even things you've dreamed of or hoped for. Sometimes they're things that come out-of-the-blue. Sometimes they're just something that ended up happening because you were being impulsive... For instance, that was pretty impulsive of you to ask Katie if you could bring both our bikes. That was a good idea..."

Erik nodded thoughtfully. "The best impulsive idea I ever had," he said, "was asking a complete stranger out-of-the-blue if she wanted to go kayaking with me..."

"The best impulsive idea I ever had," MacKenzie agreed quietly, "was saying yes..."

They both paused for a moment.

Still straddling her bicycle, MacKenzie stood on her tiptoes and leaned toward Erik. She put her arms around his neck and kissed him.

Erik moved her hair gently away from the sides of her face with his hands.

"Hi, Mac..." Erik breathed happily.

MacKenzie smiled. "Hi…" she said.

"I'm really glad you're here," said Erik.

MacKenzie nodded. "I'm having the happiest best moment I've ever had in my life…"

"Me too," said Erik.

"I remember the very first thing you ever said to me," said MacKenzie. "You told me I wasn't holding my kayak paddle the right way. You were very polite about it."

Erik grinned. "I remember the first thing you ever said to me. You called me 'surfer dude'. You were very polite about it."

They both laughed, still straddling their bikes, their faces still close together.

"I love my special necklace," said MacKenzie.

"That penny," said Erik, "went its whole life never knowing you existed. And now it loves that it's with you where it belongs."

MacKenzie nodded. "It's like me and this penny were always meant to be together."

"Just like," said Erik.

They leaned closer together and kissed again.

"I can tell you what *I've* learned," Erik whispered to her. "Now I know what The Treasure of Santa Catalina Island really is. I mean, now I know who she is…"

"Thank you…" MacKenzie whispered back. She lightly pressed the end of her nose against the end of Erik's nose as if they were two dolphins.

For a moment, neither of them spoke.

"Well, then…" Erik said at last. "I think we know what happens now…"

"Ice cream…?" MacKenzie suggested.

Erik smiled and nodded. "Exactly," he agreed. "Flawlessly imperfect after-breakfast dessert."

They both gave each other their tunnel-signal, snap-bounce-thumbs-up, and they laughed again. Climbing back up onto their bikes, they started to pedal their way toward Big Olaf's.

"Okay," MacKenzie began as they rode. "So, listen. You're not even going to believe this. You remember that Honus Wagner card...?"

ALSO BY MIKA BÓWYN

FOUR GREEK MYTHS

FROM

ANCIENT GREEK MYTHOLOGY

MIKA BÓWYN

THE MYTH OF **ARACHNE**
THE MYTH OF **PANDORA**
THE MYTH OF **PERSEUS**
THE MYTH OF **THE GOLDEN APPLE** AND
EVENTS LEADING TO THE START OF THE TROJAN WAR

Cagliostro the Enchanter

THE FIRST TALE IN THE SERIES

The Magic
Bi-Scepter

VERITAS GRATIA VERUM AMORIS

Mika Bówyn

Once upon a time
a young king seeking truth and true love
was given the power to change
bodies.

Cagliostro the Enchanter
THE SECOND TALE IN THE SERIES

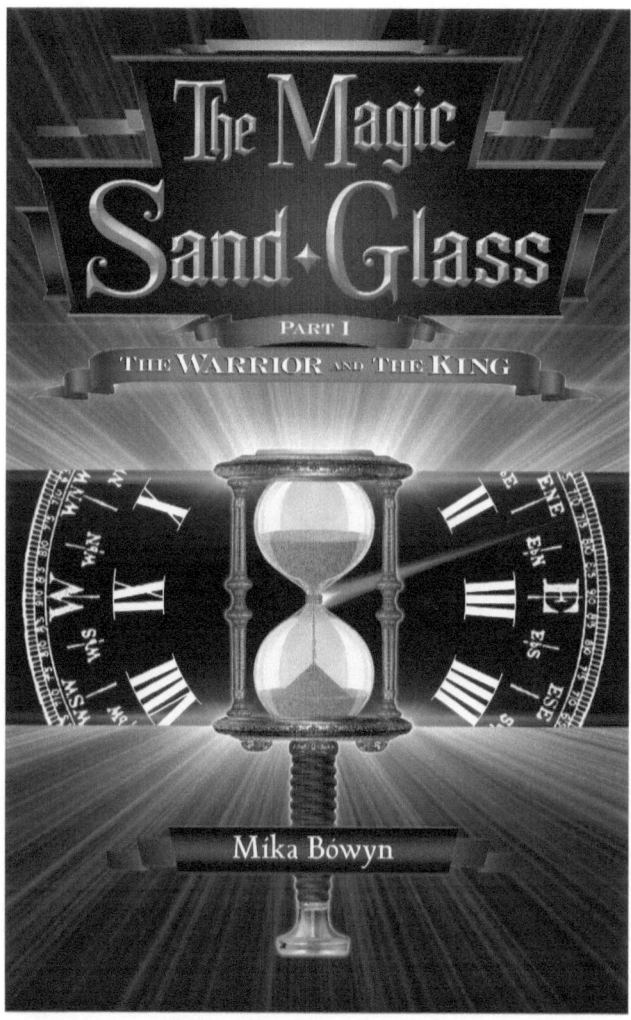

Two missions.
A young warrior on a crucial journey planned for her since before she was born.
A young king on a crucial journey to save his kingdom from destruction.
An extraordinary race against time filled with magic and peril and adventure.